THE BONES OF RUIN

Also by Sarah Raughley

Fate of Flames

Siege of Shadows

Legacy of Light

THE BONES OF RUIN

Sarah Raughley

MARGARET K. MCELDERRY BOOKS
NEW YORK   LONDON   TORONTO   SYDNEY   NEW DELHI

MARGARET K. McELDERRY BOOKS
An imprint of Simon & Schuster Children's Publishing Division
1230 Avenue of the Americas, New York, New York 10020
Text © 2021 by Sarah Raughley
Jacket illustration/photography © 2021 by Khadijah Khatib
Jacket design by Rebecca Syracuse © 2021 by Simon & Schuster, Inc.
MARGARET K. McELDERRY BOOKS is a trademark of Simon & Schuster, Inc.
For information about special discounts for bulk purchases, please contact Simon & Schuster
Special Sales at 1-866-506-1949 or business@simonandschuster.com.
The Simon & Schuster Speakers Bureau can bring authors to your live event. For more information
or to book an event, contact the Simon & Schuster Speakers Bureau at 1-866-248-3049 or visit our
website at www.simonspeakers.com.
Interior design by Rebecca Syracuse
The text for this book was set in Matrix II OT.
Manufactured in the United States of America
First Edition
10 9 8 7 6 5 4 3 2 1
Library of Congress Cataloging-in-Publication Data
Names: Raughley, Sarah, author.
Title: The bones of ruin / Sarah Raughley.
Description: First edition. | New York : Margaret K. McElderry Books, [2021] | Series: The bones of
ruin ; 1 | Summary: "An African tightrope walker who cannot die gets involved with a mysterious
society that's convinced the world is ending and is drafted into the fight-to-the-death Tournament
of Freaks, where she learns the terrible truth of who and what she really is"—Provided by publisher.
Identifiers: LCCN 2020056333 (print) | LCCN 2020056334 (ebook) | ISBN 9781534453562 (hardcover) |
ISBN 9781534453586 (ebook)
Subjects: CYAC: Blacks—England—Fiction. | Ability—Fiction. | Supernatural—Fiction. | End of the
world—Fiction. | Contests—Fiction. | Great Britain—History—Victoria, 1837-1901—Fiction.
Classification: LCC PZ7.1.R38 Bo 2021 (print) | LCC PZ7.1.R38 (ebook) | DDC [Fic]—dc23
LC record available at https://lccn.loc.gov/2020056333
LC ebook record available at https://lccn.loc.gov/2020056334

TO AUNTIE KEMI

THE BONES OF RUIN

BEFORE THE CATACLYSM

October 1, 1884
925 days since the Spring Day Massacre

A SECOND SET OF KNOCKS ON THE front door once again interrupted Adam Temple's very important business.

"All right, all right," Adam muttered, closing his hooded eyes as he stayed his hand. Ever the persistent one, that woman.

But it was no more than a minor annoyance. With the rain beating the arched windows and the wind howling in the darkness outside, providing shelter to his esteemed visitor came first. It's what a gentleman would do, even in this situation. Indeed, he'd given his servants the night off, so the door was his to get.

Straightening up, he casually tossed his bloody knife onto the mantel of the roaring cast-iron fireplace. He looked fondly up at the golden-framed portrait of his mother, the baroness, hanging above it. She'd been a puritanical woman, lovely and stoic, her braided brown hair muted by canvas oils. Her authoritarian gaze aimed daggers at him.

Now, don't look at me like that, Mother, he thought with a little grin before heading out into the foyer.

The rapping on the door made the crystals of the chandelier above him jingle brightly like bells, their light dancing along the dark carmine walls. To his left, a clay bust of his father, John Temple, cowered in the corner behind the twisting wooden staircase, but Adam spared no time for it. He would return to him later. The rapping had evolved into a frenzied pounding.

How typical of Madame. "Don't be so impatient, Violet," he whispered as his hand reached for the knob. The opened door revealed a beautiful woman standing in the granite threshold of his family manor, a woman who tried very hard the moment she caught sight of his blue eyes to transform her frustrated scowl into a pleasant, welcoming smile.

Madame Violet Bellerose was the very vision of a lady: Not a splash of rain had touched her long black gloves, nor her burgundy overdress, the same color as her gathered-up hair, because her servant—a dreadful-looking man, soaked from head to toe, with the expression and pallor of a corpse—held up a black umbrella to keep her dry. Her skirt fell straight at the front but draped elaborately at the back, billowing majestically below the waist as she crossed the doorway.

"Well," she said, her own pearl-colored parasol an unopened decoration in her hands, "isn't it always lovely to visit Yorkshire at night?" Her French accent was as solid as the pearls draped around her neck. She turned to her servant. "Pierre, you'll wait outside, won't you?"

She didn't wait for an answer before she slammed the door in the wet man's face. The wind and rain raged on behind it.

And now they were alone.

"My, the weather is just *terrible*." She inched closer to him, her boots crisp against the marble. "Feels like the end of days, doesn't it?"

Adam wasn't surprised when her slender fingers found his cheek sooner than he could blink, caressing his jawline up to his admittedly very unkempt black hair. The first time he'd met her, seven years ago, his father had entertained her in this manor. Adam was fourteen at that time, home from Eton, and she more than a decade older, but he could feel the illicit hunger in her eyes for him even then, as sure as he could now.

It wasn't a particularly pleasant experience or an unpleasant one. Her touch never shook his heart one way or another. Dealing with Madame Bellerose in any capacity required care and the utmost precaution. She was one of the more intelligent members of the Committee, after all. And while all of the members could brag of wealth, power, and an impressive body count, not all could boast of superior intellect. When in the presence of Madame Bellerose, it was imperative that he be in complete control of himself.

He was balancing on the edge of a knife.

"My, Adam, you only grow more handsome every time I see you." She rested her finger underneath her red lips as if it were the Sword of Damocles dangling above his head, her thumb caressing her pointed chin in amusement. "Beautiful balanced features, delicate and fairy-like. Soft like a woman's and yet somehow so masculine in its shape."

She admired him like a painting that she could never have no matter how many times she asked—and she had asked many times.

"Though your hair could use a bit of a comb, young man," she added in a scolding tone unsuited to her. He could feel her fingers grazing his scalp as she ran them through his hair. "Despite that little oversight, I'm sure any young British lady would just *die* to be your wife. If we hadn't killed your father, I'm sure he would have set up an arrangement immediately."

Scoffing, Adam stepped away from her, widening the distance between them to a more comfortable degree. "In life, my father was never interested in such things. He could barely stand me. He certainly didn't trust me."

"I suppose he was right in both regards."

As if she'd suddenly grown bored of his beauty, she peeked into the living room. Her blue eyes glinted dangerously, and certainly not because of the new neoclassical furniture he'd brought into the estate. She was used to expensive things; she'd inherited many from her family's part in the slave trade, the abolition of which, she always maintained, was one of France's biggest mistakes.

"Why, that *monsieur*! Might he be . . . ?"

With a gentlemanly sweep of his arm, Adam gestured for the madame to enter first.

"You are a loyal boy, aren't you?"

"As loyal as the Committee needs me to be."

"A smart boy too."

Madame Bellerose scurried into the living room. It was a spacious room, where his family used to spend much of their time together when all were alive, though the parlor in the east wing was another close favorite, a particular joy for his uncle Byron, now sadly committed. But by the sudden drop of her long face, Adam knew the carnage was clearly too contained for her taste. Golden-framed portraits of the Temple family lined the floral walls and mocked her with their spotlessness: Along with his mother sandwiched between two golden light fixtures above the fireplace, there was his cherubic little brother and beloved older sister. His grandfather. Oh, and a space where his father's portrait used to be, a painting that now lay discarded in a closet somewhere. Gathering dust.

On one side of the fireplace, a bust of Michelangelo's *David*, bloodless, with not even a scratch upon it. And on the other, a low mahogany rocking chair next to a handcrafted, gold-trimmed monopodial table, carvings telling ghoulish stories along its single leg. Clean.

No broken mirror. No intestines draped across the piano. Adam had kept the carnage to a minimum. The only blood in sight dripped from the chest, arms, and lips of the graying, middle-aged man tied to a chair in the center of the living room and collected in a respectable crimson pool on the earth-toned Persian rug. Adam was never one for a mess, but Madame Bellerose had a taste for the macabre, so he did what he could for her within reason. He picked the bloody knife back up off the mantel.

Rain continued to batter the windows from behind the dark velvet curtains. Though Bellerose was not quite satisfied with the level of bloodshed, she was just fine, as he'd correctly predicted, with the man's lifeless body. Neville Bradford—an old bosom friend of his father's.

Madame Bellerose scuttled over to his body, her heels muffled against the carpet. There, she bent down low to listen to his breathing.

"Dead." She took a step back from him, clapping her hands. "The poor man's heart must have given out after whatever you did to him." Her eyes greedily drank in the sight of his blood-soaked cotton shirt, unbuttoned at the top, revealing some of his stained chest hairs. "You've done a fine job."

Adam approached her, his hands behind his back. "I just hope it's to the Committee's liking."

"Of course. We can't afford any loose ends or open lips—not when the *tournoi* has yet to begin." She let out a whimsical sigh. "You're aware that it was your father who was supposed to be in your place. Now that both he and this man are gone, his responsibility falls on you."

"And I take on the responsibility with great honor and humility." He bowed his head ever so slightly.

Madame Bellerose's laughter was like the shriek of a crow in the night. He suppressed a wince, rather proud of his uncanny ability to keep his expression so cordial.

"Such a sweet tongue." Grabbing his chin, she drew her face to his. "Though I always imagined *silver* would taste a little bitterer."

She gave the chair a hard shove so quickly Adam's breath hitched, but it wasn't anything he hadn't anticipated. As it toppled over to the floor, taking Neville with it, Adam closed the gap between himself and Madame Bellerose, catching her lips with his. She was momentarily taken aback, but then answered hungrily, just as Adam knew she would. It was a necessary distraction. Had she not been preoccupied with his kiss, she would have been watching carefully for a yell, a gasp, any sign of life that would signal Adam's betrayal.

Adam's mouth was still wet and painted a messy red from Madame's lipstick when he grabbed her shoulders and gently pushed her away from him. Both eyes slid to Neville, lying on the floor. Madame Bellerose leaned over and waited. Nothing. He was a sack of flesh.

"You're certainly thorough," he said, maintaining his amiable expression.

"And he's certainly dead." Madame Bellerose pulled up her left glove, in danger of slipping down her elbow because of the suddenness of their exchange. "And you, full of surprises." She rubbed her bottom lip with a finger, biting down as she stared at his.

That hunger of yours was always your weak point, madame. Adam lowered his head with a little smile.

"Well, there's nothing wrong with a little surprise carnality," she said. "But if you were trying to curry favor with me just now, you needn't have. You've already earned your seat, boy. The rest of the Committee will be pleased when I relay the message at our next meeting."

"You *will* relay the message, won't you?"

"Dear Adam, I would never betray you," she said. Not at all convincing. But then, as if to remind him, she suddenly took off her right glove and flashed her palm. It was only in the moonlight that the symbol there hummed dully in her flesh—a pink scar patterned in the shape of a sword through a skull. The Oath Maker. It was meant to be proof of her word, but such a thing didn't exist as far as Adam was concerned. Still, he knew he'd have to accept it for now.

"We shall have to make sure our tracks are covered. As a political figure, Mr. Bradford's kidnapping and murder will not go unnoticed. Benini is an expert in such things. He's already agreed to take care of it. I certainly enjoy corpses, but the cleanup involved . . ." She shuddered. "Now that this particular business is over," she said, moving closer, "what shall we do for the rest of the night?"

"I must ask you to kindly take your leave," Adam said just as her hand reached up to him once more. It stopped in midair. "It's late, madame. Close to midnight. You should be getting back to the hotel. There are arrangements I've still to complete."

Madame Bellerose let her quiet fury simmer into a strained smirk. "Ever so accommodating."

She slapped him. It rather hurt.

"Madame . . ."

After her expression softened, she tapped him on the nose. "Oh, I understand, you delightful little boy."

Adam winced from pain as she suddenly grabbed his cheeks once more with the red nails of her ungloved hand and squeezed harder than she need have. He was growing tired of this.

"We shall have to have dinner soon." She brought her lips close to his. "I'm still making my own arrangements for the grand event, but while I'm in England, there's no need for us to be estranged, is there? I needn't remind you that there isn't much time left for us to enjoy the little luxuries of this world." She paused just before reaching his warm, open mouth. "You'll visit me in London, won't you?"

"As surely as the sun will rise," he lied. Wasting not another moment, he hastily showed her to the door and walked back into the living room alone, opening one side of the velvet curtain so he could watch her leave. Only when her carriage was completely out of his sight did he pick the fallen chair back up from the floor. As the legs hit the rug, Neville Bradford let out the breath he'd been holding, desperately gulping in the air as his whole body shook in pain.

"That took dedication." Adam laughed a little because he hadn't expected Mr. Bradford to take his words so dearly to heart. *Do you hear that? That is a member of the Committee, come to make sure I've killed you,* he'd told him after the first set of knocks. *But if you only* pretend *to be dead, I'll spare your life.* The kiss with Madame Bellerose would have given Mr. Bradford time to suck in another breath. A necessary evil.

"So." Mr. Bradford coughed out the words once he'd caught his breath. "You'll let me go, won't you?"

"Well, there's still the matter of the question you haven't answered." Adam pointed the tip of his bloody knife against a finger. "I wouldn't have been torturing you otherwise," he added with a shrug and leaned in so that they were at eye level, the closeness drawing a shudder from the older man. "The whereabouts of my father. We both know he isn't in the grave."

Mr. Bradford pressed his pallid lips together.

"Where has he gone to, Mr. Bradford? I need something from him."

Stubborn. Annoyingly stubborn. But since he was yet another victim of his father's carelessness, he had Adam's sympathy. He certainly wouldn't be in this position if John Temple had known to keep his mouth shut too.

"Come now, Mr. Bradford!" Adam skipped around him and gripped his shoulders as if to ease him with a massage. Bradford let out a gasp of pain. "You betrayed my father to me once." He leaned in. "Surely it shouldn't be so difficult to do it again."

"I shouldn't have done so in the first place."

Adam's jaw clenched at the regret in the man's voice. "You're in this situation now because of what my father told you and Mr. Anderson in confidence—information you thought could help procure your seat on the Committee. That knowledge now has you marked for death. If you want to avoid Mr. Anderson's fate, all you have to do is let me know where my father is. You're a political beast, aren't you? You should be able to sniff out a good deal when it comes your way."

"What happened to you, Adam?" Mr. Bradford let out a series of bloody coughs before he looked back at him, this time with an air of pity that irked the younger man. "Is it because of the Committee? You're not like them. I wanted to be so badly, but I . . ."

Yes, the two of them were once under consideration for his father's vacant seat. Now the older man's forehead wrinkled as he furrowed his brow, regret engrained deep in his pained expression. Adam sighed impatiently and walked over to the window.

"You're still young," Mr. Bradford continued as Adam leaned against the curtain. "You can still turn back. You're *better* than them."

Adam softened his gaze, considering his words, and yet still stared at the quivering man so intensely he could almost feel an electrical charge between them. The spark that separates life and death. "I'll ask one more time. Where is my father?"

Mr. Bradford's steadfast resolution was admirable, Adam had to admit. If only it was for someone more deserving. "I betrayed him once," the man said. "I will not do it again."

Neville Bradford was a man Adam had known all his life. He would come over to the Temple Estate with his bowler hat and his pipe and read the newspaper to him in brighter times. Neville Bradford and Carl Anderson had been his father's bosom friends since their school days. And so Adam's heart sank at his answer. But Adam wasn't a child anymore. He'd already murdered Mr. Anderson, and he could and *would* kill again.

There was something that mattered to him now more than anything ever had before.

The grandfather clock on the opposite end of the room struck midnight with echoing fervor. Adam drew the left curtain wide and opened the window, not at all bothered by the rain wetting his hair and clothes. Turning back, he leaned against the window ledge once more just as a pair of leather shoes landed lightly upon it.

The stranger's appearance drew a weak cry for help from Mr. Bradford's lips, but the man draped in a black cape did not respond. He only tipped his top hat and bowed.

Adam smirked. His servant was nothing if not punctual.

"Fool," Adam greeted the strange man without looking at him, though he could see his harlequin mask in the mirror on the other side of the room, split black and white down the middle with black oval eyes and a pair of golden lips pressed together in neither a frown nor a smile. "What have you seen?"

"Luck is finally on your side, my lord." Fool spoke in a voice that seemed always on the verge of laughter, pointed as the plucked string of a cello. "We've found her."

Adam's heart skipped a beat as he pushed off the window ledge. "Are you certain?"

"We spotted the girl and her circus caravan in Paris."

"Caravan?" A boyish laugh escaped from Adam's lips. *Just what has she been up to?* "Good. Don't lose track of her."

Strange. The circus? A majestic being like her—what need did she have to make money, especially in such a garish way? It wasn't what he was expecting. Then again, the assumption that he could ever ascertain her thoughts was a sin in and of itself. As the glower of his mother's portrait bore down on him, he felt the sudden need to repent.

Still. He would have Fool look into it.

For now, he was excited. More excited than he had been in a long time. His heart was beating, his face flushing, his fingers clenching as the thrill surged through him. Only for his ecstasy to be ruined by Mr. Bradford's disapproving grunt.

Bradford, who knew what he shouldn't know, and what Adam desperately needed to know.

Bradford, who could destroy everything that mattered to him with just a word.

All thanks to his father.

"Stupid boy," Mr. Bradford said, swearing through gritted teeth. "If what John told me is true, then you have no idea the kind of chaos you're about to find yourself in the middle of. Just forget all this, Adam. Forget all of it. *I* will. You have nothing to worry about from me. I swear!"

Adam shut his eyes, not wanting to see a man he once respected for his political vigor and ferocity suddenly so willing to grovel under the guise of fatherly advice.

"Just return to your studies and forget it all, my boy." Bradford's breathing was labored. "Go back to the way you *were*. Or, if you wish, we can think of another way to deal with . . . with what's to come. The . . . th-the cataclysm. The *Hiva*—"

Adam's hand twitched. Wordlessly, he placed the knife carefully on the window ledge next to Fool's black leather shoes.

"Please! Let me go, dear boy! I will go to my contacts in Parliament and—"

Adam's eyes snapped open, and without skipping a beat, he grabbed the revolver hidden in the back of his trousers and shot Bradford through the head. The man slumped over dead as the gun's smoke cast shadows across Adam's face.

Rain dripped down the back of his hair as the wind roared on.

"Was that really necessary?" Fool cocked his head to the side. "The window *is* open."

"I don't want the Crown *or* the Committee to know more than they already do. Besides, there's nobody around for miles." After tossing the gun to the floor, Adam lowered his head. "That'll be all. Leave."

Fool never needed telling twice. Dipping his top hat, he bid adieu and disappeared into the cloudy, chaotic night, his black cape fluttering with the wind.

His blood is on your hands, Father, Adam thought bitterly, taking in the sight of Bradford's lifeless body with a heavy heart. "And there *is* no going back," he whispered.

A promise made between a young man and a corpse in the middle of the night.

PART ONE
Curtains

The existence of monsters calls into question the capacity of life to teach us order . . .

The monster is not only a living being of reduced value, it is a living being whose value is to be a counterpoint . . .

The vital counter-value is thus not death but monstrosity. Death is the permanent and unconditional threat of the organism's decomposition, the limitation from without, the negation of the living by the nonliving. Monstrosity is the accidental and conditional threat of incompleteness or distortion in the formation of the form; it is the limitation from within, the negation of the living by the nonviable . . .

—GEORGES CANGUILHEM,
"MONSTROSITY AND THE MONSTROUS"

1

STRANGE HAPPENINGS

(FROM OUR CORRESPONDENTS)

London Evening Standard
12 October 1884

The thirtieth birthday of Mrs. Catherine Wells, wife of the President of the Brighthand Literary Association, abruptly ended in chaos. Held on the evening of the eleventh of October in Agricultural Hall, the forty ladies and gentlemen present at the occasion were rushed out of the venue just before dinner was served. According to eyewitnesses, a young man dressed in very meager clothing entered the hall uninvited and, with no apparent cause, promptly exploded in a burst of electricity. Somehow, the man kept his head. While the hall was in disarray, many bystanders reportedly caught sight of the strange man stealing chatelaine bags and metal coin purses from the waists and necks of several ladies as they ran. He then escaped in the pandemonium with these items in hand.

A rational man would dismiss these witness statements as the ramblings of drunkards; but while Mrs. Wells's soiree indeed provided respectable amounts of alcohol along with tea, these stories hover too familiarly close to the unexplainable events occurring throughout the city and beyond. Despite this, the government remains rather quiet on such matters, particularly these days. Much more parliamentary attention is, as of late, being lavished upon Britain's recent guests, the special envoys from Africa whose steamer docked at Plymouth two evenings ago. The delegates, said to be of royal blood, have come from the Oil Rivers region of the west coast to persuade the government to intervene in the National African Company's mining projects in the lower Niger region. Though the government certainly has a duty to manage its colonial affairs overseas, there are growing concerns that the strange happenings at home have become entirely too frequent over the past decade to ignore for much longer . . .

October 23, 1884

"She's going to fall!" a girl cried. "My God, she's going to die! I can't look!"

Iris picked the voice out from among the chaotic shouts in the alley twenty feet below her, though admittedly only because of its tone, a shriek so nasal that Iris thought she would slip off the tightrope from cringing. The rope itself was fixed from the third stories of two buildings—an old mill and a bakery. It took all her discipline not to drift along with the devilishly seductive, sweet scent of bread rising from the red-bricked chimney. The fresh aroma signaled that there were still bakers who hadn't yet rushed out of the building to witness George Coolie's carefully planned morning spectacle.

"Carefully planned," yes. *Meticulously* planned. One wouldn't typically find a gorgeous, dignified lady like herself balancing on a string between two very tall buildings without a satisfactory reason, at least not so early in the morning. The Coolie Company needed promotion for their first show since returning to England, and London in particular had no shortage of entertainment. From Piccadilly to Westminster, it was a strange town with an insatiable appetite for freakery—and Coolie, ever the businessman, did his utmost to use this fact to his monetary advantage.

Coolie . . . As if her mind was punishing her, that money-grubbing man had snuck back into her thoughts, particularly his red face shouting at her at daybreak in front of all the other performers at camp.

"You know very damn well how important this is, so I don't want any mistakes. Not *one*. We need to get those bloody butts in the seats, you hear?"

He'd seemed more agitated than usual, his square balding head dripping sweat, his gut jiggling with each swear. Coolie kept his appearance as tidy as he kept his manners.

She shivered as a chilly breeze brushed past her bare shoulders and arms. Coolie had her in one of her performance costumes: a bright peppermint-green dress that hugged her chest and fanned out in layers of tulle, leaving everything past her knees bare. Skillfully sewn, courtesy of Granny Marlow, but not her attire of choice for such a cold morning, to be sure. Not in the least a proper dress for a lady either, but the circus tended to have looser rules of attire than regular *civil* society.

Besides, Iris was sure there was not a single soul in the gawking crowd below her that truly thought of her as a "lady" according to *their* traditional standards.

"That colored circus girl is going to die for sure!" she heard a young man yell. "I'll bet you money, she's going to fall and crack her head open right here on the road."

Just the usual.

Iris sighed. The wind fluttered the boa feathers weaved into her black hair, which, despite its length and coarse texture, had somehow been pressed down and rolled up into an ordered bun at the base of her neck—once again courtesy of the hours Granny Marlow spent lovingly doting on her.

Iris was a spectacle, to be sure: George Coolie's own professed "African rope-dancer," a girl who, according to him, he'd plucked straight out of the

Congo jungles, where she'd grown up among the lions and jackals—and after rescuing her single-handedly from the "heart of darkness," he'd trained her to become the greatest stunts woman England had ever seen.

A lie. And of course people believed it. Well, according to Coolie, "Stupid people believe anything, my dear." Cruel, but accurate.

The truth was, she'd found him in his office ten years ago after he'd put on a rather disappointing show in Blackburn. He was very drunk, and to get to his desk, she'd had to quite carefully maneuver around half-broken bottles of bourbon and strewn-about paperwork, some of which documented his never-ending gambling debts.

Despite the mess, she'd asked for a job.

Coolie had quickly realized the gift he'd been given after witnessing proof of her abilities—her uncanny senses, her hunter-like nimbleness. And though this particular audience of gawking Londoners hardly deserved it, what with the unflattering names they shouted up at her, Iris completed her task as the job commanded and gave them the same wondrous sight she gave every crowd, every performance. To the gasps and screams of many, she tumbled upon the tightrope, her small bare feet gripping the rope with ease, staying in perfect balance.

Coolie had once remarked that her instincts were otherworldly. Well, of course; rope-dancing was a dangerous art that required the utmost precision and, paradoxically, a certain sense of reckless abandon, a devil-may-care attitude that allowed the dancer to at least pretend that she didn't care one way or the other whether she lived or died.

Most dancers *did* care, even if they feigned otherwise. Iris did not. And she didn't have to pretend either.

Since she *couldn't* die.

"Oh my, there goes the other one!"

The sound of an excited woman down below signaled the arrival of Iris's partner. Her foot had touched down at the end of the rope. She turned just in time to see the young man leap into the air from the ledge of the bakery rooftop, so high children were screaming. Surely he'd miss his mark, they must have thought frightfully. *Surely* the sheer force of the wind would blow him off course as he twisted his body like a gymnast in the air. Just a fraction to the right or to the left and he'd be reduced to a fleshy smear upon the pavement.

But this was a trick the young man dubbed "Jinn" had performed many times before. Over his white body-length tights was a pair of beige billowing pants that cinched in at his knees; an orange vest hugged tight against his slender chest. His white tights made it more difficult to grasp the rope, but his toes gripped it nonetheless, his feet steady.

Iris's eyes rolled quickly with just a flicker of annoyance as she heard swooning down below, likely due to her partner's striking physical features. Very few of them could resist the sight of his sandy skin glowing under the sun or his chestnut-brown hair fluttering with the breeze. It happened after every show, like clockwork. The moment the curtains closed, a good handful of audience members, women and men alike, would discreetly find their way backstage to catch a glimpse of the bedazzling young man, a boy of nineteen, to gaze upon his sharp jawline up close, his long fluttering lashes, his slender build and angular nose. And each time they saw him, his dark, catlike eyes would stare back at them with a chilling, almost hateful expression that either chased them away or enticed them further.

Iris gazed into them now, but only—as she inwardly insisted—to watch for her cue. Their routine was a complicated one.

Simultaneously, the dancers lifted their arms and waved to the crowd neither of them particularly liked. "The Nubian Princess and the Turkish Prince," Coolie dubbed the pair, because it was easy for Londoners to remember and exciting enough to bring in those with an appetite for the so-called exotic. Coolie had given Jinn his stage name for that exact reason as well.

"You have a wild look in your eyes, boy," Coolie had once said in his growling tone while balancing a cigar on thin lips. "Like a tiger in a cage. The jinn are like devils to you people, aren't they? The name will be a perfect fit. It'll make you look even *more* dangerous. The audience will love it! I'll bet they don't see too many Ottomans in the circus."

Coolie didn't much care for sensitivity or accuracy. Jinn had silently accepted the name anyway, never protesting, never sharing his real name no matter how many times Iris pestered him for it, and never speaking of the parents who'd given it to him. It wasn't as if anyone would care, Coolie had told them. Least of all the audience.

For Iris, it wasn't so fun to be inspected and dissected by the gaze of people who saw her as nothing more than a curious oddity. But she'd been given a task today, and the work she completed for the Coolie Company had so far rewarded her with food, funds, and a temporary home. That was enough for now.

She nodded to Jinn, who nodded back. Together, to gasps and applause, they wheeled their bodies sideways, their hands touching down first, their feet catching the rope at the same time. The distance and timing had to be calculated to the letter: Jinn's strong, slender legs were quite longer than hers as a man that stood above five foot ten. The top of her head brushed the bottom of his neck, and so they carefully measured out the length of their strides.

A squeeze of her hand, a strong upward toss, and Iris was in the air, flipping. She had to admit, there was something a little thrilling about the sheer terror her feats inspired in spectators who mistakenly believed she followed the same rules of life and death as they did. There was a collective sigh of relief as her toes expertly touched down upon the rope behind her partner. Their aerial routines were her favorite. Kissing the air, touching the face of the heavens even just for one moment gave her the feeling of freedom she longed for. Freedom was hard to come by for someone in hiding.

Where better to hide a freak than in a circus?

"Oi." Behind her, Iris could hear Jinn hissing amid the chatter below. "You're doing too many rotations in the air. I've told you before: if you overdo it, you won't be able to spot your landing. Or maybe you really *do* want to fall and crack that thick skull of yours?"

Iris narrowed her eyes, but it was a stretched-out, forced grin he saw when she swiveled around to face him. It never ceased to amaze her how someone who seemed so quietly feral could in reality have such a nagging disposition. A cantankerous old geezer trapped in a handsome, youthful body. And he'd been as much ever since they began working together.

"My rotations were fine. I found the rope, didn't I?" Iris insisted through a gritted smile.

Jinn smirked. "Luckily for you."

"Luck has nothing to do with it. Not when you're as good as I am." Lifting her arms above her head she twirled on one foot, adjusting for the sudden force of the wind. Beautiful and elegant like a ballerina on a stage not nearly so high. "You should be aware by now, Jinn, but I'm in *perfect* control of my body."

But her breath hitched in her throat and her heart gave a flutter as Jinn's hands suddenly clasped her waist, catching her off guard. The little smirk on his face told her he'd noticed her tremble. *Drat.*

"*Perfect* control." He stifled a laugh before lifting her high in the air, much to the audience's delight.

"Ladies and gentlemen—doesn't this sight *thrill* you? Doesn't it make you just quiver in the utmost ecstasy of excitement?"

Coolie was always a bit of a ham when advertising. Iris couldn't see him among the crowd below as her gaze was focused on Jinn's for the sake of her concentration, but she recognized the circus proprietor's voice well enough after hearing it for the past ten years.

"If you want to see more, you're in luck. George Coolie's company is putting on a show beginning tonight at Astley's Amphitheatre. Jugglers and clowns, acrobats and animals—there'll be no shortage of the wonders you'll witness!"

On cue, Jinn tossed her up as they'd practiced.

"Ah," she sighed. She could *feel* him. Jinn. There, in the sky, she could feel his warmth, his kindness, his presence. His *essence*. More strongly than a regular human should. This wasn't about some crush. This was that *otherworldliness* Coolie often spoke of when referring to her abilities. Her instincts. Her uncanny senses. Though she couldn't see him, she could feel Coolie too if she concentrated hard enough. How and why was the endless mystery that defined her life.

Jinn caught her again, keeping his hands strong and steady around her waist. She trusted him. Trusted him with her life. And though she wasn't particularly concerned about preserving it, she relished it nonetheless. Theirs was a bond not so easily broken, an assurance borne from two years of camaraderie.

No matter how far she flew, his hands would find her every time.

And so she closed her eyes, letting him throw her up into the air again.

Iris breathed in the air. Spotting of a pair of butterflies, she watched them happily, their large wings, bright orange and pink, glinting in the light of the sun. A peace always washed over her when she was high in the sky. Up there with the birds, she could feel her blood pumping through her veins, sense the gentleness of the nature around her. She could hear her own heart beating and wondered to herself, in that silent moment, how long it had actually been beating for.

The day she arrived at Coolie's doorstep was the first day of her life that she remembered. Everything that may have happened in the weeks and months and years before was under lock and key somewhere deep in her mind. An unsettling condition, one temporarily eased only when she was flying free in the sky.

When she first began working for Coolie's company, most of the other workers at the circus had believed her to be around seventeen or eighteen years old. And slowly as the decade passed, many of them began to wonder why her youthful face had not aged a day. She'd wondered the same thing. She still wondered, though she tried not to.

It hurt to ask questions with not even a hint as to the answer. Sometimes, during those lonely nights, it hurt more than death. And she knew death.

"It's the way a lot of them are, those Africans," she'd heard a juggler say one day as they were cleaning out the buckets for the caged tigers. "They don't age quickly, I swear it. I've heard Granny Marlow's hair didn't start to gray until she crossed sixty."

It was a good enough explanation for now, though another decade or so and it'd be rather difficult to hide her un-aging body, even in a place known to revel in oddities. Iris knew her time was running out. The anxiety of when it would end often prickled her skin.

"Hmm . . . you've gotten rather heavy," Jinn casually noted as he held his position underneath her.

Iris pried her eyes open for the glare she aimed at him. "How dare you," she snipped.

"Really, though. This is harder than it should be."

"Quiet, you crank." Though the corner of her lips turned upward.

With a push, he bent back and let her drop to the rope behind her. The crowd erupted. An expert routine from only the best.

"Hmph. Still speaking as arrogantly as a *real* royal," Jinn said as they both waved to their adoring spectators.

"And who says I'm not one?" she returned with a little smile.

A short-lived smile, for her eyes had just caught a curious sight down below. A young man stood apart from the rest of the crowd, watching. His black tweed sack coat was open just enough for her to see his vest and gray shirt. Well-cut trousers and pristine shoes. Outwardly, he looked like any other wide-eyed, handsome young English gentleman, worthy of the attention he drew from the women walking past him. Clean and proper—except for his hair, a black, bloody war zone upon his head. Perhaps that was what those ladies had been staring at.

But something within Iris stirred as it always did when things did not feel quite right. A kind of buzzing underneath her skin, like her nerves were on fire, like they'd been plucked and cut too many times. The hazy image of a face shrouded in darkness arose in her mind's eye.

A memory?

Before the day she met Coolie, Iris didn't have any. None. Even now, she didn't know why. But what she did have was a *sense*. A sense that she needed hide herself from something—from the world, perhaps. And also a sense that there was a task she needed to complete. A task so important, it was burned into the marrow of her bones.

There was a reason she existed. She just couldn't remember what it was.

Those two opposing instincts were each as strong as the other. They'd get tangled up and muddled when she tried to examine them too closely. She may have settled on *hiding* for now, but that didn't quiet the powerful pull nagging at her from deep within. That task she had to achieve no matter what, lost along with her memories.

An acute pang suddenly swelled up inside her. Panicking a little, she tried to calm herself, but her gaze turned back again to the young man, who wouldn't take his eyes off of her.

His eyes. A pair of powerful, shocking, glinting sapphires. On her. Only on her.

And his knowing grin.

A flash of pain rocketed through her skull. She winced, and when she opened her eyes again, she looked upon a room filled with Egyptian artifacts.

The exhibit . . . , a voice deep within her whispered. *South Kensington . . .*

Muscle latching onto bone. Flesh layering over muscle. Nerves humming. A memory of agony powerful enough for her to feel the pain, just for a moment, physically in her own body.

A *memory.*

Madame, tell me . . . are you . . . a goddess? The words of a quizzical child filled with awe.

Iris's entire body chilled. A new memory?

It rushed through her so quickly, so suddenly that when she spun around at Jinn's prodding to wave to the other side of the crowd, her feet slipped . . .

And she fell.

Iris's heart stopped, her breath snuffed out as the crowd began shouting. Jinn leaped off the tightrope in a panic, yelling her name, catching the rope with one hand and extending his other in an effort to save her. Their fingers touched, but hers slipped quickly past. It was too late.

Iris hoped the gawking men and women below would have had enough sense to catch her, but that was, apparently, the problem. As her body hit a wave of arms, her head turned too quickly. The last sensation she felt before everything turned dark was her own neck snapping from the sheer force of the fall.

Alas, she had died.

And when she came to again and snapped her neck back into place, she found herself crumpled in a large, hairy, rather *shocked* gentleman's arms. Raising a hand, she wiped the drool dribbling down the left side of her lips.

That shocking hallucination she'd seen before falling . . . It couldn't have been . . . But was it really a memory? She looked around, unable to find the man who'd caused this mess, but by now he was the least of her problems. Not too much time had passed, which made sense, since the injury itself wasn't too . . . *involved*. It wasn't as if she had to regrow a limb or two. However, she was still in the middle of a confused and terrified crowd. Children were crying. Well, Iris felt like crying too.

Out of the corner of her eye she could see Coolie gaping at her. The few times she had died in the past due to an accident or some other unfortunate circumstance, she'd always had the good fortune to do so *out of his sight*.

This was very bad.

She had to come up with a plan and fast. She was supposed to be a circus performer. She was supposed to be a freak *only* within the boundaries of human imagination.

Imagination. Yes. Like Coolie had once said, people were willing to believe anything . . .

Gathering up renewed strength, she leaped out of the gentleman's arms, landed perfectly upon the ground, lifted her arms above her head, and took a very gracious bow.

"Did I surprise you?" she asked, using her light, melodic voice to address them for the very first time, though according to Coolie's rules, she was never supposed to. "Acting is another skill of a clown, or did you forget?" And she winked. "The drama and danger you've witnessed today is just one of the many treats awaiting you at George Coolie's circus. Come one, come all!"

She waved her hands at them in triumph.

Silence.

A pregnant pause.

Then, scattered clapping.

Soon, Iris found herself once more surrounded by hoots and hollers, though she caught a nervous laugh and a twitchy hand here and there.

At first Coolie could only stare. But the man was a professional, and business was business. He puffed out his chest once more and, trying very obviously hard not to expose the aftereffects of his shock, let his booming voice reign over the din.

"Th-there you have it! The Nubian Princess and the Turkish Prince, ladies and gentlemen!"

For now at least, the crowd continued to cheer.

2

MAKE NO MISTAKE; DYING WAS PAINFUL. The first of her deaths that Iris remembered couldn't leave her even if she tried. March 17, 1876, two years after she'd joined the Coolie Company. A winning St. Patrick's Day show in Ireland filled with boisterous applause had led her to a crowded celebration at a tavern that resulted in tragedy when a runaway carriage careened into her as she staggered drunk and alone along the bank of the River Suir. The cabbie ended up cowardly running off to avoid facing his crime while she ended up facedown in the icy waters.

Worse than the feeling of her heart quivering to a stop was the sharp jolt of it starting up again as she lifted her head out of the river and expelled all the water from her lungs in the dead of night. Before then, she'd known there was something *wrong* with her. Her lack of memories. Her uncanny senses, her ability to *feel* the life, the *essence* within others.

But this . . . Coming back to life felt unnatural and twisted. A horrible lie digging through her body to poison her heart. She'd always felt at least a little tainted. Built up over years, it was more than enough to drive one off a trapeze.

In fact, it did one very painful night.

And when she let go of that trapeze bar with a silent apology to dear Granny and plummeted to the ground—she *still* didn't die.

That was also the very day she met Jinn.

"Iris?" As if on cue, Jinn hissed, snapping his fingers. *"Iris!"*

A nudge in the ribs, and Iris was back at camp in Coolie's office—a mahogany trailer stationed near one of their animal tents, held up on a pair of wheels with a short rickety fold-out staircase digging into the grass littered with . . . well, litter. His office was big enough to hold a few people, though if even Jinn's head was close to touching the ceiling, there was no possible way the eight-foot couple was getting inside. Coolie should have been more thoughtful. Although the idea of Coolie being thoughtful was almost enough to make her giggle.

Coolie was now at his desk with a bottle of vodka, half-finished, to his right, his face planted on a scattered pile of bills and paperwork. Since he was muttering incoherently, his puffy red cheeks wobbling with each ratty breath, Iris took the time to nudge Jinn back.

"I must have drifted off with my eyes open again," she whispered. Admittedly, it did happen from time to time. "Did I miss anything?"

"Just Coolie ranting about his debts."

"So nothing new, then."

The apples, figs, and medicine she'd bought for Granny on the way back to the camp were still in the handwoven wicker basket her arm was now tired of carrying. Coolie had called them into his office the moment her feet had touched camp. Without a doubt, it had to do with her fall this morning, she'd thought fearfully. But ten minutes of ranting later and her fear turned to annoyance. The man was clearly drunk. The bottles on the floor were empty for a reason.

He was usually a mess, but this was still ridiculous. It was a wonder he'd been able to run the company for this long. His face was splotched red the first day she ever *met* him, his lecherous eyes looking her up and down. . . .

Actually, the day she'd met Coolie was an odd one. There was one thing in particular she remembered: herself, standing in the middle of a chaotic scene—men, women, and children fleeing the grounds of a fair in South Kensington ten years ago, bowler hats and purses abandoned on the grass. Herself, wearing a short white dress fluttering in the breeze. And then walking in a daze through the city streets until she found Coolie. As if possessed.

Out of the corner of her eye, she caught Jinn staring at her. Quickly, he straightened his broad shoulders and faced forward.

Jinn was in his old, fading red performance attire, the worn-out leotard he now used for practice. The faint hint of sweat drifting from his toned, lean body told Iris he'd indeed been practicing before being called in by Coolie for this sorry display.

"What?" she hissed, noticing Jinn's eyes on her again while Coolie chugged more vodka.

"Just surprised." Jinn gave her a sidelong look. "You bouncing back from that drop."

Here it comes. Iris stiffened. He hadn't yet said a word to her about this morning's incident. About her almost certain death.

About the naked despair written across his face as she fell from the rope.

"What happened this morning?"

She didn't answer. She didn't want to acknowledge his suspicions—and even less, his concern. The latter made her more uncomfortable.

Concern. She hid a little smile. Such a stark difference from the day he found her, a broken doll lying lifelessly on the ground that hot day in August when she'd thrown herself off the trapeze. The day they met.

That day was the culmination of all the endless, unanswerable questions she had for herself. Like: What was she? A devil? A beast?

How old was she? Where did she come from? Did she even have parents?

Why could she remember *nothing* before that day at the fair, the day she wandered through the streets of London, found Coolie, and asked for a job at his company?

What was the uncanny instinct that told her his doorstep was where she needed to be—that within Coolie's company was a safe presence she could rely upon? That safe presence turned out to be Granny Marlow, a woman whose bright, beautiful essence felt somehow familiar to her, like the smell of nutmeg on a freshly baked custard pie. She knew she was right the moment she met the old woman knitting a headpiece for one of the trampolinists.

But why did Granny, someone she'd never met before, feel so familiar to her? Why couldn't she *remember*? Why couldn't she *age*? *Why couldn't she die?*

Back then, just like now, no one at the company knew about her secrets, and there was no telling what they'd do if they did know. Sell her for some shillings? Coolie certainly would.

That last time in Ireland was a fluke. At the top of the trapeze, she'd decided to prove it by dying this time. Her death would fix the natural order of things. That's what she'd chosen to believe. And then she would never have to ask herself a single answerless question again.

Iris could still remember it: the sweet lullaby of gravity and wood crushing her bones inside her body. And when she awoke again, her legs and arms were at odd angles, her neck slowly repairing along with her pulverized organs.

"What am I?" she had whispered once her lungs were working again and she could finally speak, though she still couldn't move even after an hour had passed.

Footsteps. Iris hadn't even been able to shift her head to see who it was. Coolie? No, Coolie's essence, or whatever it was called, was cold and slimy like him. This person was completely different from her employer. She had felt that even before he opened his mouth to speak.

"I think I'm lost."

Finally, Iris managed to flop her head to the side to see a young man wearing normal slacks and a half-tucked white shirt carrying a paper bag filled with bread. Had Coolie hired new staff? This man looked too handsome to stay behind the curtains. But even as she'd lain flat on the ground, the boy's bored, sullen gaze had barely flinched.

"Um." The boy tilted his head to the side.

"Just getting some rest," she said, answering his silent question. "What? Can't a girl lie down where she pleases?"

"Screwed up a stunt, did you?"

"I don't screw up anything," she bit back. With great effort, Iris turned her head to look up at the ceiling lights. "Do you need something?"

"I start tomorrow," the boy said simply. His voice was deep, though he looked to be in his teen years. "I don't know where I'm supposed to be sleeping."

Iris then remembered that Coolie *had* hired a new performer. She'd heard about it that morning. Wasn't he supposed to be fire-eating with Natalya?

His nonchalance at the sight of her had annoyed her more than her inability to move her legs. "Sleep on the dirt for all I care."

"Okay. Should be softer than a wooden stage, at least."

He turned as Iris gritted her teeth. But before he'd gone too far, he swung back around.

"By the way, you're bleeding." He pointed at the little pool of blood leaking out from the back of her head.

"Oh?" She'd noticed. She just couldn't move to mop it up.

"You're not going to get it checked out?"

"I told you, I'm fine. Except that I can't move," she added under her breath, but when one of the boy's eyebrows raised, she knew he'd heard her. "Besides." She paused and pressed her lips together. "It doesn't matter whether I live or die."

The boy sighed and placed his bag of bread on the ground. Then, before she could utter a word to stop him, he scooped her up in his toned arms and carried her out of the tent.

"S-stop!" Iris stuttered, heat rising in her face as he crushed her against his chest. She felt small curled up in a ball, like a kitten nestled against him. "You don't have to—"

"Tell me where your room is," he said. "And mine, for that matter. You can manage that much, can't you?" Iris scowled as he paused. "Afterward . . . I'll fetch a doctor. You need one."

After giving him directions, Iris stayed silent for some time. Her instincts had been right. This boy didn't feel like Coolie at all. His essence was quiet and calm like a gently flowing brook, though something irregular stirred deep within it. A turmoil he kept well hidden. Even still, she'd known deep in her heart—he wasn't someone to fear.

"I'm Iris," she said begrudgingly as he carried her through the grounds, the sound of his boots crushing grass crisp in the cold night air.

"I didn't ask."

A surly, rude little ass, though, wasn't he? Iris bit her lip, ready to spit back a retort.

"Iris . . . ," he said, considering the name. A name she couldn't remember being given. "Well . . . I suppose that's useful information to know. And also . . ."

Iris waited, staring up at him as the moonlight reflected off his dark hair.

"Don't say it doesn't matter whether you live or die. It always matters to someone."

It always matters to someone. Now, two years later, it was clear that her death had mattered to Jinn this morning. She could never forget the look on his face. Iris wished she could catch the flutter inside her stomach and squash it like a mosquito.

Right now there was a hint of lingering suspicion in Jinn's expression that she didn't like, but she played it off with a teasing smile. "Worried, were you? Can't live without me?"

Jinn didn't take the bait. "The accident this morning. That was a long drop."

"Tightrope dancing's a dangerous field. I've gotten out of plenty of scrapes, you know that." Iris raised her chin smugly. "I'm pretty hard to kill."

"Like a cockroach."

Jinn dodged her punch with surprising ease. His reflexes were almost as good as hers.

Eventually Coolie's slurred words began to form coherent sentences again. "And I'm telling you two, this performance tonight is important. Very. *Important.* You two are one of my top acts—no, 'The Nubian Princess and the Turkish Prince' *is* my top act!"

"I don't know, I think Larry the Lion Tamer is quite talented," Iris said.

"If you don't wow those cretins in the audience—"

"We're aware of that," said Jinn calmly, though his stiff body betrayed his annoyance. "That's why it might be better use of our time to practice instead of standing here and—"

"Do you two recognize what these numbers are?" He lifted little brown pieces of paper off his desk but then crumbled them in his hand and let them flutter back down so quickly that Iris couldn't really see anything.

"Practicing our arithmetic, are we?" Iris muttered.

"This"—Coolie pooled more pieces of paper in his hand and dropped them again as if he were showering his desk with confetti—"is *all* the money I owe to some very, *very* frightening individuals. *All*. The money." He snorted out a derisive laugh. "Lots of money."

Jinn leaned in and whispered to Iris, "They came to visit him while you were out buying Granny's medicine."

"Yes! While you were *out*! Buying *food* and *treats* for all!" His voice peaked to a whimsical, operatic point as he spoke and waved his hands as if he were practicing a magic trick for children. Then Coolie slammed his desk. The portraits of his father and grandfather rattled on the wooden wall behind him. Both of those Coolies, Iris imagined, had likely been better at handling their money than the youngest of their line. "They were kind enough to remind me that unless I pay off my debts in the next two days, they'll take my fingers instead."

Stubby as they were. Knowing where they liked to explore, those debt collectors would likely be doing a service to women everywhere.

"Perhaps gambling isn't your strong suit." Iris shrugged. "Perhaps you should . . . well, quit? Fresh starts never hurt anyone . . . if they follow the law."

The circus proprietor fell silent. Well, Iris didn't care. She knew the last thing she should be doing in her situation was to be poking the nasty little bear, but the performers and staff were the ones who worked every night only to have Coolie piss their hard efforts away on horses and hookers. They were the ones right now moving the equipment to Astley's by carriage or practicing in their tents to get ready for the big show. Instead of screeching at them to make their already perfect routines even *more* perfect, he'd be better off hiring a rather strict accountant—at the very least, one that would hide his money from him.

Coolie zeroed in on Iris, his coat sleeve sliding across the paper-filled desk. "You know who else visited while you were away?"

Iris shook her head in exasperation. "Father Christmas?"

"The press. The London *Evening Standard*, to be exact."

Iris's heart gave a little quake. After exchanging a quick look with Jinn, she folded her arms across her chest. "So?" she responded in defiance, if only to hide the fears rising in her thoughts. "Isn't that a good thing? Don't we want the attention for our performance tonight?"

Coolie's ruddy face turned very serious. "They were asking about you."

The trailer fell silent again but for Coolie's alcohol-labored breathing. Jinn shuffled on his feet and looked sideways at Iris, his eyes asking questions she couldn't answer.

"They wanted to know more about the incident this morning."

"And?" Iris lifted her head to quash Coolie's silent accusation. "Like I said, it was all an act. Or do you think I *really* broke my neck?"

"A fall from that height isn't exactly one a lady just walks away from." Coolie words were fast and sharp.

"Oh, please. How many cannons has Richter blown herself out of?" Iris shot back. "And *she* walks away just fine every time. Why can't I?"

"You should be dead." Coolie sat back in his chair, his fingers drumming against his desk. "You *looked* dead. *He* thought you were dead. Could hear him hollering from the street."

Coolie flicked his head at Jinn, who cleared his throat and shuffled again. Her partner seemed reluctant to raise his gaze toward her, but once he finally did, it was Iris who turned away from him, her face slightly flushed, biting her lip. She wasn't good with moments like these, though hearing her heart beating in her ears was always a nice reminder that she had a working one. It wasn't as if she were an undead zombie or Frankenstein's monster, then—some of her many hypotheses about her true nature.

With an impatient sigh, she gave her neck a squeeze, pressing against the high collar of her blouse. A soft squeeze, of course. It was still a bit sore. "It seems just fine to me."

Coolie raised his eyebrow. "You wouldn't be trying to con a conman, would you?"

Iris's free hand flew to her chest. "Have I ever?" Silence. "I'm telling the *truth!*"

"I've been in the business my whole life. And with the acts I've seen and paid, if something seems off to *me*—"

"Then it's probably because you're a bit too fond of the bottle," Iris said before she could stop herself. She hadn't even meant to yell, but the walls of the trailer seemed rather closer than they had before.

Without taking his eyes off her, Coolie drew out a newspaper from one of his desks. The *Evening Standard*. "Says here a man exploded with electricity and walked away clean."

"You can't possibly believe that nonsense, can you?" Iris let out a laugh that wasn't at all as confident as she'd hoped. She looked up at Jinn. "Can *you*?"

Jinn didn't answer. His lips parted but then shut once more indecisively.

"There've been a lot of rumors lately moving around the country. Especially in the city. Strange rumors." Coolie snatched one of the little slips of paper on his desk and examined it. "*Strange happenings*, as the papers say. Strange, even for me."

At this, Jinn's expression was unreadable, and yet the Exploding Man headline had clearly caught his attention. He balled his hands into fists but couldn't take his eyes off the cover story. Finally, letting out a puff of breath, he looked away. There was just no telling what he was thinking.

Iris had to come up with something fast. "Good. We'll use it." Satisfied that she'd gotten Coolie's attention, she continued. "You know how obsessed some people are with the strange and the supernatural. Honestly, the occultism people practice in these parts behind closed doors would make one wonder why there are any churches here at all except to act as a cover for their base private lives. People are bored, *thirsting* for entertainment, so we'll do what we do best: we'll give it to them."

"Give it to them." Coolie stroked his chin as he examined her like a slab of meat at a butcher's shop. It made her skin crawl. It sounded like Coolie was getting an idea. But the sly smile splitting his face felt more like a warning—that his idea was a dangerous one. A *horrid* one. The goose bumps on her arms told her the same.

"Give it . . . to them," he repeated, and grinned that evil grin of his. "Yes . . ."

Iris gulped. Quietly, secretly, and despite her best efforts to keep everything together, she sensed the situation was unraveling nonetheless. Even as a tightrope-dancing African, she'd never felt so exposed. Her uncanny instincts still mystified her, but she knew well enough to trust them.

Coolie was not safe to be around—now more than ever. And though she desperately wanted to keep her fears at bay, that was becoming increasingly clear.

"I'm glad we agree. Come on, Jinn." She grabbed his slender, muscular arm and turned him around. "Coolie doesn't need us here. We should practice for tonight." Jinn stumbled over his feet, his waist smacked by her wicker basket as she pulled him toward the door.

"My dear Iris."

Iris's hand on the doorknob froze the moment she heard Coolie's voice.

"We've worked together for a little over ten years," he told her. "You know me. You should be able to trust me too."

Iris let out a silent, bitter scoff as he continued. "You can tell me anything. Anything at all. And I'll understand." Coolie paused before delivering a line that might have felt sincere if she hadn't worked with him for a little over ten years. "You have nothing to fear."

"Good." Iris turned her head slightly. "Then with that in mind, I have an announcement to make: for no reason in particular other than my terrible pay, this will be my final show for the Coolie Company."

"What?"

Both Jinn and Coolie had said it, but Coolie's was more like a roar that shook dust from the ceiling and rattled the walls.

"Well!" Iris's face perked up. "It feels great to get that off my chest. I'll see you tonight, then, George! Come on, Jinn, let's practice."

A slammed door separated Coolie's screaming from Jinn's confused protests.

3

"YOU'RE LEAVING THE COMPANY?"

"I hope these apples aren't too ripe." Iris peered into her basket. "Never can tell with those costers and their barrels of fruit. Bet they keep the rotten ones at the top."

Iris tugged Jinn along the crowded grounds and headed for Granny Marlow's tent. Coolie had tried to follow her, but in his drunken stupor, he'd tripped over his own feet and banged his head on the trailer floor and was now being attended to by one of his assistants. Staff and circus members stomped about, moving stage equipment, carrying water troughs for the animals, and practicing tricks, though the smell of nicotine meant some were on break. Iris looked up from her basket just in time to notice a staff member carrying three metal beams.

"You're *leaving*?" Jinn spat out again as they both, unlike Coolie, skillfully avoided a head injury.

Barley, one of the clowns, stopped testing his water-squirting flower to stare.

"Will you *lower your voice*?" The only time she wanted to be gawked at was during a performance for which she was being handsomely paid.

Jinn yanked his arm out of her grasp and placed his hand on her forehead. His touch had the unavoidable side effect of stopping her breath, just for a second—though certainly not long enough to kill her and confirm Coolie's suspicions right there. "You're feeling sick. That's it, isn't it?"

"I'm dying of consumption." Iris batted his hand away.

"This morning you snapped your neck, and now suddenly you're leaving the company?"

"I didn't snap anything," she whispered furiously.

"I thought you'd died."

"You were *wrong*."

"Iris!" Jinn gripped her slender arms. She could feel her veins pulsating beneath his fingers. "Iris," he repeated quietly, though with just as much intensity. "Tell me what's going on." He hesitated. "I'm your partner. You . . . you can trust me . . ."

Partner. Iris couldn't ignore the thump in her heart. Jinn had barely said one kind word to her during their first few months together. She wasn't sure when exactly it was that they began to casually speak. To *fight*. Both felt natural.

He didn't know her secrets, nor she his. But their partnership was the one thing that didn't need elaboration. She knew his body's rhythms as surely as she knew her own.

In the ten years she could remember, she'd forged close bonds with so few people. And now, because she couldn't overlook the anxiety growing in her heart, she'd have to break one of them. Iris hid a smile remembering how Jinn would threaten to drop her whenever she teased him about his leotards. If only she hadn't revived in front of so many people—in front of Coolie—then maybe she could still stay.

"You wouldn't understand," Iris whispered. Even *she* didn't fully understand the pull of that vibrant instinct screaming that it was time to move on.

"But what if I did?" Jinn drew her closer to him. "Tell me and let's see for ourselves."

People were watching them. Iris bit her lip. She felt as if she'd been stripped of her clothes. Jinn's narrowed eyes betrayed a kind of vulnerability that made Iris blush. This was the most persistent she'd ever seen him.

Iris pushed him away and took the wicker basket in her hand, squeezing the handle. "If . . . if it's our act you're worried about, I'll help you modify the choreography before I leave," she said, continuing through the grounds as the heat rose up to her face. Granny's tent was a few strides away. Iris could hear her coughing.

Jinn followed after her. "That isn't what this is about," he said. "I—"

"Egg!" The moment Iris entered Granny Marlow's tent, she set down the basket on the sewing table and spread her arms wide. The goose waddled to her from the pile of fabrics on the grass. Likely because she smelled of figs, but Iris preferred to think they'd gained a rapport since she rescued him in Paris last year after a fussy magician almost set him on fire in a hat trick gone wrong.

"Granny!" After picking Egg up, Iris rubbed his fire-blemished white feathers in her arms. "Your food and medicine has arrived!"

The old woman was hard of hearing with a terrible cough. Though her sight was not as sharp these days, her brown hands worked nimbly as she sat on a faded blue blanket in her gray dress and hemmed one of Iris's many costumes. She didn't stop working when Iris came in, but at the sound of Iris's voice, her dark violet lips stretched her wrinkled skin in delight.

"What's that, darling?" Granny Marlow said in a hoarse voice, her tied bonnet betraying strands of coiled gray hair. "You've brought something for me?"

It was Jinn who quietly picked the basket off the table and brought it to the old woman in the center of her tent. Iris always imagined that Granny had been a stunner in her younger days; even more so than those erotic, pearl-colored beauties in Pre-Raphaelite artworks, like the ones Coolie would buy so he could spend hours in his trailer alone with them. Granny had a narrow face, the coal eyes of a deer, and a kind smile—one that always brought peace to Iris's troubled heart, though looking at it now only drummed up her guilt.

Jinn glanced over his shoulder to Iris before handing Granny her medicine, almost as if he knew what she was thinking. Leaving the circus meant leaving her, too.

"It's your medicine, Granny," Iris told her in a small voice. "Should last you a month."

Granny stopped sewing and took the bottle. "Another one of these," she said with a frustrated sigh. "They taste like they were excreted from the devil himself."

Granny had a way with words. Iris noticed, with a warm feeling, the soft, lovely expression Jinn showed the old woman as he laughed in amusement.

"Don't be so *fussy*." Iris hugged Egg as he squawked in her arms. "See? Egg agrees."

"Only because you won't let me cook him." Granny laughed and picked Iris's costume back up—a bright white-and-yellow number meant to be her Egyptian headpiece, as she was supposed to be a Nubian . . . and from the Congolian jungle. Coolie didn't much care about cultural and geographical details, and alas, neither did his audience.

Granny was far more comfortable with natural ingredients like the ones she'd used for ailments as a child living in Western Africa than with the medicine Iris brought her. Indeed, her roots could still be heard mixed in with the patchwork English accent she'd acquired while working overseas for decades.

Ibadan, a city sprawling with forests and hills. Every night, Iris would lie on the grass as the old woman told her stories about her childhood—the games she played, the gods she worshipped, the food she ate. The markets, the houses. The military warriors she would sometime see while gathering water at the well.

Iris was always fascinated by Granny's stories, especially after she happened across an old issue of a foreign newspaper, *Iwe Irohin*, years ago. A sooty-faced street boy was demanding a high price, and she paid it after she realized she could *read* it, even though it was entirely in Yoruba—one of the native languages spoken in the area where Granny grew up. The old woman had one day decided to teach it to Iris, only to discover that although Iris didn't speak it well, she already understood it. *Iwe Irohin*. The literal translation was "book telling news," or "newspaper." That she already knew the language was the kind of unexplainable oddity that drove her desire to know herself. She'd hoped Granny would provide some clues, but there were things the woman didn't remember about her *own* past due to old age.

"Iris." Granny held up the headpiece. "Come, dear. Tell me what you think of this. It won't interfere with your dancing tonight, will it?"

"Doesn't seem to matter either way, Agnus." Sitting on the ground next to her and crossing his legs, Jinn bit into an apple and eyed Iris. "She won't be needing it for more than one show."

Iris scowled at him. It wasn't his childish challenge that shook her but Granny's innocence, her obliviousness to the mess Iris found herself in.

Granny depended a lot on Iris, especially as she aged. The medicine Iris just brought her was a month's supply, but where would Iris be in a month? What would she be doing? Although she'd decided to leave, she had no plans as to what to do next. Would she ever see Granny again?

Iris was dependent on her too, for friendship—and for *knowledge*. She knew in her heart that Granny held the key to unlocking many of her own memories buried deep within her. It was Granny whose essence she'd sensed the day she came to Coolie's circus, Granny whose soul had felt so familiar . . . as if Iris had followed it like an unraveled ball of yarn straight to her.

They even understood the same language. Iris's senses told her they'd known each other in the past. But Granny couldn't recall ever meeting her before her circus days. And Iris quickly realized that asking her anything concrete was pointless.

"I really don't believe we've ever met before," Granny had told her the day Iris had finally worked up the courage to ask, and immediately afterward, the old woman was overtaken by a fit of coughing and a sudden terrible headache. Iris didn't want to cause any more.

Granny knew her *now*. Cared for her. Spoiled her. And now Iris was leaving her.

"This headpiece is fine." Iris set Egg down and let him waddle around the tent. "I can always pin it down to make sure it doesn't fall off tonight."

"Perhaps Jinn can help you, then." A devilish twinkle appeared in Granny's eyes as she delicately placed the headpiece over his knees. "Wouldn't you like to? You're partners, after all."

Jinn's Adam's apple bobbed quickly as he grabbed the headpiece and handed it back to Granny without a word, just as Iris jumped up and began to stutter clumsily.

"A-as if I would allow *him* near the hair you worked so hard on! He would just ruin it!"

But Granny only laughed. "You two, always fighting." She plucked the clothes from Jinn's hands. "You shouldn't take each other for granted."

Silence pervaded the tent but for Egg's infrequent squawks.

"She's leaving, Agnus," Jinn said, his voice strained but even. "Leaving the company."

Iris's body stiffened as Granny Marlow sat up in surprise. "Leaving?"

"Leaving." Jinn plucked a blade of grass out of the ground and threw it away absently.

"I don't understand . . ." The confusion on her old face broke Iris's heart to pieces. "Did someone offer you a better job?"

"Don't be surprised if that's true, Agnus," Jinn answered bitterly. "Money trumps loyalty for some." He smirked. "And here I thought she liked at least you."

The bite in Jinn's voice cut deep. Her blood boiled while her heart sank. Jinn's words stabbed her in too many places at once.

"Iris?" Granny rested her hands on her lap and looked up at the trembling girl.

"It's so noisy outside." Iris stepped back. "I should go see if anyone needs me."

"But, darling—"

After one last hateful look at Jinn, she ran off.

There was just no other way out that she could see.

4

IVE YEARS AGO, ONE MIDSUMMER'S EVENING, Coolie had given Iris and a few other employees the opportunity to see a show at Astley's Amphitheatre. "Surveying the competition," Coolie called it. *Stealing ideas*, more accurately.

But Iris never forgot the thrill. The smell of horses emanating from the circular stage, the feisty strings from the musicians in the pit. Granny Marlow's laughter chiming with her own as the Coolie performers sat in a crowded box. The two women let Coolie drown in his jealousy while they enjoyed a night of fellowship bolstered by grand sights arousing the imagination.

After that night, Iris had promised herself that she would come back to the royal amphitheater one day, not as an audience member but as a performer. Today Granny would be able to watch *her* on that stage. Iris was finally here.

Here for her first and last Astley's show.

The setup was quite unique. The middle of the octagonal interior was a circus arena, with a high, pea-green painted barrier separating it from the audience. The musicians' pit was tucked between the circus ring and the theater stage at the front of the house. Right now the red curtains were drawn. The chandelier dangled from the vaulted ceiling, washing light over the old decorations, the drawings and hangings all in shades of red, lemon, and gold. Pillars held up the rows of boxes, now empty, but by tonight the galleries would be filled with spectators.

With only a few hours left until the show, Iris and Jinn, both dressed in old leotards, practiced their routine with a woolen string spread across the stage to mark their movements since their usual rope had not yet been hung over the circus ring.

First, their regular rope-dancing choreography. Then came the routine Coolie named "The Bolero of Blades," in which the Nubian Princess and the Turkish Prince fought for control over Egypt. The story was a doomed one; it was to end like the tale of Mark Antony and Cleopatra: star-crossed lovers of competing kingdoms whose love devolved into blood and tragedy.

Though knife wielding was Jinn's expertise, both of them were talented with blades. Jinn packed more power behind his movements. He was fast and brutal. Iris was nimble and delicate. She approached battle as she would any other dance. Their blades—*shamshir*, Jinn had called them—clashed loudly as the two performers flipped and cartwheeled perfectly, their feet light as feathers on their marks.

They practiced for almost an hour, each silent as the grave. Despite Jinn's and Iris's professional demeanors, the tension between them was palpable.

Afterward, Jinn decided to leave first. "I'm going for a walk before the show." The first words he'd spoken to her since Granny's tent. "If Coolie asks, tell him I'll be back in an hour."

The blade's hilt hot in her grip, Iris watched his retreating figure until he'd almost reached backstage. Then, steeling her nerves and sucking in a breath, she dropped her knives, ran up to him, and gripped his bicep with both her little hands. "Buy me a present!"

That certainly got his attention. Jinn turned around, incredulous. *"What?"*

"It's my last show." She looked up at him, batting her eyelashes. "I want a present."

Jinn shook his head. "You're unbelievable."

"One of a kind." Placing her hands behind her back, she leaned in. "A hat, perhaps?"

She smiled. No matter what had happened between them, she didn't want to leave on bad terms.

Gazing up at him, Iris could count every thick lash blanketing his eyes. Not that she wanted to. But as they signaled his indecision with a quick flutter, hope suddenly bloomed within her. She half expected him to respond with something like, "How about a straitjacket?" She desperately wanted him to. It was better than the painful nothing he gave her instead.

He left the stage without a single word to her.

With slumped shoulders, she spent the following excruciating minutes not knowing what to do with herself beyond sitting on the stage and watching the other acts practice. Her thin legs dangled over the edge. Natalya the Russian Fire Eater was phenomenal as usual in her lacy green tutu. As Iris applauded, the woman asked her where Jinn was.

"He and I were going to be partners, you know," she said, her mouth still smoking. "Jinn showed off his skill for Coolie and me on his first day. He was phenomenal. A real natural." Natalya swung her extinguished fire rods. "But in the end, he didn't much like it and rejected the job. Said that while he was good at it, he actually wasn't much of a fan of fire and put in for a different act. Anyway, I think he's far happier being your dance partner. Everyone says so."

Iris's blush suddenly gave way to numb hands. Everyone says so. *Jinn* . . .

Natalya's words echoed even after Iris was ushered away by the juggling duo and the pantomimes who needed to rehearse. Backstage was even more chaotic, with everyone busy getting ready for that night's performance.

"Who brought the bloody *goose* here?!" Iris heard the riding master yell as Egg disappeared around a corner with a princely squawk.

Meanwhile, even in these narrow halls, the other performers had time to ask her the same questions every time she passed:

"Iris, are you really leaving the company?"

"Oi, someone said you broke your neck this morning. That true? Bloody brilliant!"

"How're ya still walking around, then? You in one of those cults? You a Mason?"

"You're Iris. *The* Iris, aren't you?"

The last question she *hadn't* been expecting. Everyone knew her here.

A young man had asked it just after she'd left the gallery. He stood in front of the main entrance, his face blocked from view as he held up one of Coolie's posters for their show, on which she and Jinn were drawn with cartoonish exaggeration as two little figures flipping on the rope. She could see only the man's expensive black loafers and perfectly tailored brown jacket and pants. But his very presence made her stomach flop and her skin tingle with electricity. She took a step back.

"I saw you this morning. When I told my younger sister about your show at Astley's, she begged me to get your signature for her." He dipped his right hand into his jacket pocket, folding the poster with one hand.

It was *him*. Messy black hair and deep sapphire eyes. The young man who'd made her slip and die at this morning's performance, whose very presence had turned her already precarious life upside down. She suddenly felt as if she'd been punched in the gut.

"You . . ." An acute shock of pain ran from her elbows down to her back at the sight of him. Her heart began hammering in her chest as he drew out his pen and gazed at her.

His essence was *familiar* to her, the first one she'd felt since meeting Granny so long ago. It filled her now that her attention was wholly attuned to him. The resultant quivering of her body sent her two entirely different messages:

Go to him. He'll never betray you.

And the other . . .

He smiled. "My name is Adam Temple."

Run.

Iris backed away and turned so fast she nearly tripped over herself. She gripped her head, trying to catch her quick breath.

"The exhibit," she whispered before she could catch herself.

"Excuse me?"

She heard his voice behind her. But she was already scurrying up the wooden flight of stairs to the second floor of the lobby. She had no time to plan her escape. The ladies' retiring room to the left would do, except that this

Adam followed after her, calling her name with worry. Her feet stumbled to a stop just as he cut her off, blocking the entrance.

"Miss. I'm sorry, I didn't mean to scare you."

He sounded sincere. So sincere, she looked at him once more, at his sharp jaw and high nose bridge. At his otherwise delicate, almost feminine features. Then all of it blurred, and her head once again began to ache.

Ache with a memory.

An exhibit at South Kensington. And a child gazing up at her, holding a white dress for her to wear. Gazing in arrogance, in *awe*.

Madame, tell me . . . are you . . . a goddess?

A child with messy black hair and bright blue eyes.

"It was you."

"Excuse m—"

Iris tackled the young man through the door only for the lavatory to explode with the scandalized screams of half-dressed trapeze artists. She didn't care, not even when boots began flying at their heads. Iris kept her hands firmly around Adam Temple's neck, and as he struggled to breathe, all she could think about was that new memory, barely a shadow, and this man, *pretending* he didn't know what he was doing to her.

"Stop, you're hurting him!" one woman yelled, snapping Iris back to reality. She let him go immediately, shooting to her feet as Adam rubbed his neck and began coughing. As the trapeze artists gasped in fear, he put up his hand to signal he was okay. Iris felt sweat dampen her forehead.

"No autographs . . . ," she said absently.

"You could have just told me." Adam laughed a little as he stood, dusting off his pants.

How could he *laugh?*

Iris pushed him out the door before he could gain his bearing and slammed it closed between them.

"What's wrong with her?" whispered one woman as she crouched in the corner.

"I heard she and Jinn had another fight," whispered another. "Just let her be."

They went back to dressing and doing their makeup as Iris pulled her knees up on the floor, her hand covering her mouth. She hadn't the time nor the presence of mind to parse out what had just happened before she heard Adam's voice again through the door.

"Miss Iris—"

"Enough," she yelled, burying her head in her knees. She could still remember the feeling of a body—*her* body—recomposing, muscles, flesh, and bone. And another memory: wandering through that chaotic South Kensington fair, the white dress she'd been given fluttering as people rushed past her. Other than that, her thoughts of the day were disjointed, unreliable. Painful. "I want nothing from you."

"What about secrets?"

Iris's back straightened, the air slowly and deliberately filling her lungs as she lifted her head and stared at the door separating them.

"What about knowledge?"

Adam's voice was even. Firm. Confident.

"What about *truth*?"

Iris opened the door and shut it behind her quickly, pushing him farther into the hall. The two stared at each other in silence, though only he smiled cordially.

"You don't have a sister, do you?" Iris's fingers flexed and relaxed, ready.

"I did. She's gone now. Died long ago." Genuine sadness crept into his features. He shut his eyes, and when he opened them again, only a hint of his melancholy lingered.

"That boy was you," she whispered, her throat dry. "In South Kensington . . ."

"Just as I guessed. You don't remember anything, do you? You're really . . ."

His simple words struck her nerves.

"Iris." Adam caressed her name. His deep, elegant voice made it sound beautiful. It calmed the fear instinct in her enough to get her thoughts in order. "Aren't you tired of hiding?"

He *knew* her, somehow. It was why he was at the performance this morning.

"Tell me." She stepped forward before she could stop herself. "Tell me what you know."

"I wonder if I should. It may not end very well for me." His rubbed his neck and winced. "How about this? How about you come to me when you're ready?"

He pulled a card out of his pocket and handed it to her.

LORD ADAM TEMPLE
19 MELBURY ROAD, THE CITY OF LONDON

"Of course, I'll never force you. Everything is entirely your choice." He straightened his jacket. "But when you're ready to speak of secret things, Iris, come and find me."

With a cordial bow, he left her.

A Meeting at Club Uriel

52 Pall Mall Street
947 days since the Spring Day Massacre

THE WIDE, ROUND TABLE IN THIS room of shadows was not fit for any knight. Six members of a secret brotherhood sat in their seats instead, each suspicious pair of eyes sliding from person to person, ready to react to the slightest hint of mischief.

Mischief, as it were, was Adam's forte. Which perhaps was why he was the last to arrive.

The sound of the door shutting behind him, courtesy of Madame Bellerose's butler Pierre, reverberated across the high ceiling. The flickering lights from the seven candles melted silently into their candlesticks, casting shadows across the seven banners draping the golden-brown walls.

One candle and one banner for each member.

And one candle in the center, impossible to miss; it stood as a white pillar in its bronze candlestick, towering over a man's rusted skull carefully plated. A former member, or so Adam heard. The long dagger in the skull's mouth glinted as its bones screamed a silent oath.

The silver chandelier sparkling above, along with the candle flames and the dying evening light seeping through the narrow openings in the velvet window curtains, helped Adam to better see his enemies.

The Enlightenment Committee.

It was a room no one but they could enter, on the sixth floor of Club Uriel, a building that, to the outside world, simply housed one of the many clubs that high-society gentlemen used as an escape from their domestic prisons. Only those of the most prestigious standing—politicians, explorers, businessmen—could obtain membership.

Here, the seven members that formed the upper echelon of that club planned in secrecy.

"Good of you to join us, lad," said Gerolt Van der Ven of Belgium to Adam's right, his thick, hard stomach tense as he laughed low like the rumble of an earthquake. Still in his navy-and-gold military suit despite the fact that the injuries he incurred during the Franco-Prussian War more than ten years ago had forced him out of service. The silver cane he used to walk. The silver saber he used to kill. Despite his jolly laughter, he looked as though he wanted to kill Adam now, his black eyes trained on him. "You're late." His thick black brows drew together.

Adam watched the black hairs of the impatient man's beard shift underneath an expulsion of breath. The boar upon Van der Ven's violet banner looked as if it may strike him as well. "You'll have to forgive me. I was otherwise engaged," Adam answered simply.

"Oh?" Madame Bellerose, next to Van der Ven, leaned over, her golden-gloved finger perched underneath her bottom lip. Perhaps she chose gold today to match the color of her banner. "With what? Or perhaps I should ask with whom?"

Originally, it was Madame Bellerose's older brother who sat in her seat. But that seat became hers a decade ago after she revealed he was selling Enlightenment secrets to the Romanovs of Russia. It wasn't usual to have a woman among them. In fact, Bellerose was the first. Once the Committee saw how much pleasure she took in executing her brother with a bullet to the brain, they decided to take her under their wing. Ruthlessness knew no gender.

"You're not the type to keep women company, or perhaps I have you mistaken?" Bellerose grinned. "Should I guess at who the lucky girl is?"

Adam checked the grandfather clock next to the door behind him. Six o'clock. Iris's performance would begin in two hours. Since finding out she'd been hiding in the circus, he'd been curious about what had led her to such a life. His suspicions were confirmed by their encounter today—she'd lost her memories. It wasn't an act. He could tell by the terror in her brown eyes. Amnesia . . . perhaps a result of what she'd experienced in the past. Many war veterans went through similar experiences. Sometimes the mind had to protect itself from the truth.

But that such a powerful, beautiful creation had no idea of what she was capable of only made him tingle with excitement. An elevated being traipsing about on a tightrope to thunderous applause. The very premise filled him with boyish glee. He'd been dying to watch a show of hers. Adam could only hope this meeting of monsters would be finished by then.

"Enough." A series of unsettling coughs erupted from the withered throat of Luís Cordiero, an old man whose gray hair draped his shoulders. His family founded the Commission of Africa, created to fund Portugal's plundering of the continent. He could afford his medicine. "What matters is that he's here now. Though not as punctual as his father used to be."

"The boy *murdered* his father. We're dealing with a new Temple now, don't forget."

When Riccardo Benini smacked Adam on the shoulder, he began to question the seating arrangements. Unfortunately, they were set, which meant he was forced to sit next to this golden-haired fool in his silk nightwear that looked to be made out of all the flags of Europe.

"For what it's worth, I like you a lot better, boy," Benini continued, calling him "boy" even though he was less than a decade older—the second youngest member. "John annoyed me. So many moral quandaries." He rolled his eyes. "As far as I'm concerned, you did a good thing by getting rid of him."

Adam forced a smile. "From what I understand, I've been summoned here to talk about our upcoming event. Perhaps we should get to that."

"I agree." Madame Bellerose sat back in her iron-plated chair. "The *tournoi* begins soon. By the end of the hour, I expect us to have put a finality to the finer details."

"Ah, the *tournoi*," Benini repeated whimsically, imitating her accent while twirling a long lock of his golden hair around his finger.

The Tournament of Freaks.

"We finish this quickly. Is everyone in agreement?" asked Bellerose.

She looked around the table, as did Adam. Opposite him was Albert Cortez, whose graying head barely peaked over his candle. He straightened his goatee. His family helped found the Bank of Spain more than a hundred years ago. With his short stature and whining voice, he'd always reminded Adam of the rabbit from *Alice's Adventures in Wonderland*. But Adam knew not to underestimate him—any of them. Perhaps Boris Bosch least of all.

Bosch. The scar on the left side of his face was said to have come from his pastime of hunting tigers in Siberia, the ivory teeth of one decorating his neck, tied by a thin string. A German arms dealer, owner of Bosch Guns and Ammunitions. Unlike those around the table who'd inherited their wealth, he'd earned his by trading in murder and war. Bosch was a busy man. He already had plans to conduct his usual business during the tournament, which meant Adam didn't expect to see him much. But Bosch was still dangerous in his own way. His loyalties were only to his own fortunes. Adam did well to remember.

"Then we'll start with rule number one." Benini lifted his finger. "No cheating. Oh, and rule number two: no killing each other."

"But of course." Bellerose shrugged.

"Such is the purpose of the tournament itself, is it not?" agreed Cortez.

Benini's blue banner, upon which was drawn the chameleon. Van der Ven's violet boar. Bellerose's golden swan. Cortez's green stag. Cordiero's orange bear. Bosch's black wolf. And the Temple ram, red as blood. The banners of the Enlightenment Committee hung only when they met together like this. They belonged to the seats, not the people, and so became the symbols of those who inherited them. Some years ago, the other banners had been retired once the members they represented met their bloody end. Fourteen reduced to half. From then on, they settled on having a roster of seven only. Perhaps fourteen had been too big a number for a dangerous group that wielded so much power. It was then that the Committee also realized that a massacre was not the proper way to deal with disagreements.

But a tournament? A little extravagant for Adam's tastes. Murder was far easier.

Van der Ven let out a low, rumbling breath in agreement. "And we remember the prize of the winner."

"Control over the Ark." It was Adam who spoke this time, his head resting on his left hand, his elbow propped up on the arm of his chair. His eyes were closed, but he could feel the others' ravenous gazes upon him. When he opened them again, Van der Ven's thick lips spread slowly into a smile. "Though without all the components we need, the Ark is nothing more than a rather impressive, rather useless piece of machinery."

"That's entirely *your* fault, my boy." Cortez, again with that whining, high-pitched, sneering voice of his. Adam returned his fussy accusation with a bored, sidelong look. "When you killed your father, you should have made sure to retrieve the key from him first."

True. And his father had *fled*, probably upon realizing that Adam had very much meant to pry that key from his cold, dead hands. But that was one of two important pieces of intelligence the Committee couldn't ever know.

It took a lot for Adam to fake his old man's death to the Committee. John Temple needed to stay dead while his son hunted him. The key was not for anyone but *Adam* to have. The Committee was just a means to an end.

"And what of the British Crown?" Van der Ven demanded.

Bosch's yellow brows twitched with interest. Thus far he'd been resting his pointed chin on his clasped hands, his gray hunter's cap catching the shadows that his candlelight cast across his angled face.

"The narrow-minded fools." Cortez laughed. "They have no idea what they have in their possession."

"Not yet." Bellerose brushed a strand of burgundy hair from her face. "But it's best we keep our eye on things until we can take full control of the situation."

The Enlightenment Committee and the British Crown. Adam liked to think of them as the two antagonists of a play they didn't know they were in. *Neither* side knew the full truth. Adam had to move quickly within the bounds of the tournament to ensure it stayed that way.

That meant finding his father before the truth could be revealed.

Van der Ven folded his arms over his large chest. "At the very least, we need to ensure they and the public are none the wiser while the tournament is conducted."

"Some members of parliament are also members of Club Uriel," said Cortez. Adam knew too well. Carl Anderson and Neville Bradford were as well while they were still among the living. "They're doing what they can to ensure secrecy during the days of the tournament."

Benini laughed into his hand. "Good to see the club is as excited as we are for the tournament to come." Of course, Club Uriel itself wouldn't have much of a hand in the tournament outside of spectatorship. The combined astronomic wealth and influence of the men and woman sitting around this table was more than enough to provide the resources and bribes needed to pull off a secret event of this scale. Though the identities of the Committee members were known to Club Uriel's patrons, they did not know the *true* purpose of the tournament itself. It was more than just a game. But that information was for the Enlightenment Committee alone.

"So then." Bellerose looked to the men on her right and left. "I'm right to assume that this will be a fight to the death?" She paused. "That is, as far as our champions will go?"

"In the previous meeting, we decided that the players of the tournament could do as they wished within a certain set of boundaries," said Cordiero. "Eventually, however, only one team will be left standing."

"That is, whoever's still *alive* within that team by the end of the tournament," Benini corrected, letting melting candle wax drip over his index finger. "And the one of us sponsoring that team will thus win the tournament." He grinned.

The Tournament of Freaks. Seven teams sponsored by the seven members of the Committee. A bloody battle that most would not survive. But the Enlightenment Committee was fine with the sacrifice of *other* lives.

"Then has everyone completed their roster?" Van der Ven liked to take control of things. It was the general in him. Most nodded. Some, like Cortez, sat silently. Benini, on the other hand, squirmed in his seat.

"Riccardo . . . ," Cordiero began, almost like a scolding father.

"Come now, it's not as easy as one would think, finding dependable freaks."

Benini put up his hands as if guarding himself against an oncoming animal. "And what about Adam?"

"As I just joined the Committee at the beginning of this month, I haven't had as much time as you have in finding combatants," Adam defended himself coolly. "But I'm working diligently on completing my team."

In truth, Adam had a few names in mind from the research he'd conducted during the past few weeks. But to him, the tournament was nothing more than a bit of theater to pass the time. The Committee didn't know how helpful they were being to him, keeping themselves busy with this nonsense while he searched for his father.

The moment he found John Temple, the purpose of this tournament would cease to exist.

Van der Ven grumbled. "You have three days to submit a list of your roster to the Committee—their names *and* abilities, to ensure there's no foul play. I'll be traveling to Berlin for the Congo Conference in precisely one month," he said. "I would like for this business to be done before then."

"Well, I won't be submitting tonight, I'm afraid. I have an engagement."

Madame Bellerose perked up. "An engagement with *whom*?"

"No one. It's just a bit of evening entertainment."

"You mean Astley's Amphitheatre?"

Adam tensed. Though he struggled to relax his body, he was sure Bellerose did not miss the way his gaze suddenly darted in her direction. Her grin only stretched wider.

"Weren't you there earlier today?" Bellerose stared up the long white shaft of her candle. "Hours before the show, no less. Must have been someone you wanted to meet terribly."

She'd had him followed. Adam's fingers twitched.

"Word has been going around about an act more wondrous than the human imagination," she said. "The circus proprietor—George Coolie, I believe? He's been voraciously spreading the rumor to the upper classes of society to fill his seats. Though he's been secretive about the details, many like myself are quite interested in witnessing the wonder he's referring to."

He'd been so focused on finally reaching Iris that he'd underestimated

Coolie's discerning eye for freakery and greed for profit and recognition. England was a land with an appetite for the supernatural. But whispers of the supernatural had been growing louder since news circulated of the robber who exploded with some kind of electrical current and escaped with his jewels nonetheless. That there were many more like him in this city and beyond was something few knew. Club Uriel and the Enlightenment Committee were among those few.

Well, it didn't matter to Adam if this sick world learned of the supernatural. Given that the world was ending, it would learn of the supernatural soon enough.

But Iris was different from the extraordinary beasts that stalked the streets. And she was far more precious. That morning, seeing her routine had delighted him. It was a dazzling feeling that brought him back to his early childhood days, before there was blood on his hands and bruises on his body. That sense of wonder. Joy. Whatever worry that'd gripped him when he watched her fall disappeared the moment he saw the crowd catch her. He'd left thinking she was safe. But what if he'd been too far away to realize that she'd actually died in that moment? It wasn't her safety he was concerned about but her secrets. She'd hidden well in the ten years since they first met. And now, because of him, she was on the radar of the member he trusted the least with this sacred information.

Blast it! Suddenly, with him unable to stop it, Adam's gaze turned sharp and dangerous. Only for a second, but a second was all Bellerose needed. Her own expression softened at the sight of it. She sensed his bloodlust, just enough to give her the elation she craved.

He should have realized that he'd be tailed. He would have if he hadn't been so riveted by the thought of meeting Iris. Lesson learned.

Right now, for reasons Adam could only hypothesize, Iris had no idea who she was and what she was capable of. She was like a newborn baby. Innocent. Not what he'd pictured these past ten years. He'd given her his card with the intention of providing her the time and space to gradually learn about herself in safety. But now the girl was known to Bellerose. Who was to say Madame wouldn't swap out someone among her own champions to put Iris on her team? Or recommend her to those still looking to fill their roster? Why wouldn't they want her? A fighter that couldn't die would assure their victory. His eyes slid to Benini.

At this delicate stage, he didn't want Iris in danger. Even though she couldn't die, dying was still painful. Adam knew this through witnessing the deaths of others.

That his father was still alive was one fact neither the Crown nor the Committee could ever know. Iris's *true* nature was another.

"You wouldn't mind if I joined you, would you, dear Adam?" Bellerose clasped her hands together in excitement. "It's been some time since I've enjoyed the wonders of the circus."

Adam had no choice but to nod. But as they finished their discussions of the tournament, as they slit their index fingers in ritual and let their blood put out the flames of their candles, Adam's mind was working. He'd originally planned to hide Iris while building his team without her, keeping her out of the Committee's sight. But perhaps he could hide her *within* the tournament.

"I'll retire to my room and prepare for tonight," Bellerose whispered into his ear on her way out of the room. "I expect you'll have a carriage waiting for me the moment I'm ready, won't you, my dear Adam?"

"I will pick you up promptly in half an hour."

"Oh my, that isn't nearly enough time!" Bellerose laughed, squeezing his shoulder before leaving the room with the others.

Hide Iris *within* the tournament. This was fine. No, it was an even better plan. The chaos of blood and battle may be what would finally awaken her instincts.

She'll come to me, Adam thought. He knew this as surely as he knew the end was near.

5

"CURTAINS IN ONE HOUR!"

Iris hoped Granny Marlow would finish her hair in time. She squirmed on her uncomfortable stool in the dressing room, watching Granny's fingers in the mirror plaiting her hair as if slipping through the strings of a harp.

Then again, harps didn't feel pain, lucky for them. Granny weaved the braids row by row, starting from the left side of her head and plaiting to the right. Each braid wound like a river across the back of her head until there was no more skin for it to cling to, then fell down her right shoulder, past her apple-shaped hips. That was how long Iris's thick hair was.

Granny crafted the cornrows quickly, understanding the time constraints. Elsewhere in the crowded dressing room, other women were finishing their makeup, pinning their hair, or practicing their tricks. Iris already had her silver leotard on, over which she wore a midnight-blue, pinstriped one-piece—like a bathing suit, but much shorter, as that lecher Coolie preferred. The sleeves barely reached to the middle of her forearm, lined with frilly white lace, the same fabric Granny used as a belt to cinch in her waist. The shortened Egyptian tunic she was to wear over it was for the beginning of her routine. She was to reveal the devilish little number underneath in the middle of the act.

In the center of each braid, Granny fastened one of the little gold clips she'd been using for the past five years, and so they were somewhat rusted. Iris winced as Granny worked her painful magic, and Adam Temple's card twitched in Iris's hand. She looked into the round mirror fastened to the wall. The red blush, sapphire eyeshadow, and peach lips astounded her. Sad that such beauty had to come with a generous helping of agony.

"Stop squirming and hollering, child," Granny said once again. "Pain is part of life."

"And *death*." Iris sniffed as a little tear stung her right eye. The old woman had little compassion when it came to perfecting her hairstyles. Blinking the tear away, Iris looked down at Mr. Temple's card.

When you're ready to speak of secret things, Iris, come and find me.

Despite her aching scalp, Adam remained at the forefront of her thoughts.

An exhibit at South Kensington. South Kensington had once had annual fairs during the seventies. But a strange occurrence happened at one in 1874: a gas-line explosion in the main hall. She knew because she'd been there that day. She could remember standing among the fiery chaos in a daze before eventually leaving the fairgrounds and wandering the streets. Hours after, she'd found Coolie and Granny.

But why was she there in the first place? Could she trust Adam to tell her? *Should* she? No matter how desperately she considered it, she just couldn't find the answer.

"You know, darling, it's a shame you've decided to leave," said Granny, finishing up the latest braid. "After all this time. Who will read to me and talk with me every day as you do?"

Iris's bottom lip curled inward as she crumpled the card in her hand.

"But it's *your* decision. Don't let anyone guilt you into thinking otherwise. If you've decided to move on, no one can hold you back any more than they can keep grass from growing. I just hope," she added sadly, "that you'll find a way to keep in touch with me."

"Oh, Granny. Of course."

She felt hollowed out from the inside. Would she have to leave, after all?

Even if Coolie thought she was some kind of undead vampire, if she could convince others she was simply double—no, *triple*—jointed, or some other drivel, she could stay at the circus, couldn't she?

"When you are ready to leave, make sure you come to my tent." Granny fashioned a gold clip to the braid she'd just finished and started the last one, rubbing a line of coconut oil Iris had purchased from the market down her exposed rows of scalp. "I have something for you."

"What is it, Granny?"

"Well, you'll see when you come to my tent, won't you?" Granny's teeth, slightly stained, caught the light of the lamps above them. "Consider it your going-away present."

When Granny finished, Iris admired her handiwork in the mirror. "You're very good at this," she said before falling silent. "I'll miss you so very much."

Granny laughed. "I used to braid hair in my neighborhood as a child. I suppose I should have taught you how to do it yourself instead of doing it *for* you all these years. But then, I thought we'd have more time together."

Off in the corner, their new magician practiced her magic trick. A handkerchief in a hat turned to three beautiful butterflies that fluttered through the air. Bright green and gold and orange as the sunset. Iris stared at them, admiring of their beauty, envious of their freedom.

Maybe she didn't have to leave, after all. She may feel safe if she just knew the truth of who she was. Armed with the truth, she'd be able to figure out how to better maneuver around Coolie and the other performers. Knowing her past would give her a better map of the future—and how to include in that future the people she cared for.

"Granny, come for a moment." Standing, she drew Granny into an empty corner of the room and spoke to her about Adam, leaving out the stranger details. "You know I don't know much about my past. This man said he could tell me. But I won't have to rely on him if you could just . . . remember something." She gazed up at Granny with pleading eyes. "Granny, the day I met you, I knew we'd met before."

"But . . ." Granny began coughing again, wincing and touching her temple as if too much information had come in at once. "I told you, child, we did not know each other before you began working at the company."

"That can't be true!" Iris grasped the woman's hands tightly. "My gut tells me that isn't true. We *must* have known each other in the past."

"But that's . . ." Granny shook her head slowly, trying to grasp everything.

"Thirty minutes!" A staff member's sweaty head appeared through the open door of the dressing room just to yell this before disappearing into the hallway again.

"Can't you remember, Granny? Anything about me? Where we met? Or perhaps the parents that gave me my name."

"Oh, no, darling, it was that awful man who named us," she said suddenly before blinking absently. The old woman was taken aback by her own words . . . as was Iris. So Granny *had* known her.

In truth, the name Iris had never felt like her own at all. It was as if it were nothing more than a placeholder. And now this. Her life itself was a clown's mask forced upon her until she could finally learn the truth.

Iris took in a careful breath. "Tell me more, Granny. You must remember something more."

Iris's timing was terrible. The show was about to begin. But she couldn't stop herself, even as Granny's hands began to shake in her grasp.

"Please try, Granny, *try*. Where have we met before?" Granny furrowed her brow in confusion. "Did you know me in Ibadan? Or did we meet at the . . . at the exhibit?"

"Exhibit." Granny's eyes grew wide, her lips parted in a frozen yell. *"Exhibit."*

She spoke the word as if it were a nightmare made flesh. Her chest bobbed up and down in her gray dress, faster and faster until suddenly she yanked her hands from Iris's grip, stepping back. "No. No, you're—" She grabbed her hair. "No, you're twisting things. That's not . . . You—"

Iris watched in horror as Granny lapsed into a fit of coughing, holding her head with both hands and backing up until she bumped into a table and collapsed onto the ground.

"Granny!" Iris screamed. By now everyone in the room had swarmed around them, offering Granny water, bringing clothes and towels to cushion her head. "Granny, are you okay? Granny, I'm sorry! I'm so sorry!"

Her face stained with tears, Iris fed Granny a glass of water handed to her by one of the trapeze girls. Once Granny had finally relaxed, Iris took a handkerchief from the magician and dabbed the beads of sweat from her wrinkled skin.

"We should call someone to take her back to her tent," a juggler told her. "The atmosphere of the show might be too much for her right now."

Iris asked for a staff member to arrange for a horse-drawn cab to bring her back to the grounds. But when it was time for Granny to leave, before Iris handed her off to the staff members, the old woman whispered words that left her standing in blank confusion:

"Exhibit . . ." Granny Marlow's eyes glazed over, her movements sluggish as she walked toward the door. "If those men hadn't kidnapped Sister and me, then, child, *you* would have."

"Some experiences are too difficult to face," Jinn told her from behind the doorway to the circus ring as they waited for their cue. "For some, it's easier to bury them. But when you try to drag them out by force . . ." He trailed off, shaking his head. "Whatever those experiences might be for Agnus, I'm sure she'll be okay. She's strong."

Though standing right next to her, he had to bend down and speak into her ear so she could better hear him. The boisterous, full house would have made it impossible otherwise. Iris was too distraught to care much about whatever tension still remained between them; Granny Marlow's episode had dissolved all other worries to insignificance.

Sister? *Kidnapping?* She still couldn't make sense of the woman's words, and the more she tried, the worse a blow it was to her heart. But she nodded anyway, blinking her eyes rapidly. She couldn't let her makeup, freshly redone, spoil again this close to their set.

I really can't stay here, can I?

In the dressing room, for one terrifying moment, Iris thought that Granny's heart would fail. Perhaps one day it *would* fail because of her. Granny might hold the key to her past, but Iris's search for herself couldn't endanger a life, especially one so precious.

"Jinn, you'll take care of her, won't you?" She suddenly grabbed his arm, looking up at him pleadingly. "And Egg! You have to make sure Coolie doesn't cook him!"

"Relax," Jinn said as the audience burst into applause. The lion tamer had the circus ring, and his talent for directing deadly beasts was one that easily satiated the crowd's appetite for thrills. After a slight hesitation, Jinn placed his hand on Iris's shoulder as if to keep her from floating away. "I'll do whatever you ask of me. You know that."

Iris's heart skipped. While Jinn kept his eyes out for their cue, she was captured by his gentleness, drawn in by its soft texture. It didn't appear very often. But when it did, it made her fingers tingle. She hadn't realized until this point how much she would miss it.

She hesitated before speaking next. "Jinn." She stopped. "You said some experiences are too difficult to face. Is that a personal insight from the life you've lived?" She noticed his downturned eyes. "Is that why you've never told me about yourself?"

When Jinn did not answer, Iris pressed her lips together, tugging on her headpiece absently. "I think when I leave," she started with a little whimsical smile, "I'll miss your brooding the most. Women seem to love it. Not me, mind, but I've gotten used to it over the years." Her laugh was small and lifeless. "And I'm so talkative," Iris added, filling the silence between them accordingly. "How did we ever put up with each other? A switch in partners might not be such a bad idea, after all. Maybe you'll find someone with a longer temper than mine."

Iris's eyes trailed the path up his sandy jawline, recently shaved, to his fierce gaze fixed on the circus ring. "I certainly won't miss your nagging, though," she said with another laugh, thankful her shade of skin veiled her blush.

Still nothing from him. He wasn't even looking at her. Iris's body felt numb. "I really wonder if I'll miss you at all," she muttered with a solemn tinge.

"Iris." Still he watched the stage, waiting for the applause to die. "What do you think of me?"

And suddenly Jinn was looking at her, and he was very, *very* close. In that moment, Iris could no longer hear the crowd or the roars of the tiger. Only the soft pounding of her heart, the loud rushing of blood in her veins. "W-what?" she asked.

Jinn didn't respond. He didn't speak again. He just gazed at her, waiting.

"Jinn!" Coolie entered the backstage area, waving his hands. "I want you to enter stage right. Larry's gone over time. We're scrapping the initial floor dancing and starting with the tightrope first. I need you to go to your place—*now*."

It would take some time for Jinn to make his way around the theater stage to the opposite circus entrance. But the show had to go on. Looking over his shoulder at Iris one last time, he hurried to his mark. Iris was still looking at his retreating figure when Coolie pulled her aside.

"What is it?" she asked, annoyed. "If we're starting with the tightrope, I have to climb to my platform soon." The ladder had already been set up for them, the rope ready for their routine.

"Yes, I know, I know." Coolie rubbed his balding head. "I just wanted to have a quick chat with you." Grabbing her shoulders, he forced her to look outside. "See the royal box?"

In the center of the first tier was the box that royals and other esteemed guests would sit in to watch the entertainment. Decorated with fine ornaments, it stood out from the rest.

Iris's body went limp.

"I know people in the city who know people in the city, if you understand what I'm getting at," Coolie said, very proud of himself over his connections' connections. "Some very important people have come to see you especially. Parliament members, university professors—"

And him. Adam Temple. He sat in the box patiently, his arms folded over his green vest and fitted black coat. The rowdy audience didn't seem to faze him, nor did the extravagant-looking woman sitting next to him. She wore a magnificent blue dress, her fiery hair twisting into a braided bun at the top of her head, her black gloves stretching past her elbows. Her little binoculars were trained on the performance.

Iris's heart pounded at the sight of him. "Temple . . . ," she managed, gripping her forehead, but her words prompted Coolie to search the royal box.

"Him?" Coolie said, upon following her line of sight. He grinned triumphantly, chest swelling. "A member of that illustrious gentleman's club over on Pall Mall Street. See, Iris? The upper echelons of society are here. Did you know Wilton's Music Hall on the East End is putting on a private show where each ticket costs a small bloody fortune? Only the top of society can attend and yet look at them sitting *here*. Here at *my* show."

Iris couldn't care less about Coolie's rambling. Adam made something dangerous stir inside her. But Coolie didn't seem to care about her turmoil. Instead he leaned in and whispered:

"In the ten years since I've known you, you haven't aged a day. Ten years and you don't look a fortnight above seventeen. And then this morning . . ." He paused. "Tell me the truth. You can't die, can you?"

Iris couldn't breathe. She straightened up, afraid to move.

"Do you think that by being honest with me, it would change our relationship? On the contrary, my dear, I would be ridiculous if I didn't make you and you alone my star attraction: The Immortal Woman. The Daughter of Osiris. Princess of Death." He listed off each name with the flair of a circus proprietor who truly believed each one of his ideas was nothing short of true genius. As if Barnum himself would die of jealousy.

The warm, musty air had suddenly grown heavier. Her whole body seized up in fear.

"Well, it doesn't matter what the truth is. All that matters is the money we bring in. And Iris . . . I need money. Now. More than what these shows will give me." As if she needed yet another reminder of his insurmountable debt. "Stay, Iris. The house is packed, the guests esteemed. This moment is yours! Stay and let me make you the biggest star in the country, in the world! Bigger than you could have ever imagined!"

After waiting for her heart to steady, Iris parted her lips. "I'm moving on from performing," she said in a hollow voice. "I'm sorry."

Blessed relief washed over her as Coolie backed away, his hands leaving her shoulders at last and finding his coat pockets. "Losing one of my best acts overnight. What a nightmare. A costly nightmare," he added darkly. "But I respect your decision. You have my blessing."

He turned to leave. "Thank you for giving me one last show, Iris. It will be of good help to me. Good help indeed."

Wiping her sweaty palms on her tunic, she leaped out into the ring to thunderous applause and began quickly climbing the steps to her platform. Several blasts of purple smoke shot up from edges of the ring, and their performance began. With her concentration scattered, her body moved on muscle memory alone. The smell of white horses and hungry tigers lingered in the air, rushing into her open mouth as she leaped and flipped. Tricks and lifts. Splits and twirls. Iris and Jinn danced together like they never had before, but all she felt was her rattled nerves.

At some point, Jinn's red kaftan and her Egyptian tunic and headpiece flew into the air as they both flipped and drew their weapons hidden underneath. And so they began their battle of steel, their "Bolero of Blades." The music swelled with chimes and triangles, drums and trumpets as their swords clashed and their feet gripped the rope. Jinn must have sensed her disarray because though he carried out his role, his worried expression spoke volumes.

But Iris couldn't allow a repetition of this morning's blunder. She relied on her body to know what to do while she brought herself back to the moment, to the battle. To Iris's "death" by her own sword, to Jinn's cry and loving embrace as their blades fell to the ground. And then a spectacular dismount, swinging from the rope onto the trampoline below.

As Iris waved to the crowd next to Jinn, she saw Adam grinning brightly. He couldn't tear himself from the sight of her.

"You're shaking," Jinn whispered, and her hands flew to her bare arms. Indeed, she was. But before Jinn could push forward, Coolie waltzed out into the circus ring—an unannounced, unplanned appearance that left both Jinn and Iris stunned.

"Ladies and gentlemen, the Nubian Princess and the Turkish Prince!"

As Coolie clapped, two clowns brought out a wooden board painted red and green.

"You know, in my youth, I was a performer myself!" Coolie said in his booming voice. As the crowd jeered, Coolie waved them off, laughing and holding onto his belly. "Might be a little rounder these days, but what do you say I show you lot some of my old tricks?"

The crowd hollered and stamped their feet from their boxes. They didn't know this wasn't part of the program. Even if they did, it wouldn't have mattered. In that moment, their cheering felt like the taunting of jackals, their teeth lusting for bloodied prey.

"And now for our next act, the Nubian Princess shall stand in front of the board!"

Iris didn't know what Coolie was up to, nor did she have time for him. But when she turned, she spotted several burly security men offstage blocking her exit. Iris smirked bitterly.

The longer she lingered, the rowdier and angrier the crowd became. There was no other choice. But the moment she stepped back, Jinn grabbed her wrist. Guilt mingled with an odd sort of elation as she noted his worry for her, but she had to do as Coolie directed, and Coolie knew it too; the crowd would start throwing things soon if she didn't.

"It's okay," she assured Jinn, patting his hand on her wrist, although knowing Coolie, she wasn't so sure. After sliding Jinn's hand off with a gentle sweep, she walked to the board and stood in front of it. And then, once her nerves had settled, she realized . . .

This particular board was used for knife throwing.

Panic filled her as a clown twirled into the circus ring carrying several daggers, which he gave to Coolie with a deep bow.

The crowd's bloodlust shattered the roof. Iris immediately boosted herself off the board, but the two clowns forced her back to its wooden surface with unchanging red smiles.

"Sorry," one said. Warren. "Coolie doubled our pay."

SARAH RAUGHLEY

"Let's see if my aim is still sharp, shall we?" Coolie's words made the crowd erupt.

"Jinn!" Iris cried as a knife flew, pinning her to the board through her right sleeve.

"Coolie!" Jinn bellowed in panic, violently pushing off the clowns who attempted to hold him in place. "What are you doing?"

Another knife flew. Another one. Faster than the eye could follow. Her left sleeve. Between the knives and the clowns' grip, she couldn't move. Jinn was too late to stop the next slew of knives. The murderous glint in Coolie's eyes was the last sight she spied before she squeezed her eyes tight and awaited impact. The crowd held their collective breath.

Silence.

Then boisterous applause. The knives had come within an inch of her flesh and braided hair. Finally the clowns released her and twirled away, making their stage exits. Iris tried to catch her breath. Jinn slumped to his knees from shock as Coolie roused the crowd into greater applause.

There wasn't a shadow of doubt in Iris's mind now that Coolie was unstable and his company was no longer a home for her. *That man is vile*, Iris thought as she stood pinned to the board. *Absolutely, certifiably—*

Iris heard the shot before noticing Coolie's gun, which he'd pulled from his jacket.

Then she felt the bullet pierce her skull and the impact of her head banging against the wooden board.

The knives held her lifeless body up as she collapsed and died in the center of Astley's Amphitheatre.

6

S HE WAS IN SO MUCH PAIN. Muffled screams, cheers, and gasps all blended together, indiscernible to Iris. Eventually, as her head's shattered bones pieced themselves back together, noises carried into her skull once again, filling her ears as if she were swimming in the ocean.

Distorted. Muddled.

Except his crying.

His crying.

His calling her name.

Jinn . . . is that you?

Stars burst behind her heavy eyelids. She could see galaxies. With a hush they disappeared. Finally she managed to open her eyes, and as she did, she saw Jinn's wet face leaning over her, drained of blood. When she looked at him, his dark brown eyes went wide in bewilderment, terror, relief. Tears dripped down his nose. His dry lips gaped with a soundless word.

She felt his rough hands cupping her face, trembling against her skin as her body *pushed* the bullet out of her forehead. Jinn's gaze followed the metal, still smoking, as it clattered to the ground.

A stillness fell over the amphitheater so suddenly that Iris worried her hearing had gone again. On the contrary, everything inside her was beginning to work. Her blood was flowing. Her arms and legs were slowly moving. As

Iris's daze began to clear, she forced her brain to work again, to ascertain the situation.

Jinn's breathing seemed to fill the entire silent hall. "Iris . . ."

"The knives . . ." Iris's hoarse voice crawled out of her. She coughed blood.

"Iris . . . Iris, you . . ."

"The knives. *Knives*."

When she began shaking her arms and legs, Jinn finally understood. He worked quickly, yanking the knives out of the board and tossing them away. Her body was gaining strength, but she was still weak from the pain and the sheer shock of the events. She collapsed into Jinn, who caught her, knelt down, and cradled her on the ground.

"Iris . . . ," he said again as if he couldn't say her name enough times. As she gripped his arm and took in a deep breath, he stroked her face. Iris felt blood rushing through her cheeks from the light pressure of his hand. "You're alive. You're alive . . . Iris . . ."

When she looked up and saw fresh tears dripping down his face, she wondered for how long he'd been crying. But what she saw over his shoulder made her want to cry instead. Coolie with a greedy grin, his right arm stretched toward her, revealing to the audience his latest catch.

His newest inventory.

"Ladies and gentlemen," he said in a booming voice, "I present to you our Nubian Princess Nefertiti, the *Deathless*."

So he'd settled on a name.

The realization of her survival slowly dawned on the audience. She could hear the sounds of confusion, then disbelief, then excitement and fear. Then cheering, shouting, feet stomping, screaming. It was the kind of pandemonium Coolie fed off. The hairs on Iris's arms stood on end. The crowd's lust rattled her. It was as if they wanted to take her apart and see what was inside. To taste her *exotic* blood as they swallowed her whole.

They wanted more.

In the royal box, the red-haired woman leaned over, her legs daintily crossed, staring at Iris through her golden binoculars.

But Adam. Adam Temple was mouthing something to her. The very thought that he was attempting to communicate with her so calmly in this situation was terrifying in and of itself.

Everyone. Everyone was looking at her. Everyone had seen her.

It was over.

Is this a nightmare? Her lips began to quiver. Desperately, she gazed up at Jinn, silently pleading for an answer to her unspoken question. He was looking at her too.

He was smiling.

His expression was bright despite his tears. It wasn't just relief. It was as if all of his burdens and secrets had suddenly fallen off his broad shoulders.

"I knew it," he whispered, holding her closer to him as if they were alone in this chaotic horror show of an amphitheater. "I knew you were . . ."

A rush of panic swelled inside her. Iris pushed herself away from him and jumped to her feet, her legs stronger now. The room was spinning. She could hardly take it all in: Coolie's evil. The crowd's insanity. The men and women in the royal box carefully scrutinizing her. The other performers in the wings, horrified. Jinn staring up at her from the ground.

Iris ran. So fast she barreled past security before they could catch her.

"Iris, what are you doing—?" The Bearded Woman.

"I heard rumors but . . . are you one of those—" The One-Legged Opera Singer.

"You're one of *them*!" The Swiss man who pretended to be a Cherokee chief.

Iris heard each performer as she pushed past them. Ironically, many already considered those in the circus to be "freaks." But what was considered outside the realm of the acceptable depended entirely upon the social space one inhabited—and every space had a set of rules.

What was dead was supposed to stay dead. That was simply the rule of life.

Blessedly nobody followed her as she entered Astley's main lobby. They were too terrified. But she couldn't imagine any were more terrified than she.

When Iris exited the amphitheater, she found herself on the clay entry porch, quivering in the cold, foggy night. The lamps dangling from the porch roof illuminated the darkness, and yet she still couldn't see the way forward. Collapsing against one of the columns, she wrapped her arms around it, breathing heavily, her head whipping from one direction to the other, wondering where she should run. She hadn't time to think before she spotted a cab emerging from the thick mist, the horses' hooves clomping along cobbled streets.

It was now or never.

The second the driver was near enough, Iris ran up to him.

"Take me to—" She didn't know where. "Take me somewhere. Take me anywhere!"

"Twenty pence, ma'am." The man said in a disaffected tone, scratching his mustache.

"*Twenty pence?* I don't have any money!"

"Then I'm sorry—"

She ambushed him. Because of his shock and her ferocity, it took only seconds for her to wrestle his long, black coat from him before she kicked him out of his seat, grabbing his bowler hat as it flipped up in the air. His coat was already covering her circus attire by the time the man hit the ground. Using his hat to shade her face from sight, she grabbed the horses' reins as the cabdriver began swearing and calling for help.

"Iris!" someone cried behind her.

Jinn.

"Wait!" he said. "You don't understand!"

But she couldn't wait. If Jinn was here, then more would follow. The ten years she'd spent in Coolie's company. Her life with Granny. Her partnership with Jinn.

It was all over.

"Yah!" she cried, and snapped the reins of the horses, which began tumbling through the streets, scaring pedestrians out of the way. Iris looked over her shoulder. Jinn was chasing after her, but the horses were too fast. Wincing from the agony burning inside her, she turned back and left Jinn's desperate cries to the mist.

Over the bridge.

Through this street. Through that street.

Over another bridge.

Iris didn't know where she was going. By now the police had probably been contacted. By now Coolie had sent out a search party. But she kept riding, forcing the horses harder until their knees buckled and they whinnied in protest, stopping suddenly and flinging her out into the street. There was a market nearby. She limped into the narrow street, sheathed by her stolen coat, holding her hat low so no one would see her face. The streetlamps were dim, the lights from the apartment windows faded, and yet they were blinding to her. Every woman who passed by, every man she bumped into, every dirty-faced child that sat on the steps of a store building—every one of them was a spy. Nonsensical, she knew, but she couldn't think. Where to escape? Where? Out of the city? Out of the country?

Think, Iris. Frightening men shot her murderous glances from the dark alleyway. *Calm down and think.* She needed a place to stay. To rest and recoup before figuring out her next move.

But when you're ready to speak of secret things, Iris, come and find me.

Adam. The thought unsettled her, but when she tried desperately to think of another way, her mind turned blank. Secret things. Resting and recouping wasn't all she needed. She needed the truth. Who else would give it to her?

"The card." She patted her coat before realizing it wasn't hers. She'd left his card with his address forgotten and crumpled at the theater.

Think, Iris, think, think! Hitting her scalp wasn't smart. It was still aching from the bullet—and Granny Marlow's freshly tight braids.

19 Melbury Road.

With a new surge of energy pulsing through her, she asked whoever she could for directions. It took two hours longer than it should have, what with her having to cobble together half-answers and wrong advice, but eventually her tired legs brought her to a tall, redbrick house fit for a lord: a touch of the romantic medieval. White paint coated the window frames. But the roofs were round rather than pointed, reminding Iris of the shape of a cello. Trees and bushes peeked out from behind the manor.

The black iron fence and locked gate wouldn't let Iris onto the premises. Even in the night, coaches wheeled down the roads and scattered pedestrians roamed the sidewalks. That was all she could see through the night and fog.

Iris pounded the gate until her hands were tired, paying no mind to the bewildered pedestrians passing by. The last thing she wanted was to draw more attention to herself, but her sore neck and tired legs were about to crumple; her heart was weary, her mind as thick as the fog blanketing the streets. Finally she gave up and crouched down on the dirty sidewalk, letting the coat she'd stolen cushion her bottom.

She drew up her knees and waited.

She wrapped her arms around her knees . . . and waited.

Finally she buried her face in them and began to cry.

Soon, news of her *special* sort of freakery would reach every nook of London from the East to Westminster to the bloody palace. Crouching in the night's chill, a well of despair flowed up from deep within her. Coolie had taken away her right to choose how she would live and to whom she would reveal her secrets. He'd scoffed at her free will and revealed to the world what she herself didn't even understand. And now she was alone.

She'd be kidnapped by police and investigated. Or maybe burned at the stake. Or maybe placed in an asylum. Or perhaps in a cage like that poor Sarah Baartman, whose bones were held captive, even today, somewhere in France. There was no escape for her. No future.

She couldn't even say a proper goodbye to them. Granny. Jinn.

Iris . . . What do you think of me?

Iris shook her head, her sobs growing louder, carrying into the air. There was no sense in conjuring up an answer now. She'd left him. She had no right to answer.

"Miss Iris?"

Iris blinked the tears from her eyes as she heard keys clanging inside the gate behind her. She jumped to her feet so quickly, the hat tumbled off her head as a rush of air entered her lungs.

A woman in a white bonnet opened the gate with a creak. And behind her—

"L-Lord Temple . . ."

He stood in the threshold of the manor's open door and gazed at her calmly as if he'd expected her to come. He *had* expected her to come, surely. But those blue eyes were so soft and round, so wholly, genuinely compassionate that she found her tired legs stumbling toward him nonetheless.

"Lord Temple." Tears dripped from the corners of her eyes. "Adam." Her voice was barely a whisper. She shouldn't be here. But what was that voice deep within her telling her that this was the only place in the world right now she *could* be? "Adam," she said again, her voice hoarse, her neck pained, her body weary. But her feet would not stop moving until she was close enough to reach him.

She did. She gripped the collar of his white shirt, her fingers trembling. "Help me . . ."

Adam's expression grew softer. "Aren't you tired of running, Iris?"

It was the release her aching body needed. Her face still wet with tears, she collapsed into his arms and fell asleep.

7

VISIONS OF WORLDS IRIS HAD NEVER before seen burst behind her eyelids like stars as she dreamed strange dreams.

In one moment, Iris saw a castle upon a mountain that could just be seen through the mist. A silent procession of white-robed figures carrying jewels of unknown origin climbed up the long golden staircase winding up the rock toward the palace. Gifts for a greedy, bloodthirsty tyrant. A king who'd conquered the planet and left the world below in ruins.

In another moment, Iris saw herself standing atop a tree higher than the world itself. A tree piercing the heavens: the world tree, the people had named it, with roots that dug deep into the earth, painstakingly cultivated by the altruistic technology of the world's holy priestesses. A tree originally meant for all, whose fruit kept all life alive. Now it was dying from humanity's mistreatment. She could see the continents of mankind spread out over the seas. Their brass machines and silver gadgets. Their massive, frightening black drills with the claws and jaws of a monster of nightmare, each contraption sucking the planet's life from its core.

Each world was the same. Each time the same cries burrowed into her soul. The misery of the weak. The arrogance of the strong who crushed their bones into ruin beneath boot and heel. And a cry of a different kind. Steadfast and sure. A whisper.

Niaga Ecno Emit Si Ti.

Iris gasped and shivered underneath her covers. She was alone in the darkness when she awoke, the details of her strange dream receding into the unknown. The soft bed was grand, not in size but in earthen-colored silks and pillows. The thick, dark-red curtains covering the arched windows to her left were open just enough for her to see the prattling rain and the moonlight filtering through the wet trees. Wherever she was, she must have been on the second or third floor.

Wherever she was.

Adam . . . help me . . .

She remembered now. Her flight from Coolie. She sat up, placing her hand on her cool forehead. By the window was a mahogany French vanity rimmed with gold. And tucked in the corner, taut against the dark green wallpaper, was a grandfather clock that told her it was the middle of the night.

This must be Adam's residence . . .

When she saw the glass of water and plate of shortbread cookies on the oak table to the left of her bed, her initial fear subsided. One of her earliest memories was having cookies with Granny during her first Christmas with Coolie's company. She took the glass, illuminated by the long candle burning on the table, and sipped it slowly. But the anxiety of not knowing what came next still haunted her.

Suddenly, she gripped her body—her clothes. Her circus clothes were gone. She was in a light flush-pink nightgown that draped down to her ankles. *Who'd* changed her? Her palms began to sweat at the first answer to pop into her mind.

Thunder cracked in the skies. And when she turned, she found a figure peering at her from outside the window.

He was standing on the branch of a tree nearby. A crack of lightning brightened his long physique, his black cape flowing in the wind, his top hat lowered but not quite enough to cover the harlequin mask on his face—half black and half white, the colors separated perfectly down the middle. Iris covered her mouth and stifled a scream before throwing off the covers and climbing up onto her knees. With another flash of lightning, he was gone.

"Don't be afraid," came a gentle voice from the door, which opened with a creak.

Lord Adam Temple walked across the threshold, rolling a large silver coin over his knuckles. His black coat was open, and she could see the first few buttons of his white shirt were undone, the top of his hard chest visible. His dark green vest hugged his lean torso, and the lamp he held dangled in the air, brightening his sharp sapphire eyes.

Iris looked back at the window, but the figure was gone. Had it been her imagination? A hallucination owed to the last vestiges of sleep? She crumpled over, holding her chest against her beating heart.

"Calm down, Iris," he whispered in a soothing voice. "I'm not your enemy. I could never hurt you."

His words were soft. And worse still—part of her believed him. Some deep instinct inside her kept telling her as much. Granny was the only person she'd ever come across who'd elicited a feeling of familiarity from her . . . until Adam.

Placing his coin in his pocket and the lamp atop the dresser in front of her, he pulled a boudoir chair out of the corner and carried it with him to the side of her bed.

"Were you the one who changed my clothes?" That was the first thing Iris could think to say as he sat down, her eyes narrowed and her lips pressed into a thin line.

With an all-too-charismatic smile, Adam shook his head. "I *do* have servants, you know."

Like the woman who'd opened the gate. Shifting her shoulders uncomfortably, Iris accepted his answer. He didn't seem like a lecher, not like Coolie. He remained a respectable distance from her, but his gaze itself was like a tender touch. His large hands looked like they could envelope hers completely and warmly if they chose to.

She still wasn't comfortable. She still wasn't satisfied.

"Tell me the truth," she demanded. "You said you could, so do it."

"Right to it, then." The corners of Adam's lips curled upward. Like Alice's Cheshire cat. "After the night you've had, wouldn't you rather rest and—"

"What am I?"

Adam sat back in his chair, staring at the food she hadn't touched before sighing. "The first thing I should tell you, Iris," he said, closing his eyes, "is that I *won't* give you the truth. Not all at once."

"What?" Iris balled her hands into fists. "But you—"

"Right now your mind can't handle even a hint of a memory that would reveal your true nature. Our meeting earlier today at the amphitheater is proof enough of that, wouldn't you say?"

When she nearly choked the life out of him. Iris's muscles relaxed.

Placing his arm on the table next to her, Adam picked up one of the long shortbread cookies and considered it. "My sister used to love these," he whispered with whimsy and something darker before turning back to her. "I know you have so many questions. I can't imagine how you're feeling. That's why I want to offer you a safe place to remember your memories gradually, at your own pace. That way, they'll feel more real to you than if someone simply told you." He paused. "That was what I *wanted* to do, at least."

Iris tilted her head, a curious frown playing on her lips. "And that plan changed?"

"Today it did. A little," Adam admitted. "But the general idea is the same."

At this Adam hesitated, and as he did, he stared deeply into her eyes, almost apologetically. Something within Iris stirred. He *did* know her. The "her" she couldn't remember. She could feel it so deeply that it made her chest swell with heat. Perhaps that was why she didn't flinch when he took her fingers in his.

"Iris. To be honest, there will be times when circumstances will jolt those memories from you, like shaking apples from a tree. And it may be difficult. It's not ideal, but just know this—I'm on your side. And everything I do is so that you can remember who you *truly* are." He gazed at her with sparkling eyes. "That's why you can trust me."

Was it? Or was that why she should run from here and never look back? In this moment, as she sat with her fingers gripped gently by his, it was as if there were two Irises inside her. One relished the thought of regaining her memories. The other feared what would come of it.

"And who are *you*?" Iris asked, pulling her hand away from him.

Adam stood up. "A young man with far too much wealth he didn't earn himself." With a smile, he started toward the door. "I'll tell you more once you've rested. For now, don't worry yourself and try to get some sleep."

But as the door closed behind him, Iris had other plans.

A Visitor in the Middle of the Night

IRIS DIDN'T YET TRUST HIM. WHY would she? She didn't know him. Not like he knew her. But Adam had already planned for that.

There were some charmers in this world readily adept at gaining sympathies and bending hearts to their will. And to make use of them, all one needed to do was to bend theirs.

It was two hours past midnight when a knock came at the front door. Sitting on his living room couch, Adam gestured with a flick of his head for one of the servants to get it. Instead of his father's favorite coin, it was a chess piece he had pinched between his long fingers. The board on the table in front of him was filled and alive with strategy, though nobody sat on the other side to challenge him.

When Gerolt Van der Ven waltzed through the threshold with his saber at his side, tied to his military garb, Adam knew he wouldn't be much of a match. There was no use in asking him to play. He placed the rook back in its spot.

"I assume you've come to collect your fee," Adam said, unmoved as Van der Ven's massive body sank like a stone into the red velvet chair that just barely held his weight. He was so rough with things—he'd ruin the upholstery.

Setting his silver cane down against the chair, Van der Ven let out a deep grumble in response, which Adam assumed was a yes. The old general looked about the room—at the framed portraits of his family, different from the ones in his Yorkshire country manor. At the cast-iron lanterns and lampshades. The dark rich tone of the room hid the soot from the fireplace.

Adam gestured to one of his servants, who left the room and very soon reemerged with a long instrument wrapped carefully in a white linen towel. Van der Ven grabbed it and unwrapped it greedily.

"As promised: the Carnwennan," Adam said. "Said to shroud its user in shadow."

"I don't care for legends." Van der Ven held the dagger in the light. "I care for steel."

And monetary worth—and this blade was worth many millions.

"Your father hid it well." Van der Ven's eyes hungrily took in the ruby ornament in the blade's hilt. "I wonder what other treasures he found during his many travels."

"Certainly none more useful than those artifacts unearthed by the Committee."

Van der Ven's greedy expression told Adam he didn't share the same opinion.

"You do know," Adam continued, sitting back into his couch, "that when the world ends, there'll be no use for such things."

"Foolishness!" Van der Ven's chortling laughter filled the living room. "When entering a new frontier, there is always use for tools of murder. Especially ones as beautiful as this."

Adam was all too sure that if Van der Ven won the tournament, with the Ark in his control, he would make sure to take his collection of ornamental swords, spears, and daggers with him. More than the monetary worth, more than even their capacity for violence, it was how the weapons made him feel. That pathetic need to confirm his superiority would be his undoing.

"I'm surprised that you'd trade this for information on such worthless *freaks*."

Adam slipped a yellow-tinged police photo from beneath his chessboard. The three young children receiving their mugshot in the photo had attended the '74 fair in South Kensington as pickpockets and so were brought in as criminals. Only one of them had had his tenth birthday by the time of this shot— the one on the left. He was the tallest, his light hair the longest, just past his shoulders. On the right was a kind-looking boy presumably of the Northern Eskimos. His gentle eyes seemed shaken as he huddled close to the boy in the center, holding his hand. And Adam could tell why. Even facing interrogation by police, the curly-haired boy was smiling from ear to wicked ear, almost as if to taunt the officer taking his photo. Charismatic. Incorrigible. Dangerously so. Adam had heard as much from his intelligence.

On the other side of the photo, *Maximo Morales* was written in cursive ink.

Adam had made the proposition two weeks ago, and it had taken the retired general only days to find him a list of potential champions in exchange for the dagger. Adam had special criteria for choosing this one.

"Worth is in the eye of the beholder," Adam said, and tapped Maximo's picture. "He's a cheerful one. Considering his abilities, I'm surprised you never considered him for yourself."

Van der Ven leaned back into his chair. "I'll tell you a story, boy." The old boar rested the dagger upon his lap. "Just before the war, a young man joined the infantry. The middle child of a friend of mine. His talent left much to be desired, but he was a jovial boy—well loved by peers and superiors. And because his father and I were close, he wanted nothing more than to be just as close with me." He picked up the dagger. "I had him killed."

Adam attempted to show no reaction, but his fingers pinched the photo a little harder than before.

"Being well loved is sentimental nonsense. It's far more important to be feared." Van der Ven smiled. "And the champions fighting under my banner, make no mistake, will be feared."

Being easily loved could also be a weapon. Maximo would prove to be an ace in his pocket. But before he could be certain his plan would succeed, he needed to make sure of one thing.

"Gerolt," Adam called just as the man rose to leave. "Have you ever heard of a man named Johan Adrian Jacobsen?"

"The headhunter from Norway. Yes . . . Carl Hagenbeck's man." Van der Ven wrapped up his dagger in its towel. "Last I heard, he's gone east of the Nile."

"I see." Adam had to stay aware of his location to keep that piece in play. "Thank you."

As Van der Ven left, Adam stared at the picture of the three children again. The two flanking Maximo had looked far more confident as adults when they stood in his doorway much earlier today, moments before Adam was to pick up Madame Bellerose to see Iris's show.

"We told you where Max is last week," the taller of the two had said, his blond hair spiraling down from underneath his newsboy cap. Hawkins, he was called. A young man who'd worn a deceptively innocent smile when they'd first met—a smile with a hint of loftiness perhaps better suited to men far wealthier. But just then he'd looked rather annoyed. He leaned against the doorframe. "We got you the yellow ticket and even the secret password you'll need to get into the venue. We told you all about Max, what he's like. What else do you want from us, a hair sample?"

"I want you to tail us tomorrow night," Adam confessed, fussing with his left white glove. "Myself and the lovely woman who'll be accompanying me to the venue."

"Tail?"

"To make sure nobody follows us as we go." Adam smirked. "I've had a problem with being followed recently. You could say I'm a little paranoid."

"You're a little paranoid," said Jacob, no less handsome than Hawkins, as he ran a hand through his dark hair. His brown eyes intrigued Adam—so sincere. Peaceful like a rolling river. "What you want with Max is . . . ," he started, before biting his lip. "It's . . ."

"It's the same as what your Patron wants with you," Adam said.

"No." Though his voice was soft, Jacob was resolute as he spoke, his gaze steadfast. "It's more than that, isn't it?"

Adam was taken aback. But he replied calmly. "What makes you think that?"

"People like you always want more."

Adam placed a finger underneath his lip, tamping down his amusement at the young man's perceptiveness. Well, from what Adam had already learned about this Jacob, it wasn't a surprise he'd be skeptical, even suspicious of him—and protective of his friend. But—

"All I want is to win. I'll remind you that what awaits your friend if he succeeds is the same prize awaiting you should your team succeed. Isn't that what you all want? Besides . . ." A sudden thought came to Adam. "I'm sure having a childhood friend on another team would only be of help to you. Especially such a courageous friend who would never betray you, as you assured me yourself. There are certain things you'd be able to accomplish together that the other teams might not."

Hawkins and Jacob exchanged glances.

"Are you offering us an alliance?" Hawkins asked, the right side of his lips curling at the very suggestion.

Adam returned that Cheshire grin. "I'm telling you I'd be more than supportive should you find creative ways to overcome the confines of a deadly game created by a Committee who, I assure you, will stay none the wiser of this conversation. You could overcome the tournament. Together."

The tournament meant nothing to Adam. If those friends wanted to run off with the money together, he wouldn't mind helping them for their troubles. It wouldn't matter in the end, anyway.

The two thought it over. "I guess . . ." Jacob nodded. "I guess we can take the job."

"Assuming the price is right," Hawkins said, flipping back his hair with a pride and flair that reminded Adam of a *primo uomo*.

When Adam pulled out a pouch filled with pounds, the twinkle in the golden-haired man's eyes told him the price was indeed right. "You won't see us," he said. "Once you reach the venue, we'll disappear. Literally."

"I wouldn't expect anything less from someone of your unique talents, Mr. Hawkins."

Though they were not his champions, they had looked more than capable to do as he instructed. Now, as Adam stared at their faded childhood photo, he was confident Maximo would be too. Alone in his living room, Adam picked up a black knight from the chessboard. "That's right, Maximo. You will be a useful fool, won't you?" His eyes shifted to the queen, safe on her treasured square.

An hour passed before Adam heard a knocking on the living room window. He stood.

"Welcome, good doctor." The curtains billowed with the wind after he pushed open the arched windowpane. "Come in."

Adam could tell even from behind the man's harlequin mask that hearing that title made him grin from ear to ear. But Dr. Heidegger had accepted his persona long before he was transformed on that day, along with the rest of London's *gifted*.

The Harlequin Slasher. Even in those bloody days before the explosion at the fair, he never took his mask off except to adopt his civilian persona. And now he *couldn't*, so he stayed out of sight after being scouted by the Committee, working in the shadows.

"My lord." Fool bowed ninety degrees, his head tilted at the same angle. "Your guest. She's left her room."

Adam sat back in his chair. "She has, has she?"

"She's searching the house."

"Plucky." Adam thought back to the being he'd met at the South Kensington fair, the one he'd learned about after years of poring over his father's research, and before he realized it, a chuckle escaped his lips. The texts didn't do her justice. Or perhaps the trauma had changed her. Nevertheless, the girl currently in his home wasn't at all what he'd expected.

Just who are you, Iris?

"Shall I continue to watch her? You're going to the venue tomorrow night, are you not?"

Adam smirked. Fool's special gift made him useful to the Enlightenment Committee. And though he was a freak himself, he was not to participate as a champion in the tournament; his part in all this was too special, too integral to ensuring the tournament ran smoothly. What the Committee didn't realize in their hubris was that behind every mask there was a man with a past. And in every past was the seed of vulnerability that eventually became one's weakness. Once Adam discovered Fool's weakness, the man's true loyalty became his alone.

"Yes, we are," said Adam. "But I've hired others to watch our backs. I want *you* to go to Cortez. He's been looking for a way to test the strength of his most recent choices."

"Ah, those Sparrow girls." Adam was sure Fool appreciated Cortez's cruel methods as a former serial murderer himself.

"Go to Cortez and tell him I have a proposition for him."

"As you wish, my lord."

Fool bowed and disappeared with the wind.

Loyalty was not easily won. Adam had mostly succeeded in bending the wills of men to his own. But Iris was different. It would take a little more work to win her to his side. A little longer for her to learn the purpose of her existence—and the purpose of his own. As for the latter, he certainly hoped that one day she would understand.

Since their purposes were one and the same.

8

IRIS HAD ALREADY BEEN SEARCHING ADAM'S study for half an
hour before she heard a distant, heart-stopping knock on the front door.

Just relax, she told herself. She was technically a guest. If anyone caught
her, all she had to do was say she got lost.

It did take some doing, sneaking about the narrow hallways, their dark,
floral wallpaper brightened by gas-lit wall sconces. She remained light on
her bare feet, putting her tightrope training to good use. Inside the study, the
thick curtains were closed, but a paraffin oil lamp hanging from the center of
the room remained on. Ignoring the incessant ticking of the clock on the fireplace mantel, she walked around the grand oak desk and began searching for
documents. Then she tried the cabinets. Soon she'd have to check the bookshelves sprawling across the room. All she could gather from the cabinets was
that Adam was incredibly well-read. He even seemed to like those silly, cheap
broadsides sold on the streets about vampires and robbers and such. Nobody
but little children took those seriously, and yet here were several issues of
one titled *The Fanciful Freaks of London* tucked away in his cupboards, edges
frayed and bookmarked.

He'd even written on some pages. On one, he'd marked "Exploding Man"
and circled it. With a shiver, Iris saw that the page held a drawing of a man

with sparking fingertips and remembered the headline on Coolie's copy of the *Evening Standard*.

There've been a lot of rumors lately moving around the country, Coolie had said. *Strange rumors.*

Putting it back in its drawer with a shaky hand, she searched the bookshelf. She wasn't sure what she was looking for, but a book on one of the upper shelves by a tall ladder caught her eye. She wouldn't have paid it any mind, except the surname on the spine was Adam's own.

"*A Family's Travels through West Africa*," Iris read, staring at the book cover while on the fourth rung of the ladder. "By John Temple."

Dedicated to his wife, Charlotte Temple, Baroness of Yorkshire, his small children, Eva, Adam, and Abraham, and his friends in the African Aid Society. The way in which he described some of the Africans he met during his travels certainly didn't feel friendly, though he did seem impressed by the military prowess of the Kingdom of Dahomey.

"Dahomey," she whispered, and her chest contracted with a twinge. "John Temple even spoke to their king . . ."

She wasn't sure why it had caught her attention, but indeed it had. According to Temple, through an interpreter they spoke of many things . . .

"My father was an explorer, you see."

The shock of Adam's voice behind her made her slip on the ladder, sending her hurtling into his arms. That was a narrow catch—he had to move quickly to reach her. He wouldn't have been able to sneak up on her in the first place if she hadn't gotten so lost in the text. The book was still in her grip as she stared up at Adam's alluring grin in her wispy nightgown, her legs dangling over his right arm while his left held her against his chest.

"Like my late grandfather," he continued, putting her down. "They often went on expeditions together, charting, excavating ruins, finding artifacts. Even the British Crown asked for his expertise on projects from time to time."

"Sounds like your typical plunderers," she said, coolly dusting off her nightgown.

Adam chuckled. "You're not wrong. Many men with money and

something to prove have traveled to Africa and written books about things I imagine the locals there had already known for many years." He walked around his desk, his fingers trailing the wood. "What made my father different was that he never knew when to quit. He was obsessed with his curiosity. With knowing the secrets of the world, even if it meant abandoning his own family."

That made the book's dedication more than a little awkward.

Iris folded her arms over her chest. "Well, you've caught me, so I might as well ask: That penny blood series you seem to have been enjoying . . ."

"Ah, *Fanciful Freaks*!" His eyes lit up like a child's. "You saw it while you were snooping?"

"I did. And I notice you seem particularly interested in the characters."

"They're odd, aren't they?" Adam sat on the edge of his desk, pulling out one issue of the serial. The title was written on the front page in thick lettering with a drawing of a young working-class lad lifting a carriage above his head one-handed while the lord and lady inside screamed in terror. "A boy who can stop time. A girl who can move things with her mind."

"Sounds like nonsense," Iris whispered, shifting on her feet.

"Does it?" Adam gave her a sidelong look, which made Iris keenly aware of the bullet hole that used to exist in her skull. "Written and illustrated by Chadwick Winterbottom. This first issue was published in 1877—around the time rumors of unexplainable occurrences in the city began to circulate, very secretly, among those who had access to the most secretive of networks."

Unexplainable occurrences. Like a woman who could come back to life? Like a robber who used exploding electrical currents to scare off his targets so he could steal from them? Iris chose her words carefully. "If I were to find the author . . ."

"You wouldn't," Adam said simply. "As far as I've heard, Winterbottom has been dead for two years."

Iris placed her hands on her hips, lifting her head with a challenging glare. "Then will you tell me what I want to know?"

"About the 'Fanciful Freaks'?" Adam tilted his head. "Even better. I'll show you."

Iris hated that mysterious smile of his, hated even more how his words enticed her just enough to keep her on his hook. But this bait was too tantalizing to ignore. "The rumors are true, aren't they? There are people in this city who can do impossible things."

"Does it comfort you to know that you're not alone?"

Iris had to admit that it did, though the thought terrified her at the same time. But she'd felt so alone for so long. She couldn't bring herself to believe it until she saw it.

Adam wasn't surprised to hear it. "You'll get your chance tomorrow night," he said, slipping off his desk. "For now, rest up. Tomorrow will be an interesting day."

"Adam," Iris called as he walked toward the study door. Once he stopped, she hesitated, gathering her thoughts. "I've been through hell and back. I need to know . . . *can* I trust you?"

"You're unable to die. I can't imagine there's much you should be worried about."

Iris clenched her hands, thinking of her secret being exposed so publicly. The feeling of being violated because of Coolie. The far-reaching consequences she still had yet to see.

"But if you're that worried about *me* . . ." Adam reached into the back of his pants.

And pulled out a gun.

Iris backed into the bookshelf as he approached. But to her surprise, Adam flipped the gun over. Holding it by its barrel, he offered her the golden handle.

"If at any point you feel threatened by me, you're more than welcome to kill me." He said it with the casual tone of someone commenting on the weather.

He's mad, Iris thought. He was also serious. Iris inched closer and closer. And then, snatching the gun, she pointed it at him. But Adam only answered with a cordial bow, his right hand to his heart, his arm at his back.

His head inches away from the barrel.

Iris looked down the barrel of the gun, roses and thorns stretching across the surface. Her knuckles felt numb as she held on to the weapon tightly.

"Make no mistake," she said, lowering the gun. "I *won't* hesitate to shoot you if I find the slightest reason to."

"My life is in your hands." He raised his head with an eerie, knowing smile. "Good night then, Iris. You're free to stay in my study as long as you like. There's plenty to read here. I recommend my father's book, but not too highly. He is my father, after all."

With a wink, he left.

9

THE DRESS ADAM HAD BROUGHT FOR her sometime during the afternoon was too long. A promenade toilette, the outfit was called. Dark green satin, its bottom trimmed with red-and-beige plaid. Excruciatingly tight. Over her corseted waist, the closely fitted jacket of the same dark green extended over her hips and was cinched in by a black belt. The bustle just below her waist supported the drapery at the back. Terrible to sit in, but the venue Adam was taking her to couldn't be reached by foot.

Inside the carriage, she stared at her white gloves and touched with a tentative hand the bonnet atop her head, decorated with silk green ribbons, white feathers, and hints of lace.

"Is it too uncomfortable?" Adam asked next to her.

"I look like a pine tree." Iris gripped her left forearm, her gaze to the ground. Adam chuckled. "At any rate, if Coolie's looking for me, then he's looking for a circus girl. Though not much of a disguise, it's a disguise nonetheless."

The ride had not gone as she'd expected. Actually, she wasn't sure *what* she'd expected. But tonight, Adam was suddenly interested in telling her about himself as he played with his silly coin. He was twenty-one years old as of last month. He attended Eton as a boy. Now he was a student at that prestigious law school, Lincoln's Inn over in Camden, though he hadn't much of a plan after graduation. When he wasn't studying, he lived in his Yorkshire manor alone but for the company of his servants. Oh, and he was deathly afraid of squirrels. During a visit to the countryside as a child, one had frightened him badly enough that he was now eternally scarred. He chatted with her like a schoolboy speaking to a girl he fancied for the first time, revealing seemingly everything except the one thing she wanted to know: how he knew *her*.

"My mother and siblings are gone," he told her, and though he'd said it simply, there was a moment, fleeting as the wind, when his expression became so hollow that it spooked her. It passed like a shadow. "My uncle was committed," he continued amicably. "Perhaps it's for the better: he owned and ran a series of cotton mills that were infamous for their industrial catastrophes thanks to his sickening policies."

"That doesn't surprise me."

"What doesn't surprise you?" Adam grasped his coin.

Iris caught herself once she found Adam brightened at the slightest hint of her engagement. Hesitantly, she continued. "It's just that I'm not a fan of those awful machines and what they've done to people." Quite a few of her colleagues at Coolie's company had disfigurements due to the conditions they'd been forced to work in. They'd sought out the circus for the same reason she had: as refuge from the cruelty of "civil" society.

"With each passing day, it seems that this world is heading in the wrong direction." Adam looked at a group of children huddling over a bonfire in the alleyway. "As modernity leaps forward, human civilization forsakes the natural world. Destroys it."

"A Romanticist?" Iris tilted her head.

"I'm no Wordsworth," Adam answered with a smile. "But any astute student of human history should be able to recognize that the choices mankind has made on its way to economic progress have not always been kind to *people*— nor to the natural world I so love."

"Except for squirrels, of course."

"The hideous things. Still . . ." Adam fell silent. "We've made a mess of the world."

Iris had to admit how much she loved the silence of nature. Sitting in a flowery field reading to Granny. Flying up in the air, feeling the breeze and the birds and butterflies fluttering past. But as Adam was watching her carefully, she told him none of this.

After a moment of silence, Adam asked her about her life in the circus, if she'd been fed well or if she'd made many friends. It was as if he were checking up on an old chum. Iris wasn't so keen to respond, not when he already knew her greatest and most dangerous secret.

"Coolie should be hanged for pulling that stunt last night," he said, and a glint in his eye told Iris he may have meant it. "I'm sorry you had to go through such a thing."

"I saw you and your friends up in the royal box," Iris said. "Coolie had been bragging about his 'very important connections.' Interesting that he contacted you."

"Coolie didn't contact me, but some others in my group. Then word spread."

"Your group?"

"My gentleman's club." When Adam's eyes slid toward her, they looked as if they held a particularly wicked secret. "Club Uriel. We meet every so often over on Pall Mall Street."

Iris vaguely remembered Coolie rambling about it. "What are people saying about me?"

"Oh, that you're a daughter of death, an ancient goddess revived by a primordial force, a reanimated corpse come to kill us all, and so on," Adam said flippantly.

Iris bit down into the corner of her lip. "Coolie didn't want to advertise an act to just anyone. He wanted to advertise me—my power—to those prominent connections of his."

Adam nodded. "Which means it would be in your best interest to be very careful with who you choose to trust. Of course—"

"Let me guess: 'You can trust me,' right?" Iris said before he could finish. She thought of his gun tucked inside her right stocking, making good use of her hose supporters.

Stuffing his coin back into his jacket, Adam ran his fingers through his black hair. "You said you wanted the truth. Well, here's a bit of it: the Fourth Annual South Kensington International Exhibition in 1874. You were there on the second of June when an explosion took place. As was I."

The fair. The chaos. The fires. People running. Yes, she knew. But before that?

Iris's chest felt suddenly tight as the shadow of that old memory began surfacing. He was right. Every time she reached beyond the veil to access those old recollections, it was mentally and physically torturous. Memories of flesh . . . of bone. She shook her head just as her heart began to pound. She couldn't jump into learning the truth too recklessly.

"I already know I was there," she whispered defiantly.

"But do you know what you were doing there?"

Silence. Iris clenched her teeth.

"I'll tell you more, gradually, I promise. But, Iris, there's something I wish for in return." Adam drew closer to her, touching her arm ever so lightly. "If you like, you can think of this as an honest, mutual arrangement."

Iris slid to the side of the carriage, away from his touch. "What do you want from me?"

"There are two things I need more than anything, just like you need the truth." He lifted his finger. "The first: I want you to help me find my father. Though many think he's dead, he's very much alive . . . to the knowledge of a dwindling few." Adam's eyes wandered to the brick buildings lining the sidewalk, a tinge of sorrow in them as if processing a very difficult memory. "There are many layers to your mystery, dear Iris," he said, bringing himself back to the present. "If you want to restore your memories and return to your true self, finding my father is key."

Her true self. "Why would you think that I can find your father?"

"Because you're good at finding people. Aren't you?"

Granny Marlow. Iris remembered the day she joined the company. The way she felt the woman's essence from afar. When she was calm and still, she could *feel* Granny coming to her trailer, or find her easily in the city streets, just by sensing her essence alone. Same as she could do for Jinn, and even Coolie.

But how could Adam know that?

"I told you, I know many things," Adam said, interpreting her look and resolving nothing. "Some I've gleaned for myself through years of research. Some I've seen with my own eyes." They glinted now in the moonlight. "What's clear is that you are a very special girl with very special abilities. If you would like to know why and how, you'll need to find my father."

"And the second thing?" Iris asked, afraid of his answer.

Adam hesitated. "Well, that might take a bit longer to explain," he said finally. "But I *can* explain it. If you come with me."

The carriage ride ended in the grittier part of town. "We'll be walking from here on out." When Adam lifted his hand for her to take, all she could do was stare. The truth was all she ever wanted. But looking at his hand, she felt as if she were about to make a deal with the devil.

"What you're going to see tonight might make some things clear, I assure you," he said as she stepped out of the carriage on her own, denying his touch.

For one strange moment she thought she heard footsteps behind her. But when she turned, no one was there.

She shivered. "I have to say, I don't have a great feeling about this."

"Do you still have my gun with you?" Adam asked.

With a sharp intake of breath, she nodded.

"Then by all means." Adam gave a gentlemanly bow, his hand to his heart. "Follow me."

10

AT THE END OF A DARK alleyway, the latch to a solid wooden door slid open. A sickly looking woman who covered her stringy blond hair under a simple white bonnet peeked through the resultant peephole. After Adam spoke some kind of password and flashed a yellow ticket, the latch slid shut. Then the door opened with the whining of iron.

Several narrow staircases surrounded by walls of clay took them deeper into the earth. Iris stepped carefully, holding on to the rickety railing, the sounds of cheering growing louder. Soon, Iris could hear the clamor clearly.

"Come on, knock him out!"

"Sixty-five here! Put me down for sixty-five on the Barber!"

"Sixty-five on the Barber!" Someone took the order. "Write it down, write it down."

Iris saw a stocky, white-haired man writing down the numbers on a chalkboard. No, *bets*. How else could she explain the thick swarm of men smoking cigars and hooting like maniacs as they surrounded a sunken boxing ring?

The boxers inside had no gloves to pad their bloody knuckles. They wore nothing but trousers and boots. Each punch drew floods of blood. One fighter hit the surrounding wall separating them from their voyeurs, just before returning a punch that shattered the other's bones against the stone floor. The audience couldn't get enough of the morbid display.

Taking her hand, Adam led her through the crowd, and once they reached the very front, Iris grabbed the clay barrier that separated her from the pit of blood.

"Kill him!" a man next to her cried as a heavyset fighter stood over his unconscious opponent. "Go on, kill him! Give him a good shave!"

Someone threw a knife into the ring. It clattered at the Barber's feet. He was considering.

"No killing!" cried a man from the betting board. "No killing in the Pit. Where d'you ratbags think we'll get our fighters if they get ripped into a bloody smear, eh?" He signaled to a thin, droopy-eyed man in a black suit next to him, carrying a bell.

"Winner!" Droopy Eyes rang the brass hand bell. "The Barber of East End!"

Cheers shook dust from the rafters and the gas lamps along the filthy walls.

Iris wrapped her arms around her chest, remembering the vicious crowd at Astley's thirsting for more of her blood. "Just what is this place?"

Adam thought for a moment. "Let's call it . . . an underground establishment. Where gentlemen in good health and physique—"

"Illegally fight to the death?" Iris shot him a horrified look.

"Not to the death," Adam corrected. "You heard the bookie. It isn't easy to find men of this caliber. Though I suppose the occasional accident does happen."

Disgusted, Iris turned to leave, stopping abruptly when she saw a man with sagging jowls tip his purple hat to her from the crowd, his cigarette unlit.

Adam linked his arm through her elbow and swung her back around. "I wouldn't wander too far, Iris. This type of establishment tends to draw unseemly characters."

"Clearly." Iris glared at him.

Elsewhere, the bright voice of a young woman rang out over the din. She was tucked in a corner. Iris first caught sight of her hair—the color of a pumpkin with the precise shape of a downturned bowl cut close to her skull. Her ivory face was dirtied from the smog of the city, her large, mischievous blue eyes and little mouth chatting a mile a minute as she shuffled a deck of cards on an empty crate.

"Who's up? Who's up next? Come on, you *meaters*, it's not so hard; just keep your eyes on the card and follow the red queen—and I don't mean me." As she winked at the three working-class men whose clothing style she shared down to the suspenders, she looked quite like an adorable chipmunk. But Iris had been around enough grifters to know better. She couldn't blame the girl. Where better to run the three-card monte scam than a dingy pit where fools were just itching to throw their money away?

"What are we doing here?" Iris turned back to Adam. "What does any of this have to do with what we were discussing?"

"You'll see soon enough," Adam whispered. "When he comes."

"Why, if it isn't young Adam!" came a flamboyant shout from deep in the crowd, and soon emerged a man with a long mane of golden locks that could have put a lion to shame.

Iris could tell by his swagger that he was beyond drunk, and the half-empty wineglass in his hand served as quite the clue as well. She didn't even know a place like this served wine.

The red-and-gold silk night robes, which he wore over his red vest, fluttered from the force of every rapturous shout of the crowd. He looked ready for bed, not for a blood-splattering fistfight, but he was clearly enjoying himself nonetheless.

"Do you mean him?" Iris pointed at the man as he approached them.

"Not him," Adam said quickly. "*God,* not him." And though Adam tried to steer Iris in the opposite direction, the man caught up to them.

"My boy, Adam! Why, didn't you hear me?" He swung his arm around Adam's neck before he could escape. "I've been shouting and shouting for you. My goodness, I thought my voice would . . . would *fizzle out* and just *die* from the pain and agony of it all."

It was the first time Iris had seen Adam look so annoyed, and she couldn't blame him. The man had called him only once. Iris sized him up, his long hair reaching past his shoulder blades, his blue eyes and pin-straight nose. He was shorter than Adam but seemed older, perhaps in his thirties. Italian by the sound of his accent—and his name.

"Riccardo Benini," he said, introducing himself to Iris, almost falling over and taking Adam with him as he attempted a cordial bow. "And tell me, Adam, who is this impeccably dressed creature you've brought as your consort?"

Adam grimaced, trying to loosen his grip. "Her name is—"

"Mine to give, and *certainly* not yours to know," Iris finished.

But her defiance only intrigued Benini further. He stroked his chin. "Feisty. Her contempt is as luxurious as a plundered jewel from her motherland. She has my esteemed approval."

He tipped his glass and hiccupped. Even while drunk, a patronizing sense of superiority wafted from him like the potent cologne he wore.

"Is he one of your friends?" Iris asked Adam. "From your little club on Pall Mall Street?"

Benini's eyes widened in delight. "Oh, you've told her about Club Uriel? Then that means . . . Adam, this woman wouldn't be one of your champions, would she?"

"That's not yet been determined." Adam finally managed to push him away.

"Why? Did you *ask* her?" Benini laughed. "Oh, Adam, ever such a polite, accommodating boy. Even as the newest member of the Committee, you should have known by now that we Enlighteners don't ask. We take. For example—"

Enlighteners? Iris was busy trying to work out what he'd said when the bell for the next match rang to wild applause. Benini pointed to the young man who had just jumped into the ring to face the dreaded Barber.

"Since you're here, I gather you've heard of him too, haven't you, Adam?" he said with a gluttonous smile. "We may have to draw straws for this little star."

That "star" was fit, but still far too lean to be a match for the seven-foot steel giant that stood before him. His bare chest, a light, gold-hued brown, was impeccably carved, though scarred, his tight trousers revealing a shaped physique to match his round features—eyes and nose—that gave him the distinct character of a newborn pup. His brown hair curled over his forehead, covering half his ears. But it was his reckless, lopsided grin in the face of certain defeat that seemed to draw swoons from the crowd among the shouts for blood.

"Now entering the ring, the young, the mischievous, your favorite cocky lad hailing all the way from El Salvador, Jiffy the Blink!"

The young man basked in the crowd's roars, pumping his fists in the air for a little too long. While he was showboating, the Barber landed his first punch right in his stomach.

Iris's hands flew to her mouth as "Jiffy" was launched back and hit the solid stone ground.

"Whoops?" He sat up with a wince and shook the dust out of his curly hair. Once he was back on his feet, he pumped his fists in the air again, egging on the crowd.

"A bit theatrical, isn't he? That rascal." Benini sipped his wine. "He'd make a great addition to my team."

"He'd need someone to rein in his more reckless impulses, not encourage them," Adam answered him before giving Iris a sidelong look. "Besides, I found him first."

What are they talking *about?* Iris thought incredulously just as the crowd erupted again. The Barber had landed quite the combination on Jiffy. Two more punches to the stomach, one to the chest. Soon the young man was lying flat on his back inches away from where Iris stood, coughing out blood, yet laughing as if suddenly delighted by the rats scurrying across the rafters.

"Hold on," said Jiffy the Blink. "Now, hold on just a bloody minute!"

For one second, it was a silent Adam who'd caught his gaze. And held it. But then he saw Iris. He saw her and stood up immediately. Overcome with an odd sort of youthful bliss, he stumbled to his feet and approached the barrier separating the two of them. Iris would have taken a step back, but there were too many people behind her.

"You," he said to her, amazed. "You're lovelier than I could have ever imagined." He flashed a helpless, dreamlike grin. "Marry me."

"What?"

A punch from the Barber had his blood spattering in the air and his body slamming against the wall so savagely that this time Iris *did* jump back, much to the dismay of the man behind her.

After spitting out his blood, Jiffy continued as if he hadn't just been nearly knocked senseless, "Or I could take you out to dinner tonight? No, tomorrow night! How about it? You're not the tavern type of girl, are you? You don't look—"

Another punch. The crowd collectively gasped as Jiffy stumbled back.

"Wait, hold on—" Jiffy wiped his bloody mouth and lifted up a finger. "Just a second."

"What in the . . ." Iris was baffled as the Barber approached Jiffy, towering over the young man standing in front of him, his Goliath-like feet shaking the ground with each heavy step.

But the real surprise came when she blinked.

And suddenly the Barber was stumbling from a punch Jiffy had given him right between his shoulder blades.

Wait.

Jiffy was now behind him?

"How . . . ?" Iris couldn't remember seeing him move.

Adam nudged Iris and flicked his head toward the young man now bouncing on his feet. "And now, my dear Iris," Adam said, rubbing his chin with a finger, "now begins the show."

Jiffy the Blink lived up to his name. The excitable young man, now seemingly tired of letting himself be brutalized, landed punch after punch, except neither the Barber nor Iris could see where those punches were coming from. He zipped around the man so fast he seemed to disappear and reappear at will.

"Disappear . . . ," Iris whispered as a dangerous thought entered her mind.

"His real name is Maximo Morales," said Adam. "To my knowledge, he's been fighting in this establishment for one year trying to earn money. Do you know what's made him successful?" Adam pointed at the young man. "Watch him carefully."

Iris did. At the Barber's next punch, though Maximo had his back to him, he managed to suddenly catch the man's forearm with both hands. The force pushed the younger man back, rubble flying every which way from beneath his sliding shoes. He was relying on more than just his agility and prowess.

"He's not disappearing," Iris said slowly. "Is he?"

"No." Adam folded his arms. "It's not space he's bending." He looked at her. "But time."

"Time . . ." Once Iris stretched herself beyond the limits of her own imagination—an imagination that thus far could view only herself as the center of the supernatural—it was a concept she could accept. If he were really vanishing, then he wouldn't have been able to anticipate the Barber's moves so perfectly. He was *watching* them as if, for him, they were happening in slow motion.

"Many here believe he's simply light on his feet," said Benini, swirling his drink.

"I suppose that's why they call him 'Jiffy,'" Adam answered, smirking at the name.

"Let me see if I can get a better view. Adam, my boy." Benini slapped him hard on the shoulder. And to Iris: "Until next time, my lady."

With a slight bow of his head, he disappeared among the crowd.

"He's slowing down time," Iris whispered, her eyes still on the fighter.

"Not time itself, I imagine," Adam said. "Certainly not his own, otherwise he wouldn't be able to move as such."

Iris understood. "He's slowing down *our* time? Or rather, our sense of time?" Her hand trembled upon her chest. "He can do that?"

"I wanted you to see this with your own eyes, Iris." Adam watched the fight move along at the pace Jiffy dictated. "I wanted you to see that you're not alone."

What were they? A different class of humanity? Or were they human at all? Iris so desperately wanted to speak to this boy. She wanted to ask him what he knew about people like them . . . the Fanciful Freaks, according to that penny blood. It didn't matter what they were called. What mattered was that Iris's world was slowly opening to wonders beyond herself.

"But why is he being so reckless?" So flagrantly flaunting his power in front of so many people. The mere idea of revealing her ability to others had always terrified her.

"Why *not* be reckless?" Adam faced her. "If you could use such a power, why wouldn't you?" Passion smoldered behind his eyes, turning him a little reckless himself. He took her hand and drew it away from her chest, holding it instead against his. "You have wondrous gifts too, Iris. What I hope for, dearly, is that you'll use them to the fullest."

Recklessness sounded enticing. But as Jiffy walloped the Barber, she noticed that his movements had begun slowing down, his breaths becoming more labored with each punch. Just what was he doing to himself? Iris marveled at the revelation of this young man. Just one more piece to a greater mystery. There was still so much she didn't understand.

But Adam did.

"That second task you wanted from me," she started without being able to take her gaze off the ring. "What is it?"

Adam shut his eyes as if to prepare himself. "Before I tell you, let me give you a bit of information as a sign of the trust I hope you'll come to have in me," he said. "A crucial key to your past can be found at the British Museum."

A key to her past? Iris whipped around. "Is that really true?"

"I've already arranged for the British Museum to be opened for you past its scheduled hours. One of my . . . *assistants* will be there to let you inside. If you choose to go, you must meet him in the courtyard of the museum after nightfall. The anthropological collection for the Department of Africa, Oceania and the Americas is where you'll find what you're looking for. And Iris," he said with a sudden tenderness that made her heart skip, "I need to warn you. What you see there might shock you. It might even hurt you."

Iris noticed his worry. *Genuine* worry. For her. Just what would she find there?

"And yet, without going, without seeing the truth with your own eyes, you'll never be able to understand yourself. *That* is what I want for you. I hope after you go, you'll open yourself up to me a little . . ." He drew her closer. "And then I will reveal the second task I must ask of you."

She was close enough to him now that she could feel his breath caressing her face. Iris swallowed, steadying the quickened pace of her heart, and pulled away and turned from him. That was when she saw that the man with the drooping jowls was still watching her. Only this time, he wasn't alone. Two much taller men in green bowlers stood next to him, smoking cigars with their arms folded, taking turns jerking their heads toward her.

Iris recognized them. She'd once seen them in Coolie's trailer in Manchester discussing his debts. These had to be the men demanding his money or his fingers.

Or something else he could offer instead?

With curt nods to each other, they began pressing forward. Iris gasped, her chest aching from the influx of panic.

"They're here." Iris gulped in terrified breaths.

"They?" Adam raised his eyebrows.

"Coolie's debt collectors. They're after *me!*" She grabbed his jacket. "Did they follow us? Did they follow you?"

Adam's expression turned dark. "I *assure* you, I made certain we wouldn't be."

Iris wasn't convinced. "Was this a trap all along?"

But Adam's surprise and anger were real. He looked over her shoulder to find the threat, but Iris didn't have time to formulate any kind of plan. She could see the tops of their colorful hats moving fast through the thick crowd, too thick for her to make a clean getaway.

Iris wasn't about to allow herself to be captured by the likes of them. And so she decided on the only plan of action she could think of in her state of panic.

Hiking her skirt up, she considered taking out Adam's revolver, but there were too many people in her way and no guarantee she would get a clear shot without hurting a bystander. So instead, she jumped onto the ledge of the wall and leaped into the ring.

Had she not been in such a heavy dress, she would have landed cleanly. Instead, she landed facedown in the dirt. Gasps from the crowd. The fighters abruptly stopped. She lifted her head and smirked. Ever the performer. All eyes were on her.

"Get outta the ring, wench!"

"Who's that? Where'd she come from?"

She was too *good* of a performer to be used to the sound of a crowd booing her. A little irked, she clumsily dragged her skirt up and stumbled to her feet, looking up just in time to see the Barber launching his bloody knuckles at her, his fist aimed squarely for her head.

Her scream didn't have the chance to leave her throat before Jiffy, who'd been several feet behind him, caught his arm in a flash and shoved him away with all his strength. The crowd went wild. This was certainly the entertainment they'd paid for.

"Fifty on the African!"

"Put me down for forty-five!"

"Are you all right? Are you hurt?" Jiffy grabbed both her shoulders tightly with his bruised hands. For the first time since Iris had laid eyes on him, he looked deathly serious. "What are you doing in here? Are you insane? It's *dangerous!*"

"Help me," Iris said as she tried to catch her breath from the shock. "They're after me!"

Jiffy—no, his name was Maximo—searched the vicious crowd in the smoke-filled din. "Who's after you?" he asked, watching the Barber from the corner of his eye. "Oi, I said who?"

A scream pierced the air, and soon many others followed. The crowd scattered, cigars falling from lips, beer bottles shattering on the ground. The man with the sagging jowls had just exploded with a burst of electrical current, his clothes reduced to ash while his bare body remained unharmed. Iris watched the ensuing chaos unfold in horror as the realization of who he was dawned on her: the Exploding Man.

The two men had already jumped into the ring. One tried to leap on her, but Iris ducked his swing, kicking him back against the wall. Maximo's rough grip yanked her behind him as he gave the other man a swift uppercut that knocked the green hat clear off his head.

"Who the hell are they?" Maximo shouted, stretching out his arm to guard her.

"The bookies who my former boss at the circus owed money to, and now I think they're after me as his payment instead," Iris answered plainly from behind him.

"Oh." Maximo nodded with a shrug. "Okay, then."

But the Barber was not at all impressed. "You lot are gettin' in the way of my pay!" After hitting the wall behind him with his fist, he growled and launched forward at the very same moment one of Coolie's bookies drew a gun from underneath his vest and aimed it at Maximo. All the while, the Exploding Man drew near. This was not good.

Maximo turned to her. "Remember to breathe," he said quickly, his brown eyes sparkling with both urgency and a hint of mischief.

"Wha—"

Iris blinked, her breath hitched, and suddenly she was in Maximo's arms. He carried her like a princess over the threshold, except this dark and dingy castle quaked in utter pandemonium. They were now by the betting board, overturned and long since abandoned.

"Mr. Morales . . ." Iris scrutinized his tired body. "Are you okay?"

Maximo was breathing heavily, sweat dripping off his dark brow. "Me? Oh, I'm fine," he answered with as much cheer as he could muster. He seemed to enjoy carrying her, even in his present state. "It's fine, just a bit tired. It's Max, by the way. Oh, and don't worry, I'm not breathing heavy like this because *you're* heavy. Well, your dress is a little—"

"Watch out!" Iris cried, pointing behind him as a group of terrified gamblers barreled toward them, caring nothing about their safety.

"Breathe," Max reminded her, and in another blink, they were up the second flight of stairs. When Iris noticed that Max's legs were shaking, she knew her earlier hypothesis was right. He wasn't disappearing, he was moving, just on a different temporal plane. But it was taking its toll on him. Iris hadn't the time to tell him to stop before they were already at the door, then, with one more blink, outside.

Max dropped Iris and collapsed in the alleyway, clutching his heart.

"You still with me?" Iris lifted him up into a sitting position.

"I'm fine, Iris."

A second passed. Max's exhausted smile suddenly disappeared.

"How did you know my name?" Iris asked slowly.

The question caught him off guard, or at least she thought it had for a split second. "Heard you and that fellow talking," Max answered with a cheerful grin so innocent it disarmed her immediately, much to her dismay. She wasn't sure how it was possible he'd heard her and Adam speak in that noisy dungeon. But who knew? Many things that felt impossible were seemingly possible these days, like the power Max had used to do so much for her when he didn't have to.

He shrugged, his ridiculous grin still on his face. "So . . . you want to escape?"

Indeed, his power had enabled them to beat the crowds now fighting for space up the narrow, rickety stairs. They still had a chance.

"I know a place," Iris said.

"I know several. But I'll let you lead. I'm not in any shape to." He looked at her, his expression sparkling with admiration. "And you seem like the leading type."

Iris fought back her rising blush and helped Max toward the cobbled street. That is, until a horse-driven cart filled with hay pulled up in front of them, blocking their path to the street. The driver jumped off, wasting no time pulling out his gun.

This time Max couldn't protect her. Iris shouted in pain as the bullet went through her shoulder. She dropped to the ground, taking Max with her. The man who'd shot her was young, or maybe it was just his arrogance that had given him that energy. Tall and very thin with a shaved brown head and a jaundiced pallor that matched his crooked teeth. Raising his navy newsboy cap up to get a better look at the two of them, he twirled the gun in his hands.

"Coolie said you wouldn't die even if I shot you in the head," he said. "What do you say, should we test that theory, lady? Oh, and by the way, Maxey boy: Jacob and Hawkins say hi."

Max lifted his head just as the pandemonium from the club grew louder. "B-Bately?"

"Whoops, no time." Bately must have heard the crowd too. He put his gun away.

But Iris wasn't finished. She could feel the bullet moving back through the flesh it'd just pierced, trying to find its way out of her body. With a shaky hand, she reached for Adam's revolver still hidden in her skirt.

"I said, *there's no time.*" This time, Bately's voice pierced the inner crevices of her soul. "*You don't have the strength to fight, love, do you?*"

Iris's arm felt suddenly devoid of strength. Indeed, she *didn't* have the strength to fight. Strange that she'd ever thought otherwise. Her body went limp.

"Pick 'em up, boys," he said to a group of men. "The girl's got an auction to attend. But what say we throw in Max for a few extra shillings? I'm sure Coolie won't mind."

Rough hands hauled up her trembling body and dropped her into the cart of hay next to Max. A musty-smelling blanket slid over them before the sound of a horse's trotting and wheels turning took her into unconsciousness.

11

IRIS AWOKE TO A SHOOTING PAIN in her shoulder. There were shackles around her legs and arms tying her to a chair. The bullet was out, at least, likely lying somewhere in the wagon hay.

"Finally awake, eh?" Max said, similarly shackled next to her.

"Where are we?" Iris squeezed her eyes shut and pried them open again. "Do you know anything? How long have *you* been awake?"

"Don't know. Not a thing. And about a few seconds longer than you."

Exasperated, Iris began surveying her surroundings.

They were in a parlor surrounded by all sorts of bizarre, diverse items. Priceless paintings, busts and vases on the floor, and porcelain dolls on the marble table on Max's right. In one corner, weblike spinning machines made of pearl. In another, a set of armor from ancient times. And next to the dolls were ornate cases of spices that looked imported from foreign lands.

To Iris's left, a golden pocket watch, a set of talking drums, wooden lutes from the Elizabethan era perhaps, and some other musical antiques. Behind her were "treasures" of a more morbid sort: A sarcophagus. A pickled monkey's paw in a jar. A line of skulls in glass cases and jars of teeth from specimens from Oceania, Asia, and the West Indies. They shared space with large jewels probably taken from the same homelands that the bones had come from.

"Wild collection, isn't it?" said Max, wincing as he lifted his head. "As a boy, I was happy enough collecting *buttons*." He looked up at the ceiling, squinting in the light from fixtures hanging on the walls. "Wonder where those went. Did I give them away? No, I couldn't have—"

"I think we have more pressing matters," Iris said, shaking her arms and legs. The iron chains rattled against the floor.

"Seems so," Max said. "We're tied. To *chairs*."

"For an auction, apparently." Iris stared grimly, remembering their kidnapper's words.

"Try to save a girl's life and you get auctioned off for your troubles." Max laughed.

"This isn't funny!" Iris insisted. "And . . ." She paused, suddenly feeling very sheepish. "I'm . . . I'm sorry for all this."

"Who said I was mad about it?" Max shrugged. "Far as I'm concerned, it was worth it."

Iris straightened her back with a proud huff, avoiding his irresistible smile.

"If I remember correctly, you said your boss was after you because he had debts to pay."

"George Coolie." His name tasted foul on her lips. "I have no doubt this auction is *his* scheme. He had money problems. I was one of his best circus acts, but I quit on him. This has to be his contingency plan. I guess you were thrown in as part of the bargain."

"How much do you think we'd go for? About the same as the skulls?" Max glanced over his shoulder at the glass case and shuddered.

Iris looked at the healed gunshot wound in her arm, courtesy of the man called Bately. "Higher. The two of us aren't exactly normal. Back during the match, you were manipulating time, weren't you?"

At first Iris wasn't sure what to make of Max's expression. He was hesitant. But then, why wouldn't he be? It wasn't so simple a thing, discussing one's fanciful freakery.

But soon that cocky grin returned to his face. "Oh, so you noticed? Much like I'm noticing you seem perfectly fine after being shot at close range with a pistol."

Iris swallowed. Well, "perfectly fine" wasn't entirely accurate, but she nodded anyway.

Max let out a sigh that felt more like a laugh. "So there really *are* more of us out there."

"If that's even a good thing." There was no doubt that the two of them would go for a pretty penny. Iris didn't want to think of who would be sick enough to want to *buy* them or what perverse pleasures they'd be used to satisfy.

But at the very least, looking at the boy beside her, she felt less alone.

"A man once told me that whether having a gift is really a gift just depends on how you *use* it."

His words reminded her of Adam, who she'd left in that underground ring with the Exploding Man. She wondered if he was still alive.

Max laid his head back and closed his eyes. "My mother sent me to England when I was only seven years old. Since then I've spent most of my time on the streets, stealing things and trying to survive with friends. And Bately," he added with a sneer.

The man whose words had charmed her into obedience. "He's your friend?"

"He was once. Haven't seen him in a while. He's likely a mercenary now," Max answered bitterly. "When I realized I had these abilities, it made pickpocketing much easier. Imagine having all the time you need to steal? My street friends and I had plenty of adventures. Near misses, narrow escapes, the whole lot. Ever since that day at the fair."

Fair? "The South Kensington fair ten years ago?" she asked quickly. "June second?"

Max's friendly expression disappeared into something indiscernible. "Yep."

She and Adam. Now Max. It couldn't have been a coincidence they were all there. She decided to test him. "There was an explosion that day, wasn't there?"

He fell silent, letting her words marinate for a moment before speaking. "It didn't feel like a proper one. I mean, it *was* one, but . . . it felt like a wave flushing through me. It knocked me out for a while. I was nine," he said. "My friends were there. So was Bately. They'd been affected too. When we woke up again, people were scared witless. Running everywhere."

Iris nodded. The chaos. People running. The patches of fire.

He paused. "Later I heard there'd been a murder."

Silence. He stared at the iron shackles around his legs.

"Gas-line explosion my ass," he said, snapping out of his gloom. "Something else definitely happened that day. Because after then, we all changed. We all turned—"

Fanciful, Iris thought, the picture becoming clearer. "I was there too," she told him. "I don't quite remember everything, but I know I was there."

The two sat in silence among the paintings and jewels and skulls.

"You. Me. Bately. The Exploding Man. What if we're a result of what happened at that fair?" Perhaps her lack of memories was some sort of amnesia due to the trauma.

But then why wasn't Adam affected? Or was he? Or were only a select few impacted?

"It fits," Max said. "Before then I was just a normal boy—well, as normal as a Salvadoran pickpocket in London can be."

"Now you can manipulate time."

"I can slow down others' sense of time," he corrected. "Don't ask me how or why." Max's brown curls fluttered across his forehead as he laughed. "It is what it is, I guess."

But it was more than that. Like Adam promised, it was proof she could see with her own eyes. Proof that there were others like her. And a precious clue to her own past.

Except . . .

Iris looked down at her shoes. "I don't remember my life before that day. I've been trying to remember, but my memories prior to a certain point are just . . . gone. It's probably due to the explosion. People were obviously affected differently. But still I . . ."

One step forward and two steps back. Despite what she'd learned, she still felt defeated.

"I just want to know who I am. If I've parents out there. If my name is even really Iris." She remembered Granny's cryptic words to her and shivered. "It's so painful not knowing. But at the same time, I'm scared to know. Sometimes I wonder if I should just forget about it all—"

"No, don't do that." Max's gentleness drew her attention. "Don't give up. If there's something you need to know, then what's there to think about? Just don't worry. All right? I'll help you. You can trust me. No, you *should* trust me."

"Should?"

"Well, who else can you trust?"

The image of her discarded partner flashed in her mind's eye. She shook her head. She couldn't go back to him. She couldn't draw him into this madness.

"You're very eager to help someone you just met," Iris said with a little laugh—and a hint of suspicion. But how could she stay suspicious when Max thoroughly disarmed her with that incorrigible, kind grin? It was a mysterious charm he had.

Maybe the sight of her sensitivity had touched Max in a way she hadn't anticipated. Or maybe he was just that reckless. Either way, he puffed out his chest—still bare, as Iris tried shyly not to notice. "People like us need to stick together. Believe me, I've learned that the hard way. My life hasn't been the easiest," he said with a sad smile. "There's a lot of danger out there, as you've just seen. Stick with me. I give you my word, Iris, you won't regret it," he promised gallantly, ever the hero.

"People like us . . ."

"The *good* ones," Max added. "Not the nutters like that exploding gentleman."

"People like your friends?"

"Yeah. Jacob, Hawkins—I hope they're fine. Bately better not have . . ." As he frowned, Iris remembered how the mercenary had mentioned them. "And Cherice." Suddenly his face drained of blood. "Cherice, oh *damn*." Max groaned as if he'd just been punched in the gut, and when she told him so, Max let her know that a punch in the gut was precisely what was waiting for him when the girl he'd left behind in the Pit found him again.

"But forget all that. Once you and I get out of this mess, I'll do whatever I can to help you. You're not alone in this." Max rattled his chains. "As you can see."

Iris's shoulders relaxed and her whole body breathed with relief. Knowing that she wasn't alone was invaluable to her. "Thank you." She paused. "In that case, we really should try to avoid being auctioned."

Max's laughter chimed like music. "I'll agree with you there."

After some time, Iris could hear footsteps. "Someone's coming! Max, anything yet?"

An exhausted Max slumped over on his chair. "I've been trying for hours," he said in between breaths. "Scuffling around while chained to this bloody chair. I couldn't find anything that can break or unlock them."

She was more distressed by the way he was sweating and breathing heavily than by his failure. "Okay. Don't use your abilities for the time being."

The corners of Max's lips curved only slightly. "So you've noticed my weak point, have you?" He winced as if a sudden shock of pain flashed through him.

"Don't damage your body any further," Iris warned. "I mean it."

"Thank you for your concern." Max rested his head back against the chair. "I mean *that*."

The door opened, and a few men who worked for the auction house walked in behind a physician's assistant from Cambridge University dressed in a vest and a perfectly straight brown bow tie. Not that he'd bothered to introduce himself to Max or Iris. She heard from their conversations. He didn't address them at all even as he set down his tray of tools on a table.

"We'll measure the male specimen first," said the assistant. Iris's stomach churned. The stick he was given . . . It was a horse measuring stick.

Their chains were double locked, first to fasten their limbs, then to tie their limbs to the chairs. But Iris still had Adam's gun. The fools hadn't even bothered to check. She just had to wait for her moment. If she could just untie herself . . .

Carefully, one of the men unchained Max from the chair, but his feet and wrists were still too tightly bound for him to move freely, especially in his exhausted state.

"Stand," ordered the assistant.

"Want me to dance a little jig for you too, mate?"

A whack to his left shin with the wooden measuring stick sent Max doubling over.

"Max!" Iris yelled as Max trembled with pain.

"I said, 'stand,' not '*speak*,' you filthy *wog*."

Max's decision to remain sitting earned him a beating. Iris screamed, struggling against her chains, her blood boiling, cursing her own inability to save him like he'd saved her.

"Try the other one," suggested one of the auction employees with a sigh when Max proved too difficult to crack. "She'll be weaker than the male."

"Now, I don't know about that one, lads." Max laughed, blood dripping from his lips.

The tool the assistant took off his tray looked like two long fishing hooks fused together at the ends. It wasn't until he aimed the sharp ends at her forehead and chin that she realized he was trying to measure her skull.

"We'll start with craniology, then," said the assistant. "Looking at the shape of the specimen's skull and comparing it to others of her race will be good information for those bidding on her. With the right precision, we can determine the female's level of intellect as well as her predilections toward theft and other pathologies."

Except Iris kept squirming. She wasn't about to let that ridiculous tool near her precious skin. "If you're curious about how smart I am, you're better off *asking* me, *idiot*."

"Oof," Max said with a chuckle.

"Don't touch me!" Iris spat in the assistant's eye. "I said, don't touch me, you sick—"

The door opened and slowly creaked closed.

Light footsteps. And yet there was a heaviness to each step, an impact that Iris felt deep in her immortal bones. Out of the corner of her eye, she saw the old man's great white beard, his dark eyes behind brass spectacles. His long black jacket. His bow tie, a blood red.

His clinical gaze on her.

Iris didn't know why she felt as if her lungs were filling up with liquid. Or why the skin of her arms was sizzling with an electric charge, or why the acidic contents in her stomach were now threatening to rise up through her throat.

"Good afternoon, Doctor Pratt!" One of the auction's men gave his hand a brisk shake. "Your assistant told me you were running a little late. Thank you again for volunteering to do this work for us on such short notice."

The assistant gave up on trying to measure her. "Maybe you'll have better luck, Doctor."

Doctor . . . Pratt . . .

"When I heard of the treasure in your possession, I had to confirm it for myself," the old man answered.

His maliciously blank stare seemed to mock the sudden swell of anger inside her. The dead air of the room weighted her shoulders, and darkness fell over Iris's sight. Her body began to shake.

This feeling . . . The chains were hot against her skin. *This feeling . . .*

Fear. Yes, fear. Panic, rising up through her sweating body.

And rage.

He touched the square crystal cuff link on his sleeve and, without even an evil grin to match, raised his chin. "So you've returned from death, Iris. Hello, old friend."

Iris's head nearly split from the sudden shock of memories that flooded her. Of blood. Of hands on her skin. Of her flesh burning. Of her veins flushed with drugs to keep her mind clouded and addled. Tears and screams. Each memory was nothing more than a quick flash, but each flash was a painful blow stirring her rage to frenzy. The sight of his white crystal cuff link pushed her further. The white crystal drew her in, calling to her. Taunting her. Asking her, *Do you know what I am?*

This feeling . . . She gritted her teeth. *This man!*

Doctor Seymour Pratt, standing inches away from Iris, reached for the craniometrics tool.

And he leaned in.

"You should know this," he whispered. "Now that I've confirmed you're alive with my own eyes, this auction is meaningless. Regardless of who wins you tonight, you'll end up back in my possession sooner or later." He straightened up. "Then shall we get started?"

Iris's throat could have ripped apart from the force of her scream. Blind rage possessed her, and in that moment she launched forward, her mind empty but with one command: *Kill him. I have to kill him!*

With her ankles and wrists bound, she grabbed the pointed tool away from the assistant with her teeth, forcing the blades open where they joined. Then she brought her wrath down upon the doctor.

"Iris!" Max yelled somewhere as the assistant gave a cowardly yelp, oceans away.

But the doctor caught the tool in his hand. And smiled. "You haven't changed."

It was as if every part of herself had vanished except for the bloodthirsty anger driving her. She let go of the tool and bit his arm instead, screaming and struggling. The assistant tried to pry her from him, but she wouldn't go, not until the doctor was a bloody mess on the ground.

"How dare you!" the assistant cried. "This man is a physician! A surgeon! A scientific, ethnological genius! You will show him some resp—" He cried out from the blow Iris gave him to his nose with the back of her head.

Iris did not know Doctor Seymour Pratt.

At least, she could not remember him.

But she *hated* him. So much she could die from the poison of it.

"Stop, you *animal!*" The assistant threw her to the side. She crashed into the table to her right, her chair breaking off an arm. And as she fell to the ground, a small, heavy object dropped onto her head and clattered to the ground in front of her face. She gasped from the shock, the feel of blood dripping from her mouth slowly bringing her back to herself.

The object—it was the golden pocket watch. It popped open on impact. Clockwork, metal, and pins plucked the teeth of the little comb.

And played music.

A melancholy, romantic tune filled the room with the sound of tinkling bells.

"Iris!" Max was frantic. "Iris!"

Iris could hear Max hopping in her direction. The assistant backed off immediately when Max made a threatening move toward him.

"Sir," said the assistant to Doctor Pratt, who simply held his wounded arm to stop the bleeding. "Sir, I shall mend your—"

"I can tend to myself," said the doctor with a dismissive wave.

If only Iris could reach the revolver still bound to her thigh, covered by her billowing dress. Tears stung her eyes, but she would *not* let them fall until those disgusting men were gone.

"The sedative!" said the assistant.

"The one we have isn't quite strong enough to knock them out . . . ," said another man.

"Never mind that," the assistant shot back. "Hurry!"

One among his group pulled out a needle and shoved it into her arm without the slightest bit of kindness. Iris gritted her teeth as she forced herself to bear the pain. From the sound of Max's grunt, they'd given him the same treatment before finally leaving the room. Doctor Pratt's small black eyes were the last to disappear behind the door.

"Damn, they really got me good." Max knelt beside her, still chained. His face was drained of blood. The sedative would likely kick in soon for both of them. But for Iris, despair had already extinguished whatever fire she had left.

"Iris?" he said softly, trying to see her face. "Iris . . ."

The music within the pocket watch filled the silence.

"That was dangerous. You know that, right?" With labored movements, Max lay down beside her. "You could have been killed."

"I can't die," she answered softly.

"Ah, really? I thought you just healed quickly." He chuckled. "If I'd known that in the Pit, I would have asked *you* to save *me*."

Iris appreciated his attempts, but her heart was just too heavy for his cheerfulness. Though the wisps of new memory faded from her, she could still feel blades piercing her skin. Were they once held by his hands? That Doctor Seymour Pratt?

She didn't know. How could she? She didn't know anything about herself.

Coolie shooting her in the head, hunting her down like a dog, and auctioning her off to the highest bidder. Pratt's assistant measuring her as if she were some kind of specimen . . .

"This body is mine," Iris whispered, tears dripping down her nose. "This body is *mine*. Why won't they let it belong to me?"

Her weeping added the hint of despair needed to complete the pocket watch's light tune, turning the music minor. Max was quiet for a moment.

"My mother," he said finally. "My mother sent my sister, Berta, and me to England because a merchant had promised her that he'd give us an education."

Sister? Iris listened.

"As it turned out, we were to be displayed in an exhibit. Somewhere along the way, my sister and I were separated. She was only five years old. And I was seven. Too young to try to find her. I couldn't even speak the language here. I couldn't do anything for her." Max paused, collecting himself. "I don't even know whether she's still alive."

Iris blinked back her tears, thinking of the two tiny siblings in a foreign land.

"I do not know the depth of your despair, Miss Iris," Max told her. "But I understand despair quite intimately."

Despair. Iris stared at the tearstains on her ripped dress. How silly she must have looked to those men, dressed as an aristocrat when they didn't even view her as human.

"It's why I've been trying so hard to raise money," continued Max. "Now that I'm old enough, I'm going to find her. I'll . . . I'll do anything." He stayed quiet for a long time. "Maybe that's why I was given these powers. To reunite my family. I have to, no matter what the cost."

Iris gazed at the clockwork gears shifting inside the pocket watch.

"When I lost my sister, my world ended," Max continued. "I don't expect to be understood. Or even . . . even forgiven for what I choose to do to get her back." He rolled over and stared up at the ceiling. "One thing I do know is that you have to do what you can to keep your world from crumbling. That goes for you too, Iris. Don't lose hope. It's all right if you don't know yourself yet. You'll find it one day. I'll . . ." He paused. "I'll help you however I can."

The sedative was starting to work, sapping the dwindling energy within her. Iris shifted her head, looking over her shoulder. "Find it?"

"The truth of your world."

The watch's music played on.

12

B Y THE TIME THE SEDATIVE BEGAN to wear off, it was nightfall. Rough-looking men in suits unlocked their chains, leaving only their
wrists bound. And so began their march toward the auction hall. Max
was whispering to himself in Spanish. Praying? Swearing? Iris couldn't tell.

While the men dragged them by the chains, the haughty auctioneer walked
behind.

"Why are you doing this to us?" Iris demanded him. "This can't be legal."

"The clientele we're serving tonight is of a special kind," he said. "With special tastes."

Special clientele. The "esteemed guests" Coolie had invited to their Astley's
show, perhaps. And she was right. As they entered the auction hall, she could
see them in their black jackets and petticoats, with their canes and white gloves,
holding the program for this evening's entertainment. Benini, Adam's eccentric
colleague, sat in the front row, now in a brand-new robe: sparkling emerald
green over his unbuttoned white shirt and black trousers. With a wineglass in
hand, he used the auction program to fan his face in the stuffy room.

His golden locks blew into the face of the woman on his left—a woman
she recognized: the wealthy-looking heiress-type who'd sat next to Adam at
Astley's. Her flaming burgundy bun clung to the base of her neck, a black hat
with white feathers finishing her look.

"Will you stop it, you fool?" The woman smacked his program to the floor.

Benini huffed. "Such a violent woman you are, Madame Bellerose. I wonder how your husband even stands you, you *beast*!"

Madame Bellerose, as she was called, folded her arms, exasperated.

The auction hall was divided into two columns of seats. Paintings and extravagant light fixtures adorned the walls along with busts of naked Greek men who watched over the macabre proceedings with their hollow white eyes.

The guards pushed Iris and Max onto the platform. A painting of green hills and valleys, so very nostalgic for industrial England, hung behind the wooden podium where the auctioneer was to stand. And in front of the podium—

Iris narrowed her eyes. "Coolie."

Coolie shifted awkwardly to the side as she was shoved to the front of the stage beside him. What could he be thinking, she wondered, as he saw her bound up in chains, a former employee treated more cruelly than the animals in his own company?

"Why, Coolie," she said once the men had dropped her chains and left her standing in front of the hungry crowds. "I thought slavery had been abolished? Or didn't you hear?"

At the very least, he showed a little bit of shame, his puffy cheeks swollen red as he stepped off the platform to further the distance between the two of them.

"Thank you, my dear guests, for coming tonight," said the old auctioneer, taking his position at the podium. His voice echoed off the high ceiling, moonlight streaming through the windows above him. "We here at Wilson and Wilkes Auctioneers welcome you."

"How could you *do* this?" Iris hissed at Coolie. "I gave you ten years of my best work."

"*You* were the one who left me no choice," he hissed back, straightening his bowler hat. "I told you I needed the money, and yet you *still* stabbed me in the back. The debtors and I came to an agreement. They get paid *double* what I owe, and I keep the rest."

"A heartwarming collaboration."

"Well, unlike you, I can't survive without my fingers."

The auctioneer continued. "First, I'd like to say that unfortunately, we have not yet been able to install the new security system purchased from the Bosch Guns and Ammunitions Company."

Disappointed grumbles.

"Yes, yes, I know." The auctioneer put up his hands to calm the crowds. "It's a complicated system designed by a complicated inventor. But rest assured, even without it, there shall be no intruders." He gestured to the thugs meant to be their security. "And because I know your esteemed time is valuable, we won't waste another moment. I introduce to you the first lot of the evening, courtesy of Mr. George Coolie, owner of the Coolie Company."

At this, that crook Coolie *dared* to take off his hat and bow as if it were their last call. The only upside to this sick show was that the more he made Iris seethe, the more she could feel her strength returning. She looked over at Max, who was cracking his neck from side to side. The sedative was gradually wearing off.

"Now, these specimens—"

"Excuse me." Coolie held out his hand to stop the auctioneer. "Allow me to explain these fine treasures to our illustrious guests." He cleared his throat. That was how Iris knew his pitch was coming. "Ladies and gentlemen, we've all heard the rumors, haven't we? They've even made the papers. Rumors of strange happenings. Rumors of strange people."

Max and Iris exchanged glances.

"The girl before you has a wondrous gift. You've seen it yourselves, I reckon, if you had the incredible luck of being present at the Coolie Company's legendary show at Astley's Amphitheatre—now playing every night for the next seven days, tickets still available."

Max raised an eyebrow. "*This* was your boss?"

"Don't remind me," Iris grumbled.

"A girl who can't die." Coolie waved his fingers as if telling an old ghost story. "An oddity stranger than anything Barnum can conjure up with his cheap parlor tricks. A *true* oddity confirmed in front of your very eyes. Confirmation that dark powers truly *do* exist."

Interested murmurs filled up the room.

"Is she an angel?" Coolie paused for dramatic effect. "Or is she a devil?"

"What about the boy?" someone shouted from the audience.

"Oh, I have magic powers too," Max confirmed with a nod. "As for whether I'm an angel or a devil . . ." His smile turned wicked. "Well, that depends on whether I fancy you or not."

"Are you *trying* to get sold off?" Iris whispered angrily into his ear as some ladies began fanning themselves.

"I just don't like being left out of things." Max shrugged. "*You* know."

"No, I do *not*!"

The front doors opened and slammed shut with gusto. In walked Adam Temple, the weight of his black boots echoing across the red walls and ceiling.

"Adam . . . ," she whispered, prompting Max's attention. So he'd survived, after all. Iris wasn't sure whether she was relieved or upset. Like the rest of them, he carried in his gloved hand a bidding paddle. He *was* here to save her . . . right?

When Madame Bellerose saw him approaching her, she looked delighted to see him, so much so that she shoved the mysterious figure sitting to her left out of her seat.

That figure was an odd one. Dressed in a black coat, she'd been sitting between Madame Bellerose and a ghoulish, withered man who'd handed Bellerose her paddle. Pierre, Bellerose had called him. Iris couldn't see the girl's face underneath her wide-brimmed black hat, as it was shaded by a yellow veil affixed by pins to her hair. But she could see her long, tiny black braids, a river of them, stretching almost to her hips. After Bellerose snapped at her in French, the woman went and silently stood next to the wall. Perhaps they were both servants. Pierre certainly looked miserable enough.

At Madame Bellerose's prompting, Adam took the seat that the veiled woman had left vacant, but his blue eyes were on Iris and Max. As Coolie prattled on about how she was an ancient goddess of some sort, Adam started mouthing something to her.

"Max," Iris whispered, nudging him in the ribs with her elbow—bare ribs, as the poor boy was still shirtless. "The man who just entered—"

But Max was shifting uncomfortably, avoiding her eyes. Eventually, he cleared his throat. "Ah, you mean the man you were with in the Pit?"

"Yes, him. Can you make out what he's saying?"

Max squinted. "T . . . all. Tall. Is that it? Tall? Must be referring to me, then."

Iris watched the curves of his lips carefully. "Stall," she whispered. *"Stall!"*

Stall? Stall for what, exactly? Just what did he have planned?

"Without further ado," the assistant chimed in, interrupting Coolie, "I believe we should start the bidding. First, on the girl, as she is the main feature of the night."

Iris looked anxiously at the crowd of wealthy bidders all holding their paddles at the ready.

"Who will bid five hundred pounds?"

"Five hundred *pounds*?" Max balked. "I don't know whether to feel disgusted or proud."

"Five hundred."

Adam. Perhaps winning her was the only way out of this mess. His grand plan.

"Five hundred, thanks." The auctioneer pointed his gavel at Adam, who looked deadly serious. "Do I hear six hundred?"

"Six hundred."

The old man who'd spoken was at the opposite side of the room, several rows back, so short Iris wouldn't have been surprised if his feet didn't touch the ground. He stroked his graying black goatee with satisfaction as the auctioneer took his bid.

"Cortez." Adam shot daggers at the man behind his shoulders.

"Turns out he's looking to fill his team too," said Benini. "Who was he trying to fool staying silent at the meeting? At any rate, you might lose your champions, Adam."

Champions? Iris frowned as Madame Bellerose shot him a withering glare. "Some things are better not discussed out in the open," she hissed.

"Do I hear seven hundred?"

"Seven!" Adam raised his paddle, almost lifting out of his seat before staring at Iris again. "Stall," he mouthed again, and nodded up toward the ceiling windows.

Nothing lay beyond the windows but the moon, but Iris could see that the man named Cortez meant business. That made her nervous. As they say, the devil you know.

And so she stalled. "Oh. Ooh, my fate! My cursed fate!" She whipped her head to the side. "How could this be that I would end up in a battle with my love, my own heart? Why, oh why are the stars so cruel?"

The auctioneer stumbled over his next words. Stunned silence. Iris had the room's attention, a fact of which she took full advantage. "Whether this land is yours or mine, can't we rule it together, hand in hand? Ah, my dearest love! My Turkish Prince!"

"Hang on." Coolie's large nose scrunched as it clearly dawned on him: this was the dialogue for "The Bolero of Blades," written by Coolie himself, though eventually scrapped on the agreement of the whole company because of how unabashedly horrid it was.

"Or we can flee together to the Valley of the Kings and there share our lives as eternal, passionate lovers. Ah, my Turkish Prince! Can it really not be done?"

Without Jinn as a partner, Iris turned to Max, throwing herself against his bare chest. He didn't seem to mind at all. In fact—

"I'm here, my princess!" he shouted, extending his hard pectoral muscles and adopting a very serious expression.

"*Nubian* Princess," Iris corrected him quietly.

"I'm here, my Nubian Princess!" Even without any context, Max clearly understood Iris's plan and surpassed her ridiculous airs as if it were a competition to see who could act worse. With a hawklike gaze, he surveyed the bewildered upper class. "And I shall never leave you. For ever since I laid eyes upon you, I knew you were destined to be my eternal love. You are my sun, my moon, my stars, my—uh, my . . ." He searched for the word.

"Galaxy!" Benini offered, positively delighted.

"Yes, galaxy!" Max would have pointed if his hands weren't tied. Benini gave him a thumbs-up. Even Adam's lips had quirked into a helpless grin.

"Just what is this nonsense?" someone cried from the audience. "Mr. Wilson, get ahold of your stock. We don't have all day."

Iris froze in fear before she spotted Adam spurring her on with a wave of his hand.

Right. Stall. "My esteemed lords and ladies," she cried over the confused babble, "don't be so rash! This is but a demonstration of what you'll be getting in the deal upon your purchase!"

Iris steadied herself. Max's inclusion left her no choice but to improvise, using Coolie's dreadful dialogue as a guide. "My love, do you really mean it? We do not have to die in this bloody battle for possession of the ancient lands?"

"Why no, my dear. I suspect not." Max gazed into her eyes. "Because . . . Because I *love* you, my princess."

His intensity was palpable. Without realizing, Iris withdrew a little from him.

"I loved you when first I laid my eyes upon you. In that very moment, your beauty captivated me more than any living thing has ever done in my lifetime. Your strength. Your courage. Your grace. Your intelligence. Your vulnerability."

Their audience fell into a hush. Iris opened her mouth but had no lines to recite.

"Is it rash, my love, to have fallen for you so quickly?" Max continued with the utmost tenderness. "You might say so. Others may indeed disapprove of it. 'It's unrealistic,' they would say. Yes, I understand how silly it all seems. Yet, I am but a rash man. A rash and foolish man who cannot help but be so easily captured by love."

There was something dangerous about his enticing gaze and incorrigible smile. That she couldn't tell whether he was being serious or not made her shiver.

Benini stood and clapped. "Bravo! Encore!"

Iris's eyes darted from side to side. Pushing herself off his chest, she turned and fell to the ground, much to the gasps of the audience. "Oh, my Turkish Prince! Who am I but, uh, a slave to destiny," she said, her voice more stilted than before. "How I've missed you all these long days and nights! How I've longed to see you!"

How I've longed to see you . . . Iris's lips pressed tightly as she thought of *him.* That cranky young man who would sometimes look upon her softly when he thought she wasn't watching. "How I've longed to—"

"Enough of this nonsense!" An unimpressed Madame Bellerose stood. The veiled woman hadn't moved from her position next to the wall, though Iris could tell her shrewd eyes were fixed on her. Madame Bellerose raised her paddle. "Four thousand pounds! Four thousand pounds on the girl *alone!* That should be enough, should it not?"

Iris snapped her head up in shock. The audience was in an uproar.

"Four thousand pounds?"

"Ridiculous!"

"Then I shall bid two thousand on the Aztec." Standing on his chair, Cortez really was quite short. "Give him to me *now!*"

"*Aztec?*" Max repeated. And then, after a short moment—"Hold on, why is my bid lower than hers?" He shot the man a withering look. "Come now, I'm worth more than that, old man."

Adam was on his feet. "I bid my entire family's fortune on the girl!"

"My, my," said a man Iris couldn't see. "What would the late Lord Temple say if he could see his son throwing his inheritance away for a Negro witch?"

Iris clenched her teeth. Adam's knuckles were bloodless as they gripped the handle of his paddle in fury. "Isn't that what you're all here to do?" he spat back. "Or am I mistaken?"

"Unfortunately, Mr. Coolie has asked for all bids to be made in specific dollar amounts, good sir," said the auctioneer.

But Adam wouldn't give up. "That fortune is more than enough—"

"Then how about *forty thousand pounds?*" Madame Bellerose seemed to relish the gasps and murmuring that descended upon the auction hall. "Far more than her worth."

Adam's grip tightened around his paddle. "A hefty sum no doubt won through your family's spoils in the slave trade," he hissed. "You're willing to give it up?"

"This girl's powers would make her an unstoppable piece for me to play," she answered. "Isn't that why you want her so desperately?" Iris could see the challenge in the woman's eyes as she added, "Outbid me. Then I'll outbid you. Let's see how far we can go, shall we?"

Silence. Adam was seething. The auctioneer cleared his throat. "As of now, I have forty thousand pounds on the girl. Do I have a higher bid?"

The realization that he now had at least that much in his pocket drove Coolie into a fit of giggles, stopping only once he caught Iris's eyes. He dared not look at her when he said, in a hushed tone, "I'm sure they'll take care of you, dear girl," before straightening his shoulders.

"A job well done, Coolie," she shot back bitterly. "A job bloody well done."

"Forty thousand pounds!" said the auctioneer. "Going once?"

Murmurs from the crowd. Adam stared at his paddle, perhaps wondering if it was worth it. If *she* was worth it. But then, curiously, he looked up at the ceiling.

"Fifty thousand," Adam called.

"Sixty thousand," Bellerose replied instantly. They glanced at each other, their fierce battle raging. All the while Coolie had to stop himself from dancing where he stood.

"Sixty thousand. Going once?"

Adam shifted between anxiously looking up at the ceiling and hesitating to lift his paddle.

"Going twice?"

And then, suddenly, Adam unknitted his brows, his scowl easing into a wicked grin.

He lowered his paddle at last.

"Sold to Madame Violet Bellerose!"

Just as the auctioneer lifted his gavel, the thunderous sound of glass shattering above them sent the whole room into chaos. Max and Iris jumped off the stage and dove for cover, as the shards rained down upon the pulpit.

Iris couldn't see the figure crashing through the ceiling—only the stream of fire exploding from his mouth, aimed at the bidders, sending them screaming in terror through the front door. It wasn't until he'd leaped from the stage and landed catlike in front of her that Iris's chest swelled with emotion. She couldn't believe it. It couldn't be true.

THE BONES OF RUIN

"J-Jinn? *Jinn!*" she cried, stunned at what she was witnessing.

Jinn did not look behind him at her. But she'd recognize those old worn-out trousers and dull brown vest anywhere. In his hands were the curved blades he'd used in their bolero, just as sharp and deadly as she remembered them. He gripped them tight with determination.

Fire. Breathing fire. He was breathing fire . . . The words repeated in her mind again and again until they jumbled into a stream of nonsense.

"Who's he?" Max wondered, in awe of the mayhem that Jinn had just created.

Even in the midst of her pure shock, an overwhelming feeling of hope brought an open smile to Iris's lips and tears to her eyes. "My Turkish Prince."

13

JINN. IT WASN'T A DREAM. JINN was standing in front of her. Real. Flesh and bone.

Her partner had returned to her.

But this couldn't be Jinn, *breathing* fire from his *mouth*. She could see the smoke rising from the burning chairs and drapes. Her heart pounded against her rib cage. How? Jinn wasn't—he *couldn't* . . . could he?

"Run!" someone screamed. "Run, man, run!"

She heard cries as gentlemen and women ran for their lives, Coolie and the auctioneer along with them. Jinn had aimed for the empty seats in the leftmost row. It was clear he didn't want to kill anyone. Indeed, for one fleeting moment, he stepped back, and Iris could see the quiet terror in his eyes, as if he were seeing something more than just a flaming auction house. But he gathered himself quickly, his resolution clear in his expression.

"Enough!" Adam cried as Jinn's mouth smoked again. His front row had been spared, but Iris wasn't sure for how long. "Jinn! Enough!"

What? Since when do they know each other? Iris glanced between the two.

At least Adam had the good sense to run out of the way. Madame Bellerose couldn't move with Benini holding on to her, screaming and cursing his fate. Her servant Pierre had tried to stand, but instead tumbled backward, taking his seat with him.

It was the girl in the yellow veil who leaped to action. With her black hat flying back behind her, she took off her jacket with one sweep to reveal a yellow skirt down to her chestnut-colored shins and a brassiere made entirely of pearl beads, woven tightly together—even the wide straps that held her brown chest up. The girl was fast, but nimble enough that the yellow veil pinned to her hair did not move even as she charged forward. She wore it like a fencing mask, shielding her mysterious identity.

Even with all that Iris had already seen, she still couldn't believe her eyes. As the girl ran toward Jinn, her chest smoked with fine, white dust, revealing the wooden hilt of a blade.

It *was* a hilt. And it *was* a blade—a very long blade, emerging from her chest where her heart should have been. She pulled it out. It was bloodless in her hand. Its surface gleamed immaculate and bright in the moonlight, white like the cuff links that demon Pratt had worn on his sleeve. Jinn was too stunned to move.

Iris didn't have time to think. Pushing Jinn out of the way, she held up her arms. The girl's blade sliced through the chain binding her wrists. Now free, Iris grabbed the chain, doubled it up for extra fortification, and blocked the girl's next swings. The mysterious girl hesitated at Iris's prowess, her instincts. Iris was stunned herself, but she didn't complain. She bent back, watching the white sword swiping the air just above her nose. Then, tearing her dress for easier movement, she slid behind the girl, whipping her shins hard with her chains as she passed. The girl cried out in pain and flipped onto the row of chairs. Iris finally grabbed the revolver strapped to her leg and shot at her, but the girl deflected each bullet with her massive sword. Once Iris's onslaught had ended, the girl jumped out of the way just in time to avoid the stream of fire billowing from Jinn's mouth. Adam, Benini, and Bellerose ducked for cover as the painting of Immanuel Kant on the wall beside them burned.

"Iris!" Adam called, and out of the corner of her eye she could see him trying to reach her before she quickly shifted her focus back to her opponent.

Iris had always been good with blades, had always been agile, but up to this moment, she'd used those skills for entertaining. There was no audience to please this time. Only the boiling of her own blood that somehow remembered the euphoria of battle. Something about this girl had dragged that curious feeling out of her. But Iris was not as quick as this girl. She leaped at Iris. When Jinn met the girl in midair, he slashed at her chest with his left blade, then tackled her to the ground, only for her to strike his forehead with her own—

And launch her sword straight into Iris's stomach from afar.

"Iris!" A frantic Max tried to reach her, but the auctioneers' thugs had just snapped out of their stupor and begun lumbering toward her, hesitantly of course, because not even they could believe the battle transpiring between Iris, Jinn, and Bellerose's guard. As Max readied himself to take them on, Iris collapsed, her body crumpled in Adam's arms.

"I'm fine," she said, though her sight was dimming. "The sword . . ."

Such a strange sensation, the sword embedded deep inside her flesh. Perhaps it was the pain numbing her senses, but the blade felt familiar to her. The warm pool of her blood dripping down its length felt welcome there. A blade of solid white . . .

Slowly, she lifted her arm, her fingers hoping to touch it just once . . .

Dropping his blades to the floor, Jinn carefully yanked the weapon out of her stomach with trembling hands. Blood splattered out of her mouth, the torment unbearable. The mysterious girl flipped to the second row and balanced perfectly on top of the wooden rail of a chair. From there she watched Iris die.

"I'll be fine." Iris managed a smile for both shaken men before she died in Adam's arms.

She awoke again to the grunts of battle. Iris wasn't sure how long she'd been gone. She didn't bother to ask Adam, whose expression was one of reverence.

"Iris . . . ," he started, taking in the sight of her in a way that shook that memory in South Kensington from her. An awestruck boy with blue eyes. "Your power. You really are . . ."

"Adam." His expression made her uncomfortable.

"You're ready." Adam cupped her face with a hand. "From here, you know where to go."

Iris had no patience for his cryptic words. She pushed herself away from him the moment she was strong enough. Jinn was dodging the woman's sword, which she must have taken back while Iris was dead, meeting her swings with his blades. Iris's stomach ached, but it didn't matter. She needed to help him. The girl was too fast. And the more Jinn sprayed the room like a dragon, the more the walls around them cracked and the air dragged with smoke. They couldn't afford to stay inside the building for much longer.

Breathing heavily, Iris grabbed her chains, the only weapon she had left, and charged at the two of them, blocking the girl's sword once again. The girl quivered at the sight of Iris, reborn. But then, slowly, she lowered her head.

"Isoke," the girl said in a voice so youthful it surprised Iris. "It *is* you, isn't it? Just as Bellerose said. The one called Child of the Moon Goddess. She Who Does Not Fall . . ."

Iris could just see the outline of her dark lips trembling in fear behind her yellow veil.

"I . . . I . . ." The girl caught herself, gritting her teeth. "Isoke, you're coming back with me to Dahomey. Back to King Glele. I will make you fall today." She bore down harder on Iris with her sword.

Iris grunted as she struggled against the force of the girl's strike, her mind scattered in confusion, not only because of the indecipherable words the girl spoke, but because Iris could understand her at all—the girl hadn't spoken English. Not Yoruba, either. And yet Iris could understand her perfectly. She'd learned this language before. But when? It was another mystery from her past that she couldn't afford to ignore.

With a yell, Max crashed into the girl, sending her flying back into the front row of chairs. The sword sailed out of her hands, shattering into white crystal the moment it crashed into the ground and disappearing into pearl smoke. The girl had knocked her head on one of the chairs and was struggling to move. It wasn't a sight Iris enjoyed. The girl seemed so young, despite her tall frame, and so afraid when she saw Iris's revival. Iris still couldn't see her face, only her tiny braids fanned out about her, a blanket of obsidian spread upon her veil and the marble floor.

"Jinn!" Iris helped him up. "Jinn, are you all right?"

Jinn gazed up at her, wild emotions writing too many stories across his dark eyes.

"Iris . . . ," he started, reaching up to touch her face.

"I don't know what the hell is going on," said Max, "but I *always* know when it's time to go." Max looked down the clear path in between the chairs. "Come on."

"Who's he?" Jinn asked, getting to his feet.

Max shot him his cocky grin. "Her *Salvadoran* Prince, friend. Nice to meet you."

Iris was entirely uninterested in the tension between them. Instead, she peered around the room. In the midst of the chaos, Bellerose and Benini had already escaped.

And Adam. Adam was gone too. When had he slipped out? Was it really his plan to leave her there in the burning building?

You're ready. From here, you know where to go. Adam's words.

And he was right. She suddenly did know where she had to go next.

The museum.

Max held out his hands to Jinn and waited, tapping his foot.

Jinn raised an eyebrow. "What do you want?"

"Burn these off."

"Excuse me?"

"Come on, you know. With your—" Max blew into the air as a demonstration. Jinn gave Iris the uncomfortable look of a boy who'd just realized his secrets had been revealed.

"Go on," Iris said. "We can discuss the details later. Right now we have to move."

After placing his blades behind his back, tied to him by a brown belt, Jinn obliged Max's request. This time a controlled stream escaped from his lips until Max, shouting from the heat, managed to break the chains himself.

"Thanks, mate," said Max, blowing on his wrists.

Jinn scowled. "I'm not anywhere near close to being your *mate*."

One of the beams in the corner of the building cracked, threatening to collapse. Grabbing Iris's hand, Jinn pushed Max out of the way and began running, leaving behind the mysterious girl still trying to move.

"Jinn—" Iris started, surprised at her own worry for the girl's life. But he wouldn't stop until he'd pulled her outside and far from the burning auction house, Max following close behind.

"Jinn, stop!" When they were far enough away from the flames, Iris finally pulled herself out of Jinn's grip.

"What are you doing?" Jinn balked. "We need to go."

"Where?"

"Out of this city. This *country*." Sweat dribbled from his forehead. "Anywhere."

Iris shook her head. "I'm sorry, I can't do that."

"Don't worry, we'll take Granny with us," added Jinn softly.

Iris felt ashamed in that moment that Granny wasn't at all what she was referring to. And yet at the same time, that Jinn had thought of Granny made Iris's insides feel warm.

"Who's Granny?" Max asked rather brashly, leaning over to catch his breath.

Jinn gritted his teeth. "Why are you still here?"

"Because she *needs* me," Max said teasingly, and patted his shirtless chest almost as if he wanted to see Jinn's eyes burn with quiet anger. He seemed to relish it.

"I do," Iris replied, surprising her circus partner. "I need both of you. Because I'm going to the British Museum even though I don't know what I'll find there."

As Jinn stared at her, confused, Iris pulled him into an empty alley and began, as fast as she could, to explain what had happened since she'd run from the circus. Max listened carefully.

"A key to your past?" Jinn stroked his chin, deep in thought. "The Department of Africa, Oceania and the Americas . . . And you trust that man?"

"You obviously did," retorted Iris. "Otherwise, how else would you have found me?"

She had a point, and he knew it. Jinn shifted on his feet. "He came to me after you were kidnapped, and we came up with the plan. I'm not sure he knew

I had these . . . abilities." He swallowed. "But he knew I was your partner. When he asked me if I would do anything to get you back, I—" He stopped, turning his face from her.

"Your abilities." Her conversation with Max filled her thoughts. "You were at the South Kensington fair in 1874, weren't you? June second, the day of the explosion."

When Iris locked eyes with her stunned dancing partner, it seemed for a moment as if time had slowed . . . as if perhaps Max were playing his tricks, though she knew he wasn't.

Finally, Jinn confirmed it.

"So was Max." She pointed at him. "And me. I have every reason to believe that all the people at the fair that day . . . changed. *Transformed*. You too."

"That's what I was trying to tell you before you ran from the amphitheater," he said quietly, and just then Iris remembered his pleading as she drove away in the carriage she'd stolen, his words disappearing with him into the fog. "That we're the same!"

"Why didn't you say anything?" Iris accused. "You can breathe *fire*?"

Jinn looked away. "I don't like having to . . ."

His expression darkened, and he looked suddenly so vulnerable. But Iris couldn't let this go. "You can breathe fire, Jinn. Ever since we met. There was plenty of time to tell me, not just then! Why didn't you say anything?"

"I could ask the same question to you," Jinn said. "Instead of being honest with me, instead of confiding in me, you *ran* from me."

"I ran from *Coolie*," she corrected, feeling attacked and guilt-ridden all at the same time. "There's a difference."

"Not to me."

"Oi, come on." Max watched the street carefully. "That's enough. I know emotions are still high after our adventure at the auction, but this little spat isn't exactly helpful considering our present situation."

"Our present situation is this." Iris's hands balled into fists. "I'm going to the museum. Whatever key to my past is there, I'll find it. With or without you. I won't stop. I can't."

The South Kensington International Exhibition. Adam. The girl with her sword of pure white. Granny's cryptic accusation. And—

Doctor Seymour Pratt. Simply thinking of him made her stomach heave.

She needed to know what mysteries were locked tight deep inside her subconscious. The secrets piling up would soon kill her.

Max nodded. "So we go to the museum."

"We won't." Jinn grabbed Iris's wrist. "Temple said he made 'arrangements.' Who knows what he's planned. It's too dangerous."

"That's why I'll go with her," Max retorted, grabbing Jinn's wrist.

"I said it's too *dangerous*."

"Don't listen to him, Iris," Max insisted, shooting her a quick glance. "Go. Follow your instincts. And you—" He smirked at Jinn. "If you're too much of a coward to risk your life for a beautiful girl in distress—for your *friend*—feel free to run. I'm staying right here."

"*What* did you just say?"

"*Enough!*" Iris yanked her hand away before falling silent. She knew Jinn was only worried for her well-being. And she was encouraged by Max's support. But she was tired of being talked *at* and *about*. "Jinn," she whispered finally. "You've never told me about your past. But you at least *know* your past, don't you?"

Jinn stayed quiet. It was enough of an answer for her. Without being able to stop herself, she gripped his shirt and stared up at him, her eyes large and pleading.

"I need to know mine." Tears stung her eyes as the memory of her rage in the auction house haunted her. The sword-wielding girl's words. The names she called her: Isoke. She Who Does Not Fall. "I need to know. Please help me. *Please* . . . I need you. You're . . . you're my partner, aren't you?"

For all those many moments the circus pair locked eyes during their routines, it was never this desperate, never this naked with emotion.

"You're my partner," she said. "Before. Now. Always." She buried herself in his chest. *With or without you* was a lie. She needed him, now more than ever. "Don't leave me . . ."

Trembling a little, Jinn covered his eyes with his hands and turned from her quickly, but before Iris could push any further, he let out a little laugh.

"You win, Iris. You win," was all he said.

A beat of silence passed as the three stood in the alleyway under the crescent moon.

"To the museum, then," said Max.

Iris nodded. There was no turning back now.

14

A T THREE PAST MIDNIGHT, THE BLACK gates of the British Museum opened slightly to Iris's touch, startling her.

"It's unlocked." In the cold of night, Iris's fingers trembled around the iron. *Aren't they afraid of thieves?*

But Adam had told her to come here tonight. He'd had everything prepared for her beforehand. That must have been why the cobbled streets were empty. How Adam managed these feats was beyond her imagination. The power of wealth and resources, perhaps? Or the power of the mysterious club he belonged to. That *Committee* . . .

Jinn and Max pushed the gate open and let her walk inside first before shutting it behind them. Two columns of white stone held the gate in place, and from its sides stretched a black fence around the museum, each black rod narrowing to a tip, piercing the night. The tall white columns shielding the shadowy southern entrance reminded her of the Greek buildings of ancient times.

The three stood in the courtyard facing the triangular pediment upon the building's flat, cast-iron white roof. Supported by the columns in accordance with classical fashion, it featured fifteen sculpted figures. Bodies of white stone depicting humankind through the ages as it acquired the knowledge and capital that would make people the undisputed rulers over life and land, whether life and land desired it or not.

Power. Perhaps this was the story the museum wished to tell to those who passed by it, but for Iris it was an ominous symbol. The hubris of the stone men and women looming over her made her body tremble.

According to Adam, a man would be waiting to greet them at the entrance. But though the gas lamps stationed atop the gate columns were lit, the wide walkway to the entrance remained empty. Iris, Max, and Jinn made their way down the stone path, checking the grassed areas at their sides, but no shadows lurked in the darkness.

Iris tied her shawl around her waist. "There's no one here."

Max, still shirtless, shivered in the night as he peered around the columns. "That Temple bloke didn't seem like the type to be pulling your leg about something like this."

Jinn checked the gates behind them. "I wouldn't trust him. We still don't know what his real intentions with you are."

Indeed, Adam had too many secrets. He dangled his half-answered questions like worms on a hook. But the underlying sincerity in his eyes whenever he spoke to her, however darkly mischievous their expression, couldn't be brushed aside.

Adam Temple . . . She just didn't know what to make of him. He said he'd prepared something for her. Prepared *what*?

The answer to that question came sooner than she expected.

The two barely adolescent girls emerged from behind the Grecian white columns at the south entrance, hand in hand as if partners on a stage. They were twins in more than just their round faces, mannequin bodies, and sedated brown eyes. The extravagant black dresses they wore were the same, their skirts fanned out like open umbrellas, their stockings as black as the curls swiping their waists. They descended the entrance's stone steps, perfectly in sync, until they came to a stop and smiled the same sleepy smile.

"What is this?" Iris whispered as Max and Jinn closed ranks with her immediately. "What's happening? Who are you?"

"Three extraordinary questions."

The voice had come from above. That man . . . Iris had seen him outside the window in Adam's manor. She'd thought she'd just been imagining things. She was wrong.

He'd appeared from seemingly nowhere, standing at the very tip of the triangular pediment with his black cape covering his body, his harlequin mask hiding his face and his top hat tipped forward.

"I don't imagine they'll answer, unfortunately," he said. "They don't speak."

"Who in the blazes are you?" Jinn squeezed his hands into fists and stood closer to Iris.

"I am but a messenger—the *official* messenger—for the illustrious and powerful Enlightenment Committee. How do you do?" The man bowed with a sweep of his hand. "Much like Miss Iris, the name I hold now is not my true name," he continued, his black leather boots curled upward at the tips. "But some have correctly dubbed me a fool, and I must say, I find it quite suits me."

"Certainly dressed like one," Max muttered.

"Congratulations, Miss Iris and company," said Fool. "I welcome you to your preliminary challenge of the Tournament of Freaks!" Reaching within his black cape, he threw up sparkling confetti into the air that exploded like little firecrackers into colors of every kind. "The first of many battles to come."

"Tournament of Freaks . . . ?" She stepped back from the twins' doll-like grins, brandished like a weapon.

"Survive this test, Miss Iris," said Fool, "and you will gain many of the answers you seek. Answers dutifully promised by Lord Temple. But beware. Misses Faith and Virtue Sparrow are not as fragile as they look. Otherwise they wouldn't be under consideration for Mr. Cortez's team of champions."

"Cortez?" Max said, and turned to Iris. "The little man at the auction?"

Iris remembered him standing atop his chair to bid on them, his black goatee reaching well past his chin. Like Benini, like Bellerose, like Adam . . . he was a member of the Committee.

"Champions," she whispered, now having heard that word for the third time. And as she stood in the museum courtyard, she knew without a shadow of a doubt that if she wanted to know what Fool had meant, she'd have to get past the Sparrow twins.

By the looks of the two, it wasn't clear to Iris if they even cared about winning this fight. They seemed to simply do as they were told without a word. What had Cortez done to them?

At once the girls raised their arms with blank expressions. A chilled fog rose from beneath Iris's feet as snow descended upon them and began blowing around the courtyard with increasing ferocity until Iris could no longer see the Sparrow girls at all.

Iris shielded her face from the blizzard. "What's happening?" she just barely had time to ask before the earth began to quake beneath them. Yelling, Iris managed to stumble out of the way. A long, thin icicle burst through the ground where she'd stood. Another one. Another three, right at her side. With each explosion of ice and stone debris, Iris flipped out of the path of danger, putting her tightrope training to use, but by the time the courtyard had settled, she'd lost track of the others. She could only hear the sound of their struggling.

"Jinn!" she called frantically. "Max!"

"Iris!" Jinn called back. "Where are you?" He sounded so very far away.

"My sense of direction's been blown to hell," said Max somewhere behind her. "All this dodging. I have no idea whether I'm facing left or right."

If the Sparrow twins' plan was to separate and confuse them, it succeeded. Ice and snow. The girls worked together to cause the kind of mayhem Iris had never witnessed before. Their only chance was to get to the girls themselves.

"Max, Jinn, can you hear me?" Iris cried over the pandemonium. "We've got to—"

Iris felt the point of an icicle lifting her off the ground. Her boots slipped off the surface, but the freezing tip pierced her flailing hand. Iris let out a cry as the icicle continued into the sky, carrying her up with it. To take the pressure off her hand and keep it from ripping in two, she lifted her skirt and hugged the thick icy skewer with her entire body, holding on for dear life as its momentum carried her higher and higher.

And then stopped.

Wincing in pain, she pried her right eye open, then her left. The icicle was gone. The pain in her hand vanished. The wound disappeared.

And then she saw herself. For a split second when she gazed into the courtyard. She saw . . . *herself*. Yes, she was there down below, holding on to her head. What was going on?

And then she was falling, falling back into the blizzard swirling around the courtyard of the British Museum. Iris felt her bones break upon impact. What an annoying, painful inconvenience. She waited patiently for her body to mend itself before sitting up with a haggard breath, attempting to figure out what had just happened to her.

She checked her left hand. The wound and pain were back. Somewhere in front of her, a stream of fire and an explosion of steam told her Jinn was fighting the dangerous ice skewers in his own way. But what about the one that had launched her up into the sky? Why did it disappear the moment she—

The moment she left the snowy fog.

After jumping back to avoid another icicle bursting from the ground, Iris racked her brain, trying to remember what she'd witnessed while in the sky. Up there above the museum, she saw it for only a moment. The blizzard raging on inside a large but limited area, like a bubble. The Sparrow twins stood directly under the full moon, their arms trembling as they held each other tightly. Red mist swirled around their linked hands.

And when she had looked down from that vantage point, no fog or snow blinded her sight. Jinn and Max were dodging icicles that didn't exist. The courtyard was just as pristine as how they'd left it.

But she'd seen herself too . . . *So you've noticed my weak point, have you?*

Max's words came to mind as she remembered. No matter how powerful the Fanciful Freaks were, their power always came with limitations. Iris had thought the twins were controlling the weather. What if it was nothing more than a snow globe of illusions—one they could make only while their hands were joined?

Then the icicle. Being carried into the air. It was all in her head . . .

But there still had to be some kind of tenuous connection between reality and fantasy. Though it'd taken place in her own mind, the illusion the Sparrow twins had given her nonetheless gave her a true perspective of what it'd be like to be outside their field of influence—what she would see if she were truly in the sky looking down.

Iris wasn't sure. But it was time to put her theory into practice. "Max, Jinn!" Iris cried, whipping her face away from a lash of snow. "Get to the twins. Break them apart!"

"What?" Iris heard Max grunt in pain.

"Just trust me!"

Iris peered up at the full moon just above the south entrance. As long as she didn't lose her sense of direction . . . "Follow my voice, Jinn! Find me!"

She started running, calling to the boys whenever she could accumulate enough breath. The icicles always announced themselves, shaking the ground before breaking through. She timed her jumps to avoid them cleanly, each time with better precision.

"Iris!" Jinn. She'd found him. She reached out to him and grabbed his hand.

"We need Max," Iris said. "Jinn, use your fire!" And when his dragon's breath exploded an icicle behind them—"Max!" Iris called. "Follow the steam and you'll find us!"

Running at this speed, they should have crossed the courtyard in a minute at most, but Iris and Jinn ran toward the moon for what felt like ten minutes or more. Iris's hypothesis was right; this truly was an illusory world. But it was a world with boundaries. As long as they could exploit the boundaries, they'd have a fighting chance.

"I'm here!" Max said finally, jumping through the steam and shards of ice bursting from Jinn's attack. He grabbed Iris's other hand, and Iris pulled him toward her.

As they ran, Iris explained as much of her theory as she could. "Do what you can, Max. We need to separate the twins!"

"That I will, but I'll have to work fast," Max said. "I can't hold my breath forever."

Hold his breath? Was that how it worked? His weakness? Iris didn't have time to ask.

Max took in a deep breath.

"Remember, follow the moon! That's—"

Suddenly Iris felt the wind knocked out of her, her sense of time skewed. She blinked, and Max was on the steps of the museum, breathing heavily. The veins in his forearm bulged as he held the girls up by their wrists, their feet swinging childishly in the air as they shrieked like bats. The red mist chaining them together had disappeared.

The illusion collapsed. The blizzard, the fog, the icicles. The museum was exactly how they'd left it. Their wounds and pain vanished. But for Jinn, this wasn't over.

"We have to finish it," Jinn said, striding forward.

Iris grabbed his wrist, holding him back. "Wait, what do you mean by that?"

Jinn's eyes glinted dangerously. "You know what I mean."

"Jinn!" Iris was horrified. "They're children!"

"I know. I *know* that." Jinn cringed at his own suggestion, the emotional battle raging inside him stiffening his body as he watched the girls struggle in Max's grip. "But they almost killed us. They *still* could kill us!"

Iris looked down at her dress, where Adam's revolver seemed even heavier.

"Iris." Jinn grabbed her hand wrapped around his wrist. "Even if you can't die, death isn't the only thing to fear." He squeezed, gazing at her desperately. "I won't let them hurt you any further than they already have. That's the promise I've made to myself."

Even separated, the girls bit and kicked Max, trying to join their hands once more. But *kill* someone? She couldn't imagine it. It was wrong. It was unthinkable.

But sometimes such things are necessary, a tiny, nasty voice from deep within her whispered. *You wanted to kill that man at the auction house, did you not?*

Doctor Pratt. Just thinking of his calculating beady eyes made something vicious in her stir. But that was different—an uncontrollable thirst, a need she couldn't explain. Standing here in front of the museum entrance, Jinn expected her to make the choice to end someone's life . . .

Humans are such awful things, the voice within her said. *Maybe it would be better if they all—*

Iris let go of Jinn, shut her eyes, and covered her ears. "There has to be another way!"

"Indeed, there is!"

Fool. From atop the museum, the cloaked man threw two long copper needles into the necks of Faith and Virtue, who slumped over lifeless in Max's grip.

A wide-eyed Max placed the girls gently on the stone steps. "You didn't—"

"Never you worry, my boy. They're only asleep. I may be a fool, but I boast expertise in the holistic practices. Rejoice! For they live."

Max checked their pulses and nodded. They were indeed alive.

"They're no longer your concern." Fool straightened his white gloves. "It'll be up to Cortez to decide what to do with them after I lay his champions at his feet."

Iris's fingers curled into fists. "Champions, champions, *champions*! You keep mentioning it. What do you *mean*?"

"As you've passed your test, you'll find out soon enough, sweet girl." Fool swept his arms to the side with a welcoming gesture. "The British Museum is yours to explore. You are free to enter . . . and abandon hope. Follow the trail, and you'll find the answers you are looking for. But a word of advice." He touched the rim of his top hat. "From here on, strengthen yourself. For the journey to the truth is not for the faint of heart. Especially a truth such as yours."

15

W HAT A HAM," MAX SAID AS they stared at the trail of purple
flower petals leading them down the marble hallway. *Irises.* How
quaint. "What a *large* ham."

"Fool? Or Adam?" Iris asked, for she didn't know which of them had
arranged this.

Fool was sure to have taken the twins to Cortez by now. Just what kind of
monster was Fool? Was he a product of that fateful fair too?

Iris wondered if he was hiding a scar behind that harlequin mask. Or maybe
he was just a fan of theater. Either way, even with him gone, they had to stay on
their toes. They could be walking into another trap.

The petals led them into a library with rows of white bookshelves filled
to the brim with more books than Iris could ever read in a lifetime. Their footsteps on the wooden panels echoed across the ceiling. Iris's fingers trailed the
round mahogany tables, her eyes on the flickering lamps stationed on the tall
wooden chests of drawers pushed up against majestic columns.

Upon the very last table was an open book, iris petals held between vari-
ous pages.

"Feels good to be led by the nose, doesn't it," Jinn said sarcastically as Iris
drew the book closer to herself.

Iris bent over to read the golden text on the green cover. *"Essay on the Theory of the Earth* by Georges Cuvier."

Iris swept a crushed petal across the introduction and found another on the one hundred and forty-sixth page.

"Oh, we *can't* be meant to read all this," Max said, making a face once Iris sat down at the table. *"Seriously?"*

It wasn't such a big deal. After ten years of reading to Granny anything she could get her hands on, she'd become quite the proficient reader. More important: Would some truth about herself emerge from these pages?

"Not the whole book," Iris told them. "The flowers are bookmarks. Let's start there."

Max and Jinn pulled up seats next to her and waited, Max with his head rested against his hand, Jinn quietly watching to make sure no shadows slipped between the bookcases.

This man Cuvier referenced a few other places, histories, and narratives. Babylon, Egypt, Greece. Alexander and Moses. The Bible and Hellenistic writings. Each time, he alluded to . . . "events," as he called them. By way of fire, by way of flood. Acts that made plants and animals in parts of the world extinct, which would then be followed by repopulations of fauna and flora. Extinction events. Catastrophes.

Cataclysms. Many of them.

Iris read enough to know these theories intrigued her, but she wasn't sure what to make of it. Cuvier's disdain for many of the cultures he referenced gnawed at her as she read, but Iris was drawn nonetheless to the idea of cataclysm. Especially interesting were the extensive notes she found in the book's introduction, notes written by a man called Robert Jameson, responsible for translating Cuvier's French work into English. Jameson's interpretation of Cuvier's work extended to the concept of a *divine* deluge that had come multiple times throughout history to wipe everything away like the biblical flood of Noah. His was a geological justification for the flood in Genesis as well as glacial events that, in his estimation, shaped and reshaped the earth.

Extinction and rebirth. When she spoke of it to Jinn and Max, they could do nothing but sit in confusion along with her.

"But what does this have to do with us?" asked Jinn. "Us . . ."

"Fanciful Freaks?" Iris finished with a smile.

"No." Jinn refused with a deadpan expression. "*No.* Anything but that."

"Fanciful Freaks, eh? A friend of mine wrote some penny bloods with that title." Max kicked his legs up onto the table. "Begged him to change that title."

Iris blinked, shocked. "A friend of yours?" She thought back to the author on the issues she'd found in Adam's study. "Chadwick—"

"Winterbottom, yeah!" Max lit up as he rested his arm around his chair. "Glad you've heard of him. He wrote about us: Hawkins, Jacob, Chadwick's sister Cherice. When we were street kids, we were all part of the same crew."

The Fanciful Freaks . . . an idea ripped straight from real life. She stared at Max in awe.

"Question remains," he said, "if this is all about evolution, are *we* the evolution?"

The mysterious explosion at South Kensington had transformed so many, probably even more than Iris knew. But how was it connected to the theory of cataclysm?

Iris, Jinn, and Max turned their heads toward the double white doors ahead of them where the trail of petals stopped. The doors were shielded from potential visitors by a red velvet rope plus the words STAFF ONLY and UNDER CONSTRUCTION painted in black letters on each door.

Iris stood from her chair. "Let's find out, shall we?"

Max moved the stanchion holding the velvet rope in place. The door opened to Iris's touch. With a hesitant glance exchanged between the three of them, they stepped inside.

The only light within the long room came from the four paneled windows above. Moonlight streamed through them, washing over the glass cases lining the wall. The flora in them needed the light: the infant palm trees, neem, orchids, cacti, bamboo, and mangrove. The showcases in the center of the room carried artifacts: pottery and wood carvings of African heads. Or else glass jars of baobab fruit, lemongrass, and herbs and seeds.

Adam Temple stood at the very the end of the room, tossing up his favorite coin and catching it. So this was where he'd gone after the auction. He stood with his back to them in front of a glass display of bones. After catching his silver coin for the last time, he buried it within his jacket pocket before placing his hands behind him.

"What is this all about, Adam?" Iris demanded. Next to her she felt Jinn clench his hands into fists while Max, on the other side of her, shifted slightly away.

It was a moment before Adam answered.

"The Hermetic Brotherhood of Luxor," he said without turning to look at them. "They believe in clairvoyance, astral projection, and scrying through the use of magic mirrors." Iris could see his delicate face reflected in the glass display, imprinted on the human skeleton hung up on a rack between the remains of monkeys and gorillas. "On the other hand, the Order of Knight Masons believes that by communicating with celestial beings through Cabbalistic ritual, mankind would once again regain primordial unity lost with the Fall of Adam."

Iris stayed near the door. "And what does your order believe in?"

Adam kept his gaze on his white-gloved hand, his palm turned upward to catch the moonlight. "The end of the world."

Iris's heart shook at his words. "Cataclysm."

"Evolution," Jinn added, placing his arm out in front of Iris as she stepped forward.

"And the renewal of mankind." Adam turned to face them now.

"You mean that nonsense you had us read out there." Max flicked his head toward the door. "You people actually believe it?"

"Catastrophism is the foundation of the formation of Club Uriel, and its upper echelon: the Enlightenment Committee," Adam said. "The continual annihilation and regeneration of populations."

Max's usual hearty laugh would have bounced off the glass cases. He seemed somehow more subdued, however, in this room with the four of them as he muttered, "For how important and rational you lot think you are, you seem oddly susceptible to your own imaginations."

"It's funny, isn't it?" Adam ran his hand through his black hair, closing his eyes as he considered it. "Even Cuvier was a scientist. Doctors, authors, astrologers. How can people who believe so much in *reason* become so easily enraptured by what they outwardly consider to be reason's opposite? But perhaps that's the paradox of the modern age."

"Excuse me, but what does that have to do with the fact that you sent little girls to *kill* us?" Iris frowned. "What's your business with us . . . us—"

"Fanciful Freaks?" The crook of Adam's mouth turned into a teasing grin. "Though that's not the term I would use to describe you, Iris. You're very different than they are."

"Answer the question," Jinn said as Iris's fingers twitched. He swiftly moved in front of her, almost blocking Adam from view.

"The Enlightenment Committee was created long ago, before Club Uriel. Indeed, the club is a front. The Committee is an exclusive order of the wealthiest and most powerful across Europe. Fourteen members once upon a time." He smirked and looked at his right palm again. "As far as Club Uriel is concerned, catastrophism is a bewitching scientific concept despite its contradictions and inconsistencies—an intriguing alternative to other theories of evolution and, for some, an exciting hypothesis of what may one day become of us. They don't know the truth that we Enlighteners do. We were formed on the foundation that the world would end, and after decades of painstaking research, we alone now know this to be humanity's future beyond a shadow of a doubt." His eyes glinted. "And we know what to do about it."

Something in Iris stirred, something dangerous and secret. After a moment, she felt faint, but she refused to show it.

"The world *will* end. In that case," he continued, "who would guide the regeneration of mankind? We in the Committee already use our resources to steer political and economic developments across the continent. Boris Bosch, for example—"

"The arms dealer?" Max said, and leaned into Iris. "There was someone in the Pit who used to work in one of his factories," he whispered. "Terrible face, that poor bloke. Half of it got burnt off in an accident. Never had the heart to fight him."

"The leader of Bosch Guns and Ammunitions Company has sold weapons and many new technological innovations to political leaders around the world," said Adam. "Including my family's contacts in Parliament."

"So basically," Jinn interrupted, "since you people believe the world is ending, you want to lead whatever's left behind, and you seem to think you have a right to." Jinn shook his head in disgust. "You're nothing but an egotistical doomsday cult."

"After everything you've seen, is it really so hard to believe in the end of days?" Adam calmly pushed back. "Do you really think your supernatural existence is a happy accident?"

Jinn clenched his fists, his eyes downturned in quiet anguish. "There was nothing happy about that day." Iris watched him, worried. What horrible memories taunted him?

"Oh, but there was." Adam cocked his head, amused at the expression Jinn showed. "It's always a happy day when one's theories are confirmed."

Iris gently pushed Jinn aside and stepped forward. "As far as I'm concerned, nothing's proven," she said.

"And as far as I'm concerned, it doesn't matter what *I* believe. It doesn't matter what the Committee believes. It doesn't matter what they believe." Adam flicked his head toward Max and Jinn. "What matters to me, Iris, is what *you* believe." He stepped aside. "And what you see."

In front of the glass case of skeletons was a museum label, a plaque affixed to a kind of wooden podium. A summary of the contents inside, though to Iris it looked more like a tombstone. Max grabbed her wrist, shaking his head. Of course the display was horrible, but she was compelled to see. The skeleton hanging in the center of the display was of average height, with long legs and wide hips. It was female. There was something delicate about the small skull. That it was displayed next to the skeletons of apes disturbed Iris. That the skeleton was in front of her at all, defenseless against her gaze, disturbed her more.

But when Iris reached the podium, it wasn't the label's description of the objects that caught her attention first. It was the picture next to it. A photo stained yellow. Three women dressed in grass skirts that barely hid their bodies in a zoo display crafted to simulate their "natural" habitat, what with the monkeys and imported palm trees. Written in cursive beneath the photo . . .

GORTON ZOO HUMAN EXHIBIT
MANCHESTER, 1832

It was a photo of herself.

Iris's body went numb. There she was, carrying a staff that held her steady against the ground, her face, her body the same as they were now. Though her brown eyes were hardened, it was unmistakably *her*.

Slowly, Iris turned to the description on the plaque:

GORTON ZOO'S HUMAN EXHIBIT ENTITLED "SPECIMENS
OF THE NIGER REGION." BEGAN 23 AUGUST 1830.
DISCONTINUED 3 AUGUST 1832.

Heart racing, she skimmed until she saw words she recognized. Names.

"'The human specimens from Africa were the Marlow Sisters, named thusly by Thomas Jones, captain of the slave ship *Marlow* that brought them to England's shores: Anne, pictured at age eleven. *Iris—*'" Her breath hitched. "'Age unknown. And Agnus Marlow,'" she said, throat dry, "'pictured at age eight.'"

Marlow. Agnus Marlow. Iris checked the picture again. Looking closely, she saw Granny's kind eyes and heart-shaped lips, this time on the face of a child.

But there was a darker truth to reveal.

"'And on display is . . .'"

Iris couldn't go further. For a moment, she swore her heart stopped beating. Her fingers twitching as they traced along the plaque, she read and reread, hoping the words would make a little more sense every time her sight ran over them. She opened her trembling lips again, tears in the corners of her eyes.

"'On display,'" she said, her voice hoarse, "'are the remains of Iris Marlow.'"

"That's impossible!" Jinn cried as he and Max ran up to her.

She would have collapsed to the ground if Max had not kept her steady by the shoulders.

"It's okay," Max whispered, but though she could feel his hot breath on her ear, she could barely hear him. Granny, more than fifty years ago. And this Anne with her butterfly barrette clasped firmly in her woolen hair. Iris was the oldest among them. It was impossible. It was unthinkable, and yet here it was in front of her. Her past. Her—

She looked up. Her bones.

Her *bones*.

"No," she whispered as the skeleton mocked her from behind its glass cage. "This can't be true. Those bones aren't mine."

"They *are* yours." The shadows crossing Adam's face danced almost playfully as he lowered his head, his black hair shielding him from the moonlight. "They are yours, Iris."

"They are not!" she cried, so loudly she felt her throat rip.

If those men hadn't kidnapped Sister and me, then, child, you would have.

Granny's words. What did they mean? She was a kidnapper? Those men— they were slavers? Granny's sister, Anne. But how could Iris even attempt to kidnap anyone? Just how long had she been alive? Just what—

Shaking, Iris bent down and reached into her stocking, and suddenly she was pointing Adam's revolver at his head.

"Iris!" Max and Jinn yelled at the same time, but Iris could only hear her own heart thumping in her ears.

"What does it mean?" She desperately tried to hold her aim steady, but her arms felt so weak, her hands heavy.

"Colonial exhibits, you see, are quite popular," Adam said calmly. "Especially now, they're flourishing across the Western world—in Europe and even the Americas. Men and women who revel in the opportunity to affirm their own civility come from all over to see displays of colonized tribes from Africa, India, the Americas, and so on. Maximo surely knows what the experience is like."

Max's grimace answered to the affirmative. It held within it so much pain.

"Don't worry, Iris. Nobody today would link this Gorton exhibit to you, even if they happened to see you in one of your circus performances." Adam leaned against the glass case to the right, the wide leaves of a palm tree shading him from above. "How could anyone believe that a girl of seventeen was seventeen half a century ago?"

Iris lowered the gun. Was this the traumatic experience Granny had refused to remember? The three of them exhibited in a . . . a human zoo? Granny had felt familiar to Iris all those years ago because she'd *known* her back when Granny was still a child. Fifty *years* ago.

Iris brought a trembling hand up to her mouth and stepped back in fear. She was wrong. She wasn't like Jinn and Max at all. She was . . . *different*. "How long have I been alive? How can I be standing here if my bones are . . . if my bones are . . . ?"

Encased in museum glass. Prepared for viewing. They would be a learning experience for visitors. They would seem a wonder to others. But to Iris's eyes, they were bones of ruin, worn and dented, taken from her body—a horrific reminder of just how cruel this land truly was.

"Important questions," said Adam. "But there's so much more to ask. Why do you have no memories from before the explosion in South Kensington? If that explosion created the Fanciful Freaks, then why do *your* abilities predate that day? And the girl who fought you in the auction house: Why did she seem to know you?"

Isoke. She Who Does Not Fall . . . Iris shuddered.

"You're not like them. The Fanciful Freaks. You were special long before that day. Who are you, Iris Marlow?" Adam asked, and she felt intensely pulled in by his hawklike gaze. "Who are you, really? No one in the Committee knows. No one in the government. But *I* know. And I can help you know too."

Iris Marlow. Perhaps it was madness setting in, but she couldn't help but smile ruefully. So she had a last name—the name of a slave ship.

"In exchange for what?" Jinn demanded.

At that, Adam grinned. "I've already told Iris this was a mutual arrangement. She performs two tasks for me, and I will help her unravel the mystery of her own life. In fact, I daresay she'll never truly understand who she is unless she completes those tasks."

Iris felt like her soul had left her body. If she even had a soul. "I know the first," she said, sounding as empty as she felt. Find his father, John Temple. Another key to her identity. "What's the second?"

"Oh, that?" Adam tugged his right glove. "I want you to be my champion." He looked at her. "I want you to fight for me, under my banner, in the Tournament of Freaks. The Tournament crafted by the Enlightenment Committee. That's all, really."

Iris lifted her heavy head. *"What?"*

"You've met the Sparrow twins. The Exploding Man. Bellerose's guard. They're all players in this game. But I still have yet to complete my roster of warriors."

"This is madness," said Jinn. "Why in the world should we *fight*?"

"Why do you fight, Maximo Morales?"

Max wasn't ready for Adam's question. He couldn't answer.

"What about those men and women who watch you in the Pit? Why do they draw lots on you fighters?" Adam tugged his glove again. "To win. This is nothing more and nothing less than the same. The Enlightenment Committee was created to guide this world: what it is now and what it will be. But who among us will lead? Our previous efforts to decide resulted in a dreadful massacre. The Spring Day Massacre of 1882." Adam laughed. "Well, that was before my time. However, our numbers were reduced by half—from fourteen to a mere seven. After that day, the Committee swore that such a slaughter would never occur again. That they would find another way to decide. A fairer way." He took off his right glove. "It was a promise I was forced to make as well, as the newest member of the order."

He showed them his palm. "This is the Oath Maker." Faded pink scars there traced out the shape of a skull and a sword piercing it through its center.

"Forcing people to fight your battles for you." Iris could feel her blood pumping through her fists. *"That's* your way of resolving things?"

"Not *my* way," Adam confessed. "But if I don't participate, it'll look suspicious. And there are many powerful people who know of you now, Iris."

How could she forget the auction? Iris shuddered.

"Having you on my team means I can better protect and guide you. And nobody will look deeper into our connection if they think you're simply my champion."

"Connection . . . ," Jinn repeated, glaring at Adam, who returned it with a coy shrug. "A tournament," Jinn said instead of perhaps what he wanted to. "What are the rules?"

Iris looked up at him in surprise. "Jinn?"

"If Iris is to join, then so will I," he said simply.

Max nodded, stepping toward Adam with a challenging lift to his chin. "And me."

At that, Adam only smirked.

Iris grabbed them by their wrists. "You two—"

"No, it's what I expected." Adam fit his hand back into his glove. "It's what I wanted. I can't participate without a team of three. And as for the rules, you'll be given them in due time. That is, if you all accept and agree with this contract."

Iris felt heat rising up through her body, turning itself to a quivering anger. "And if I don't agree, I can't imagine the Committee would leave us all alone knowing as much as we do about them. Am I wrong?"

"You're not," whispered Adam. "But that's why I want you, Iris. I want you to stay with me, under my protection. Learning of yourself. With these men as your knights."

Just as Adam lifted himself from the glass, a bullet came flying for his head. It pierced the case instead, which shattered. A split-second decision to miss that followed a similarly emotional decision to aim. Nobody moved as the smoke wafted from the barrel of his gun in Iris's hand.

Adam didn't react. He only watched her.

"I'll do it." Her voice was barely a shade of itself. Hoarse with fury.

"What was that?"

"You heard it," Iris said, her eyes burning. "I want the truth. I want an end to this hell. So I'll do it. I'll find your blasted father. I'll become your champion. And you will *not* betray me. Because if you do, I promise you, Lord Temple: I *will* kill you. And unlike me, you will stay dead."

None of the men dared to speak. But Adam Temple calmly met the rage bubbling up inside of her. No matter how neutral his expression, she knew he was probably satisfied. This was what he wanted. He seemed to want her to know her true identity almost as much as she did. That little boy at the South Kensington fair. His wonder.

Madame, tell me . . . are you . . . a goddess?

"Am I, Adam? A goddess?"

"You are to me."

Her grasp weakened, until Adam's gun slipped from her fingers and dropped to the floor with a clatter. Adam started for the door, picking up his gun along the way, emptying it of its bullets, perhaps so no one would get the wrong idea. Glass shards crunched beneath his boots as he walked, but then he stopped and turned back around. "The winning team of champions will receive twenty-five thousand pounds each," he announced, sucking the air out of the room. "You can see why others have agreed to fight. As for you, Iris, I imagine the truth is more precious than gold."

It was. *It was*, but . . .

As the weight of everything fell upon her, she began unraveling. "This is insanity." Iris shook her head, avoiding the sight of her bones hanging in the case. But she'd already agreed. How could she have agreed to such madness? "I can't possibly . . . How can I?"

"Iris."

Suddenly Iris felt Max's hand on her shoulder, lightly, with a hesitance that was uncharacteristic of him—almost as if he wasn't sure it deserved to be there.

"We can do this," Max said. "Let's do this. Together." And, after casting a dark look toward Adam, he bent down and whispered so only she could hear. "There's a lot you can do with the truth. And there's a lot *we* can do with this money. I can find my sister."

Max's sister. That's right. Max had his own hopes and dreams. She couldn't think only of herself. Her chest was still tense when she looked up at him and finally nodded.

Adam appeared pleased. "Well, it seems you've accepted. Go to Club Uriel at 52 Pall Mall Street on Sunday, the twenty-sixth of October. You're to check into the building, as it's where you'll be living for the duration of the tournament."

"*Living?*" Jinn and Max exclaimed at the same time.

"Oi, nobody said I'd be giving up my rat hole to take part in this thing," Max added.

"You can back out if you'd like." Adam gave him a sidelong look that Max couldn't seem to return. "Though I'm surprised, Maximo. I thought there'd be something you wanted more than anything."

A shadow fell upon Max's expression. Jinn smirked. "Money," Jinn guessed.

"No." Max whipped up his head, meeting the other boy's eyes, his own simmering. "*No.*" He looked from Adam to Iris and then turned from all of them. "I get that you're Iris's friend and all, so I won't sock you in the jaw for that. But don't think you know me."

"*Stop*, Jinn," Iris chastised him. "He already said he wanted to help me."

Max was silent.

"After all of the champions check into their new lodgings, you're to go to Wilton's Music Hall at six in the evening."

"The one on the East End?" Max raised an eyebrow. "Catching a show now, are we?"

"Indeed, you are. A very exclusive show. You'll be given further instructions there. Until then, Iris, you're welcome to stay at my residence tonight."

"No, thank you," Iris breathed, suddenly feeling weak again. Her lips trembled.

Adam's hand rested on the doorknob. "This may all seem terrible to you," he told her. "But one day, you'll understand. One day, you'll believe." He looked over his shoulder. "And one day, you'll know beyond a shadow of a doubt that I *am* on your side."

And so he left Iris to her determination and despair.

A Young Man Thinking

ADAM'S HOME FELT ODDLY EMPTY WITHOUT his former guest, but he couldn't blame her after what she'd just learned. She'd been so distraught. In truth, for many years he didn't believe she was capable of *feeling* distraught—not a supernatural being such as herself. She was always surprising him, that girl. Adam could still feel the flare of the bullet that singed his ear.

The lost look in her eyes had made him uncomfortable at first. Later, as he returned home, he began to consider, then feel the bitter bite of her pain as if their emotions were connected. This wouldn't be an easy path for her, but such was the path she was on, like a train rushing along its tracks until its predetermined stop. From here, things would only get worse before they got better. She had to prepare herself.

Iris Marlow. Or so she was presently called.

"Lord Temple?" said one of the two gentlemen standing at the threshold of his living room.

Adam lay down on the red velvet sofa, his head on a soft pillow, his legs so long that his ankles balanced atop the edge of the sofa's arm. He stared up at a portrait of his mother, the Baroness Charlotte Temple, a leather-bound copy of the Bible open on his stomach.

"You had something to report?"

"Yes, Lord Temple. Cortez has taken the Sparrow twins to the Crystal Palace."

The Crown's domain.

"I see." That didn't surprise him. Cortez only wanted winners on his team, and those poor little girls he'd kidnapped from their Bristol orphanage had failed the test he'd given them. Melee battles were how Cortez had decided to choose his champions, and it just so happened that Adam's team needed assessing too. It was a mutual arrangement between the two Enlighteners.

After Adam had returned home from the museum that night, he'd found Cortez waiting at his doorstep. Once they were inside, Adam had then turned in his newly completed roster.

"Preposterous!" Cortez had crushed the little note in his hand. "A girl unable to die fighting in a tournament to the death. An unfair advantage, wouldn't you say?"

"You must not have thought so at the auction, otherwise why bid on her?"

Simple logic seemed to embarrass the older man. He spat haughtily on the floor, which Adam didn't appreciate.

"There were no restrictions on the type of abilities each champion can have," Adam reminded him. "Therefore, I'm breaking no rules."

Cortez's face turned red. "But—"

"*But* you can tell this to the Committee: Having Iris will ensure I make it to the final round. However, should Iris die even once during the final challenge, I will forfeit." Adam looked at him. "I swear upon my life."

"And it's precisely your life we'll take if you try to go back on your word."

Once Cortez left, Adam was again left alone to his thoughts. But even though Adam wasn't surprised to hear what Cortez had done to the Sparrow twins, he found that the news did bother him. One had to be cruel to be a member of the Enlightenment Committee. But sending the twins to the Basement was *too* cruel, even for that evil little man. Such young, innocent girls.

For a moment Adam thought of his sister, Eva. Brown hair like their mother's. The memory of her face flashed by, causing his muscles to seize so quickly that the gentlemen rushed over to see if he was okay.

"I'm fine," Adam said, waving them off. They backed away immediately. Yes, he was fine. There wasn't much Adam could do about the twins without drawing attention to himself.

Besides, in time, all suffering would come to an end.

"Speaking of the Crystal Palace, what of Bosch?" Adam asked. "Is he still up to his usual business deals?"

"Concerning the Crown? Yes, we believe so," said one of the men. Both looked like unassuming middle-class gentlemen who would never come off as spies to those seeking moles. That was important. For many years, the Committee had placed a number of spies within the Crystal Palace to keep tabs on the Crown's experiments. Double agents. His father was once one, many years ago.

But when the British Crown approached Bosch a few years ago, it presented an even better opportunity. Bosch would sell them the weapons they so desperately wanted while feeding them false information on the strange, ancient machinery they were currently studying, keeping them in the dark as to what they *truly* had in their possession—and the cataclysm to come.

So far, Bosch had done his job. The Crown was solely fixated on building their artillery. But if Adam's father could turn traitor, no one in the Committee deserved the benefit of the doubt, especially one so driven by greed. Adam would have to watch the movements of the Bosch Guns and Ammunitions Company. And their head of Weapons Development too—Uma Malakar, that mad genius whose only true allegiance was to her own frightening intellect and curiosity . . .

So many pieces in play. Adam sighed as he dismissed the spies. However did he keep track of it all? He supposed he wasn't his father's son for nothing—as much as he hated the man.

"My lord?" After several minutes, a servant timidly entered the living room. "Is there anything you need? Tea, perhaps?"

"No thank you. You're free to retire tonight, Miss Danielle."

Though he didn't look at her, he was sure she bowed before leaving him to his loneliness. He'd been surrounded by such servants, men and women, his entire life. And school friends who knew of his family legacy and treated him accordingly. Different from them—different from all the inane, self-enamored club members or the bloodthirsty Enlightenment Committee—was Iris. Iris challenged him. With strength. With nobility.

With innocence.

She was not like what his family's research had described. She was not quite the woman in that old yellow-tinged photo, the warrior trapped in a human zoo, judging from behind her discerning, hardened eyes. *This* Iris was spirited and daring. Soft and unsure, but determined. She truly must have changed the day they met at the South Kensington fair. Without any memories, she would have had the space to develop a new persona.

Fascinating. But that warrior was still inside her. He knew as surely as he could still feel the heat on his ear from the bullet that narrowly missed it.

"She's truly something." He smiled almost boyishly to himself. "She completely exceeds my expectations. She's . . ."

He stopped. There was no point in speaking aloud. He was alone but for the portrait of his dead mother. He let out a little laugh, resting his hand atop the Bible on his stomach.

His mother still wouldn't have approved. She was staunchly puritanical right up until her death, and more so than ever after his siblings were brutally murdered.

And then he saw it. The brains of his ten-year-old sister and three-year-old brother splattered across the sidewalk. As surely as he could see the coffee table in front of him. He sat up quickly, the Bible slipping onto the floor. There in the intense silence, he stared at his own dark memories, dumbfounded, the anger slowly building up inside of him until he couldn't stop himself from pounding his leg with his fist, again and again until he'd tired himself out.

Calm down, he scolded himself as he had many times in the past when his anger and despair got the better of him. Fool wasn't the only one with a mask to wear.

Adam lowered his head, ignoring the biting pain in his thigh. "What do you think of this world now, Mother?" He flicked his head toward the window. "Not too far from this place, there are children languishing on the streets. Elsewhere, the disease-ridden are being left to rot. Men and women are being thrown into asylums simply due to their differences. Murderous men live a hundred years and the innocent die in an instant."

An instant was all it took for his younger brother and older sister to be butchered by robbers after an outing in Yorkshire. Another two years for his mother to hang herself in her bedroom from grief. That was all it took for Adam's world to end. And all the while John Temple was on an entirely different continent on one of his expeditions. He didn't even attend their funerals, the *bastard*.

Adam breathed in deeply to calm his hatred for the man simmering in his chest.

Industry destroys nature. Men conquer kingdoms, and civilizations fall to ruin. Just next month, Van der Ven would be among those representatives from countries across Europe congregating at a conference in Berlin to decide how to further terrorize a continent that did not belong to them. This was a cruel and terrible world. The Enlightenment Committee knew that it would end from years of researching the civilizations that came before. But as far as Adam was concerned, the world *should* end. He was sure Eva and Abraham would have agreed if they'd lived.

But first came the tournament. Let Club Uriel and the Enlightenment Committee gorge themselves on that silly bit of theater. It didn't matter who won.

He stared at the chessboard on his coffee table. A queen and two knights. But as his fingers ached to take the king, he thought better of it. He had no right to think of himself as such. When the time came, when Iris finally regained her memories, he would gladly take his place as that girl's pawn.

"Matthew, chapter twenty-six, verse fifty-two." Though he picked the Bible back up off the floor, it was merely out of respect. He did not need to flip to the page. Thanks to his mother's brutal teachings, he could recite it from heart. "For all they that take the sword shall perish with the sword."

Such was the fate of this wicked world.

"And what of you, Iris?" he whispered. "Will you be ready?"

He stared out of the living room window into the quiet night.

PART TWO
Tournoi

The glances of the other fixed me there, in the sense in which a chemical solution is fixed by a dye. I was indignant; I demanded an explanation. Nothing happened. I burst apart. Now the fragments have been put together again by another self.

—FRANTZ FANON, *Black Skin, White Masks*

16

October 26, 1884

56 years, 1 month, and 6 days since the Day of Darkness

WILTON'S MUSIC HALL CLOSED DOWN THREE years ago due to its inability to meet fire regulations. However, just a few months ago, an "angel investor" funded what was supposed to be its short-term survival. Iris wondered which member of the Enlightenment Committee had put up the money.

The music hall's opening show was to be entirely private, which, of course, made envious would-be customers eager to be among the chosen few regardless of the quality of the show. But even if the show was open to the public, the price of a ticket was *astronomical*. Not even the wealthy could afford it. This was to be an exclusive show. One with a very special set of customers. Which is why on Sunday morning, before they were to check in at Club Uriel, Iris decided to go to the theater first to learn what she could.

"Everyone ready?" Iris said as she and her two teammates left Max's apartment and stepped out onto Goulston Street, making sure not to wake the old woman who'd fallen asleep on the building's wooden doorstep.

Nobody'd had much sleep at Max's one-room apartment. Iris had spent each night on her cot tossing and turning from what she'd learned at the museum. Worse still, living with two men had its challenges to say the least. Especially two men who couldn't stop bickering.

"Shut the door, will you?" Max ordered Jinn, carrying all his meager belongings in a sack he held over his shoulder.

Jinn balked. "*You* were the last to leave."

"Yeah, but it's my apartment," Max said, moving in front of him. "You were my guest. Now hurry up and close the door and don't wake Gertrude."

As Jinn scowled, the cries of a colicky baby by a nearby newspaper stand wouldn't be soothed even by his frantic mother's exhausted singing as she held him to her chest.

"Oh please, child, stop crying!" She began bouncing the baby up and down in her arms. "If you're good, I'll buy you a toy from Whittle's. Would you like that?"

Max had given Jinn a violet vest to wear atop his brown shirt. He took a brown sack with him, tied over his shoulders with rope, hiding his bolero blades inside. The tournament would soon begin, and they each needed to bring what they could to Club Uriel—though Iris didn't have much except the ruined green dress she still wore. At least Max had finally found some new clothes: his brown trousers were held up by chestnut suspenders over a dirty beige top.

"Wilton's, eh? Snooping's a good idea, Iris," Max said as they walked down toward Graces Alley. His mauve newsboy cap shadowed his amused expression. "Can't wait to see what's up."

"Provided everything goes well." Jinn kept a short pace ahead of the two of them. "The Committee may have something planned to keep us away until Monday."

Iris had considered it. Still. "*Any* information that'll give us a heads-up on the competition can't hurt."

"Don't worry, Iris." Though he was speaking to Iris, it was to Jinn that Max shot a cheeky look. "I'm a master at sneaking and breaking into things. With me around, you'll get all the information you need."

"Oh right, from what Iris told me, you were a thief," Jinn said, looking back at Max. "Thieving, lying, conniving—"

"*Conniving?*" Max turned to Iris, who shook her head quickly.

"I didn't say that!" Iris let out an anxious huff and looked between the two of them. "Look, stop. We're officially a team now. We have to work together."

But could they with these two constantly at each other's throats? She sighed as they started down the street. At least she had a few shillings in her vest pocket. She'd asked Max for them so she could buy some new clothes with the promise that she'd pay him back. He'd given it to her on one condition: she take him with her to the store. Iris rolled her eyes. The boy was relentless.

The bickering between the two boys continued until they turned left onto Whitechapel.

"Coolie?" Iris grabbed the back of Max's shirt with one hand and held Jinn back with another. No, not Coolie, but his debt collectors. With bowler hats on their pudgy heads and cigars in their fat lips, they stood at the corner of Whitechapel and Old Castle Street, feigning idleness as they sneakily peeked through the passing carriages for any sign of her.

Coolie had lost his chance to use her to pay them off when she escaped the auction. But if they kidnapped her *themselves*, then they could hold her for ransom for even *more* money . . . or just have their own private auction. The dastardly possibilities were endless.

"Someone must have tipped them off that we were staying at Max's apartment," said Jinn through gritted teeth. He took her hand. "We'll have to go another way."

Keeping their heads down, they changed course, turning left on Mansell Street.

From a distance, Iris could see a crowd building outside Wilton's Music Hall, many of them impeccably dressed and wealthy.

"'The Fanciful Freaks of London,' eh?" One man read the ridiculous-looking poster clinging to the rusted red walls next to the doors.

"The Fanciful Freaks of London." Max laughed. "Well, this is interesting."

A poster for a *private* show. Adam's friends sure loved arrogantly hiding their secrets right underneath people's noses. It was all a game to them.

"Give me a ticket," demanded the man. "I'll pay double the price!" As if he had the money. But the little bald man in a gray suit guarding the door simply twitched his white mustache and shook his head, denying him.

"Probably a terrible show anyway," an old maid grumbled to her friend as they scurried away from Graces Alley.

"You learn this on the streets," Max told Iris. "The more you tell folks that they can't do something, the more desperate they are to do it. All that money they're willing to pay for a show adapted from a penny blood."

"Maximo." Jinn nudged him in the ribs. "Over there." He flicked his head behind them toward a darkened alleyway. "I'm sure I saw the debt collectors."

Iris whipped around. "You think they followed us here?"

"It's possible." Jinn turned to Max. "You up for a little canvasing?"

"You mean surveying the area?"

"Just to check things out."

Max folded his arms across his chest. "Will Iris be okay if we leave her alone?"

"*Iris* is standing right here, gentlemen." Scoffing, she placed her hands on her hips. "And she'll be more than fine on her own given that *she* can't die, unlike her two strapping bodyguards here."

At her cheeky grin, Jinn and Max exchanged a sheepish glance and nodded.

"We'll be back soon," said Jinn before leaving with Max. He couldn't help himself.

Iris drew closer to the crowd. To her surprise, on the other side of the street, some men were howling in anger.

"Three-card monte! It's a bloody scam!" one of them screamed as a boy hurriedly slid his cards off a wooden barrel and slipped them underneath his sleeve.

No. Not a boy. Iris squinted. She was wearing boy's clothes, but her rounded, soft features were unmistakably feminine. Not to mention that Iris had seen that pumpkin-colored bowl cut and suspenders before. Down in the Pit.

"I demand you give me back my money, you shameful *rat*."

"*Rat?* I resent that," she said in her cockney accent. "I prefer adorable little mousey."

"Mousey—?"

"It's what my brother used to call me, and now here you munchers are, desperate to watch a bit of theater that stole the title of *his* story, which none of you deigned to waste a *penny* on when we tried to sell it to you on the damn streets."

Brother? Iris stared at her.

"What the hell is this stupid boy going on about?" someone said.

"Stop babbling and give us back our money! Police? Police!"

There were a few officers some ways away. But by the time part of the crowd began calling for them, the girl was already halfway down the street, coming toward Iris.

"Really, these people are just ridiculous, aren't they?" the girl said to her. "Always demanding this and that. So entitled, am I right?"

Iris generally agreed, but then again, "Yes, but . . . well, you *did* cheat them."

The girl shrugged as she passed. She was actually quite pretty, though she smelled like a combination of apricots and fish. "Wouldn't you?" she said before walking on rather quickly.

The police were now looking Iris's way as the gaggle of men pointed in the thief's direction. Iris turned around fast. Policemen, thieves, and debtors. She didn't expect her plan of snooping to go awry this early. Maybe she was better off shopping for a new dress, after all.

Sighing, she put her hand in her pocket.

Her breath hitched. Her money. It was gone.

She patted her dress again. Did she drop it on the way? Or—

The shock of realization made her head snap up. The girl. That *girl*.

How *dare* she?

"You!" Iris screamed at the thief retreating quickly down the street. The girl turned, saluted, and began running just as the police with their clubs followed suit.

Except Iris was going to get to that rat first. *Nobody* stole from her.

It was a merry chase, one Iris didn't have the shoes for. An odd procession of a thief followed by an immortal tightrope dancer, a group of Metropolitan policemen, and a few angry victims who wanted their pound of flesh along with their money. The girl weaved through carriages, jumped over tables of fresh food, and dodged horse-drawn wagons carrying blankets and hay—hay the thief threw in Iris's face once she began to close in.

Enraged, Iris wiped her face and looked to her right only to find Coolie's debt collectors, pointing and grinning at her.

You've got to be kidding me! With gritted teeth, Iris followed the girl into a narrow street, empty but for a few dirty pigeons on the ledge of an apartment window above. It was underneath the apartment window that the thief finally stopped.

"None of you want to be doing this," she said rather confidently as if she wasn't just under five feet tall and facing a dozen or so burly men. "You may regret it later."

Iris watched the debt collectors—likely hoping to snatch her in the midst of the chaos. "Maybe you shouldn't have started this mess in the first place, eh?"

Instead of answering, the thief gave a curious birdcall, high, sharp, and far too close to a real hawk. She waited, but only silence followed. Iris scrunched her face, confused, as the thief tried again and again, only growing more frustrated each time.

"This boy's gone batty!" one of the policemen said, voicing Iris's thoughts perfectly. "Check him for opium!"

"Hawkins, damn it, where *are* you?" the thief cried, stomping her feet.

Hawkins? Iris turned around, trying to find whoever the thief was waiting for, until suddenly she felt the girl's back press up against hers. "Oi, my name's Cherice," she whispered. "Cherice Winterbottom. And I've got a proposition."

Winterbottom . . . Hawkins . . . Iris almost gasped. She was Max's friend.

But first things first. "And that is?" Iris began backing away from the crowd, but Cherice stuck close to her like a shadow.

"I see you've got your own stalkers, mate." Cherice nodded her head toward the debt collectors, their nasty eyes glued to Iris. Perceptive, this one. "What do you say you help me get these folks off *both* our backs, and before I make my getaway, I give you back your money?"

"You're *giving* me my money either way," Iris hissed, spotting a stray wooden stick leaning against the dirty apartment building. "But I agree. We take care of them first. Then you apologize. Deal?"

The men began charging.

Cherice smiled wickedly. "Deal!"

Iris went for the wooden stick by the bricks, grabbing it and turning around just in time to see Cherice's cards fly from underneath her sleeve and fling themselves at the attackers. It was a targeted assault, each card nicking faces and beards, necks and suits just deep enough to cause eyes to dilate in horror. Just what kind of cards were these? And how was she moving them? Iris would have to consider it later. She used the opportunity to swing her stick at the debt collectors, who'd braved the pandemonium to get to her, whacking one in the shins, tossing the stick up in the air, kneeing his stomach, catching her weapon, and slamming it against the other's face.

"I'd duck if I were you, girly!" Cherice yelled at her, just in time for Iris to see the thief's cards turn sharply in midair with a flick of her fingers, switch directions, and cut back toward her. It was as if she was moving them with her thoughts alone.

"What in the bloody hell is going on!" a policeman cried as he ducked for cover.

"Witches!" one of the scamming victims screamed, avoiding the sharp edge of Cherice's cards. "Bloody witches! The rumors are true!"

"Not witches," Cherice corrected with an evil little grin. "Fanciful Freaks."

Iris gaped along with them.

Most of the men in the alleyway turned tail to run. But a few stragglers continued to try their luck, including Coolie's debt collectors.

"Coolie's still got a price on your head," one said, holding his face where Iris had smacked it. "We're getting our pay one way or another."

Iris flipped her stick around, her blood pumping. She was ready. She was hungry. Oh, how she'd been wanting to hit something for so long. And my, how she was good at it.

But it was then that Cherice's birdcall was finally answered. A birdcall in a lower voice coming from the apartment window four stories above. There behind the open window were two figures: both young men, the shorter partially obscured by the taller, who stood on the ledge with a book in hand, his back to them. His blond hair fluttered as he let himself fall backward.

Iris's breath hitched as his heels slipped from the ledge, as he took the hand of the other boy to pull him down as well. Ridiculous! They were both going to fall and break their necks!

They both fell indeed—through a dark vortex that swirled open beneath them in the air, swallowing them whole before collapsing into nothingness again. Iris stared, shocked, as the vortex reappeared above the ground, spitting out both boys. While the shorter landed gracefully upon the asphalt, the taller landed on the back of one of the debt collectors with a crunch. Long and lithe, with a sharp face and impeccable black leather shoes, golden hair tied at the base of his thin neck, and that single book in his hand, the pages of which he had yet to tear his eyes from.

"Hawkins!" Cherice cried as she willed cards back into her sleeve. "You idiot! Took you long enough."

"What was 'at?" The blue-eyed young man flipped a page as he casually stepped off the back of Iris's assailant. "I didn't hear a thank-you." His voice had a whimsical lilt that seemed uninterested in much of anything. "How disappointing."

"Damn it!" The other debt collector grabbed the arm of the man Hawkins had landed on, but he was knocked out cold. He looked at them. "Y-y-you think I'm scared of you freaks?"

Judging from the sweat dripping from his brow, Iris thought yes. That's when the shorter boy stepped forward, causing the debt collector to squeal in fear. A handsome, olive-skinned, and wide-faced young man whose hooded, gentle eyes stared at the debt collector. He tried to look serious, though it was clear he was hiding his amusement.

The debt collector readied his fist. "Don't come any closer, you filthy—"

A dodged punch followed by a cool brush of the throat. Cherice's olive-skinned friend didn't strike Iris's attacker per se. But Iris could tell that he'd done something once the collector clutched his throat after throwing out a few hurtful, dehumanizing slurs.

"Wh-what?" The man stepped back. "What am I saying? Why can't I understand what I'm saying—?"

"Oh dear, he can't understand English anymore, can he, Jacob?" the one called Hawkins said as his partner scratched his head with a shrug. "I wonder what it sounds like in his head."

"What are you all saying? What is this?" The debt collector balked at the group of them, eyes bulging as if he were going mad.

This Jacob—though he looked serene, there was no sign of pity in those clear eyes of his. "It certainly hurts to not be able to understand your own language, doesn't it?" he said. "By the way, what were you calling me just then?"

Just as the debt collector began gripping his head, Iris heard footsteps approaching.

"I wouldn't try anything more, mate," came a voice from the entryway of the narrow street. "These lot aren't ones to be trifled with. Believe me."

"Max!" Cherice and Iris cried at the same time, and then promptly looked at each other.

Max strode up the street with Jinn in tow. The debt collector knew he was beat. Lifting his unconscious colleague by the arm, he dragged him out the other end, swearing revenge like they all do.

"Everyone all right?" asked Jacob in a soft voice. That hint of cruelty was gone.

"Jacob!" Max greeted the young man with a wave. "Hawkins!" The blond-haired boy saluted him. "And Cher—"

The moment he was close enough, Cherice grabbed his shoulders and kneed him in the groin. The pain was so visible on Max's face that Iris could feel it in her own immortal bones.

"That's for leaving me in the Pit, you stupid arse!" she cried as Max whimpered and nodded, accepting his punishment. But then, as if to give them all whiplash, Cherice wrapped her arms around Max's neck while it was low enough for her to do so and gave him a deep, long kiss—on the lips, no less. "It's good to see you again, though," she said as Hawkins, Jacob, Jinn, and Iris looked on, thoroughly baffled.

Max nodded again, his face blood-drained, his jaw slack. "I think I need to sit down."

17

S O THIS WAS YOUR LITTLE GANG?" In the alleyway, Jinn leaned
against the brick wall of a building. He didn't look impressed.

"Gang?" The tall, willowy young man, who introduced himself
as Lawrence Hawkins, coolly ran a hand through his sun-kissed blond hair.
"Hmm . . ." He paused, tracing a long finger down a thread of his beige frock
coat, mismatched with the rest of his shabby clothes. Stolen, likely. "Gang?"
This time, he said it with a knowing grin. Iris could tell he was the type to take
his time even when it infuriated others. "I suppose you could say that."

Judging from the scars on his hands and narrow, princely face, he'd been in
a fight or two in his day. Even Cherice's chipmunk features were marred with
indents and discolorations implying varying stages of healing. Jacob's black
hair lay loose on his shoulders, his brown-and-yellow plaid pants stretching
down just past his knees. His white shirt was dirty with the soot of industry.

At Jinn's scowl, Max waved his hand. "You're getting us all wrong. We're not
so bad. Just trying to survive."

"I heard you loud and clear." Jinn shot him a withering look. "Tell me, how
many other kids did you beat up and steal from while you were 'just trying to
survive'?"

"You're taking this rather personally, aren't you?" Max stood up straight, all signs of peacemaking gone from his expression. "There something you want to share with the group?"

Jinn pressed his lips together, his eyes darting to Iris, but then darting away just as quickly. It made Iris curious herself, but there were more pressing matters. Iris sighed, trying to think of a way to break the tension.

It was Cherice who managed it, wrapping a strong arm around Max's neck, forcefully bringing him back down to her height once more. "Well, let's just let bygones be bygones, shall we? Who are these lovely people? Not thinking of replacing us, were you?"

Iris wondered if Cherice realized by the red turn of Max's face just how tightly she was squeezing his neck. Or if she cared.

Max's friends. While holding Max hostage, Cherice explained their abilities, though Iris wasn't sure if she'd caught it all. Apparently, using her will alone, Cherice could move her cards, even sharpening the sturdy paper to a point where they became as deadly as knives. Her powers strangely didn't work on anything else. Hawkins—well, Iris had seen with her own eyes what Hawkins could do, while Jacob could make anyone speak and understand—or *not* understand—any language he pleased. There were likely limits to their powers, as with Max. But it still made them a fearsome group.

"Wait," said Max suddenly, freeing himself from Cherice's steal grip. "Hawkins, Jacob—did you come across Bately recently?"

The two young men stared at each other quickly. Then, curiously, at Iris. As Jacob rubbed the back of his head, Hawkins cleared his throat. "Yeah, a few days ago. He put the whammy on us. You know his usual game."

That silver tongue. The one that had compelled Iris into submission.

"But it's nothing to worry about," Jacob said quickly. "We've gotten out of plenty of scrapes, you know that. Truthfully, I was surprised to see him. I heard he skipped town."

"Doesn't matter," Hawkins said in barely a whisper. "One day, we'll finally get that bastard and make him pay." His expression was suddenly menacing. Cherice's too. Even Max's features grew dark as a worried Jacob looked on. There was something Max wasn't telling her.

"At any rate, let me introduce myself properly." Iris tossed her stick aside. "My name is Iris. Iris . . ." She paused, remembering the photo from the British Museum. "Iris Marlow . . . I suppose."

"You're a long way from home, aren't you, lovely girl?" Hawkins inspected her in a way that was all too familiar to Iris.

"So am I," Jacob said quietly. "And Max. Or did you forget?"

As Cherice nodded in agreement, Hawkins shrugged. "Didn't mean anything by it. You know I'm the type to be interested in everyone's stories."

"Even though you'd have to pull out his tooth to get him to share his own," Cherice added with a smirk.

"Jacob's from Labrador, *far* across the pond," Max explained to a confused Iris.

"Oh, an Eskimo?" Iris asked, recalling the act Coolie had tried to produce while they were performing somewhere in Germany: "The Wild Eskimos," he wanted to call it. Except in Germany he couldn't find anyone to fulfill the role.

"Inuk," Jacob corrected quietly with a kind smile.

"O-oh, I'm sorry." Iris felt a sheepish flush in her cheeks.

"He was born far up north, so it would have been cold as all hell," Max said. "Totally opposite from my old home—at least, from what I can remember of it."

"I was brought to Europe with my parents as a baby, so I have very little recollection of it," Jacob said.

Iris noticed the tinge of loss in his eyes. Maybe that was why she hesitated before asking: "How . . . Why did you come here?"

An uncomfortable silence pervaded the group. Max waved away the question with a little laugh. "Like Hawkins said, we all have our stories. In any case, let's get out of here before the police gather up some courage. Besides, Iris, you and I have some underwear to buy before we head on over to Club Uriel," he added, wincing from Iris's blow to the head while Cherice's wide eyes narrowed, her face red.

"Club Uriel?" Cherice stared at the three of them: Max, Jinn, and Iris. "Don't tell me."

"Fanciful Freaks," Iris and Cherice said in unison.

It didn't take long for Iris to catch up. Cherice's strange abilities. Two groups of three. Two teams. The tournament.

Max's childhood friends were their competitors.

A thick tension descended upon them. Iris, Max, and Jinn had fought the Sparrow twins and Bellerose's guard just yesterday, surviving by the skin of their teeth, and the tournament hadn't even started yet. What kind of bloody mess awaited them all?

What kind of bloody mess would they have to inflict on each other?

But Hawkins and Jacob didn't look so surprised. They exchanged glances and nodded. It didn't exactly inspire Iris with confidence.

Quickly, Max slid through his friends, standing in the middle of the two teams. "Okay, it seems we're in a bit of a predicament."

Understatement. Iris scooted closer to Jinn without realizing it. And of course Jinn noticed, as he noticed all her little movements. She felt his gentle grip around her elbow as he pulled her closer to him.

"Not a predicament," insisted Hawkins. "An *opportunity*. To be honest, we had a feeling you'd join the tournament."

"You did?" Cherice placed her hands on her hips, flustered. "Really?" Seemed they'd kept her in the dark.

"A man named Adam Temple heard about your record in the Pit and asked about you. Told us he was looking to build his team."

Max shifted on his feet uncomfortably, and Iris couldn't blame him. A man keeping tabs on you, researching you for however long just to see if you were fit for his supernatural team? Adam had taken Iris to the Pit to meet a potential teammate, and all the while her potential teammate was clueless about him and his intentions. Iris could relate.

"The tournament isn't ideal, but if we win it, we'd never have to look for money again," said Jacob. "You wouldn't have to fight in the Pit for chump change anymore."

"But now he's exchanging the Pit for a tournament in which we're all enemies," said Iris quietly.

"No, not enemies," said Max, suddenly more serious than ever before. "Doesn't matter why or how or when we all signed on to do this tournament.

I trust all of you. Even that glum bloke." He flicked his head toward Jinn, who rolled his eyes in response.

Hawkins smiled. "Thought you'd say that. That's exactly why I'd call this an opportunity. We don't need to see each other as rivals. We're friends. We have a positive connection. We can help each other."

"A partnership?" Cherice said, scurrying closer to them.

"A pact." Jinn finally moved himself off the building, his catlike eyes watching them carefully with a quiet note of distrust. "That whatever happens, we won't harm or sabotage each other. That's the least we can do."

"More than that. We can game the system and run off with the cash together." Hawkins grinned. "Not like we haven't done that before."

Max returned that grin with conspiratorial glee.

A strategic alliance. It was only the smart thing to do.

"I'll start," Iris offered. "By sharing some information about the Fanciful Freaks of London."

At the sound of that particular title, Hawkins looked rather stiff. Iris couldn't help but notice Jacob's gaze sliding toward him with a hint of worry.

"You mean Chadwick's penny blood series or the Committee's oh-so-exclusive show?" Cherice said, wriggling her fingers mockingly.

Pressing his lips together tightly, Hawkins flipped loose strands of blond hair over his shoulder. "If it's the latter, save your breath. I heard it's tacky and cheaply produced. An insult to my refined tastes."

"*Refined.*" Cherice rolled her eyes, her lips curling teasingly. "Always talking like a baron as if you aren't deep in the dirt with the rest of us."

"Max told me you were all at the South Kensington International Exhibition ten years ago. June second," said Iris. "That's when an explosion happened. We think that explosion may have caused a lot of people at the fair to change. Us included . . ."

Except that wasn't right. Iris was a Fanciful Freak long before that day at the fair. Adam had made that clear. And the exhibit. The sight of her ancient bones hanging behind a glass case. She would never be able to forget it.

"Your theory, Miss Iris?" Jacob asked.

"Theory?" Iris lowered her head sheepishly. "Well . . ."

"We're working on it," Max offered, giving Iris a little wink. Cherice scowled. "But as far as I'm concerned, we should try thinking of it together. Part of the alliance."

"I've never much cared." Hawkins shrugged. "Things are what they are. No reason to dig any further."

Iris gave a quiet little huff. How nice to have such a blasé attitude about the truth. Meanwhile, it kept Iris up at night.

"Why don't we gather our things and head over to Club Uriel," said Jacob. He seemed rather comfortable in the role of mediator.

It was Hawkins he looked to for confirmation. The golden-haired boy just shrugged.

Max nodded and turned to the others. "What do you say?"

Although Iris wasn't quite as confident as she'd let on, she couldn't help feeling relieved that they may have already found a strategy to get through whatever bizarre horrors they were about to face during this tournament. She nodded.

"Then, to Club Uriel." With a princely bow and sweep of his hand, Hawkins gestured them forward. "Ladies first."

Cherice and Iris made the same impatient face before striding out of the narrow street. Theories. Iris narrowed her eyes as she thought. A gas leak couldn't be responsible for what gave the Fanciful Freaks their powers. But if not that, then what?

18

THOUGH IT WAS LATE MORNING, DARK clouds had already begun to loom. The teams took two separate cabs to 52 Pall Mall Street. Team Iris, as Iris had dubbed them teasingly, had their own carriage, but it was hardly big enough for the three of them. Max had happily offered his lap to her, much to her chagrin. Then, to escape her knuckles aimed at his gut, he sat on Jinn's lap, much to *his* chagrin.

Soon, they were all standing with their meager belongings in front of a red-brown brick building on Pall Mall Street. Iris read the black letters scrawled against a mahogany plaque screwed into the white front door: CLUB URIEL. ESTABLISHED BY PROFESSOR RODERICK HAYES, SEPTEMBER 3, 1812. MEMBERS ONLY. Their temporary home during the tournament.

They glanced at each other. Iris placed her hands on the knob and, swallowing the lump in her throat, pushed open the door. The scruffy-looking teams baffled the doorman, who was even a little incensed when Iris showed him her invitation card, courtesy of Adam. But the rules were the rules. He begrudgingly let them inside, Cherice sticking out her tongue as she passed.

The club had all the trimmings of wealth. The steep wooden stairs they climbed were swept clean and had smooth railings, located in a colorfully wallpapered, spacious lobby. The walls were pearl and ruby-rimmed at the bottom, perfectly matching the second floor's red velvet carpeting. And from the bottom steps if Iris looked up, she could see a golden-framed portrait of a white man in a black suit and tie, his furry dark mustache warming his thin lips. Professor Hayes himself, maybe. A gentleman's club, to be sure.

"We're really meant to live here?" Cherice said in awe.

Likely. From outside, it was clear the building was six floors in total. A gentleman's club and temporary hotel for the supernaturally gifted. Hawkins looked thoroughly satisfied.

The sound of chattering grew louder as they ascended the stairs.

By the time they'd rounded a corner, the chatter turned to screaming.

Shocked, the six followed the sound into a room fit for the upper echelons. Golden-framed portraits of important men lined the white walls. Brass chandeliers hung on the high ceiling buttressed by white classical columns. Two rows of red leather couches bordered each wall. Ferns and other potted plants brightened the room with color.

At the front of that room, a bearded man gripped a wealthy woman's neck with one hand, his other inches away from the side of her face. He looked like a grenade ready to detonate.

And his hand *glowed* red-hot.

"I said, give me the key to the bloody safe!" he screamed in front of a roaring fireplace, his black hair limp on his creased forehead. He looked sick with his red face and dilapidated clothes. One of his brown eyes was clouded and pale, the other clear but unfocused.

"I'm not gonna ask twice. Unless ye want to see Mrs. Cordiero's brains melted all over this lovely carpet! Eh? Oi, are you listening to me?"

Iris made a move, but Jinn held her back, shaking his head. The situation was dangerous. The man sounded not just malicious but *desperate*. Sweat glued his hair to his pink forehead while his glowing hand fidgeted. A volatile situation, to be sure.

But the members of Club Uriel were not impressed. Most continued their discussions, sipping from their wineglasses, or else watched the hostage situation with amused curiosity. Even the hostage herself, a big-boned woman with curly black hair, looked annoyed, as if she were more concerned with being touched by a sickly, filthy man than being harmed by him.

"Cordiero?" one member said. "But he's your Patron, is he not?"

"It's always interesting to see a dog bite the hand of his master, isn't it?" another said, followed by smatterings of laughter.

The man was incensed, and Iris couldn't blame him. Even with his power, the members of Club Uriel couldn't be bothered to take him seriously.

"I'm no one's dog, not anymore. I told you, I'm finished with you lot!" The pupil of his bad eye quivered oddly as he looked around. "Open the safe and give me my money, or—"

Bang.

Iris smelled gunpowder but didn't see the gun. The man drooped to the floor with a hole in his head.

After the stunned silence had passed, conversations resumed. Servants, dressed in red vests and trousers, continued weaving through the chairs offering drinks. As two of them carried the man's dead body away, Mrs. Cordiero straightened out her dress with a huff and stalked back to her seat.

The only smoke Iris could trace came from outside the room. Just around the corner, Iris could see the swish of black robes, the back of a man's shaved head, and a white collar around his brown neck. But by the time Iris ran to the entrance, he'd already disappeared.

"Iris," Adam called from one of the leather seats close to the fireplace. "Oh, and another team. Welcome."

The club members glanced at the six of them, muttering and chuckling as they drank.

"Look," said Hawkins, disgusted at the display—or maybe the indignity of being stared at. "Just tell us where to put our things."

"Third floor," answered Adam. "Mr. Alva will show you to your room."

An aged servant bowed and gestured for Hawkins to follow him. After one last anxious look toward Iris, Max, and Jinn, Cherice followed Hawkins and Jacob out the door.

"Iris, come sit," Adam said. "Of course, Jinn and Max are welcome too."

They did. Adam flipped his silver coin across his knuckles as he watched them approach. A snap of his fingers brought a servant rushing to give them three small glasses of liquor. Brandy. Max took his in one shot.

"Blokes getting a hole in the head," Max said, setting his glass down on the wooden table. "Part of the fun, is it?"

"Oh, that. Yes, that was unfortunate." Adam leaned back into his chair. "He was a champion like yourselves," he said. "I didn't expect him to take a hostage. Now Cordiero will have to replace him quickly or stick with the two he already has."

"Oh, poor *Cordiero*," Max spat.

"Sometimes getting one's hands dirty is a sad but unavoidable necessity." Adam stared at him. "Wouldn't you say, Maximo?"

Max had no response.

"Champions." Iris's bottom lip curled as she remembered the helpless desperation of that man, only to be met with apathy. But then, even the Colosseum warriors of ancient Rome were owned by their masters. So this was Club Uriel.

"None of these people were surprised in the least to see what that man could do," said Jinn, folding his arms over his dull brown shirt. "I thought you said there were only seven members of your Committee."

"There are."

Jinn grimaced at Adam's affable smile.

"I told you before: Club Uriel has many members who share theories about evolution, rebirth, and the end of mankind over drinks," Adam explained. "They have the privilege of being spectators of this tournament. But they're not Committee members."

Iris recognized at least two from the auction. Every now and then they shot her greedy glances but didn't dare interrupt while she was in Adam's presence.

Adam pinched his coin between two fingers and dropped it into his pocket. "I'll eventually tell you more of what you need to know. But first, Iris, would you accompany me somewhere? Meanwhile," he added after seeing Max and Jinn react quickly, "Mr. Mortius will show you to your room on the third floor."

"Third floor?" Max raised an eyebrow.

"Don't worry, the other champions are scattered on different floors. But even if they weren't, I assure you: you'll be taken care of in Club Uriel."

Either that or get a bullet to the head. And Iris didn't want another one of those.

With that, Adam stood. "Well, Iris. Will you come with me?"

Simmering in their locked eyes was a battle of wills. The challenge in his grin. Her hands squeezed into fists on her lap.

"Iris?" Jinn stood quickly along with her, but she put a hand on his wrist to assure him.

"It's fine," Iris said, though she wasn't quite sure how true that was. Reluctantly, she turned to Adam. "Lead the way."

Adam placed a hand on Jinn's shoulder. "Loosen up a little. She's in good hands."

The scowl on Jinn's face was a loud enough response.

Iris looked at her two teammates behind her before leaving the room.

Iris never thought she would see a garden indoors. What the rich wouldn't pay for. The room had a stream of wide windows. If not for the gray clouds, bits of sunlight would have been showering the plants and flowers on tables and hanging in pots on walls. On opposite sides of the room were framed portraits of two men: Carl Anderson, a portly, long-nosed, bearded man in a fine suit. Deceased August 24, 1884. And to Iris's left, Neville Bradford, his blond hair graying around the edges. Deceased October 1, 1884: less than a month ago.

"Esteemed members of our club," Adam told her when she asked about them. "Mr. Anderson was a member of Parliament. Mr. Bradford was formerly the Colonial Secretary heading the Colonial Office."

"Both men of empire." A breath of disdain escaped Iris's lips.

"Both men of *power*," Adam corrected. "Using whatever means in their control to gain it. Alas, both met with unfortunate accidents that took them from us far too soon."

Iris raised an eyebrow. "Unfortunate accidents?"

Adam's back remained to her as he approached the center table. "Their donations to Club Uriel will always be remembered, at least. Right this way."

Adam led her outside. It was even chillier than before, but she relished the outside air. As dirty and polluted as it was in this city, at least the breeze was refreshing.

"Some conversations are better held in private," Adam told her after shutting the glass double doors behind them.

"Then will you answer me now?" Iris said. "About those men and women who watched a man die in front of them and barely blinked?"

"Ah. Club Uriel." Adam placed his arms behind his back and walked over to the balcony's railing. "As my grandfather once told me as a child, joining associations and clubs is a way for men of means to gather resources and connections. Club Uriel is a secret society with access to knowledge most in the world could only dream of. But the Enlightenment Committee is even more exclusive, operating from within the club. The members of the club may know our identities, but they don't know how we came to be, the extent of our power, or our true aims. Not until a member dies is a new one chosen from among the club. There are men who would kill to be among our ranks. Or die trying."

Adam seemed to be speaking from experience. His eyes told too many bloody stories.

"Some are helping to fund our little tournament," Adam continued. "Many have already cast their bets."

"So they're the audience. How fun for them." Iris felt sick to her stomach.

"You are what you've been for many years, Iris," Adam said. "A performer. I simply want you to perform. Do you have any other questions?"

The breeze blew Iris's hair as she stared out over the skyline. She could see the bridge in the distance, steam rising from ships. Donkeys pulling wheelbarrows and horses drawing carriages down the lanes. Men and women in bleak attire sitting in wooden chairs on the street corners in front of their shops. Children laughing and playing through the roads. Normal life. She wondered what that felt like.

"How many know of us?" Iris asked. "Us Fanciful Freaks?"

"Rumors are becoming more rampant, though some are trying to keep it under control," answered Adam. "With our funding, independent research is being conducted across the country to learn more about the abilities of those changed ten years ago in South Kensington. Meanwhile, the Crown is conducting their own studies here in London."

Iris frowned. "What . . . kind of studies?"

"All I'll say is that the Committee only use corpses for their experiments," said Adam. "The same can't be said of the Crown."

Live subjects. Iris shivered. And yet the thought of corpses being exhumed and trifled with in the name of science made the hairs on Iris's arms stand on end as well. That desperate man, newly dead. Was that his fate?

"So I perform." Iris walked over to the balcony, gripping the ledge. "I participate in this game under your banner."

"Find my father along with that and you'll get what you've been wanting. And more."

Iris let go of the railing and turned to him. "But how?"

"Instinct," Adam answered. In two strides, he was closer than he should have been, but she was fixed to the spot nonetheless. "You use your uncanny instincts, Iris."

Iris touched her chest, feeling her heartbeat. "There was one time I found an old friend. Agnus, if you recall." Iris thought of Granny's childhood photo in the British Museum. "I felt her. Her life. Her soul. That day at the fair, I tracked her all the way to Coolie's. It was as if her blood was pumping through my veins."

"Has it happened again since?"

"Sometimes." But only through some fluke, when she was quiet and still. And there were times she could sense Jinn even when he was off camp. She'd never dared speak of it.

Adam nodded. "You're feeling the vitality, the *life force* of someone close to you. If you learn to hone that ability, you can use it to track someone from yards, miles, even countries away. Those are your abilities, Iris, waiting to be wielded like a sword."

A sword. Iris flinched a little at the word, watching as Adam pulled out his coin, flicked it into the air, and caught it again. Soon, he began turning his coin across his knuckles.

"This was my father's coin. Watch it carefully," he told her. "Hone your concentration."

She watched the coin tumble over his knuckles, soar into the air, and land in his palm. An endless cycle until Adam snapped his hand shut, enclosing the coin inside.

"Now close your eyes."

Iris broke out of her trance and stared at him in disbelief. "I think *not*."

Adam's expression seemed to make him younger. Like a boy admiring the pluck of a friend. "I promise not to do anything you wouldn't approve of."

Pursing her lips, Iris folded her arms over her chest. "You'd better not if you want to keep your fingers."

Once she closed her eyes, she heard his voice.

"Agnus Marlow," he said. "You felt her presence. Her life. Her soul. If you can feel one living thing, you can feel another. Take these plants, for example."

She heard his footsteps retreat from her and then the soft opening of the double doors.

"Can you feel them?" Adam said from the doors.

It was humiliating, but she tried anyway. For a long moment, she felt nothing, but then . . . something warm slipped up to the tip of her fingers. Something calling to her. Life.

"Breathe and let it consume you."

A kind of peace washed over her. The same sense of oneness she felt whenever Jinn tossed her up into the air during one of their routines. Up in the sky among the birds and butterflies flying free. Nature. Beings with a vitality detached from the industrial world. It was faint, but she could feel them.

"This world has many secrets, and there are many who've tried to discover them," said Adam, and she could feel his arm brush against hers as he leaned against the railing next to her. "Some anatomists, geologists, and paleontologists believed that different cataclysmic events cleared the stage for new forms of life. They looked at patterns of extinction throughout history, fossil records, faunal successions. But what about a grand *cataclysma*? One that can destroy civilizations—*humanity*—as a whole? Robert Jameson was a scientist who tried to prove the divine nature of Cuvier's earlier theories. And my grandfather, a member of the Committee, built upon *his* work. His conclusion was that, indeed, this world has experienced a history of total planetary annihilation occurring periodically and without fail. But different in nature to what others in the scientific community believed. Gods and demigods once walked the earth. Then extinction. Then rebirth. A cycle like the coming of spring. That is what the Committee believes. In fact, that is what we know to be true."

"And your cult thinks that a new dawn is upon us?" Iris scoffed.

"Yes. But my father had a theory. What if this cycle isn't caused by different events?" He looked at her. "Not by flood one time or fire another. What if the grand *cataclysma* is the same event over and over again? If the world is to end, then how will it end? And what will end it? The Committee ordered my father's assassination for withholding key information from them. Information in that precious journal of his."

"They tried to kill him?"

"Before he could share his secrets with other entities. Imperial rivals. The government."

"The British government is the Committee's enemy?" Iris thought of the portraits in the room. Carl Anderson and Neville Bradford. Men of the Crown.

"As is any entity with power," Adam said. "Knowledge and power are dangerous commodities when one monopolizes them. The Committee believes he's dead and gone. I know he's not. But those secrets are precious, Iris. They are the key to understanding what comes next . . . the cataclysm awaiting us. That's why I need you to find him. You could say I'm a little like my father: I don't want those secrets falling into the wrong hands either."

"Even the Committee's?"

"The Committee is nothing more than a macabre birthright," Adam answered flatly. "And a means to an end."

But before Iris could fully digest Adam's words, he plucked open the top buttons on his white shirt, grabbed her hand, and placed it firmly upon his chest. There, as her body warmed, as her cheeks flushed, she could sense his heart pulsing steadily beneath his skin.

"Now feel me, Iris," he whispered. "Concentrate on the beating of my heart. The blood pumping through my veins. My father's blood."

As Iris's blood pumped, it was hard to concentrate on much else other than his thin hair prickling her palm.

"Try, Iris." He wrapped his arm, gentle but firm, around her waist and drew her to him to finally close the distance between them. His body was hard, his grip steady. He wouldn't let her go. "Concentrate. Get a feel for me to get a feel for him."

Like a bloodhound sniffing a bloody rag to pick up the trail of a killer. It wasn't a comparison she liked. But truly, she *could* feel Adam beyond his body.

Madame, tell me . . . are you . . . a goddess?

Adam's voice as a child, despite his awe, was just as discreetly ravenous as it was now. Feeling him like this drew her back into that memory . . . a memory of flesh latching to bone.

Her heart jumped into her throat. She pushed him and ran to the balcony doors, turning her back to the glass, holding the knob behind her.

"Don't look at me like that, Iris," he said in almost a whisper as her pulse raced. "This is just part of what you'll need to face to get your memories back. I told you it wouldn't be easy. But I also told you that I'm on your side. I meant that. I still do."

The breeze ruffled their clothes, their hair, marring the silence of the moment.

Iris turned and faced the door, her eyes on the plants. "I'll hold you to that."

"We'll practice again soon," she heard him say behind her. "Sometime during the tournament, when we can be alone."

Iris snorted. "You seem confident the other tournament champions won't get rid of me."

"They couldn't even if they tried," said Adam. "You know that. You *know* you'll survive. Soon, you'll come to understand the full extent of what you can do. You who feels the thread of life so powerfully, you can't die even if you desired it."

Without looking back at him, Iris fled.

19

T HIS IS OUR ROOM?"

Iris stared wide-eyed at her team's lodgings. Room 308 was an odd combination of a mini-parlor and a bedroom with nothing to separate the two except the thick green curtains that slid on a hinge around a large four-poster bed—the biggest and most lavish of the three beds in the room. Max had already claimed that one.

"No, he hasn't." Jinn grabbed him by the collar and threw him off. "That's Iris's bed."

After landing rather badly on the checkered rug, Max rubbed his back. "Who says? I say we cast lots. It's only fair." He looked back with a cheeky grin. "Right, Iris? Or I'd also be willing to share with you."

Iris leaned against the door. The chairs around the table to her left arched to a point, with Gothic carvings in the dark wood. Mirrors hung upon the walls above the cabinets with standing lamps strewn about for lighting. The long sofa in the corner was adorned with ornamentation. Shades of pink were used for the wallpaper to contrast with the floor's dark woodwork, and floor-length brocade draperies were tied back to let the light stream in from the window behind the three beds.

As for the beds, Iris could understand Max's slight frustration. There were two very plain ones with white cotton sheets pushed up against the far right side of the wall. They looked like hospital beds. The other was as extravagant as you'd find in a noblewoman's bedroom: a four-poster bed frame, a large headboard and footboard without a single crack in them, and thick, lavish bed-sheets of violet and soft blue.

Iris felt a prick of annoyance at the sight of those sheets—again with the iris theme?

"The three of us are sharing this room . . . together?" Heat rose to her face when she saw the washstand and towel rail next to her. Staying in Max's apart-ment was an awkward arrangement she didn't want to see repeated.

"Makes sense. We're a team, aren't we?" Max seemed rather chipper as he jumped up to his feet. "This place is *expensive*. I wonder if there's anything here I can steal."

"She's back?" cried a chipmunk from behind the door. "Lemme at her!"

The door burst open; Iris had to stumble out of the way to avoid being flung across the room. Cherice's small face was red with fire as she stomped into the room.

"You *see*? What's that, then? Look at that bed!" She pointed at the lavishly decorated four-poster on the right wall. "It's clearly meant to be hers!"

"Meant to be hers," Jinn repeated with a shrug while Max rolled his eyes in response.

But Cherice was talking to Jacob and Hawkins, each taking one side of the doorframe.

"Meanwhile, *our* beds look like the kind you put corpses on!" A huff from Cherice's lips blew up her apricot hair.

"It all depends on how much our Patrons are willing to spend on us, I sup-pose." Jacob pointed at the plaque to the left, hanging on the wall close to the sofa. A plaque with a ram carved into the wood. "It's your team's symbol," he explained. "If Adam Temple's your Patron as you say he is, then—"

"Then he must fancy the *hell* out of you." Cherice laughed as Iris's face flushed with heat. "He in love with you or somethin'?"

"No!" Iris couldn't have screamed it louder. She turned quickly toward Jinn, ready to explain, not knowing why she had to explain, feeling it was ridiculous to explain in the first place. Except Jinn had taken one of the books from the shelf next to the window and was already flipping through the pages while lying on the cotton sheets of the bed he'd chosen for himself. Now she was silently furious and couldn't explain it.

"Do you love *him*?" said Jacob as Hawkins giggled behind his hand next to him. "It's okay if you do."

Iris whipped around and practically bared her teeth. "What business is that of yours? Okay, so what about you? Who do *you* love, Jacob?"

That shut him up fast. Hawkins noticed Jacob's sudden change in demeanor and, after an awkward shuffle of his feet, played off his own slight blush with a frustrated sigh. "Well, this suddenly stopped being amusing," the blond boy said before pushing off the doorframe. "I'll leave you to sort it out, then."

Jacob swallowed, his throat dry. "U-uh, L-Lawrence, wait!" And he closed the door after them. Cherice didn't seem to care. She was still glaring at Iris, hands on narrow hips.

"So are you in love with Max, then?" Cherice asked.

"Yes!" Max answered, hopping onto the extravagant bed once more.

"*No!*" Iris answered at the same time. This had to be some kind of humiliation ritual.

"As her professional partner, I can tell you she's more likely to be in love with herself," Jinn answered flatly, flipping a page of his book. "And pretty things. Jewelry, hats."

"*Excuse* me?"

"Didn't you ask me for a hat?"

Iris had half a mind to pick up the vase on the table and throw it at his head. There was that childishness she saw in Granny's tent the day she ran from the circus, rearing its ugly head.

"What about you?" She pointed at Cherice with a little bit of childishness of her own.

"Me?" With a smile, Cherice skipped over to the lavish bed, jumped onto the covers, and after landing on her knees, threw her arms around Max. "Maxey's the only guy for me."

She said this so confidently, so openly, that it shocked Iris into a timid silence.

Max, however, returned Cherice's affections with an awkward laugh and a smooth removal of her arm. "She's kidding," he explained to Iris, shaking his head. "She was always the youngest in our group when we were kids, so she's turned into a bit of a brat. Don't pay her any mind."

But Cherice certainly didn't look like she was kidding. The stiff expression when Max patted her on the back said otherwise.

"Are you finished?" Jinn closed his book and, getting up, tossed it onto the bed. He looked up at the wooden clock on the cabinet. "Half past one. I think I'll have enough time."

"Time for what?" Iris asked, suspicious, as he walked to the door.

"Just some business," he said, passing her and shutting the door behind him.

Iris folded her arms, staring at an oblivious Max and a forlorn Cherice. What a mess. But she had a way to fix this.

"You know, there are things I need in the city," Iris said to Cherice, sauntering over to her. "Clothes and whatnot. We can use the money you stole from me to get them. How about it?"

Iris didn't wait for an answer. Grabbing the short girl by her sleeve, she pulled her out of the room, ignoring her protests.

Maybe Jinn was right: Iris did have a taste for the good stuff. But many of the stores she tried to drag Cherice into wouldn't even let them in—Iris for the shade of her skin, and Cherice for her dilapidated, working-class clothes and unique musk. Max had come along, if only to carry their things, but it didn't seem like he'd have much to carry.

It was more important to Iris that she square things with Cherice. She'd been surrounded by annoying men for so long; it was nice to have another girl to talk to. But what a hard shell to crack.

"Some of those store owners could use a smack in the face," Iris said as they stalked down the streets, Max strolling along behind them. "That combination of curse words you gave one was brilliant though. You'll have to teach me that one."

"I'm not the teaching type," Cherice said, her lips pursed. "Ask one of your boy toys."

Iris sighed impatiently but didn't give up. Hooking her arm around Cherice, she swiveled her toward the next store on Regent Street.

The skies had cleared, and the streets were unusually bright and bustling with children rushing past. Somewhere on the streets a newsboy was peddling papers: "The African ambassadors met with the queen yesterday! Read all about it!"

Inside the store, Iris could feel a little tension vanish from her body. Sometimes the act of looking at pretty things was therapeutic. Jinn really did have her pegged. Though, as she noted with annoyance, he still hadn't bothered to get her a hat when she'd asked him for one.

Cherice seemed to enjoy it too—at least when she thought Iris wasn't looking. And then when she caught Iris's amused smile, she turned around in a huff, trying very badly to remain cold as stone. It was actually adorable. Iris could see why her friends doted on her.

Unfortunately, her good mood turned sour when the shopkeeper shooed them out of the store, though not before hurling a terrible word at Iris like a grenade. Her stomach dropped out as the door slammed behind them.

"What was that, you slime ball?" growled Cherice. "Open up and fight us face-to-face, coward!"

"N-no, forget it." Iris managed a weak smile as her shoulders slumped. She was an African tightrope dancer who performed primarily across Europe. It would have been a miracle if she hadn't come across such words before. They still hurt.

Eventually, Iris was able to find a dreary black dress and Cherice a new pair of slacks. As Cherice hungrily eyed the café on the other side of the street, Max kept a watchful eye on Iris. She noticed but she didn't know how to respond. Because he'd wait outside while the girls were in each store, he hadn't seen how rudely they'd been treated—until that last encounter. His expression had turned uncharacteristically solemn afterward.

Then suddenly—"Come on, you two. Iris. Cherice." Max grabbed Iris's hand and tugged her down the sidewalk, Cherice scurrying close behind.

"J-just wait a moment," Iris said as she stumbled along past throngs of children.

"See these kids?" He jerked his head toward a group of them. "I think I know what all the commotion's about!" he said.

Many of the children were still in their Sunday church finest, the girls in their bonnets and doll-like dresses, the boys in their cloaks, tam hats, and sailor suits. Some carried pinwheels and slingshots, others carried dolls and strange toys Iris had never seen before. And eventually, Iris realized where they'd gotten them.

"Whittle's?" Iris read the extravagant sign on the storefront window, nearly tripping over her own feet as Max pulled her into the redbrick toy shop.

The busy shop buzzed with children's delighted cries, the floor bustling with energy. A flock of children surrounded the red pedal cars and tricycles in one corner. Another held Pulcinella marionettes, strings, and beautifully painted boxes so children could put on their very own Punch and Judy acts. Iris swirled around on the spot, following a little red train as it buzzed around the beige walls of the shop atop finely built railroad tracks.

"New deliveries!" one child cried, her eyes stuck on a silver-rimmed toy theater of porcelain dolls.

"You hear that, Cherice?" Max jumped up and down, clapping. "New deliveries!"

"Oh, shut up." Cherice rolled her eyes, but not even she could hide her excitement.

"Remember how we used to take you here? Chadwick, Jacob, Hawkins, and me?" Max leaned toward Iris and "whispered" in a very loud voice, "One time she wouldn't stop crying until she got something. Saw some Protestant boy with a pinwheel and nearly beat him up for it."

"His snotty arse deserved it," she said, folding her arms.

Another seemingly new delivery caught the children's attention—a giant Punch puppet about the size of an average boy: rosy cheeks; wide, pointed nose; extravagantly large black eyebrows, curled up at the tips; with a red cap and pin-striped pants. Though a puppet, it stood upright on its own two feet, solid as a statue. How in the world had they created such a thing?

Iris turned to Max, bewildered, but with a helpless wide grin on her face nonetheless. "Maximo Morales." She couldn't but laugh at the unbridled boyish passion curling off Max's whole body like smoke as he took in the sights. "Why did you bring us here?"

"It's *Whittle's*!" Max declared. "The most famous toy shop in the city."

While Cherice pushed through throngs of children to get to the merchandise that had caught her eye, Max beckoned for Iris to follow him to the wall nearest the cashier.

"I always loved coming here as a kid," he continued. "When the others weren't around, I'd stand outside the window because I couldn't afford anything."

Iris raised an eyebrow. "You didn't steal anything? Even with your abilities?"

Max looked *intensely* offended, enough to draw a laugh from Iris's lips. "Hey, unlike what that bloke Jinn might think, I didn't *always* spend my days engaged in crime." He paused. "Well, I usually did. But not here. Okay, a few times."

Iris folded her arms by a pearl-painted wooden rocking horse.

"One time was to get Cherice a doll. It wasn't easy for her, growing up the youngest and the only girl among a bunch of smelly orphan boys." Max smiled a little. "You know, deep down, I always hoped that someday I'd step inside these doors with . . . with my little sister."

"Berta, you mean," she whispered.

Max's expression became warm as he gazed back at her. "You remembered."

Iris's face flushed. "Of course. Why wouldn't I?" She fidgeted a little. "I still don't understand why you took me here."

It was then that Max grabbed a puppet off a shelf before anyone could see him. It had the armor, long boots, goatee, and brown hard hat of a Spaniard of the early modern era.

Iris tilted her head. "Don Quixote?"

Max's hand flew up its back.

"Why did Max bring you here?" Max repeated her question in such a ridiculous, high-pitched voice, Iris burst out laughing. "Why, it's because you were looking so distraught before, I figured you needed a reason to smile!"

Swallowing her laughter, she pressed the backs of her fingers against her lips. "But why should the great Don Quixote care about how I feel?"

Puppet Quixote shook its head sternly. "Oh, sweet young girl. Don Quixote always cares."

Iris grabbed its little white hand. "But why does he sound like an old maid?"

Max cleared his throat and placed the toy back on his shelf, and grabbed a cat puppet and threw it to Iris.

"You're a fool," she said.

"I'm not a fool but a trickster." Max winked. "That one's on the house. You want it, just say the word, and I'll sneak it out."

So he hadn't entirely forsaken his life of crime. Iris giggled as Max went off to browse the merchandise. And when she turned, she could see a little apricot head peeking out from behind a shelf. The moment she called to Cherice, it bobbed out of sight. Iris giggled. These two.

Might as well give it a try, Iris thought, pulling on the puppet and catching Cherice before she could scurry off. But the second Monsieur Cat tried to introduce himself, Cherice began barking at him like a dog. Iris's eyebrows shot up. Parents and kids alike were staring.

"Wassat?" called Max from another part of the store. "Cherice, you barking again?"

Gulping, Iris tilted her head with a shrug. "It was a good dog impression."

Cherice didn't seem to have the energy anymore to put up a front. Grabbing the puppet off Iris's hand, she stared at it with a pout. "Maxey seems to like you," she said finally, strangling Monsieur Cat a little.

"Never mind him," Iris said with a dismissive wave. "I want to know about you."

Cherice blushed, taken aback. "Me?" She paused, lowering her head. "What's there to know? I was the youngest of a pack of street kids. My mum died of cholera when I was six. Chadwick was my older brother, but the rest might as well have been."

"I saw his penny blood series," Iris said. "He was a great storyteller."

At this, Cherice smiled. "He loved drawing. Used to draw things for me all the time. It'd cheer me up after Mum died. But then he died." Her expression turned dark. "Because of Barry Bately. That rat bastard sold us out to the police for some shillings."

Remembering that man's jaundiced teeth and silver tongue, Iris shivered.

"There were others in our group, you know? They got sold off to workhouses. Hawkins was going to be one of them. Chadwick fought 'em hard, and—"

Iris put a hand on her shoulder. She didn't have to go on.

"Well, that was two years ago." Cherice straightened up. "No use crying over the dead."

"That's not true," Iris said, noticing Cherice discreetly wipe a tear from her eye. "I'm sure the dead want us to cry for them *sometimes*. Just not too often."

Cherice looked at Iris, her expression softer than before. She seemed like she was going to say something but thought better of it, settling for patting Iris on the back.

"Come on," she offered. "Let's steal a bunch of things."

Iris supposed that was a peacemaking gesture.

Iris turned to see a schoolboy at the other side of the busy cashier counter staring at the two of them with intense, bright green eyes. He looked older and far more serious than the other children here, old enough to be sent off to boarding school. If Iris could have guessed, he was a maybe one or two years younger than Cherice.

A gray newsboy cap fit his round head of light brown hair, though it certainly didn't cover those large ears. Along with his silver eyeglasses and the large leather book under his arm, his features were charming enough to make her want to pinch his cheeks, but his calculating expression drew Iris's apprehension.

"Henry!" called a cheerful but overwhelmed old man packaging toys at the front counter. "What are you doing, boy? Don't just stand there, help out, will you?"

"Yes, yes, coming, Granddad," answered the surly boy, and joined him behind the counter.

"My, what a gloomy young man Whittle's grandson is," gossiped a nearby woman to another, one hand carrying a puppet, the other being tugged by a little boy. "Meanwhile, Whittle himself looks as happy as ever. Likely not a family trait."

Iris assumed they hadn't noticed the little smile Henry gave when his grandfather nudged him to show a perfectly tied gift box.

"David Whittle only *looks* happy," said another woman with two brown bears tucked underneath her arm. "His debts aren't exactly a secret. No matter how many toys they sell, it won't be enough to keep the store from closing."

They were talking too loudly. Though his grandfather seemed preoccupied with the children, Henry shot them a stiff glare before he went back to packaging toys.

Just as Max returned to them, Iris tugged his arm. "We should go," she said. "We're in everyone's way. Besides." She lowered her head. "I already feel a little better. Thank you, Max."

"Good," he said, his eyes shining. "And as for some new clothes, let's try it the good old-fashioned way, shall we, Cherice?" He wriggled his fingers.

Cherice grinned wickedly.

20

EVENING. AS IRIS SAT UPON HER princely bed in her new pale violet dress, she wondered if all the teams had checked into Club Uriel by now. Adam only said Sunday. But the show at Wilton's Music Hall would start today at six in the evening. If they weren't here, that's where Iris would meet them—the place where they'd learn the rules of the tournament.

Max's light snoring from the other side of her drawn curtain had become almost soothing, certainly more so than the clock ticking away. He'd decided to take a nap before going. But as Iris stared at the clock, she wondered where Jinn had gone and how long it would take him to return—or *if* he would return. Iris remembered his cold expression earlier and bit her lip in frustration. That annoying old crank letting stupid things bother him. She hated that about him.

Iris pulled her knees up to her chest and waited.

Tik. Tok. Tik. Tok.

So many things had happened during the past few days she could hardly imagine they were arguing over routines just days ago. Only because Jinn nit-picked everything. Acting like he was above it all. Even now, after she'd drawn him into this bizarre tournament, he was still acting above it all. After she'd put him in harm's way with no idea what would come of it, he still acted like he didn't care. Like he could handle it. Like it was nothing.

Iris squeezed her eyes shut, wrapping her arms around her knees. "You stupid old cr—"

The curtain opened with a swish. Her heart stopped. Jinn stood at the side of her bed, a heavy sack in one hand and a long white gift box balanced in the crook of his arm. She wasn't even sure when he'd slipped in.

"Who's a stupid old crank?" he asked in a flat voice, dropping the box onto the bed.

Iris shot to her knees. "Jinn!" she exclaimed, and then, keenly aware of Max sleeping on his bed, cleared her throat, blushing. "Y-you're back," she added, feigning nonchalance. "Where did you go?"

"The circus camp." The sack fell to the floor with a clatter. Peeking out of the burlap was the shimmer of a blade. Bolero blades. "These are yours."

Iris blinked. "Coolie's?"

Jinn rolled his eyes. "No, Barnum's. I flew to America."

Iris folded her arms with a huff. Most of the lamps were off so that Max could rest. Only the sun's dying light streamed through the windows, dancing along Jinn's handsome face. It was then that Iris realized with a slight jolt in her chest that the two hadn't really been alone since she ran from the circus. There was still much left unsaid. At least, that's what Iris felt.

"Needless to say, I quit," he told her. "And gave Coolie a message."

"A message?" Alarmed, Iris slid off the bed and grabbed his hands, much to his shy surprise. She noticed the sores and bruises on his knuckles.

"Coolie had his debt collectors with him. Two birds, one stone," Jinn said. "He actually got off easy, but that's what happens when you hide under the desk wetting yourself."

Iris smirked. "I would have dragged him out anyway." But it wasn't just that. Some of these bruises looked older. She wondered how many he'd gained scaling the building of the auction house and crashing through the windows to get to her.

"I'm sorry," she said. "Everything's turned into such a bloody mess so quickly."

"At least I found you again." Jinn gave her a rare smile. "You really thought you could run away from me, eh? I'm your dance partner, for goodness' sake."

"No matter how far I fly . . ." She stopped and blushed as the room fell to a gentle lull for too long. She tried to let go of his hands, but Jinn wouldn't let her. His grip kept her in place.

Iris looked from his clavicle to the strong muscles of his long, sandy neck, to his Adam's apple sliding up and down his throat. She stared at the buttons of his vest. When she finally looked into his face, she saw his mouth half-parted and still wordless despite his best efforts.

He didn't express himself easily. Neither did she. But in that moment, when he pulled her off the bed, closer to him, she realized there were many different ways to express emotion. She felt the outline of his hard body as the memory of what he'd once asked her filled her with an odd warmth.

What do you think of me?

A sudden flutter in her chest caused her to rip herself from his grip.

I'm such a coward, she thought bitterly, sitting back down on the bed, waiting for her pulse to slow. "A-and Granny?" she said too fast, stumbling over the words. "She's okay, isn't she?"

Jinn was left dazed by the quick change in mood. But after swallowing and taking a deep breath, he followed along. "Granny is all right. Except, I suppose, that she misses you."

Iris smiled softly. She wished she could go back and let her know she was okay. But for now, it was too risky to return; she was facing a bigger enemy than Coolie. One day.

"In case you were wondering, that goose of yours is just fine too," Jinn added. "Fed and watered. Living the charmed life."

Iris could imagine Egg, the bird prince, squawking about the camp, ownerless.

"Thank goodness they're both okay." After dabbing a tear from her eye, she recalled the last moment she and Granny saw each other. "Jinn, about those strange things Granny said to me before we had her taken home. That I would have kidnapped her if those men hadn't—"

He shook his head. "She must have been confused. She was in a human exhibition as a child. Put on display and gawked at for the amusement of the English. What she went through in her childhood, needless to say, would have been traumatic. Sometimes you get details mixed up when you remember trau-matic experiences."

"No, something's not right about this," Iris insisted. "There's something she knows that I don't." She put her hand to her heart, trying to find the right words. "Something about me."

"That you were once a kidnapper?" Jinn shook her head. "Iris—"

"I'm over fifty years old at least!" Iris reminded him. "Isn't anything possible?"

Bellerose's guard had known her too. She'd called Iris "Isoke." There was much more to her mystery than she realized.

"Shadows of the past . . . ," Jinn whispered.

"More like demons." Placing both feet on her bed, she drew up her knees again.

"Enough." Jinn gripped her shoulder. "If you start worrying like that, you won't be able to stop, you know that. Just look at what's right in front of you. The pieces will fall into place."

But what was in front of Jinn? An immortal witch? A monster?

"Jinn . . ." She chose her words carefully. "Aren't you . . . Aren't you scared of me? Everything that I am . . . Everything that I could be. Everything you've found out. Doesn't it scare you even a little bit?"

"Not at all," Jinn answered without skipping a beat. "You're Iris. That's enough for me. I'll stay right here until it's enough for you."

Her chest began to swell with so much emotion, it almost overtook her. For one fleeting moment, she wanted to fall into his arms and cry. Instead, she lifted her head. And upon seeing his strength, his honesty, she gave him an exhausted smile.

Jinn looked at the clock behind him. "It's almost six. I'll bet the other teams are already at Wilton's. We need to go. But before that, there's something I need to pass along to you."

Iris tilted her head, confused. "Pass along?"

Jinn flicked his head at the white box on her bed. "Granny's parting gift. She still wants you to have it." Jinn must have noticed the hitch in Iris's inhale because he gave her shoulder a gentle squeeze. "And there's also a message she told me to give you."

Iris held her breath, waiting.

"'No matter what happened in the past and no matter what will happen in the future, I will always love you.' That's what she said."

Jinn looked deeply into her eyes, the hand on her shoulder providing a warmth that seemed to come from two people: both himself and the woman she still considered to be her closest friend. She breathed in deeply, letting the revelation of it sink into her bones.

Inside the box was a beautiful new set of clothes. Hand-sewn with experience and love. Worth thousands more than what she could have ever gotten in any stupid dress shop.

"Granny . . . thank you," she whispered, placing her hand on his, just for a moment, before a twitch of his fingers sent a wave of fluttering embarrassment through her.

"I'll save it for later," she said. There was no telling what was awaiting her. She didn't want to ruin Granny's hard work. "Let's wake up Max and go."

To Wilton's Music Hall.

21

TEAM IRIS AND TEAM HAWKINS—AS IRIS inwardly called his band of three—passed the old man at the entrance, who ushered them in with a bow. The crowd Iris had seen that morning was gone. The Committee's doing? Much smaller than Astley's, Wilton's still thrilled with a respectable amount of red velvet seats and a brass-colored balcony that stretched along the rectangular space. The sunset-orange lighting added a mystic feel to the thin columns and the painted walls.

Iris had her bolero blades in a large embroidered work bag Cherice had "picked up" for her on their way back to the club. She held it close to her, dreading the moment when she'd have to loosen the cord strings. Max had entered first—which is why a fight erupted immediately once he spotted Barry Bately at the front of the hall, leaning against a seat and smoking a cigarette.

"Bately," Max said, his fists ready. "So it's true. You really are in this mess..."

Just before leaving Club Uriel, Adam had given them names to memorize. Important information before the first round. But some of the names had caused a shock:

Adam Temple (England)
Maximo Morales, Iris Marlow, Jinn

Riccardo Benini (Italy)
Freddy Frasier, Blake Sanders, Kyle Leakes

Boris Bosch (Germany)
Lawrence Hawkins, Jacob Josefiub,
Cherice Winterbottom

Gerolt Van der Ven (Belgium)
Gram, Jacques

Albert Cortez (Spain)
Mary White, Henry Whittle,
Lucille Bouffant

Violet Bellerose (France)
Rin, Martin Leclaire, Robert Staunch

Luis Cordiero (Portugal)
Barry Bately, Torrence Cairnes,
Doug Waters

"Whittle?" Max had said, rushing over. "Of the *Whittle's* Whittles?"

On the back was written details of their abilities.

But another name had turned Max's expression dark. "Bately. That bastard would sell his own sister to the highest bidder. Iris—" Max was very serious. "Be careful of him."

And now there Bately stood inside the music hall, lazily tilting his head to the side and running a hand over his shaved brown head. He gave a salute. "So you've joined the freak show too. Good to see you, mate. Cheers!"

Max and Cherice started barreling toward him.

"Stop!" Iris caught them by the crooks of their arms. Every time Bately spoke, it caused her heart to hammer harder against her chest. And Bately seemed to know it. He relished it.

"Why?" Hawkins stalked down the center aisle as Jacob hung back, watching his friends warily. "Whatever beating he gets, he deserves."

The mercenary chuckled. "Still mad I used my mojo on you and Jake a while ago, eh?"

"You know I'm mad because of more than that."

"Aye, shaddap," came a slow, deep voice next to Bately. "Show's about to start."

A man in a purple hat with sagging jowls sat next to Bately's empty seat, his cigarette balanced upon his lips. The Exploding Man.

"What kind of mad reunion is this?" Iris said as an exasperated laugh escaped her lips.

A *mad* one, for sure: leaning against the leftmost wall was the girl from the auction house. Iris's blood froze at the sight of her yellow veil, her black coat. Her rivers of braids.

Madame Bellerose's guard. She had survived the fire. Iris's throat tightened, and she wasn't sure if it was in relief or fear.

"Now, now," said the doorman, who walked in after them. "There will be no fighting here at Wilton's Music Hall. Not without dire consequences."

The old doorman was an employee of Club Uriel. He had to be, based on his wicked, knowing smile. "Take your seat, take your seat, and wait for the show to begin."

Two men identically dressed like detectives strode into the hall and took their seats in unison, completely in sync right down to crossing their legs. Iris's head was starting to ache.

Stretching out his neck, Max took a seat to the right, several rows behind Bately, and didn't take his eyes off his old acquaintance who had betrayed them and caused Chadwick's death. Cherice's little body shook as she sat down next to Hawkins and Jacob with a huff.

But Iris kept her eyes on Bellerose's guard.

"Come," Jinn touched the small of her back and went to sit next to Max. In her aisle seat, Iris tore her eyes away from the girl and scoped out the rest of the hall.

Near the very back, a cigarette smoked between a man's long, spindly fingers, but because he kept his head downturned, Iris couldn't see his face. His stringy gray hair mopped his shoulders from underneath a black top hat. His pale, frigid-looking hands peeked out from his long, dark gray jacket, which he kept buttoned to the very top of its lapels. If it weren't for the cigarette still sturdily in his grasp, Iris would have thought he was sleeping. Or dead. Perhaps *undead* if his pallor was any indication.

Next to him was a man of Iris's skin tone, but he looked to be a priest. A *priest*? Involved in this insanity? There wasn't any end to the surprises. She could tell by his white collar and black robes that he was Catholic. She could see only the side of his face—a side riddled with scars.

White collar and black robes. Iris flashed back to the man who'd been shot earlier that day at Club Uriel . . . and the figure in black robes and a white collar who'd disappeared behind the doorframe after shooting him.

She shivered. What the hell had she gotten herself into?

"Mr. Whittle, it seems that we're the last team to arrive."

Whittle? Iris whipped around and found a fidgety blond girl who looked no more than fifteen or sixteen standing next to the boy Iris had seen at Whittle's toy shop.

"Oi." Max couldn't nudge her as Jinn was sitting between them. But he'd gotten Iris's attention nonetheless. "Henry Whittle, right?"

Light brown hair. Silver eyeglasses. Newsboy cap. Surly expression. It was him—the toymaker's grandson and heir to the Whittles' debt. Iris could guess why the cash prize would be appealing to him, but such a young boy taking part in this tournament . . . Her stomach churned.

But worse still was seeing the old woman behind him.

"Goodness me, everyone's looking!" The old woman appeared thrilled by that, though she could barely straighten her back to see the rest of them through her clouded brown eyes. After a series of coughs, she brushed back a few strands of gray hair and turned to the young girl. "Mary, my bag."

Mary seemed to have forgotten she was carrying a small burlap sack. The sound of her name jolted her back from the sights of the music hall.

"Oh, uh . . ." Mary sounded as bashful as she looked, squirming and staring at her feet. Her French braid stretched down her back, tied in a blue ribbon. "I-I'll hold on to it for now." With how tightly her hands gripped the bag to keep from trembling, her decision wasn't a surprise.

As the final, strange team took their seats, Iris turned to Jinn. "What do you think?"

But Jinn didn't respond. Instead, he was staring oddly at the man with stringy gray hair, the man who seemed all too peacefully unaware of or uninterested in anyone's presence. Jinn stared at the cigarette in his hands and swallowed a sudden, deep breath before shaking his head.

"No," Jinn whispered to himself mysteriously, shaking his head before concentrating on the stage. "It couldn't be." He didn't elaborate.

Moments after all teams were settled, the curtains spread apart, giving way to an explosion of white smoke and the earsplitting shriek of a woman in terror. It gave the group a start, though Max seemed thrilled, leaning over his knees with a big grin, awaiting the spectacle. Maybe a bit of theater was needed to ease the mounting tension.

Once the smoke cleared, a woman with loose blond hair in a yellow dress appeared before them, lying woefully on the stage with the back of her hand pressed against her forehead.

For a moment, it seemed like the woman had "died." But gradually, with gentle movements, she began to stir, staring at her rosy hands in wonder.

"I, fair Alice, who thought I was not long for this world, have escaped the clutches of death!" The woman felt her heartbeat. "I am alive! What is this mercy that has rescued me from the ferry headed for the underworld?"

"Her acting's as bad as ours." Iris smirked, nudging Jinn in the ribs. "Remember that 'Bolero of Blades' script Coolie scrapped?"

Jinn grimaced. "I try not to."

"I kind of had fun improvising it with Max the other day, though."

"What?" Max and Jinn both said at the same time but for different reasons.

Max seemed to perk up at the sound of his name even if he hadn't heard the context while Jinn responded to Iris's offhand remark with an awkwardly stiff expression.

"Shush." From her seat behind Max, Cherice put a finger to her lips. "Quit the chatter." She punched Iris in the shoulder a little too hard to get the message across.

"I *said*, what is this mercy that has rescued me?" The actress looked annoyed. Iris couldn't imagine she was part of the club or the Committee. The poor thing looked like every other struggling actress in the city, taking whatever role she could get. Iris hoped they paid her a pretty penny to be part of this terrible show.

The sound of thunder. Iris knew from stage experience that someone in the fly rails was shaking a thin sheet of metal to produce the sound. A trapdoor on the stage opened and, rising out of the black square hole in the floor—

Iris's blood ran cold.

"It's *him*," she whispered, just as Jinn's and Max's bodies tensed next to her. Fool.

Jinn's hand instinctively reached for the brown sack he'd placed on the floor at his feet, the sack Iris knew carried his weapons. But she touched his arm to stop him. Fool didn't seem interested in any kind of mayhem, at least not yet. The actress wasn't at all stirred by his presence. He was part of the play. The man had kept his mask, top hat, and black cloak, so Iris could only assume that he was playing the role of himself.

Then again, isn't this all theater? Iris asked herself as the stage settled and Fool bowed deeply to his scant audience.

Fool's harlequin smile flashed dangerously underneath the gold lighting.

"Was it a mercy, my dear Alice?" Fool spoke in his usual musical tone, always on the verge of laughter. "But then that would suggest that such a thing as mercy exists in this cruel modern world of power and hubris. No, Alice, what saved you was fate."

The actress gasped too loudly, as if she was afraid the audience couldn't hear her. She was clearly new at this. "Fate? But who are you, dear sir?"

"I am Fool." He introduced himself with another bow, much like he did the night the Sparrow twins attacked Iris, Max, and Jinn. "And you, my dear little rabbit, are chosen."

Well, he was a better actor than she was at any rate. Perhaps because he wasn't acting.

It was then that the theater's fly rail system sprang to life. Another explosion of white smoke. Then, with the combined workings of ropes and sandbags, the actress was soaring through the air, screaming in both terror and joy. Iris caught glimpses of the stagehands holding the ropes off to the side behind the drawn curtains.

"What is this?" the actress cried. "I can fly! But how is such a thing possible?"

"Of course it is possible, young Alice. Were you not at the South Kensington Exhibition on June the second, ten years past? Were you not changed by the mystical explosion that transformed others? Of course you can fly, Alice. You were chosen for a grand destiny."

The ropes set the actress down, and after unhooking herself, she collapsed at Fool's feet. "Oh, the mysterious explosion that wrought such a terrible destiny upon me! Oh, the sorrowful decision I made that day to visit the fair, the day that changed my fate forever!"

Fool crouched down next to her, lifting her face up with a white-gloved finger. "Not terrible, my dear, but *glorious*. For with your new abilities, you, who've been poor and destitute since you were born, now have a chance to begin a new chapter in your life—one of wealth and fortune. But—" he added upon seeing signs of hope on the actress's face. "You can only do so if you participate in the game."

The actress blinked innocently. "Game?"

"The Tournament of Freaks."

From the fly rails dropped seven majestic banners. Each looked like a coat of arms, but each bore its own color and had its own animal caged within the heraldic shield.

A wolf on a black banner.

A boar on a violet banner.

A stag on a green banner.

A swan on a gold banner.

A bear on an orange banner.

A chameleon on a blue banner.

And a ram on a blood-red banner. The same ram drawn upon the plaque in Iris's room.

"Under one of these seven banners must you fight if you are to claim your prize of unbridled riches." Fool swept his arms across the stage. "Each banner represents a Patron from the esteemed Club Uriel. And you will be their champions. Seven teams of, at the most, three in number. Three rounds in which you will battle for supremacy. The winners of the first two rounds will receive an *irreplaceable* advantage for the third, after which only one winner will emerge. Whichever team wins the tournament will receive riches that will last them a lifetime. Simple, yes?"

The actress stood and glanced around the stage, taking in the banners with what was supposed to be an expression of horror and awe but to Iris looked more like constipation. "But what are the rules of this strange game?"

"Rules?" With two strides of his long spider legs, Fool leaned into the actress, lowering himself to her eye level before holding up his fingers. "There are but three."

This is what Iris had been waiting for. She listened carefully.

"Rule one: The battles to be fought between the teams are to take place within the jurisdictions chosen by the Patrons. In the meantime, champions are not to attempt to leave the city of London of their own volition until the game is complete. Any attempt to flee the game will result in very *disastrous* consequences."

Iris shivered, getting his message loud and clear. Well, Coolie's Astley run was a month. After that, they were heading back down to continental Europe. Iris hoped the tournament would finish and she could learn the truth about herself before Granny was taken from her.

"Rule two: There are two areas in which battles and acts of aggression cannot take place under any circumstances. First, Club Uriel at Pall Mall Street, where the gentlemen responsible for these esteemed festivities gather. And second, this theater, open to all champions at any hour of the day and night."

Fool swept his hand across the musty air. "You may think of them as neutral zones. Those who desire respite would do well to come here."

"Oh, how wonderful," cried the old woman behind them before letting out a hacking cough.

"Rule three: Your esteemed Patrons, who are fortified with the utmost of security and protection, hold the right to change and add to said rules at their discretion as the game unfolds."

"What? Bollocks! So then what's the point of having rules at all?" Max barked, causing the actress to jump a little where she stood.

"Calm down, Maxey, you're scaring the little dove," said Bately, looking behind him with a smirk that earned a hateful glare from Max.

Fool was unperturbed. He cocked his head, touching the rim of his top hat. "It is this in exchange for the illustrious future that awaits you should you succeed."

Selling an illustrious future seemed quite ironic for a cult that believed in the impending end of the world. The money was nothing more than cruel bait to lure in desperate players willing to amuse the rich and powerful.

No. This tournament had a deeper meaning. If not for the club, then for the Committee, who, through their painstaking research, truly believed the world would soon end.

Who among us will lead? Adam had asked at the British Museum. Instead of slaughtering themselves, they would slaughter others. Whichever team was left standing would receive their prize money, and their Patron would win the right to guide the regeneration of mankind.

Nonsense. No, it was insane. What did the "regeneration of mankind" even mean? If the world was ending, then there was nowhere to go—that is, if the world was truly ending. Iris needed more proof. More important, she needed to find the proof for herself.

But not today.

"The first round begins this very midnight," continued Fool.

Iris's heart thumped in her chest.

"Midnight?" Cherice squeaked behind them.

Iris's gaze slid toward Bellerose's guard by the wall.

Entering stage left were two clowns, one in red and one in white, each holding a small golden treasure chest. They danced and twirled, stopping center stage with a deep genuflection.

"The rules of this round are simple," said Fool.

The red clown opened his box. Inside were seven golden tickets.

"First, you will choose a number. And then—"

The white clown opened his.

"Each team will choose a key in the order of the numbers on your tickets. The key must be in the possession of one member at all times. There are seven, forged of different materials: diamond, ruby, coal, sapphire, emerald, iron, and gold."

Iris couldn't see them from here. She sat, uncomfortable and waiting, in her seat.

"At half past eight, a train will be leaving from King's Cross to take you to the destination of the first round. There, starting at midnight, you will have three hours to steal a key from another team and return to Club Uriel with a set of two. That will determine your success. Oh, and as for how you obtain the second key? Well, that will be left up to your discretion." Fool shivered with excitement.

Iris tensed, suddenly and keenly aware of the other Fanciful Freaks sitting and listening to Fool in this otherwise empty music hall. Her only solace was the pact. As long as Team Hawkins stayed true to their pact, she had less to worry about.

Then again, any rule can be broken. Iris stiffly remained in her seat.

"Remember," said Fool, "stay alive and you move on to the next round, even if you don't obtain a rival's key. But stealing a key will be to your extreme benefit. And that is for certain."

"I have made up my mind, dear Fool!" said the actress. "I will join this merry game." She stood at the edge of the stage, her whole body bursting with excitement. This really was simply a job to her; if she truly knew this was all real, she would either be terrified or grinning evilly like Fool surely was behind his mask. "I shall build my team, and after we succeed, I will be rich beyond my wildest dreams! Oh, Fool, do you have any advice for a young girl such as me?"

Fool gave his advice, but not to her. He looked directly at the crowd. Maybe Iris was imagining things, but she could feel his gaze on *her* when he spoke once again. "Try very hard not to die, my dear little rabbit."

The actress scrunched up her face in confusion. "That wasn't in the script," she hissed. But as the play had come to a close, begrudgingly she bowed anyway. The curtain fell. The players disappeared.

All vanished but the two clowns with their chests of treasures.

One member of each team began to line up in front of them.

"I'll get it." Jinn walked to the stage without hesitating. Getting the key was all well and good, but soon they'd have to decide who among them would carry it. If she possessed the key, she might inspire the others to target her assuming she was the weakest of the three. They didn't know she couldn't die—at least she didn't think they did. And she would rather have them target her than either Jinn or Max.

Hawkins's hatred was palpable as he stood behind Bately waiting for his ticket and key. Bately couldn't care less. This tournament would be the perfect excuse to settle an old score.

Henry waltzed up to the stage with a confidence that exceeded his young age. Meanwhile, the ghost-skinned man finally moved. Putting out his cigarette on the red chair in front of him, he crushed the stick between his fingers, letting it drop to the floor before leaving the hall without a word. His partner, the priest, drew ticket one, grabbed the charcoal key, and then left, muttering as he passed.

"For the sake of His sorrowful passion," was all Iris heard.

Bellerose's guard did not take the key, but rather one of the scruffy-looking men who seemed to be part of her team. As the girl left the hall, Iris could feel her watching.

Eventually Jinn, who'd drawn the number four, returned with a ruby key. Red as the ram, shining under the stage lights. It was small, with two perfect rings overlapping and interlinking; a sun and its shadow, perhaps—one passing the other. On its head rested a small crown to which a silver chain was affixed. It was as beautiful as it was extravagant.

Stranger still, Iris felt drawn to it. The two rings pulled her into them as if teasing her with a whisper. *A sun and its shadow* . . .

"Carriages await outside to take you to King's Cross," said the red clown once all the teams had chosen their keys.

"Then if you'll please," said the white clown.

Bowing, they exited stage left with a twirl.

The seconds ticked away. And midnight drew near.

22

THE TRAIN SPED OUT OF LONDON in the middle of the night. Each red-and-gold-painted rail car was finely furnished and built for long travel, with tables, upholstery, gold roping, and leather seats. They were expensive cars, made for politicians and the wealthy. Clearly a donation from Club Uriel. A luxury train ride—and a last supper of sorts for some.

Each team had taken their own car, with guards placed to ensure they kept to the rules—no mayhem until the appropriate time at the appropriate venue.

Team Hawkins and Team Iris had to keep a lower profile. That's what Iris realized. They couldn't announce their pact to the rest of the teams, not so early in the tournament. It would come in handy during the first round—a surprise tactic they could use. Though Team Hawkins was in the next car, they'd made sure to meet secretly inside the train station.

"A stage play," Iris had said once the two teams had gathered in King's Cross. She shook her head. "I'll give 'em points for creativity at least."

They were inside a bathroom. For men. Iris could tell by the dirty urinals. Max had barricaded the door. Iris just hoped nobody caught cholera from this.

Jinn looked at Hawkins. "Have you learned anything about Fool?"

"From our Patron," Hawkins answered, passing his fingers through his hair.

"He's a Watcher of sorts. He's to take stock of the events of the game and relay information to the club."

Iris bristled. Spectators indeed.

"That's how it works," Hawkins said, almost amused. "We do the fighting. They hear the stories the next day without ever having to risk themselves in the process."

"But depending on how big the battleground is, with seven teams, how could Fool take stock of it all?" Iris asked.

Jinn stroked his chin with a finger. "He must be like us."

Iris nodded. "Which means he was at the fair that day too." And instead of a player, he was a servant of the Committee. But what was the full extent of his power? That's what Iris wanted to know.

"By the way," Jinn said, his dangerous gaze sliding to Hawkins, "who's your Patron?"

An awkward silence followed. Thanks to Adam's list, Iris's team was well aware. But this was a test.

Jinn doubting his friends' loyalties clearly annoyed Max. "Come on now, mate," he said with a sour expression. "You don't need to—"

"Maximo, your friends were the ones who suggested this alliance, weren't they?" Jinn replied without taking his eyes off Hawkins, who returned his suspicions with an amused look.

"Boris Bosch," Jacob finally answered. "The arms dealer from Germany. Under the banner of the black wolf."

From what Adam had told them in the British Museum, Bosch was a man who sold weapons to the powerful, even leaders of countries. That was the type of person who made up the Enlightenment Committee.

"Thanks, Jacob," said Max. Jacob nodded.

The old friends seemed to have a lot of faith in each other. She wasn't sure whether that was something to worry about. But Jacob radiated a sense of genuine kindness, quiet and pure, that relaxed her suspicions nonetheless.

"And you have Adam Temple." Cherice tapped her chin. "Didn't we see him at Club Uriel the last time we were there? He's a handsome bloke."

"Very handsome." Hawkins's expression was mischievous and bright. "I'm jealous." Jacob responded with a slight roll of his eyes but said nothing.

Adam . . . handsome? An uncomfortable sensation prickled Iris from the inside as she remembered him holding her close to him.

"See that?" Max snapped his fingers. "We're getting along well, aren't we? I knew an alliance could work. To be honest, we've memorized a list of teams Temple gave us."

"Oh, he really fancies you," Cherice said with a mocking smile as Iris blushed and Jinn grimaced. Max gave Cherice a soft knock on the head.

"We'll fill you in. For now, all we have to do is help each other pass this first test."

"Just a shame you ended up with a key that sticks out so much." Hawkins seemed to enjoy prodding Jinn, flinching not in the least when he was met with the latter's steel glare. "You should be careful. Shiny objects tend to lure predators."

"Don't concern yourself with me," Jinn responded coldly. "I'm always careful."

"By the way, anyone know where we're headed?" Cherice asked.

"A zoo in Manchester," Jacob answered. "I overheard one of the other champions. Belle Vue, I think it's called." And after that, the group dispersed for the train, Team Hawkins to their own car, with Max and Jinn following Iris to another.

Belle Vue Gardens . . . Iris now sat on the leather seat in her train car, watching out the window as the countryside rolled by under the night sky. Her thoughts began to turn to the British Museum, to her bones in the display. The first tournament would take place inside a zoo, just like where she and Agnus had been trapped so many years ago. *Gorton Zoo.* She shuddered. Surely that was part of the reason she was filled with such dread.

Jinn must have felt her trembling beside him. He took her hand. His touch made her breath hitch, but her body warmed as the reassuring look he gave her melted some of the tension within her. Large hands and such a gentle touch. Iris was thankful for it, for *him*, though the thought of telling him so made her slightly embarrassed. While Max looked out the window, Iris placed her own hand over Jinn's, giving him a helpless little smile before pulling her hands away. Now was the time to concentrate. Now was the time to be strong.

But as the train took them into Belle Vue through the arched Longsight Entrance, a wave of dread returned to her. Her heartbeat quickened and her palms began to sweat. It wasn't just the tournament or what awaited her here. There was something . . . off about this place. Something she couldn't quite put words to, though her body reacted to it as if recoiling from a menace.

What was this place, really?

Outside her window, Iris could see gardens and groupings of trees everywhere, and a long exhibition hall through the window to her right. She was sure the Committee had arranged for the zoo to be empty of staff in the dark of night. But what about the leopard and bird houses? The bears, elephants, and monkeys? Wolves, ostriches, and giraffes? From what they could glean of the map they were given by one of the guards, the zoo boasted many beasts. Iris couldn't be sure they'd all be kept in their cages.

They exited their cars in the order of the ticket they drew at the music hall. Five minutes separated the exit of each team, giving them all enough time to hide in the zoo. Even after you stole someone's key, the first round wouldn't end until the three hours were up. There were no guarantees until the clock ran out. It meant every team had to have a strategy.

Unlike Cherice's knifelike cards, Jacob's and Hawkins's abilities were more suited to escape than battle. She knew they'd be hiding well.

"Stay close to me," Jinn whispered to Iris, his blades in hand, as they stepped out onto the grass. Iris had tried to memorize all the information Adam had given them, but now as fear and trepidation hollowed out her insides, there were some names and abilities she couldn't quite remember. Worse still, she could focus on little else but the disturbing feeling she'd had from the moment she'd seen Belle Vue . . .

"Remember," said Max as they passed a children's playground, the domed metal climber glistening under the moonlight. "We stay together. Under no circumstances will any of us go off alone." Max sounded a little like a general giving orders to his troops. Living on the streets with other urchins must have been good practice.

Jinn nodded. "Divide and conquer is the most obvious tactic," he said. "They won't know who has the key, so it'll be easier to try to force a one-on-one. Iris," Jinn added with a hint of urgency, "in that situation, they'll likely go after you first."

Of course, because she was a woman, a few idiots would assume she was weaker than the rest and thus easier to take out. From their perspective, even if she didn't have the key, they'd be reducing the team's numbers.

Bring it on, then, Iris thought, the blood starting to pump through her veins. She gripped her bag of blades tighter.

Em Ees Uoy Od?

The voice came in a whisper within her own mind.

Em Ees Uoy Od?

No, she wasn't imagining it. And her teammates hadn't heard it. Iris searched her surroundings until, out of the corner of her eye, she noticed a little girl with dark brown skin hiding behind a tree. Bellerose's guard? No . . .

Anne?

Iris blinked, shaking her head. Anne Marlow? The blood rushed from her face as Anne Marlow stepped out from behind the tree, reaching out to her, her solid white eyes pupil-less.

"What is this?" Iris hissed suddenly, causing Max and Jinn to look back, since she'd fallen behind. "What is this nonsense?"

But Anne Marlow simply kept her hand outstretched. *Niaga Ecno Emit Si Ti,* she said in Iris's mind.

"Iris?" Jinn touching her cheek caused a shock that pulled her away from Anne and back to her teammates. She hadn't even realized she was breathing so quickly. And when she looked again, Anne was gone.

"You all right?" Max asked.

Gone. Anne was gone. Iris placed a hand on her forehead. She was more affected than she'd originally realized by that revelation at the museum. That was it, wasn't it?

She swallowed and nodded. "I'm sorry. Don't worry."

Yes. There was nothing to worry about.

They kept themselves concealed in the bushes and shrubs, erasing their presence while they searched for enemies behind the houses and halls. But the other teams hid themselves perfectly. It wasn't until they came to a locked cage with lions that Iris heard a horrible scream coming from the east, where she remembered seeing a small lake.

Because Iris whipped around, she didn't notice the colorful marbles rolling toward them.

Max gulped. "Guys?"

Everyone looked at their feet. Little wooden ducks on wheels surrounded them. Tiny Elizabethan men straight from a Shakespearean play choppily marched their puppet legs through wind-up devices on their backs. So many toys. But no children.

"Get out of the way!" Jinn suddenly grabbed Iris's hand and pulled her away as the toys began exploding one by one. But if it weren't for Max's power, neither of them would have made it out without a missing limb. After dodging the attack, Max bent over, breathing hard, while the pink, orange, and red smoke dispersed through the air.

"What is this?" Max coughed, covering his mouth. "What's happening?"

"Exploding toys . . ." Iris coughed into her sleeve.

Toys. It could only be one person.

And then Iris felt the point of a knife pressed into her back. She sighed.

"Is this Henry's doing?" Iris asked her assailant.

"My, my, you've done your research." It was the voice of the old woman she'd seen in the theater.

Before the woman could stab her, Iris elbowed her in the face and kicked her in the shins, then once the woman was off balance, Iris gave her a fast forearm across the jaw.

"We're not going to hell, are we?" Max said, scratching the back of his head at the sight of the old woman heaving. "Even as a kid, I never hit old ladies . . ."

But Iris had no qualms about doing it and didn't feel bad at all about the guttural yell that escaped the woman's throat.

"Miss Lucille!" a girl cried from behind the cage. Mary. "Stay right there, I'll heal you—" The girl gasped and covered her mouth. Apparently she was meant to keep her own powers a secret.

Lucille rolled her eyes and charged in with her knife again, only to be blocked by Jinn's blades. After flipping her aged body back, she smirked. "My, my, this first attack was quite the failure," she said.

The more Iris thought about it, the faker her "old maid" voice sounded. And then she remembered what Adam had written.

"Shape-shifter." Iris's accusation was met only with a twinkle in the old maid's eye.

"Shall we retreat, then, my doves?" the woman said.

Team Iris had been so focused on the unusually nimble old lady that they hadn't spotted Henry sneaking out from his hiding spot. Now he was out in full sight next to the lions' cage. "Not before causing a little mayhem." He spat gum into his palm and stuck it to the lock.

His team bolting from the area was enough cause for Iris to realize his plan. And once the cage lock blew open, Team Iris was running as well, with ravenous beasts hot on their trail.

"Max!" Iris cried, and she didn't have to say another word. Iris blinked twice, sucked in several breathes—and suddenly the three of them were behind a refreshment stand watching the lions barrel down the cobbled path toward the elephant house. Out of sight.

"You realize how heavy you are, mate?" Max said, his back against the wall next to Iris.

"*Excuse* me?" Iris said, trying to catch her own breath.

"I meant *him*." Max flicked his head toward Jinn. "You still have it?"

Jinn nodded. *It*. The key. As long as they had that, they were still in the game.

Iris bent over. Exploding toys, knives, lions. It hadn't even been an hour yet. Well, Fool did say anything goes. Seemed like everyone had decided to set their morality ablaze if it meant getting that massive cash prize. Or maybe it was easier to do if you thought everyone else would be doing the same. How were they going to keep this up to the end?

"Iris," Jinn hissed, and when Iris looked up, her blood chilled.

Fool. Fool was crouched in the tree directly behind them, curiously writing in a pocket book. His cape billowed in the wind, which grew stronger by the minute, as the gold paint on his harlequin mask glittered beneath the stars. He was recording the events for the club.

"Enjoying the show?" Max spat.

At this, Fool stood up on his branch, bowed, and made his way through the branches.

"We can't hide here forever," said Jinn after a while. "We need to think. Get on the offensive and start doing the hunting."

It was all well and good but proved easier said than done. Someone dashed out from the shadows just as a flash of blinding light burst around them. Iris protected her eyes with her arms, but soon she could tell something was wrong with her vision. The zoo was shrinking and expanding, the starry sky above closing in on her with a shocking suddenness. She dropped her bag. The grass shifted one way and the ground another. Dizzy. She felt dizzy—too dizzy to fight off the hand that gripped her mouth and began dragging her away from her team.

Someone was yelling for her, but she couldn't tell who. Her mind swirled as the stars above dipped and danced around her, making a mockery of her senses.

Her senses. It was like they'd gone haywire.

And as if to confirm it, her sight went dark.

23

IRIS'S SENSES RETURNED IN TIME TO feel a thick rope tying her to the rough bark of a tree. She could see bits of the moon between the treetops. Once her dizziness subsided, she realized she was sitting on the grass and could hear the rough panting of a deep voice, followed by a smack and a grunt.

"Stop heaving like a fat bloody hog in heat, it's *disgusting*."

Two goons in dark suits argued with each other, one holding his bald head from the blow it'd just received, the other holding onto his bowler hat as his partner prepared to retaliate.

"Stop."

A young woman stepped out from the darkness. Deep brown skin. Long golden skirt swishing back and forth across her shins as she moved elegantly into Iris's line of sight. A black jacket open just enough so Iris could see her brassiere of pearl-colored beads. Long rivers of braids streaming down her back, stray strands loose over the yellow veil covering her face.

It was *her*.

Her black hat and yellow veil covered her well, but Iris could still see the scars of battle on her hands as if lovingly crafted. Iris tensed. Even if she weren't tied up, this would be a pickle to get out of. This girl wasn't one to fall so easily.

She Who Does Not Fall, whispered the girl's voice in her memories.

"Oi, Rin!" The man with the bowler hat grabbed her arm, which, though toned, was slender enough to almost fit inside his grungy palm. It was then that Iris remembered how young she must have been, though her delicate ferocity seemed ages beyond her. "We brought the girl here."

"Almost killed myself in the bloody process," muttered the bald man, still holding his head. The flash of light and the disruption of her senses. It was their doing, without a doubt. Iris remembered those two from Adam's list.

"Now what?" Bowler waited, but received only a slight shift of Rin's head in response.

"Idiot, she doesn't understand English, remember?" said Baldie, only too happy to return the strike he'd received. "Just keep using French like you did before. Bellerose said she understands a bit of that."

"I already told you I'm not fluent. Damn it. Feels like I'm gargling cotton balls. Whose stupid idea was it putting this filthy wog on the team?"

"Bellerose said she's an *Amazon*." The bald man smirked. "Bollocks. Just remember, once we win, we'll kill her and take the money for ourselves. Beats grave digging."

It was astounding how brazen people were when they thought those around them couldn't understand. Perhaps the girl called Rin really didn't, but she wasn't stirred much either way. After the hatted man tried to speak to her in French, she turned so sharply toward him that he nearly stumbled back and fell in horror.

"Her teammates will be looking for this girl, but I will *not* be interrupted." She spoke in the same language she had in the auction house. A language Iris understood—a relic of her past. "Separate them and attack individually using the dark as your cover."

She gave orders like a seasoned general, but it didn't matter to two thugs who had neither the language skills nor the intellectual capacity to understand them. At the look on their dumbfounded faces, Rin let out an almost imperceptible sigh—the only time when her youth seemed to crack through her icy veneer. "Divide," she said in broken English. "Attack." And for good measure, she grabbed their shoulders and shoved the both of them in opposite directions, using short hand gestures to make it clearer.

"I think she wants us to attack the others," said the bald man.

"Hold on a bloody second." Bowler angrily wiped his long nose with the back of his hand. "Why do we even need to take orders from her in the first place?"

At that, Baldie gave her a shining grin. "Might just kill her now and be done with it." He moved toward her, flashing yellow teeth. "What do you say, old bo—"

Iris wondered why he hadn't noticed the long blade strapped to the back of Rin's jacket. Long with a large wooden handle, its razor edge was now pointed at his neck, grazing the tip of his nervously bobbing Adam's apple.

But Iris knew from their last battle—that was not her true sword.

The two men stumbled back and ran, disappearing into the trees. Iris hadn't the time to worry about the others; Rin's gaze had already returned to her.

Quietly, Iris reminded herself as she continued to search the dirt until she found a sharp little rock she could use as a makeshift knife. Living in a circus, she'd seen enough escape artists to pick up a few tricks of her own. But she'd have to be extraordinarily careful not to be caught by the girl watching her from behind the yellow veil.

"My name is Olarinde," said the girl in her native tongue, easily flipping the heavy sword around so its tip pointed toward the grass. "Rin. Youngest among the Nyekplohento."

The Reaper Regiment. That was what the word meant.

"Oh-laa-rin-day," Iris whispered, committing the name to memory.

"I've been waiting for this opportunity to speak with you, Isoke."

There was that name again. Familiar and foreign at the same time. Iris tried to keep her heart rate steady as she continued cutting her binds.

"I know you can understand me." She lowered her head. Iris kept her lips pressed tight. "Do you know why I've come to this gaudy land of gears and sickness?"

"I remember," Iris said. "To bring me back to your . . . your king."

"Stop speaking that *ridiculous* language," Rin spat out in disgust. "You are from the Kingdom of Dahomey. Speak your tongue: Fon. Or are you ashamed?"

Fon. Yoruba. What other languages did Iris know? Just who *was* she in the past?

Rin took a step closer, inspecting her with interest. "No. You've been in this land for so long you've *lost* your tongue, haven't you?"

There was no contempt in her tone; only the sympathy that came from understanding loss. Iris tried to form words in Fon, but she simply did not have the muscle memory to speak the language.

What she wanted to ask was: Why? Why did this girl want to take her? Rin was a clue to who Iris was *before* that fateful day in South Kensington. She was a piece of the truth that Iris both feared and wished for.

"Half a century you've been missing from the Kingdom of Dahomey. Some believed you'd died a final death. But the king, the military—those who'd seen you in battle—always believed we would find you again. Who else could survive but She Who Does Not Fall, the warrior who could withstand any blow dealt to her? And now you reappear here like a lost animal caught in a thicket. But you're not as I expected." Rin straightened her back. In that moment, she understood. "You've lost your memories."

It was not just her quick assessment of her situation that surprised Iris, but how casually Rin accepted that a woman could live for fifty years without aging.

Rin held the wooden pole of her blade with two hands, staring down its sharp length.

"Ever since I was transformed, I've been able to sense the white crystal, faintly," Rin told her.

White crystal? Iris furrowed her brow.

"I followed it to the mining site in Yorubaland. Then to this land, where I met Bellerose. When she told me about this tournament of monsters, I somehow knew I would find you here. You who once fought more monstrously than anyone." Rin turned her back to her, just as Iris felt the rope loosen. "Tell me. Why do you fight *now*?"

Finally, the ropes fell. Iris rose quietly, nimbly to her feet. Her goal was to slip behind the tree while Rin wasn't looking, but she hadn't taken two steps before Rin spoke again.

"It's to know yourself, isn't it? To know your past."

Iris froze. Rin didn't turn, even though by now she must have heard Iris move. The light of the moon continued to filter through the treetops.

"What else could you want?" Rin said.

And, after spinning around, *launched* the sword at her.

For a moment, Iris's heart stopped, but the blade dug into the ground just at her feet.

Then Iris saw it—the hilt of Rin's sword, her *true* sword, burrowing out of her chest until the bloodless white blade exited her body, sparkling under the starlight. A sword as tall as Rin was.

"If you wish to know who you are, then pick up the sword at your feet and fight me."

Iris hesitated, staring at the weapon.

"No? Then let me give you further incentive." Rin reached into her jacket pocket and placed her skeleton key around her neck. The iron rested flat against her dark chest. "You need this to win the first round. Me? I couldn't care less. I have my mission in front of me."

Iris's hands squeezed into tight fists as her eyes lapped up the sight of the key.

"Fight me, Isoke," Rin said again. "You may not remember your true self. But trust me: your body will."

24

AS RIN EXPECTED, IRIS'S BODY REMEMBERED: how to hold the heavy wooden handle—long like a pole, with a razor-sharp blade at the top; how to wield it so she could meet each of Rin's blows with surprising precision. It was a one-on-one battle in the night, both of them dodging and charging, aiming and searching for vulnerabilities.

Iris's blood began to boil from the thrill of it as something dangerous stirred deep within her. She could tell Rin was holding back. Somehow knowing that *angered* her. And as her weapon clashed against Rin's pure-white blade, Iris's body shook with dread, fear, and excitement; her bones were telling her something: a secret from her memories.

Soon, Iris cornered Rin against a tree. Without hesitating, Iris launched the blade at her, shocked at herself the moment it left her hands. What was she thinking? Iris wasn't interested in a battle to the death. How had her excitement turned into a lust for bloodshed so quickly?

Rin easily dodged with a leap and the blade plunged into the tree. Landing catlike upon the ground, she flipped over her sword and waited. Struggling to regain herself, Iris moved quickly over to the tree and pulled the weapon out only to be met with Rin's sidelong look.

"Once upon a time," Rin said, "there were two girls who lived in two different eras under two different kings but were given the same name: She Who Does Not Fall."

Iris's weapon trembled in her grip, her breaths short as she tried to calm herself. But Rin, far more in control of her body and emotions, used Iris's hesitation to attack again.

"The first girl was kidnapped and taken to the Dahomey people from a neighboring Yoruba tribe." Rin cocked her head. "That was sixty years ago. Do you remember, Isoke?"

Shaken, Iris lunged for Rin, only for the warrior to jump and land on top of Iris's sword hilt with her thick black boots, causing Iris's arms to buckle. As the tip of the blade plunged into the earth, the girl pointed her sword at Iris.

"She was trained as a warrior, a raider. She was a woman who could not die no matter how many battles she fought. An unimaginable and *terrible* power that many thought was gifted to her by the moon deity, Gleti."

Iris swung the pole again, using her nimble body to force the girl back.

"Favored among the *ahosi*," Rin continued after meeting Iris's blade with hers. "Favored by the previous king, King Ghezo. She Who Does Not Fall. Child of the Moon Goddess."

Iris *didn't* remember, but she knew Rin wasn't lying. She could feel it. They clashed swords again, Iris leaning back when Rin charged, dodging by the skin of her teeth.

"But *was* it the goddess who gave her these gifts or the necklace of white crystal, always around her neck, that kept her safe?"

Iris's eyes followed the unnatural white of Rin's blade, then suddenly remembered Doctor Pratt's cuff links. Blinding-white stone.

"And so brings us to the second girl." Rin jumped back, pointing her sword to the ground. "I too came from the Yoruba tribe. Captured in a raid and marked as a slave. It was only after I transformed, after I was gifted this soul sword, that I was given a chance to survive. With this sword, I became unstoppable in battle. Another She Who Does Not Fall, of sorts. I was trained to surpass you who had disappeared all those years ago."

Iris shook her head. It was too much information to take in at once. She stumbled back, the pole nearly falling from her grip.

"It wasn't until an explorer visited our lands that my king began to believe you were still alive. That explorer seemed obsessed with your mystery. His name was John Temple."

The pole finally fell from Iris's hands. She stared into the girl's yellow veil.

"You've heard of him," Rin said. It wasn't a question. "Isoke, did you know that you were brought to the Dahomey merely weeks after the Day of Darkness?"

"The Day of Darkness?" Iris repeated in a faint whisper.

"A global eclipse that plunged the world into night. Our astronomers had their theories. It wasn't until Temple came to us that we were able to corroborate them. So is it a coincidence? Or is your very existence foretold by the gods?"

"Stop it." Iris gripped her forehead.

"And yet you belong to the king. To the Dahomey Kingdom. You're for us alone to use."

"Use." Iris bowed her head. "*Use.* Everyone thinks they own me, don't they? But this body is mine . . ."

She thought of Coolie. The auction house. The Committee and their tournament. And—

Doctor Seymour Pratt. Memories of him fell around her like shards of glass, a man of science grinning over her body as pain flooded her senses. His white crystal cuff link . . .

"This body is *mine.*"

Iris trembled with frightening rage until her weapon was back in her hands and she was slashing at Rin's body with a bloodlust that felt as natural as it did otherworldly. Even Rin was unprepared. The girl did her best to meet every lunge with her sword, but Iris could tell that she was overwhelmed. Good. *Good.*

"Stop toying with me," Iris grunted, and then threw her weapon to the ground. "All of you, *stop toying with me!*"

She lunged at Rin and, with one guttural yell, grabbed the girl's yellow veil and pulled it violently from her face. Rin stumbled back in shock, her sword flying from her hands and shattering into smoke against a tree. Then she fell to the ground when Iris leaped on top of her. Iris looked into the girl's surprisingly delicate young face. She couldn't have been more than sixteen. And it wasn't until she noticed those features—the small chestnut-brown nose, thick brows, and a scar rendering her right eye useless—that Iris snapped back to her senses, realizing her hands were around Rin's thin neck.

Iris loosened her grip. "Your eye," she whispered. The long purple scar was deep, creating a crevice in the closed lid.

Rin must have understood the word "eye," because her lips trembled into a smile. "Though we were given the same name, I was never as good as you, Isoke."

A flash of light burst in the distance, and then an explosion of fire. The commotion grabbed both Iris's and Rin's attention, but Iris responded faster. With one swift movement, she punched Rin in the face, knocking her out.

Her team was in trouble. She couldn't stay here any longer. She had to go help them. It was the one clear thing in the thick muddle of her mind as she yanked the skeleton key off Rin's neck and ran toward the light.

Iris wanted to call out to Jinn and Max, but if she announced herself, it would give away the one advantage she had: the element of surprise. She saw the two of them as she entered a small clearing next to the zoo's refreshment hall, and Hawkins's team as well. Hawkins and Cherice were struggling with their senses, courtesy of Rin's teammate, no doubt.

"Max!" Cherice called out, holding her head and falling to the ground. "Where are you?"

"Jacob!" Hawkins yelled. "Are you okay?"

Jacob was nearly passed out by a nearby tree. Max and Jin were tending to him, struggling to lift him up.

"It's all right," Max said. "It's gonna be all right."

Iris surveyed the area. Their enemy must have been hiding somewhere and probably got the jump on Team Hawkins first since Max and Jinn were fine.

Darkness, Iris thought, remembering Rin's command. *Use the dark as your cover.* Iris began to search the trees.

"Found you," she said, spotting Baldie's large bottom peeking out through the branches. She wasn't sure if he was the guy who'd scrambled their senses or blinded them with light. Either way, she'd have to be careful getting to him.

As quietly as she could, she threw a small pebble with surprising precision at Jinn's head. He frowned, his fists up and ready to fight until he spotted her behind an empty firework stand. They didn't need words. She flicked her head toward the tree, and with that, Jinn left Jacob to Max and followed her.

Iris and Jinn snuck around the tall tree, and Jinn already knew what to do.

"Ready?" he whispered.

"Aren't I always?"

Jinn smirked. Then, using his hands, he boosted her into a lift they'd done a thousand times. Iris flipped up so high it almost surprised her, but Jinn had meant business. She caught Baldie's branch one-handed.

The bald man's pupils dilated at the sight of her, and he cried out in a jumbled-up language, sounding pained just speaking it, as if his throat were on fire.

Jacob. At some point, he must have tried to make sure Bowler and Baldie couldn't communicate with each other. Who knew where Bowler had escaped to.

She launched at him before he could attack her, swinging around the branch and kicking him out of the tree with all her might. He landed with a horrible crack just as a purring brown cat slinked out from behind some roots. As she stared at the little animal, baffled, Jinn knocked Baldie unconscious.

"Iris!" cried Cherice, loud and shrill from the clearing. She stumbled back and sat on the ground with a thump. "Iris! Girly, is that you?"

"You okay?" Max stood, wiping the sweat off his forehead.

Iris nodded, showing him Rin's key. But before she could say anything, the brown cat jumped at her, grabbing the key with his teeth and scurrying away.

Adam's list. She forgot—there was someone other than the "old lady" among the champions who could shape-shift.

"You've got to be kidding me!" Iris looked at Max and nodded. "After that cat!"

Iris gave chase with Jinn by her side. But Max didn't move. The supernaturally fast cat continued toward the lake, but when Iris looked behind her, Max was talking to Hawkins. Then, before she could call out to him, Hawkins grabbed Max, Cherice, and Jacob and pulled them out of sight into the darkness. They disappeared. Hawkins's power.

Damn it, Max, where did you go? Iris gritted her teeth. Jacob had his own teammates to look after him, didn't he? With Max's power, she and Jinn could have caught the cat by now.

Past the trees and animal houses. The cat finally slowed down from fatigue enough for Jinn to launch himself forward and catch it right on the bank of the small lake. The moment he did, the cat transformed into a chubby man who struggled in his grasp. Which one was he? As blood pumped in her ears, she couldn't remember his name. Guess it didn't matter. As long as they got their key back.

Jinn had his blades strapped to his back with a rope. He wouldn't need them to take care of this guy, whoever he was. But Cat was far spryer in his human form than Iris realized. With a cowardly yell, he kicked Jinn back, slipping from his grip, and darted past Iris, dropping the skeleton key in fear several paces behind her by some thick bushes.

Jinn picked up the key. She could see his grimace from here. "It's still slobbery," he complained.

"Well, it was in a man's teeth."

"It stinks."

"At least we have it back," Iris said with a little laugh. Max was still nowhere in sight.

"That makes two keys," Jinn said, patting his pocket.

"Good." Iris turned toward the lake. The tournament was three hours long and she couldn't tell how much time was left. They just had to wait things out until it ended.

She looked at her reflection in the lake, and as it rippled gently, she could have sworn she saw Rin's face instead. The girl had told her that Iris was once a warrior in Dahomey, kidnapped from a neighboring region. It explained why she understood languages from a time she couldn't remember. But what was this *white crystal* Rin kept talking about? What did it have to do with her?

"Jinn," she said, her eyes still upon the water. "There's something I need to tell you."

But her mind blanked the moment she turned around and found the man with the sagging jowls slipping out from some bushes behind Jinn.

"Jinn!" Iris screamed, but it was too late.

The Exploding Man grabbed Jinn and, before Jinn could escape his grip, set off an explosion of electricity.

25

THE EXPLODING MAN WENT OFF LIKE a bomb. It was over in an instant, the damage done, and now he was squatting above Jinn's burnt body, ready to pluck Rin's key from his twitching fingers.

Iris launched at him, shrieking. It didn't matter that he jumped back and began sparking once again. Iris wrapped her hands around his neck, screaming in pain from the electrical current, howling in fury but refusing to let go.

The Exploding Man couldn't breathe. As if her vise grip were a candle snuffer, the electricity evaporated, and he fell back. Iris stood over him, body and clothes in a shambles, with an expression that would terrify a demon. He could see her body was already healing. Scrambling back, he ran off, leaving Jinn with the keys.

She would heal, but Jinn couldn't. His shirt and pants were torn, his naked, exposed back bloodied and burnt. Tears welled up in Iris's eyes as she turned him over. He was only just breathing.

"What do I do?" Iris wiped her face, still throbbing in pain from the electrical burns. "Jinn, what do I do?" Her whole body trembled as she held his head against her lap.

Cold water. Cold water! Whenever she burnt herself cooking, Granny would always bring her a pack of ice, not knowing that her wound would heal on its own.

Shaking terribly, Iris wrapped Jinn's arm around her and stood, leaving the key on the ground, forgetting it entirely. She dragged him as fast as she could toward the lake. Then, wrapping her arms around him, she jumped into the icy water.

Bobbing in the waves, she lifted up his head while keeping one arm linked around his waist, examining his unconscious face, his dark hair floating around him. She was relieved when he started coughing. But he was still barely conscious. It took all her strength to keep them both floating, hoping with everything she had that the chilly waters soothed his pain like it did hers, but he needed more than this.

"I-Iris . . . ," he croaked as she dragged him back onto the shore and laid him against the thick bushes.

"It's okay," Iris lied, watching his eyes struggling to open. His lips were trembling, his throat sounding sore with her name on his tongue. Water. She could get him water.

She ran to the lake and held as much as she could in her mouth. Then, as carefully as she could, she tilted Jinn's head back and pried apart his lips.

Jinn . . . She couldn't stop the tears trailing down her cheeks as she cupped his face, lifted it toward her, and emptied the water into his mouth. Slowly, gently. Jinn's long lashes fluttered rapidly, his hand weakly rising up against her arm.

"Jinn," she said, noticing a bit of his strength return. "Are you okay?"

His hand continued moving up until it touched her face. Then his other hand. His eyes, half-open, stayed on her as he kept her face near his.

"More," he whispered hoarsely, and drew her face closer. "I need more . . ." And closer. Iris shivered, her heart crashing against her chest as her lips drew so close to his that his breath slid into her mouth. "Iris . . ."

His body gave out as he fell unconscious.

Shaken, Iris left him for a moment to grab the key she'd left behind, but then returned to his side immediately. She needed help. Someone. Anyone!

"Iris! Are you okay? God!" Max. He ran up to her and turned her around, gripping her shoulders tightly. "I'm sorry, Jacob was hurt, and the others needed me." He was speaking so quickly, she could barely understand. He checked her face, hands, and arms before he finally noticed Jinn behind her. "What?" He gaped. "What happened?"

"*They* needed you?" Iris grabbed his shirt. "*We* needed you!"

Max took in the sight of Jinn, horrified. "Well, I . . ." He paused, guilt killing his words.

"*Jinn* needed you!" Iris gazed up at him, tears streaming down her face. "I thought we were a *team*."

Max shifted, his breath heaving, his eyes darting around, not knowing where to look. "What should I do?" he asked with a hollow expression.

Iris held her head and thought. "The girl . . ." A deep intake of breath brought the girl's image to mind. "The girl with the blond French braid. On Henry's team. Mary! She can heal. Max!" She pierced him with a glare, the very sight of him making her furious. "You have to find her and bring her here! Do whatever you can!"

Swallowing, Max nodded. "What about you?"

Iris's lip trembled. "I won't leave him. I'm not like *you*."

Iris was too angry to regret what she said, even seeing the look that crossed his face at her words. Max stood up, his body stiff, his lips flattened into a thin line. He didn't argue. Didn't retort. He simply took off, disappearing with the blink of her eye.

Iris wiped her tears as quickly as they fell because she had to stay alert. They had two keys, but there was still time left in this hellish round. There was no telling how long it would take Max to find that girl, Mary, or if he'd find her at all. Until then, she had to protect Jinn.

"You'll make it, Jinn," she promised, removing a strand of wet hair from his cheek. "You have to—you still haven't told me your real name."

And for just one fleeting moment she let herself break down, pressing his head against hers.

Thirty minutes. No, closer to an hour. Max hadn't returned yet. Jinn was still breathing, but for how long?

Iris didn't dare move him any more than she already had. Instead, she kept watch for any approaching enemies. At this point, even if one managed to sneak up on them, all she'd be able to do in this situation was guard Jinn.

Her nerves flared, the hairs on her arm standing on end as she waited.

But she didn't have to wait long.

He sauntered up to them, whistling. A few marks on his face but otherwise none the worse for wear.

Barry Bately.

Iris shot up to her feet, fists ready.

"Come on, woman." He tilted his head to the side, amused as he swung a pair of keys in plain sight. "You know that won't be much use against me."

He was right. But what confused her was the fact that he already had a pair of keys. So what business did he have with her?

"Oh, these?" Bately said when he saw her staring. "Can never have too many, can you? Especially if you don't want anyone else to get that mysterious advantage for the final round."

Iris gritted her teeth and squeezed her fists tighter. She had to think, and think fast.

Bately seemed to relish the moment before he used his power. Seemed to love choosing the most evil words he could think of. And she could smell the bloodthirsty malice from here.

"Do me a favor, love," he said, his voice now sounding deep and hollow as if it'd fallen down a well. "I'm Queen Victoria of this here England, you see. So take that rock over there—yes, that sharp one. And prove your loyalty by stabbing yourself in the neck." He paused and then could barely contain his laughter when he added, "Oh, and while you're doing it, I want you to say, 'God save the queen,' all right? Just for the fun of it."

Iris didn't struggle with her arm as it reached for the sharp rock at her feet, didn't fight it when her mind went blank and her smile widened into a dream-like grin. What a strange request. But he'd requested it, after all.

That's why she yelled, with all her might, "God save the queen!" And stabbed herself in the neck.

"Good show!" Bately yelled as Iris fell to the ground next to an unconscious Jinn in a pool of her own blood. It was the last she saw of him before she died.

The wound was easy enough for her body to heal. She kept her eyes only half-open after she awoke to the sound of him rolling on the ground in laughter. "Amazing! 'God save the queen.' Bloody *brilliant*!" She wondered how long he'd been rolling there.

Soon he was on his feet. Dusting himself off, he quickly approached Jinn, just like she knew he would. As he squatted down to grab the keys, Iris's foot came flying to his face.

Bately stumbled back, wiping blood from his busted lip. Iris still wasn't completely healed. One wrong move and it felt as if her head would sever. And Bately was serious now. She could tell by the look in his eyes that he was readying his silver tongue yet again. So Iris did the only thing she could think of.

She covered her ears and started singing. *Loudly.*

"God save our gracious Queen! Long live our noble Queen! God save the Queen!"

While he was staring in shock, she leaped and kicked him in the face again.

"Send her victorious!" She kneed him in the stomach. "Happy and glorious!" Kicked his shins. "Long to reign over us!" A nasty headbutt that nearly split his forehead in two. "God save the *Queen*!" And one final punch to send him flying.

Iris checked Bately's immobile body on the ground. Unconscious. Served him right. She held her neck in pain, its flesh still weaving itself back to perfection. "The queen." Iris scoffed.

She tore off a piece of her dress and shoved it in the mercenary's mouth. Then she took his keys for good measure. "Can never have too many," she said with a smirk before going back to Jinn's side.

It wasn't long before Max came back, Mary flat against his chest, his hand over her mouth. He dumped her at Jinn's feet.

"I-I don't have our key!" Mary said, her eyes glistening with tears. The poor thing was terrified, but Iris wasn't in the mood to care.

"We don't want your key. We want your powers." Max pointed at Jinn. "Heal him."

Mary looked at Jinn's burns and pursed her lips. "Wh-why should I?"

"Because if you don't, *I'll kill you slowly.*" Iris's blood was boiling, her eyes blazing. She truly didn't care. If this girl wasted any more time, Iris would tear her apart.

Mary trembled, her hands pressed against her chest. Max sighed. "Look. Just do this for us, and we'll help you out later, okay? It's a promise."

Iris was incensed at how polite Max was being. It wasn't until she saw Mary weave her magic, running her hands just above Jinn's body as if playing a harp, that the murderous blood in her finally calmed and she was back to herself. She sat and watched the gold trails Mary's fingers made in the air. Like shooting stars.

"Why in the world are you involved in this competition?" she asked Mary suddenly. "A girl like you . . ."

Mary shot her an angry look. Of course she would. The captor asking the captive a question. "That's none of your business."

"Looking for a better job than being Mr. Whittle's servant?" offered Max. Mary inhaled in surprise, but he shrugged. "Why else would you call a boy younger than you *Mister*?"

Mary bit her lip. "I would never leave the Whittle family. Not after they gave me a home. I would never betray them. And you won't make me!"

She must have mistaken this for an interrogation because there was a defiant lilt to her tone to go along with the fear. But all Iris could think about in that moment was Jinn and Granny. The two who'd given *her* a home. Her eyes softened as she watched Jinn's wounds heal.

Em Ees Llits Uoy Od.

Iris's head snapped up, and she searched around her. Anne? Iris thought she saw the girl standing on the lake, but she had to be wrong. It was a mistake, a trick fueled by trauma. After squeezing her eyes shut, she concentrated solely on Jinn and refused to look anywhere else.

Finally, Mary stood. "He should be okay in a few days."

Iris raised an eyebrow. "Why isn't he okay *now*?"

But Iris understood. Leverage. Mary didn't want three champions chasing after her. It didn't matter. Iris was done. She just wanted this to end.

"Thank you," she said with an exhausted sigh. And when she waved Mary off, the girl didn't waste any time. She ran from them as fast as she could.

A few more agonizing minutes of waiting by a sleeping Jinn, and suddenly Iris heard footsteps approaching. Not a competitor.

Fool.

"The three hours are up," he told them, probably grinning under his harlequin mask. "Good show, good show! Please make your way to your private car, if you have the strength to."

Fool bowed, indicating the way with a gentlemanly gesture. Iris could have spit in his face.

She passed by him without a word instead. Max carried Jinn on his back after placing the two pairs of keys around his neck. She was glad to finally be rid of this place, this tainted zoo that played tricks on her mind.

They began the slow march back to their train, neither of them saying a word. The weight of everything she'd experienced kept her pace languid as she trudged along. Her mind's chatter grew fainter and fainter with each step.

But then, once her mind was fully blank, her body began to move on its own.

"Iris?" Max called to her, but she ignored him.

The panic of battle had dulled it, but now with her body calmed by extreme fatigue, it flared up again inside of her—*familiarity*. Like when she had found Granny at Coolie's.

Anne appeared in front of her again, her hand outstretched, and Iris could no longer fight her. Anne wasn't *Anne*. Now that Iris had let her mind go, she knew it deep within her soul. But whoever this was—*whatever* it was—it was something entirely close to her, compelling her, drawing her in. She followed Anne off the central path into another wooded area, this time filled with bright wildflowers and plants.

"Iris? Oi, Iris?"

She knew Max couldn't see what she did. He sounded very far away as she passed the flowers, plants, and trees as if in a dream. She could feel it more keenly now. The sense that she knew this place. Yes, she knew this place. She'd been here before.

"Belle Vue . . . in Manchester . . . ," she whispered. The lock in her mind began to open and ghostly wisps of a memory slipped out. A memory of three girls in an exhibit—well, two village girls . . . and the warrior who'd tried to kidnap them in a raid.

"No." She squeezed her head. "Stop it." She tried to *will* herself to wake up, but her feet continued walking forward.

"Iris!" Max called again. "What are you doing?"

The smell of blood filled her nose, slipped down her throat, and flowered in her lungs. A strong scent. It wasn't hers. Neither was the singing she could hear from the clearing.

"Belle Vue," she whispered again. But that wasn't its original name, was it? As she approached the clearing, another memory flashed in her mind's eye. An old memory of blood. Of pain.

Of massacre.

A massacre that had taken place in this very spot when the zoo had a different name.

"Gorton," she whispered, and looked up into the clearing. "Gorton Zoo."

In the clearing lay a *heinous* sight.

The vampiric man she'd seen at the music hall was covered in blood, quivering in ecstasy. Body parts lay about him as he lapped at blood from the body's open chest. The corpse was in such shambles, she couldn't even tell who it was.

Next to him, the dark-skinned man in a white priest collar and black cloak swung a golden, smoking thurible by its chain, but the incense rising from it was not strong enough to cover the smell of blood. Indeed, it was the blood that saturated her senses.

"Iris, let's go!" Max hissed, fear and urgency clear in his voice. "I said, let's *go*!"

But Iris was numb. Numb from shock and from strange, horrible feelings with no source but the shadow of memories. Gorton Zoo. This very spot now awash with blood had been home to a similar atrocity fifty years ago. The memory wasn't clear, but the *feeling* was. Something evil had happened in this exact spot.

Maybe that was what this creature who posed as Anne Marlow was trying to tell her. "Anne" stood behind the two monsters, though they couldn't see her—her thick, bristly hair a beautiful moon around her head, a single hairclip shaped as a monarch butterfly pinned near her right brow just like in the photo. It was just as she thought: only *she* could see Anne, who looked as real as flesh and blood. But *this* Anne's round eyes were white, her button nose gray, her plump lips cracked and dried. Though the air was still, her white dressed fluttered lightly.

"Anne," Iris whispered. "No. You're not her. What's your name?"

The girl only stared at her.

Iris stumbled toward the scene, but Max, focusing only on the two bloody champions, dropped Jinn and grabbed her by the elbow, pulling her back.

"What are you doing?" he yelled at her, because now the bloody vampire's eyes were on *them*. But she didn't care about the beastly man or his partner. Not when Anne was trying to tell her something. Not here in this place where she used to stand with the true Anne and her sister, Agnus, in a human exhibit, now long forgotten.

Rebmemer Lliw Uoy Yad Eno Tub. Nettogrof Evah Uoy.

Anne reached out to her, kindly. Waiting.

Nekawa.

"Iris!" Max yelled, holding Iris tightly in his arms, for she had started screaming.

The two monsters began to move toward them, stepping over the bloodied body parts strewn about the clearing. Grabbing Jinn's wrist and keeping Iris tucked in his arm, Max took a deep breath and disappeared.

INSIDE THE
LIBRARY OF RULE

THE BRITISH MUSEUM WAS WILLING TO provide as many secret areas as a powerful order was willing to pay for. The Enlightenment Committee liked to hide in plain sight. And since the museum's directors had been members of Club Uriel since the start of the century, interference from the British Crown was not an issue.

The directors did not share any information on the contents of these secret areas with the rest of the club. They also worked quickly: the Marlow display had originally been property of Paris's Museum of Man. On Adam's orders, its transfer was swift and covert, finished in time for Iris's innocent eyes. All so she could remember. If Iris hadn't taken the picture of the three Marlows with her, Adam would have destroyed it anyway to protect her.

The directors liked to imagine that they were of a higher class than a normal member. Some were even foolish enough to believe that they were already part of the Committee. Since no one in the club truly understood what being included in the Committee entailed, it was an easy enough ruse to continue—a ruse fueled by men's arrogance and desperation for status in equal parts.

Such men annoyed Adam. Those who clung to status lost sight of the truth. The power they sought was a mirage, as weightless as sunlight. The Crown. The club. The Committee. They were all the same. Ironically, it was his father who understood his feelings the most. Which was why Adam still needed to hunt him down.

Five among the Enlightenment Committee stood in the Library of Rule, deeper than the basement of the museum: Madame Bellerose, Gerolt Van der Ven, Luís Cordiero, Boris Bosch, and himself. With no windows, only lit candles hanging from candelabra on the wall brightened the glass displays showcasing the ruins of ancient civilizations kept safe from prying eyes. They'd been given the report from Fool: Most of the champions had survived the first round. Only Bosch's, Van der Ven's, and Adam's teams had managed to secure multiple keys while the other teams finished with none. Among the dead: Both of Bellerose's men. One from Benini's team who once shape-shifted into beasts. And two of Cordiero's champions—including Doug Waters, otherwise known as the Exploding Man. There wasn't even enough of him left to bury, not after what Van der Ven's men had done to him.

Gram and Jacques. Though one of Bellerose's men had been killed by Cordiero's man Bately, all the other deaths had been at the hands of those two. Adam had known what Gram and Jacques could do, but the horror of their work still chilled him to the bone. And now, much to the annoyance of the others, Van der Ven was boasting about his boars as he boasted of all his bloodied treasures.

"Beasts, the two of them. I told you I would have the strongest team. Their assassin work for King Leopold made them prime agents for the job." His thick chest bounced as he let out his rolling, gaudy laughter. "We should end the tournament now. Give me the Ark, and I'll have more time to think about how to rule the New World."

Adam shook his head but held his tongue. Van der Ven was wrong. On the other side of the apocalypse would be no "New World" for them. Only beautiful nothingness.

Adam closed his eyes and remembered attending the funeral of his sister and brother at the tender age of six. The caskets had been closed because what was left of them was too horrid to look upon. That's what the priest had said, forgetting that Adam had already seen the insides of his siblings' heads scattered upon the ground the night they were murdered.

His uncle Byron hadn't much cared about what it had done to Adam. After Adam's mother died and his uncle was given temporary custody of him while his father was out traveling the world, the drunk was quick to drink and quicker to beat Adam silly. It had taken Adam some time to get rid of Uncle Byron, but if his father hadn't left him alone to indulge his adventurous curiosities, perhaps Adam wouldn't have had to send his uncle to that asylum. Everything in Adam's life had gone wrong so early, he didn't know what was right anymore.

Except this: The Committee didn't deserve to escape to the New World. And brutes like Van der Ven were the reason the world *needed* to end.

After receiving their reports on the sixth floor of Club Uriel, Benini and Cortez had gone home, one sulking, the other planning. But here, the rest of the Committee had summoned the museum's director. It was the apocalypse that they wanted information on.

On the front wall were stones excavated from the Black Sea four decades ago by an expedition led by Julius Temple, Adam's great-grandfather and a former Committee member. Made of a substance that had the look of pure gold, each stone was only the size of baked bread, and yet together they seemed to tell a story—a tragic one, as evidenced by the chicken-scrawl drawings of faces in agony.

Julius Temple's team had estimated that the civilization the stones were made by existed twenty thousand years ago. According to Adam's grandfather, Sir Isaac Temple, the stones Adam now looked upon, trapped in their glass display, were something of an amalgam of copper and quartzite. Plato had called it orichalcum, a metal theorized to have been used to build sprawling cities, palaces, and shrines as far back as 9000 BC and found in places as far spread as the North African Atlas Mountains, Morocco, and even deep in the Atlantic. This had once been an extensive, prosperous civilization indeed. And its people had a name: the Naacal.

The Temples had spent their lives exploring, researching, and translating the strange writings inscribed upon these particular ruins. This civilization worshipped the sun—that much was clear given how prevalently solar symbols appeared on the heavy tablets, believed to be used in religious spaces.

But what drew Adam's eyes was the symbol that appeared on only two round tablets, joined together even after thousands of years. Faded, but still omnipresent. Two rings linked, one bright, one dark: a sun and its shadow. An eclipse. A nightmare, John Temple had once guessed, for a civilization that regarded the sun as the source of life itself.

An eclipse meant the end of the world. Such was the tale the circular tablets told.

"Have you been able to discern how much time is left?" Cordiero asked the director, who pored over an ancient scroll laid out on a wooden table next to a stone tomb. Adam's father had believed that the dust inside the tomb had once been a high priest of the Naacal named Nyeth. It was his writings on the table being inspected under a magnifying glass by the director.

"The Temples led the charge in deciphering the Naacalian linguistics," said the director. It was not an answer. "But everything to do with this symbol"—he pointed to the sun and its shadow—"was written in code by the Naacal. It's as if they wanted to warn future populations and yet keep what destroyed *them* a secret."

Madame Bellerose cooled herself with a luxuriously embroidered hand fan, exasperated. "Why on earth would they do that if they wanted to warn us of our own demise?"

"To test us, perhaps." Adam straightened his gloves. "To see if we're a civilization worthy of being saved. Based on my father's research, we know the Naacal were as arrogant as they were advanced. They were kind enough to warn us of the *cataclysma*. Just not kind enough to tell us when it would strike, or how."

"To think your father burned all of his research before he died." Van der Ven glared at Adam as if he were the man himself. "He was a traitor."

Not all his research, Gerolt. John Temple still had his journal. Adam stepped closer to the scroll, eyeing the drawing of a skeleton key. After seeing it for the first time in the Library of Rule, Benini had fallen so deeply in love with its unique pattern that he'd ordered blacksmiths to create several replicas from every material that suited his fancy. After Benini lost a bet to Cortez, seven of those priceless keys became the central point of the tournament's first round. But the one described here in the scrolls—*that* was the true treasure.

A skeleton key partly of pure white crystal. "The Moon Skeleton," it was called. Now in John Temple's possession.

The Committee was still hunting for it. Adam needed to get it first at all costs.

"Your late father was probably best suited to deciphering this text, Lord Temple," said the director, scratching his snow-white beard. "But I have been able to decipher the name of this symbol—the one that appears on those circular tablets behind you." The sun and its shadow.

Adam's eyebrow raised. He'd been confident that nobody but his father had been able to make sense of those symbols—a code within a code. If he hadn't had access to his father's research notes growing up or the acuity to understand them, Adam wouldn't have known either.

"And that is?" said Cordiero on the other side of the table, his arms behind his back. Adam knew that with his old body, Cordiero wouldn't be able to stand for too long.

"The Hiva," he answered.

Adam's fingers twitched, but he remained very still as the director explained his theory as to the word's meaning. It wasn't accurate, but he'd come close enough to worry Adam. He would have to keep an eye on the situation—or even have the director "replaced" if needed.

"We're sure the Crown is still clueless as to these developments?" Van der Ven demanded, and turned to Bosch, who stood in a dark corner of a room. "Well?"

Bosch was a quiet man. If Van der Ven hadn't turned to him just there, he might have gotten away with spending the duration of the meeting not speaking a single word. Sometimes he did. His words were precious—tools he used for the primary purpose of selling weapons and making his riches. He did speak, though, this time.

"It's going according to plan: The Crown believes I'm working with them. *For* them. All the while, whenever Malakar visits the Crystal Palace to inspect the wares I've sold them, she gives them false information. False information on that Helios of theirs."

The word "Helios" sent a chill through Adam. The tension in the room became thick. The greatest of the Naacal's treasures.

A doorway to the impossible.

"*Their* Helios?" Van der Ven scoffed.

"It was the Crown that found that ancient machine in Lake Victoria," Adam reminded him. "It's in their custody, so it's theirs. But without the key, there's no way to use it. And as long as Malakar continues to mislead them, they'll never figure out how."

But what if *she* one day figured out how? Uma Malakar, the head of Bosch's Weapons Development Team, was not to be trifled with. She'd been studying the Helios under Bosch's and the Committee's orders based on the specifications she'd received from the Crown. If she somehow figured out a way to operate the Helios without needing the Moon Skeleton, then Adam wouldn't need to search for his father anymore. *Malakar* would be the new threat he'd need to snuff out.

But except for her periodical visits to the Crystal Palace, the genius worked outside the country in secrecy and seclusion—and under intense security. It wasn't easy to get to her.

He was getting ahead of himself. For now he'd continue to keep his eye on the situation.

As Van der Ven pushed for more information from Bosch and the director, Madame Bellerose pulled Adam aside.

"What is it?" Adam watched Bellerose touch the white frills of her fan against her lips.

"Just a question, my dear Adam." Bellerose tilted her head. "On your request, we changed the location of the first round at the last minute."

"This is true." Adam folded his arms. "And? Were you unsatisfied with the results?"

"Not at all. I was just curious as to why."

Adam showed Madame Bellerose a tiny smile. She liked to be challenged.

"Why, madame, had I noticed you'd fallen asleep at the meeting, I would have woken you up immediately. You'll have to forgive me."

Bellerose smirked. "Oh right, you mentioned something about the obstacles, cover, and mayhem a zoo would provide."

"And wild animals," Adam reminded her. "Much more interesting than an empty field."

"But why not a zoo in the city?"

"Having them take the train, randomly drawing their turns." He shrugged. "It was a nice bit of theater. Plus, I'd been to Belle Vue as a boy. Fond memories. And the Committee accepted. So . . . any other questions?"

Madame Bellerose gave him a look he knew all too well, as if she were calmly assessing which wing to pluck off a trapped fly. "You went there as a boy. But your father went there as an adult—for his research, did he not?"

She's watching for a reaction, Adam reminded himself. *Don't give it to her.* "I didn't know you studied my father's work so closely."

"The Temple mind is a thing of beauty. It would be much stranger if I didn't, no?" Bellerose began to tap her chin with her fan. Elsewhere, Adam could hear Van der Ven and Cordiero calling his name. But Bellerose wouldn't be interrupted.

"I found out through my networks that there was a terrible tragedy in that area many decades ago," she continued. "One of those *horrid beasts* went wild and killed the visitors. Aside from that, for the life of me, I can't figure out what else about that silly zoo might have been of interest to anyone."

She was trying his patience. "You said yourself, madame. The Temple mind is a thing of beauty. But I never could figure out my father's." Adam straightened his jacket. "Now, if you'll excuse me."

Whip fast, Bellerose gripped his arm, pulling him back so violently his breath hitched in his throat. "But I'm not finished with you yet," she hissed with a candied smile on her face.

"Madame!" Cordiero approached slowly, his hands behind his back, his weak knees keeping him up longer than Adam had anticipated. "Your seat on the Committee might have you confused. Though Adam is the youngest and the last to join, he is still a Temple. And you are still a woman. Know your place."

Despite his relief at Cordiero's intrusion, Adam knew she was seething inside. That practiced smile didn't fool him. She let him go with a little bow of her head. "But of course, monsieur," she said sweetly. "In fact, it may be better if I take my leave. Lord Temple." She spread out her fan with a flick of her hand. "I'll see you soon."

Cordiero shook his head as he watched Madame leave. "A pretentious brat, she is. This is why I was opposed to women joining the Committee." He turned to Adam as the door shut with gusto. "Adam," he started as they approached the table. "You must continue to search for whatever of your father's research he may have left behind. Based on what the director has discerned, the nature of the Hiva needs to be understood more fully. I won't rest until I do. I'll devote all my resources to it."

You will, will you? Adam nodded stiffly and joined the other men at the table. As the champions fell, the competition between the Committee members narrowed. Which of them would lead humanity into its next stage of existence? The thirst for that power came with a thirst for knowledge—to reveal every secret still unknown to them. To leave no stone unturned.

Cordiero . . . what a nuisance, Adam thought, running a hand through his messy black hair.

He may have to move his knight soon, after all.

26

J INN WAS SHIVERING IN THE NIGHT, sweat dripping from his forehead as he healed from his wounds. Max had gone to bed.

"There's no point in worrying," he told her after he placed Jinn on his bed in Club Uriel. "Nothing we can do now but trust that girl, Mary. As for tonight, just try to get some sleep."

After the first round of the tournament had finished, a guard in each train car made note of how many keys each team had collected and promptly took the keys into their custody. Max had managed to sneak one of their keys to Team Hawkins beforehand so they had a pair to hand in. Afterward, the guards and teams went to Club Uriel's gentlemen's gathering room on the second floor. There, the teams saw them deposit their keys inside a solid oak box held by Fool while a subcommittee of club members played their role in the tournament by monitoring them from the corners of the room.

Iris could tell from his lingering, narrowed gaze that Max was more worried about her than Jinn. Why wouldn't he be at least a little worried after what he'd just seen? Even she couldn't explain it. A moment of temporary madness owed to three hours of battle. That's what she'd told Max on the way home, but she wasn't sure. She just wasn't sure.

She gave him a nod and went to bed. But after he'd gone to sleep, she found herself sliding beside Jinn, feeling his body quivering while he fought for each breath. Iris wrapped her right arm around her partner's firm body, wiping the sweat from his brow before pressing her head against his.

"You'll be okay," she whispered, closing her eyes.

Closing her eyes was a mistake.

The second she did, she saw Gram, dripping with blood. And the Anne who wasn't Anne reaching out to her, speaking in tongues.

Shivering, she opened her eyes and concentrated instead on the uneven rise and fall of Jinn's chest.

"You'll be okay," she said again and again, until she finally fell asleep. And there, lying next to Jinn, she dreamed—dreamed of the last time they slept side by side. A sweet dream of a sweet memory.

It was the second of January, 1883. Iris hadn't known if it was the snow falling from above for the first time that season or the memory of the thunderous New Year's applause she'd received the night before. But that morning, she'd been so content—so *happy*. And when she was happy, she couldn't help herself. As the sun came up, she looked out over the fresh, hard sheen coating the grass and jumped out into the grounds from her trailer in her worn black slippers, relishing each crisp crunch beneath her feet.

Her dress and shawl were quite thin; Granny would have her head. But that day, she didn't care about getting sick. It wasn't as if it would *kill* her.

After all, if she was truly a monster, might as well enjoy it sometimes.

It wasn't Granny but Jinn who found her jumping about. She could still remember his exasperated stare.

"What are you doing?" he demanded with a tired yawn. If she hadn't looked up and seen him, she would have heard the rumbling thunder from that dark, rainy cloud that seemed to trail him everywhere he went. The crank. "Our last performance is tonight. You think you'll get paid if you're too sick to do your stunts?"

"Stop your *worrying*, old man." Iris bent down and made an imprint of her hand in the hard snow. "I heal quickly."

"You didn't drink Jack's vodka last night, did you?"

It was just that she loved New Year's. The celebrations at the circus weren't anything to scoff at, of course. But to her, this time of year meant new beginnings. It signified hope, however small. Maybe this year would be her breakthrough: the year she'd learn who she really was.

"Oh, come on!" She lobbed some snow at his unsuspecting face. "Good shot, woman!" Iris congratulated herself, pumping her fist.

It took a while for an unamused Jinn to catch her and plop her over his shoulder like a sack of potatoes. Unfortunately, "a while" was too late. Jinn's prophecy came true that night with one small caveat—they both fell sick. It wasn't enough to dismay Oxford's drunken audience, but any professional could see that the two tightrope dancers, usually perfect, were off. By the next morning, Coolie had them placed in a spare trailer away from the rest of the performers.

The trailer was as bare as one could imagine. Not even a bed. Granny had directed some staff to provide them with blankets, but they were given only one.

"At least I have my own pillow," Iris thought bitterly as she lay next to a sleeping Jinn.

She shifted her head, staring at his face before turning back around as fast as a strike of lightning. Her head had already been throbbing since last night, but the delirium from the strange concoction Granny had fed her must have been the cause of her sudden, erratically rhythmed heartbeat. Placing a hand on her chest, she looked at him again. Now, upon closer inspection, she could see the line of sweat above his chestnut brows and dripping from underneath his bangs. He was sicker than she was. And it was her fault.

Pressing her lips together, she reached for the bottle of Granny's medicine beside her and nudged him awake. "Jinn, have you tried this? Granny made it."

Jinn's mumbling was indecipherable at first. Still lying down, she placed a gentle palm on his cheek and watched him swallow before he repeated himself. "The stuff with the garlic?"

Iris handed it to him. "Yes. You never know, it might—"

Jinn placed the bottle on her face before turning his back to her and falling asleep again. She gritted her teeth as the bottle tumbled onto the hard wooden floor between them.

A day later, she still wasn't well. She hated being sick. She was susceptible to common colds, she just couldn't die from them. But the snot and the head-aches were annoying.

"It's you!" Looking for a way to vent her frustration, she pointed a finger at Jinn's slim form, his back flat on the floor. "I bet it's your fault. That's right. You keep reinfecting me! That's why I'm still sick! I blame you!"

"That's not how it works," Jinn replied coolly. "Neither of us has gotten over it quite yet. It is what it is. Stop speaking nonsense and just be patient."

"Well . . . ," Iris grumbled. "I still blame you. Old crank."

"Then get rid of me," Jinn said simply without moving an inch. "I know you've thought about it."

Iris sat up and grabbed her pillow, but rather than smothering him, she poked him. Poke, poke. Poke. His ear. His cheek. She wanted to know how he'd react.

He reacted by taking her pillow and placing it firmly underneath his own head. Double cushioned. And she reacted, in a childish huff, by using his legs as a replacement.

"I truly hate you," he said, and yet he seemed to place falling back asleep above shoving her off. And so Iris stayed.

"French," she said, breaking the moment of silence that followed.

"What?"

"I haven't said this before, but I've noticed a bit of Parisian in your voice." She'd performed in Paris enough times to know. "Your British accent is stronger— or more practiced?"

Jinn said nothing.

"You were born in Paris." Silence. "Well, you must have spent most of your life in Europe. . . ." She trailed off. She'd never told Jinn about her lack of memories. He also never asked. Whenever anyone at the circus was curious about her past, she would simply make something up. It was better than the truth.

Iris was but a simple product of her environment like everyone else. With no memories of her life before Coolie's company, and since she spent most of her time performing in England and many a lonely night reading roman-tic British novels by the flicker of candlelight, her environment was largely

English—for better or for worse. Which explained her own accent. It was one of the reasons why she wanted to know about her life before.

But Jinn remained silent. She supposed he didn't have to tell her. Innocent curiosity still stirred within her. "What of your parents? I don't really know much about mine." Which was why she liked to hear stories from others. "Did they used to read to you—?"

When Jinn sat up and cupped her face with a hand, her body flushed quickly and furiously. It was the fever, she convinced herself, as he leaned in slightly, as her breath became shallow. For too long, he looked at her. The quiet between them felt thick, palpable. Before she could say anything to diffuse the soft but exhilarating tension between them, he scooped her up, placed her back where she'd been on the floor, and returned her pillow.

"Sleep," he said with a yawn, turning away from her.

And after *that*, she very well couldn't.

Iris awoke from her dream with a jolt. She was back in Club Uriel, still lying next to Jinn on his bed. She wondered for a moment what had woken her, and then Jinn gave a loud moan.

"Ugh, no . . . please, no!"

"Jinn?"

She sat up. In their room, as Max slept beside them in his cot, Jinn had begun to stir, but he was still barely conscious. She felt his forehead with the back of her hand, beads of his hot sweat warming her skin.

"You're going to be okay," she said when she noticed his shivering becoming more violent. "Jinn? *Jinn?*"

"Don't take him—" Jinn's voice was hoarse, his head flopping from side to side. Squeezing his eyes shut, gasping for breath, he looked as if he were fighting something within himself. Was he dreaming? Caught in a nightmare?

"Father!" Jinn's hand flew up to his forehead, his breaths coming fast and furious as he began shaking his head, thrashing about.

"Jinn!" Iris didn't bother to call for Max or to even check to make sure he was still asleep. She sat on top of her circus partner, her legs straddling his lap as she held his wrists. "You're going to be okay."

She might have been embarrassed under any other circumstances. Her bare legs hugged his pelvis, her short nightgown, courtesy of Cherice's shoplifting, rode up to her hips. But watching Jinn struggle, nothing else mattered. She bent over, pressing her forehead against his, still holding his wrists, and willing him to calm down.

"It's okay," she said again and again. "You're okay."

Eventually, his breathing softened. His body stilled. And then she could feel him slipping his arm out of her grip.

"Iris," he said, this time with a gentleness that made her shiver. She sat back up. Jinn's eyes were still closed, those long eyelashes fluttering. His breathing came more steadily; his lips opened slightly. "Iris . . . your voice . . . you . . ."

Maybe his nightmare had finally become a dream. She watched him, his delicate face, with curiosity and relief until jolting with surprise as his rough palm suddenly found her naked arm. As his fingers began trailing up her skin.

His eyes were not even half-open when he lifted himself up.

Iris's hands found his chest, her face flushing with heat as he laid his head against the crook of her neck.

"Iris . . ." A hot whisper.

"Jinn?" she said, suddenly unable to move as Jinn's face began caressing her cheek. His lips touched the sensitive part of her neck so lightly she thought she might have imagined it.

Her words caught in her throat, her heart pounding rapidly as Jinn slipped his arm around the small of her back.

"J-just what kind of dream are you having?" she stuttered, but her thoughts went blank as she felt herself being drawn closer to him.

A second kiss against her neck. Then another one. Jinn's lips trailed up her neck skillfully as he held her body flush against his.

"Iris . . . ," he said again. She was only barely listening when he added, "You can't leave . . . I won't leave either . . ."

Her body burned with a sudden craving that frightened her. She tilted her head back, looking up at the dark ceiling, her legs still gripping his waist.

"Leave? The circus?" she breathed. Had her escape from Coolie that night affected him that much?

And then Jinn winced. Iris realized that her arms had slipped around his back. That she was holding him too tightly. With a jolt her mind began to work again. As he convulsed a little in pain, she pushed him back down gently and lifted herself off of him.

"Sleep," she told him, glancing at Max with a blush to confirm he was still asleep before climbing back into her own bed.

Sleep. Neither of them would get much with her lying next to him. Least of all her. It was a lesson she'd already learned long ago.

It was going to be a long night.

27

THE NEXT ROUND WAS NOT FOR a few days. Officially, it was to give the remaining champions time to heal, but also to give Club Uriel time to lap up the stories Fool told them about the first. Iris was sure they were gossiping like hens on the second floor or in their parlor rooms at home after their business meetings or Parliament sessions.

In the meantime, the next morning Iris stayed mostly in her room, tending to Jinn while he was on the mend, trying to forget their nighttime ... incident ... while waiting for him to wake up and be his grumpy self again.

Max, rather unsettled from the first round, had decided to go out for a walk and didn't return for most of the day. During this time, she changed into the gift Jinn had brought for her. Granny's going-away gift had been a simple one: a peach blouse, its high guipure collar sheathing her long neck, its sleeves tighter around her arms than at the elbow. No corset, thank the heavens. Granny knew her. And a long skirt the color of green moss, the frills at the bottom brushing the bottom of her ankles. The embroidery along the front of her shirt, the intricate patterns. It was a sign of Granny's love. No matter what their past had been, Granny loved her in the present. This gift, painstakingly sewn, was proof. And as Iris's fingers played with the black ribbon around her neck, sewn in as a little bow tie, she knew that as surely as she knew her own love for the old woman. That love was a lifeline for her during these dark times.

After the brutal first round, knowing that the other champions were living in the same building made the hairs on the back of her neck stand on end. Even if they were on different floors, there was always a chance they'd bump into each other.

Like this morning.

"Cherice!" Iris saw the girl as soon as she left her room. "You all right?"

Cherice held her bicep, swinging her arm around like a prizefighter. "Still a bit worn-out, but otherwise, I'll live. *Phew!* All this for a little money!"

A lot of money. But it was more than that. With money came freedom. Freedom from poverty, from hunger. From the limitations chaining them. And power. *Resources.* She was sure that was how the Committee baited most of their champions into this gruesome tournament. Only those with a damn good reason to put their lives on the line could agree to join. In that way, Iris shared something in common with everyone here—even those who had tried to kill her.

She looked at Cherice, returning the girl's friendly smile. Only one team could win the tournament. How brutal would this get? How long before friendships dissolved into bloodshed?

But the two girls chatted anyway as they left the hallway and reached the staircase.

"Hold on—" Cherice put her hand up to stop Iris. Iris had seen them too. Harry Whittle and the Whittle maid, Mary White. Only, the boy didn't treat her as a servant at all. As soon as he spotted them, he grabbed Mary's wrist and kept her behind him. It didn't matter that she could still see over his head. He guarded her nonetheless.

Team Hawkins had only just managed to survive a run-in with Henry's team during the first round. Cherice and Henry stared each other down.

"G-good morning," Iris tried, lifting up a timid hand to greet them. It wasn't what Henry was expecting.

"Good morning?" Cherice spat. "Didn't this dumb kid sic some tigers on you?"

"Lions," Henry corrected with a smirk as Mary bit her lip behind him. "We're going up to our floor. Kindly mind your business."

Iris tensed as the two continued up the staircase. This boy couldn't have been more than fourteen. But even he had something he was willing to risk his life for.

"Your grandfather," Iris said suddenly, freezing Henry's feet to the steps. "I saw him at Whittle's the other day. The toy shop, I mean." Iris cringed at herself. Of course he knew the name of his own family store.

"I saw you both too. And?" He was curt and straightforward. But as Iris looked closer, she could see beads of sweat lining his forehead. He wasn't as confident as he seemed. It was a stressful situation for all of them.

"What are doing?" Cherice hissed, but Iris tapped her arm to calm her.

"You know, I'm not really interested in hurting anyone," Iris admitted. "When I decided to become a part of the tournament, I knew I'd have to fight. I had a taste of it earlier." She remembered the Sparrow twins. "But . . ." She shook her head. "I really don't like seeing so many people get hurt," she admitted. "It's just that . . ." She paused. "There's something I need more than anything."

"Money?" Henry guessed.

Iris couldn't tell him. Couldn't tell him of her search for self. Couldn't tell him that even though she was terrified with each clue she learned, she wouldn't stop until she'd gathered them all. She wasn't just another Fanciful Freak like them. Her past connection to Granny, her battle with Rin, her breakdown at Belle Vue, formerly her personal prison—all pieces to the puzzle of her identity. She was right to be in this tournament. She'd never have had this opportunity otherwise.

It was also why she was heading down to see if Adam was around—to ask for his father's book: *A Family's Travels through West Africa.* Somewhere between the words of those Temples, her own experiences, and her independent research, she would come to the truth of who she was.

"There's always something that matters more than money," Iris finally said, and then looked at Mary behind him. "I'm really sorry for how I treated you before. But I'm so very grateful you healed my friend."

"She didn't exactly have a choice, did she?" Henry spat, then gasped a little when he felt Mary's hand on his shoulder.

"It's okay," she said, avoiding Iris's eyes. "I'll accept your apology. You made a genuine one, after all."

Henry blushed a little at Mary's touch, but his expression quickly soured. "What's the point of acting all nice now when we're in a tournament like this?"

"I know," Iris said. "I know it's a contradiction. Everyone has their own reasons for being here. But I can't stand the thought of people dying."

Henry pressed his lips together as if he was struggling with her words. Maybe he was. Maybe being in this tournament was an existential crisis any champion with even a hint of a conscience had to contend with. It was only natural. It *should* have been natural. But then—

"Stop with the nonsense and get out of our way," Henry barked. "And by the way, the next time you threaten anyone on my team?" His young eyes narrowed to slits. "You'll regret it."

"Little pisshead," Cherice growled as they went on their way. She hadn't noticed Mary's small smile of gratitude as they passed.

"Cherice," Iris said, looking at the girl. "Doesn't it bother you too? That people are dying in this tournament?"

"People have *been* dying, girly," she answered. "Just that most of us aren't important enough to mourn. I've seen plenty of corpses in my day. Starved. Diseased."

As she trailed off, Iris could see, just for a moment, the deep well of loss in her eyes.

"Don't worry though!" She slapped Iris on the back rather painfully. "When it's just the two of us teams, we'll find a way to split the pot. Hawkins has been thinking of a plan," she added, lowering her voice. "We never leave our own behind. That's our code."

Henry was right. The tournament could have only one winner. Being kind to the other teams felt pointless, but deep inside her heart, Iris still wanted to find a way. A way for everyone to get what they needed without playing into the club's hands. Without any more tragedy.

She just didn't know what that way could be.

———— • ————

Iris couldn't find Adam anywhere in the club. After Mr. Mortius let her know he was otherwise disposed at home, Iris and Cherice decided to go for a walk around the area. Both needed the air.

Cherice was far more open today than the last time they traipsed around London. Iris told her about some of her favorite circus performances while Cherice told her about her older brother's gambling habits, which she learned through years of seeing him lose money. Hawkins would watch Chadwick draw for hours while Jacob laughed at Max's terrible attempts at coming up with stories for his pennies. They'd all tease their youngest when she wore dresses—except for when those dresses helped her get away with theft. Cherice's hair was longer in those days, and proper English gentlemen never suspected girls of being capable of criminal activities until it was too late.

"Stupid as hell, if you ask me. It's like they've never heard of the Forty Elephants," Cherice said, sighing wistfully at the thought of London's all-girl crime syndicate. But they were a bit too big and organized for Cherice's tastes. She liked the homey feel of a small gang of robbers.

Iris was happy to hear all about Cherice's friends. She was happy to make some friends herself, especially now when she needed them the most.

Later that night, Iris felt comfortable enough to visit Cherice, hoping to ask if she had another one of her pig-bristle toothbrushes. But as she stood in front of Team Hawkins's door, she heard light gasps and moans around the corner. She peeked her head around to see Hawkins and Jacob locked in a passionate embrace, Jacob with his head tilted in ecstasy while Hawkins's lips traced his cheekbones, his hand firmly inside the shorter boy's trousers, descending confidently, devilishly . . .

Iris turned around quickly with a blush, her body suddenly hot as she remembered Jinn in their bedroom. Strange thoughts began to slip from her mind and down her body like warm honey. She wasn't a Peeping Tom. She *wasn't*. But for some reason, she couldn't move.

"Wait, Lawrence—"

She heard the two separate.

"What's wrong?" Hawkins said, annoyed. "Isn't this what you want?" Iris could hear the sudden princely arrogance in his voice when he added,

"Always stealing glances at me like a love-struck puppy. Isn't this what you're *desperate* for?"

"What's that all about? I'm not now nor will I ever be desperate for any-thing—or any*one*," Jacob fired back indignantly.

"Oi, oi, it was a joke." Hawkins laughed rather nervously, but Iris couldn't help feeling a little miffed on Jacob's behalf. It reminded her of Jinn's constant deadpan insults. Some men were so . . . "Come on. It's been a while since we've had some time alone, hasn't it?"

"This is not funny to me," Jacob said. He was clearly hurt. "And I don't want to hear about me being love-struck, not from someone still in love with a ghost."

Silence fell upon the two of them just as Iris realized she'd been stand-ing there for far too long. They'd catch her. This was a private conversation. Everyone had their secrets, their stories. But those stories were theirs to give. She was invading their privacy. They didn't deserve that. And she wasn't about to lose the friends she'd just made.

Iris wasn't sure if one of the boys would stomp off or if they'd choose to let their tensions subside, reconcile, and continue their night. She somewhat hoped it would be the latter, but Iris descended the stairs before she could find out.

28

ebmemer Lliw Uoy Yad Eno Tub. Nettogrof Evah Uoy.
Niaga Ecno Emit Si Ti.
"Iris!"

Later that night, Iris awoke in Max's grip, her throat sore as if scraped by a knife. Her wide eyes stared in blank horror as he knelt by her bed.

"Iris," Max said. "Are you okay?"

Iris took a moment to catch her breath and then looked around the room. The sun was just beginning to peek through the closed curtains. Jinn was still fast asleep in the corner. If what Mary said was true, he would be fine soon. A needed solace.

"I'm sorry," she apologized quietly. "Did I wake you?"

At the sound of her voice, his hands loosened but remained on her shoulders. "I've been awake for a while. Still got my mind stuck on that first round, I guess."

The first round of the tournament. As much as Max continually insisted that she get a proper night's rest, how could she after what she'd seen? Those two men—one a priest, the other a ghoul, both demons. The body parts littering the ground.

And that Anne, who tried to reach out to her only to have a terrible riddle spring forth from her lips instead. A riddle that now haunted Iris's dreams.

"Are you all right?" Max took her hands. "You're cold."

"As a corpse." She laughed bitterly because she felt like one. "Fitting considering how many times I've died already."

"That you *know* of." The corner of Max's lips curled in mischief. "A woman who can't die. You really could be an ancient queen for all we know. I hope you know that would make our relationship wholly inappropriate."

Iris managed a small smile, but it was the truth in his words that bothered her. Her past as a Dahomey reaper. Her capture by slave traders. Her own work as a raider . . .

If those men hadn't kidnapped Sister and me, then, child, you would have.

That was it. Rin herself had been from a neighboring region, taken by the Dahomey in a raid and eventually trained as a warrior. What if Iris had meant to do the same to Granny and her sister all those years ago . . . only for all three of them to be kidnapped themselves?

Iris's hands trembled. A queen or a kidnapper? Certainly a monster. That was her life fifty years ago. But could she have had a life before that?

"Come now, Iris, don't cry."

Max's words surprised her, because she hadn't noticed it until then, but she really was crying. Tears silently streamed down her face.

"Seeing you cry just makes me want to bother you even more—you *do* know that, right?" Max scratched his head impatiently. "Okay, hold on."

Quickly, he ran over to his bed, slipped something Iris couldn't see out from underneath his pillow. He kept it hidden behind his back as he knelt down by her bed. Then—

"Oh, it's you again," said Iris, her eyebrow raised.

Max's Don Quixote puppet was staring her in the face, chatting away. Telling awful jokes. Recounting old tales of glory. The moment Iris finally laughed, Max's eyes lit up.

"There it is." Without looking, Max threw the puppet behind his shoulders and leaned in. "I really hate seeing girls cry. It's why I stole that doll for Cherice all those years ago."

"You'd better not tell her that." Iris wiped a tear from her eye with a sad smile.

Max put his arm on the bed and thought, his eyes staring at the gorgeous lace of her covers. "Iris," he started, but stopped. He shut his eyes, his shoulders rising and falling with his breath. "As for Cherice and the others . . . I'm so sorry."

"For what?"

"For not helping Jinn." He looked toward the other boy, fast asleep in his bed. "For not helping *you*. You're right. We're supposed to be a team. But I . . ."

As he trailed off, Iris's hands tensed on her lap. Her anger last night felt like a distant memory. But as she thought of it now, as she tried to consider Max's own circumstances, she couldn't help but soften. She shook her head.

"Max, they're your friends," she said simply. "They've been your friends for years. You've only known us for a few days."

"But I gave you my word," Max insisted. "That I would help you. That means something. If not to anyone else, it does to me. I don't like to go back on it. I'm not like *him*," he added, and in that moment Iris knew he was imagining Bately's smug face. "I won't betray a friend."

The ticking of the clock filled the silence between them.

"I felt like I betrayed her," he said finally. "My sister. When we were separated. Mother had counted on me to keep her safe. She was just a child with no understanding of the world."

"So were you." Iris could see the surprise in Max's eyes as she placed a hand on the side of his face. "So were you, Maximo. So you shouldn't blame yourself anymore."

As Max's large eyes glistened, she felt suddenly much older. Well, she *was* older. She just didn't know by how much. Maybe this was how Granny felt whenever she placed a hand on Iris's face to stop her from crying after a bad show or an awful fight with Jinn.

"If your sister's anything like you, she's learned to survive. And she's out there. We will find her—together. I promise." She smiled. "We're a team, aren't we?"

Max gazed up at her, saying nothing, for a long time. And then, "You really are beautiful, you know that? Inside and out."

A fast blush made Iris turn away, but Max had already pulled back. "I don't want to see such a beautiful girl's face twisted in horror. So you'll have to have sweet dreams from now on. Okay?"

Iris's smile turned bittersweet. She looked down at the purple-and-blue sheets of her bed. "I did have a bad dream," she whispered. "A very bad dream."

Max cocked his head. "Care to tell me what this dream was about?"

Ghosts of the past. An unknown future. "Not especially." She gave him a teasing grin.

"How mysterious." He pouted a little. "Well, it's up to you, as it should be."

"Max." Iris stared at her hands, remembering Anne reaching for her. "Sometimes I'm not sure this is all worth it."

"It is," Max said. "It will be."

"This will all work out in the end, won't it?"

Max gave her a thumbs-up. It looked silly. Silence passed between them.

"Doesn't inspire much confidence, does it?" Max looked at his hand and rubbed the back of his head. "Well then, what about this?"

Max pulled something from his trouser pocket. Something Iris hadn't seen in a while—and didn't think she'd ever see again.

"The pocket watch." The golden pocket watch from the auction. She remembered its tune before Max even opened it. The honey and romance. The quiet grief underlying it all.

"Nicked it before we went out onstage," Max said.

Back when they were both chained and about to be sold.

"You *are* a good thief," Iris said, impressed.

"I am." He handed it to her, watching her listen to its music for a time before speaking again. "Soothing, isn't it?"

Iris nodded, holding the watch in both of her hands, letting the chain dangle in the air.

"Keep it." Max stood. "Every time you have a nightmare, listen to it. And don't forget."

"Don't forget what?" Iris said, looking up as he reached for her curtain.

"You're not alone." He smiled sweetly before drawing the curtain around her bed.

———•———

Later that day she finally had the opportunity to meet Adam at Club Uriel. There in the gathering room on the second floor, she asked for his father's book. He readily agreed to have someone send it to her immediately. But despite this, Iris was in a bad mood.

It was the gentlemen in the room with them, watching the *little champion* who'd appeared before them so abruptly. Every now and then she'd catch one turning from her to gossip excitedly with his friends like schoolboys.

Adam had noticed too. With a sigh he leaned back in his red leather chair. "I hope you're keeping well, Iris," he said with genuine concern.

Was he concerned? That so many were risking their lives in this tournament?

"The second round won't start for a while." He eyed her intently. "Maybe you and I could play a round at the new Gossima parlor in town. A game of whiff-whaff should help you relax."

"You just keep up your end of the bargain," she said. "By the end of all this, I expect to know the full truth about myself."

"And you will," Adam promised. "Participating in the tournament. Finding my father. I promise you, by the time you've completed both tasks, you'll know yourself completely."

Iris frowned. Telling her the truth would've sufficed, but he'd once said that hearing the truth all at once would be too much for her—and as she remembered her breakdown at the zoo, she couldn't help but agree, though it pained her to admit it to herself. Then again, it was also clear that Adam wasn't ready to give up this game between them. He picked up his wineglass and considered it with interest.

"No matter what happens, Iris, I'm on your side," he promised once again.

"My dear Adam! I hoped I'd find you here, and here you sit."

Iris had heard that French accent before. Behind her stood Madame Bellerose, the French heiress, as Iris understood her to be. More important, she was the woman who had been willing to bid on Iris at the auction as if she were some exotic spice from overseas. Her burgundy hair was twisted in a bun at the back of her head, likely to make room for her wide-brimmed hat.

"Madame." Adam flashed her a practiced smile. "To what do we owe this pleasure?"

Iris noticed, equally annoyed, that Madame Bellerose did not spare her a glance.

"Why, I came to invite you to my soiree, my darling boy."

She looked extravagant in a red-and-pink triple-flounced skirt, its drapery following her as she walked around the red leather couch Iris was sitting on.

"Guard?" she turned, calling down the hall. "Guard? *Viens ici.*"

Into the room walked Rin. Iris's blood drained from her face, her fingers curling in her lap. Rin's black jacket was properly buttoned to the top, her yellow skirt swaying as she walked. And her face, Iris noticed, was now covered by a new red veil as dark as Bellerose's hair, so dark Iris wondered if Rin could even see. She hoped not. If Rin could, would another battle between them ensue?

Relax, Iris thought. *Fighting's not allowed in Club Uriel. Those are the rules.*

But of course, rules could be broken.

"Adam, do tell this one to stand to the side." Madame Bellerose brushed strands of hair with a black-gloved hand. "I'm tired from the carriage ride and I'd like to sit."

"Iris is my guest. And my guests sit." Adam gestured to the empty seat at his right. "You're welcome to do the same."

The woman's expression stiffened, her red lips thin as the blade of a knife. "How uncouth," she said, but sat down nonetheless.

Somehow seeing Rin standing in the same spot even after her Patron had sat stirred a sense of camaraderie that went beyond whatever residual fear was left over from their battle. Without a word, Iris shifted to the side and patted the seat next to her.

It caught Rin by surprise. But slowly, as Adam grinned secretly and Bellerose scowled, disgusted, Rin took her seat next to Iris.

"And so here we all are," said Adam. "Iris, let me formally introduce you. This is Madame Bellerose. Her family has vineyards across Europe and has long manufactured luxury goods in Paris, but they're also known as being quite the philanthropists. Madame herself has donated a fair amount to women's groups across France, Britain, and America."

"We're at the dawn of a new era, after all. Old money can have new values, no?" Bellerose's long gloves were spotless, the seams intricate as if especially sewn for her.

Adam turned to Bellerose. "Madame, let me introduce to you, Miss Iri—"

"Oh yes, I recognize that one from the auction," Bellerose said with a bored sigh.

New values, huh? The irony. Iris could hardly hide her amusement.

Adam rubbed his chin. "In that case, what party are you referring to?"

"I stumbled upon an old friend I haven't seen for some time," said Madame. "And so I'm throwing him a welcome back party at my residence—next Tuesday evening."

Adam sipped his wine. "I think I'll be busy that night," he said shortly. "So, if that's all."

Bellerose adjusted her shoulders. "You seem in a hurry to get rid of me. Can't we just gossip like the rest of them? About the dead and dismembered bodies left behind from the tournament? Poor Douglas. He never did stand a chance against Belgium's boars."

Douglas. That was the dead man's name. The Exploding Man, according to Adam's list. Even after everything he'd done to her, Iris shivered violently at the thought. But as her stomach heaved, she gritted her teeth to calm herself, noticing Bellerose's and Adam's eyes on her.

"Those two grave robbers I employed were useless, of course. Dead already."

And so Bellerose had one champion left.

Adam looked at Rin. "I'm terribly sorry for this," he offered.

"Oh, dear boy, please." Bellerose dismissed him with a wave. "The little beast doesn't understand what we're saying. She's useful for little more than her savagery in battle."

"And what are *you* useful for, Madame Bellerose?" Iris glared at the woman, her skin burning hot. But Bellerose's shock slowly turned to a viciousness that simmered underneath her smile.

"My, my, Lord Temple, do you have no disciplinary skills?" Bellerose snapped her fingers at a waiter carrying a tray of champagne. "Careful now, or you may end up in the same predicament as Portugal."

Portugal? She must have meant the man named Cordiero.

Adam placed his glass down. "You mean that incident here the other day."

"The man who made a fuss and had to be put down like a dog. Such an unnecessary loss for the tournament." Bellerose's smile turned wicked. "But punishment is to be expected for those who speak out of turn to their superiors."

"Such barbarity," Iris whispered, shaking her head, her fists clenched so tight she could feel her blood pumping through her veins.

Bellerose's eyes slid toward her—a cordial glance. "Did you say something, dear?"

"He's here, no?" Adam said quickly, successfully stealing back Madame's attention.

"Perhaps. I don't see him." Bellerose pinched the thin neck of her wineglass. "But there are other things I'd like to discuss with you, my love. Alone." She looked at Iris. "If that's okay with this one, of course."

"More than okay." Iris stood. "I don't want to spend another second around you."

Bellerose's laughter sounded like shattering glass. Iris grabbed Rin's arm.

"Come with me," she said to a surprised Rin. She had things she wanted to talk about too.

Rin, the fierce warrior, now stumbled behind her awkwardly as Iris pulled her away.

Rin wasn't comfortable standing outside. Different from the seasoned fighter Iris knew, Rin folded her arms, impatient, turning her back on Club Uriel as tipsy men streamed in and out, laughing garishly and smoking cigars. But the second Iris grabbed her elbow, Rin's well-trained muscles moved in a flash, pulling out of her grip and facing her menacingly.

Iris put up her hands. "I'm not here to fight," she said. "Just needed the air. And thought you did too." Especially Rin, who had to be around that disgusting woman so often.

Rin understood her body language, but lifted her head in defiance none-theless. "If you want to speak with me, use our tongue," she challenged. "You still understand it, clearly, so you can speak it if you try."

Iris cleared her throat. "All right," she mumbled in English. "But if I do that, will you show me your face? You want to speak with someone. I want to look you in the eye when I do."

She pointed at Rin's veil. Rin must have understood, because she turned away from her, keenly aware of the two men who'd just lumbered out of the club.

"Don't worry about them." Iris guessed her embarrassment. "I've already seen your face. Even on their best day, those wankers can't match your loveliness."

She tried her best to say it in Fon and must have flubbed it entirely, for Rin burst out laughing. It sounded beautiful.

"Beauty means nothing to me," Rin said. "It's Bellerose who makes me wear this veil when I accompany her. She says my face is too horrid for her to look upon."

"Her entire *existence* is horrid. I wouldn't put much stock in what she has to say." Iris had spoken in English, but just so Rin understood her meaning, she said Bellerose's name and made a comically disgusted face that had Rin giggling.

Rin continued. "I decided to wear the veil myself because secrecy is always helpful in battle. But I suppose here it only makes me stand out. Besides—"

She unpinned the red veil from the braids that kept it in place.

"As you said, you've already seen my face."

Delicate, youthful features—a small, round nose and thick, straight eyebrows—contended with the scars of battle on her face. Her large, focused brown eyes shone fiercely bright—that is, the one that was still unmarred. Iris's gaze traced the dark violet scar down the center of her right eye. Without meaning to, she reached out to touch it, only realizing when Rin twitched that she had no right to from the start.

278

"You could have killed me after our last battle, but you showed me mercy," said Rin. "You *should* have taken my head. That's what you and I were trained to do." Outwardly, Rin spoke proudly of the act, but her little shiver didn't escape Iris's notice. "Why didn't you?"

Iris only shrugged, smiling. It caught Rin off guard. After a moment passed between them when it was clear Rin may not speak again, Iris decided to interject.

"What happened to you? Your face?" Iris tried to ask in Rin's language.

Perhaps Rin understood. Perhaps she didn't. Either way she didn't answer.

That was when Iris remembered the story Rin had told. That she was kidnapped in a raid and taken to the Dahomey. This girl was not at the South Kensington Exhibition that made the rest of the Fanciful Freaks. That's when Iris began to wonder: when it came to the birth of the Fanciful Freaks, perhaps it wasn't the place that mattered so much as the method.

She tried to ask her. "Your powers," she managed in Fon. It took a few tries to get the pronunciation correct enough for Rin to understand.

"You once had a necklace of white stone," Rin said, and Iris remembered her mentioning it among the trees. "You left it inside your household when you disappeared. It was the same household I came to live in when I was first brought to the Dahomey. They believed the stone to be the secret behind your power. That's why I swallowed it."

"*Swallowed* it?"

"To keep me safe after my household decided to send me to the *ahosi* for training. Because of my nervousness, it went into my windpipe instead, but I didn't choke. It simply stayed there in my chest. That's how I knew the crystal was wondrous." Rin placed her hand upon her chest. "It was while working for the king that I learned of his experiments in the Forge."

The Forge . . . Iris covered her mouth with her drumming fingers but said nothing.

"Behind the palace complex, deep within the mountains, was a secret workhouse made of stone. Inside was a hearth they called the Forge. There the kingdom's top military warriors conducted experiments with it—the white crystal, just like what your necklace was made from."

Iris frowned. "Experiments?" She almost held her breath as she heard the answer.

"Because of the rumor that your white crystal necklace had caused your wondrous powers, the king had sent spies to find more of it. They correctly guessed it would be where they'd originally found you and took just enough so as not to raise suspicion. In the Forge, they conducted many experiments to see if they could meld it into different weapons, if it would react to other kinds of ore, to steam pressure, to *vodun*. I don't know *all* the details. At the time, we trainees were ordered to keep watch for thieves at night. But because of the experiments, the Forge was often volatile. And an accident happened the night I went inside the workhouse alone. A strange explosion. That's all I can remember from that night. And when I awoke . . ."

"You had your sword," Iris said.

Just like at the fair. Iris was right—the method mattered more than the place.

"I was the only one there at the time, so no one else could have been affected," Rin continued. "When the Forge exploded, I felt the force of it reso-nating inside my chest. It was as if the little crystal inside me were buzzing . . ."

So the key to everything was this mysterious white crystal? And Rin was an important piece of this puzzle too. Together, they could make sense of it all. But she was also a dangerous warrior with a mission of her own.

Iris thought carefully about what to do before finally offering her hand.

"I want to know the secret of the white crystal. If you get any more infor-mation, please, *please* let me know," she said. "And call me Iris," she added. "You and I are sort of like sisters, aren't we?" As strange as their relationship was, Iris truly felt a kinship with her that she couldn't express with words. She only needed the one to translate for Rin to understand her meaning.

"Sisters?" Rin stared at Iris's hand, a little annoyed, a little embarrassed. She folded her arms and turned away. "After I manifested my sword, I was told many times that I was like you. The reincarnation of the great Isoke. I trained with my life on the line all while chasing a ghost."

She looked down at her own calloused palms. "And then I was told to bring you back alive. You, a ghost who should have been long dead. The king's true reason, I don't know. When I came to these lands, I didn't know what to expect. But now . . ." Rin's shoulders drooped a little. "If I take you back with me, I wonder . . . what will happen to the two of us?"

Iris smiled even wider, her hand still out for Rin to shake.

Rin placed her hands in her pockets with a defiant huff. "Your language skills are terrible, Isoke," she scolded. "But don't stop trying . . . When I was first taken to Dahomey, I too found it difficult to learn."

"Rin—" Iris started, before a bloodcurdling shriek from inside the building cut her off.

Stunned, Iris and Rin ran inside only to find an old man tumbling down the staircase. The blood pouring from the man's mouth stained his white beard, his cloudy blue pupils dilated as he continued to flop down each step until his body rested at the bottom. A trail of blood followed behind him, one of his leather shoes abandoned in the middle of the stairs.

"Cordiero! He was poisoned!" someone screamed from the railing of the second floor.

Everyone ran to see the man's undignified end, gasping and whimpering. Among them were Adam and Bellerose, both staring with an intensity that frightened her.

"My husband!" A woman barreled down the steps: Mrs. Cordiero. Once she'd reached the dead man, she threw herself upon him and began wailing.

Cordiero. A member of the Enlightenment Committee. And now he was dead. Poisoned.

Mrs. Cordiero's wail echoed off the high ceiling, but neither Adam nor Bellerose seemed to notice Iris glaring up at them as they turned and left the scene.

So which one of you did it? Iris thought to herself. The Enlightenment Committee was a frightening group indeed.

29

IRIS HAD TO GET OUT OF Club Uriel. And so she told Max to look after Jinn as she spent the rest of the day on the grass by the River Thames with the book Mr. Mortius had delivered to her: *A Family's Travels through West Africa*, by John Temple. Courtesy of Adam. It was good to know that murdering Cordiero hadn't made him forget the little things.

Or maybe the culprit was Bellerose. The woman looked ruthless enough to do it. Adam at least had helped Iris enough to earn the benefit of the doubt.

Well, there was no proof either of them had committed the crime. Besides, the death of a Committee member had nothing to do with *her*. So she focused on what did.

Like many explorers, John Temple's father, Sir Isaac, was interested in the Nile, which took him to Eastern Africa, specifically Zanzibar and Nairobi. John had once gone on an expedition with his father, funded by the British government. He spent a number of pages detailing from experience Lake Victoria, one of the great lakes of the continent. More curious was an offhand line that seemed to flow by quickly and yet stick out of the page all the same.

Later, while my father was recovering from sickness
in Yorkshire, the Crown sent another expedition, one

that cared more for the treasures within the lake. And

treasures they found, indeed. That they'd made such

an important discovery without him bothered Sir

Isaac until the end of his life.

Maybe it was her imagination, but Iris felt the sting of mockery in those last few words. The Temple men seemed to have a long history of hating their fathers. But what was this about "treasures" within the lake? Maybe they were just categorizing fauna and flora. Still . . . it made her uneasy.

John detailed his experiences in West Africa, including his travels to the Oil Rivers Protectorate in the lower Niger region, where the local authorities had sanctioned a special mining project. But according to a newspaper Iris had just bought on the street, that project was now under British control. It was why some envoys were here in England right this very moment.

John Temple also spoke of the Dahomey Kingdom:

The ahosi. *Or the* mino. *That is what they call*

themselves, though we Europeans call them Amazons

because of their resemblance to the Amazons of Greek

mythology. They are women military warriors who

serve their king. An elite force known for their prowess

in battle.

And Iris was once one. It was still difficult to believe. John Temple spoke to the king of Dahomey about his travels. It was his work that had brought him there in the first place.

It wasn't until an explorer visited our lands that my king began to believe you were still alive. That explorer seemed obsessed with your mystery, Rin had told her as they'd fought under the stars. John Temple. He was researching her.

Why? Did the stories of She Who Does Not Fall reach as far as Europe?

"A global eclipse," Iris whispered, trying to remember all that Rin had said. She scanned the chapter. Indeed, it was one of the topics that John Temple spoke about with the king. The king's predecessor, King Ghezo, had once believed that the eclipse was a sign that the gods favored the Dahomey. The existence of Isoke was proof enough for him. It was something King Glele believed even now. About that eclipse, John wrote:

> *Different cultures believe a solar eclipse to be an act of aggression, like the Vikings, who once believed that sky wolves were chasing the sun. But in the Americas, the Navajo believe eclipses to be a part of nature's order. What if it is both? A display of the Earth's predilection toward order and balance and also a sign of the divine?*

The natural and the supernatural working together. Maybe even one and the same. Iris put the book down and stared into the black waters of the River Thames. White birds and butterflies of gold, orange, and blue flew above her. Free of fears. Free of secrets. Free of worries. *Free.*

She and Rin gained their powers in different places and times than the other Fanciful Freaks of London. What if there were more like Iris around the world? Maybe there had been Fanciful Freaks throughout history—only *her* powers had allowed her to survive a little longer than the rest, that's all. There could be an entire society of them that she didn't know about. If John Temple knew the truth, he didn't reveal it in this book. If Adam wasn't going to tell her outright, maybe she *would* have to find his father.

Iris had been so wrapped up in her thoughts that she didn't hear the light footsteps behind her. And so when she let herself collapse to lie upon the grass, she collided against someone else's back instead—someone strong and slender, with sinewy muscles.

"Tired from a hard day of reading?"

"Jinn!" She whipped around, a sudden swell of emotions drawing tears from her eyes the moment she saw him sitting upon the grass, his back to her. She hugged him from behind, burying her face in his hair. "Jinn, you're okay!"

But the memory of the last time they embraced made her flush. She quickly turned back around, wondering if he remembered his fingers trailing up her arm. His lips on her neck . . .

"Been in the vodka again, have you?"

He clearly did not. Well, he'd been more asleep than awake, then. Half in a dream . . .

Still.

She hit him in the back of the head.

Jinn grunted, holding his head with a wince. "And that was for?"

"I'm just glad you're okay," she said, turning around with a blush. "Don't be stupid again. Watch your back next time."

That frantic moment she'd pulled him out of the lake during the first round. She still remembered the way his hands had reached greedily for her face as he pulled her closer toward him, his lips cracked, his consciousness slipping away from him . . .

Iris shook her head quickly, warmth still rushing to her cheeks. Probably didn't remember that one either. "G-glad to see you up and about. You know, I've made some progress on this mystery of ours since you've been out. The mystery of the Fanciful Freaks."

"Oh?" was all he said.

Iris was more than a little annoyed. "You don't care?"

"I have other things to care about," Jinn answered simply.

It was then that Iris noticed Jinn had something in his hands. By the time she turned to look at it more clearly, Jinn's hands were already at the base of her jawline where her braids had gathered. She reacted sharply to his touch, her breath hitching. Working swiftly and softly, he bound the braids that Granny had weaved in a purple ribbon, forming a perfect bow.

"Wh-what's this?" Iris asked, the heat in her cheeks spreading across her face.

"Didn't you tell me to buy you a gift?"

At Astley's. Iris bit her lip. "But . . ."

"I bought it that day. Before you ran from Coolie," he said. "I just . . ." He paused. "I just didn't know how to give it to you."

"Why now?"

She could feel Jinn raise his head toward the sky. "I guess I realized that sometimes it's better not to hesitate."

And yet hesitation was already ingrained in their relationship. Words not said. Secrets kept. It was the mountain between them that Iris didn't know how to cross. Even thinking of closing the gap made her body flood with an anxious kind of energy she could only dispel by being happy with this moment. Just a moment like this, without asking for more.

But didn't she want more? *Could* she without even knowing who and what she was?

Tenderly, she touched the bow. "It's not a hat," she whispered.

"Don't be picky. I remembered, didn't I?"

Jinn's smile brought more warmth to her body, warmth that made her feel less like an eternal corpse. She remembered what he'd told her before the first trial—that it was enough that she was Iris. There was another option to all of this. Taking Granny, running off. But something in Iris just wouldn't let her move from this spot.

She still had to *know.*

"Jinn . . ." She fell silent for a long time before continuing. She thought of the words Jinn was crying out in his dream—something about his father? "Do you cherish the memories you had with your father?"

Jinn was taken aback. She could tell by the way his muscles tensed.

"I'm sure there are memories you like to think back on," she continued, looking up at the sky. "There have to be. He was your father."

"That's what makes it hurt all the more," Jinn answered. Iris could hear his quiet anguish.

Iris let her fingers touch his softly. And together they stayed like that, sweetly, gently, tenuous in their intimacy, intimate in their silence as the minutes passed. Jinn lowered his head before speaking again.

"That day at the fair, I saw him lying on the grass beside one of the flames. Like me and so many others, he'd been knocked down by the explosion. I saw him gasping for breath . . . and a man standing over him."

A man standing over him? Iris bit her lip but remained silent.

"I can't quite remember the man's face. Sometimes I think I—" He paused, struggling with himself. "Sometimes I *think* I can remember, somewhat. That pale skin. Contours, shapes. Sometimes. But . . . I'm just not sure. It was ten years ago. I was nine, and I was terrified. But I do remember his cigarette—and the way he glanced at me before he dragged my father away by the leg through one of the flames. And I remember the flames. I hate flames. I *hate* them."

Jinn touched his throat bitterly, as if his own fire was clamoring to erupt. All the time he'd used his abilities to help her without her knowing how much it pained him to do it. She should have realized it by now. It must have been why he'd opted out of being a fire-eater at Coolie's company. Just because you *could* do something well didn't mean you liked doing it. But when you had no choice . . .

"That was the last time I ever saw my father. I couldn't do anything to stop it. I don't even know what that man did with him . . ."

Jinn's voice broke. He raised his knees, gripping his head. "You asked once where I'm from. I was born in Paris after my parents moved from Istanbul." He paused. "No, not moved. *Exiled*. My father was part of a political group of intellectuals dissatisfied with the Ottoman Empire. I think they called themselves the Young Ottomans."

"Young Ottomans." Iris listened intently, absorbing every bit of information. After years without knowing, each new detail brought the young man known as "Jinn" to life in a way that captivated her.

"Many Young Ottomans were exiled to Paris in those days. My mother died shortly after giving birth to me. And after my father's death in South Kensington, I lived in London. On the streets. I had to learn the language. Avoid danger. From criminals. From gangs my age who beat me and stole my money."

As Jinn frowned, Iris thought of Max and his friends and swallowed. It explained his distrust, at any rate.

"Once I discovered my abilities, I joined different circuses, fire-eating, before finding Coolie. But that memory of my father burning—of my kind father being dragged away . . . Eventually, I just couldn't do it anymore. I turned down the job and became your partner."

Jinn fell silent. Opening up to another meant making yourself vulnerable to pain. And she could feel his throbbing in her own chest.

"My father was a gentle man," he insisted as if he needed to convince her. "A writer. A thinker. Calm and understanding. If I didn't know him at all, I'm sure I'd be at peace today. Sometimes not knowing is a kind of peace, Iris." He stifled a sob, shaking his head. "I wish I didn't remember him. I wish . . . I wish . . ."

Iris heard his breath catch in his throat as she enveloped him with her arms once again from behind. "It *can* be a kind of peace," she answered. "It can also be a kind of hell. I'm sorry, Jinn." She didn't know what else to say. "From the bottom of my heart, I'm sorry."

"My mother used to say that when we lose something, we gain something in return," a voice cut in.

Max. He was approaching with a sack of potatoes balanced over his right shoulder. Iris and Jinn shot to their feet in surprise.

"When things go wrong, I try not to think about what I'm losing. Just what I'm gaining." He gazed at Iris with a soft smile before he lowered his brown eyes to the grass at his feet. "Though I seem to be losing a lot these days."

Max seemed unusually pale, his characteristic cheer forced. Iris wondered if anything had happened to him.

"What are you doing here?" Jinn said. "You weren't around when I woke up."

"Had things to do." Max looked close to sticking out his tongue. "Thought I'd stop by."

"What things?" Jinn pressed.

Instead of answering, Max dropped the potatoes unceremoniously on Jinn's feet, grinning wide as his teammate began cursing. "I hate that fancy stuff they cook at the club. Can you believe they bring us everything but good old hearty *potatoes*?"

Cherice *had* mentioned that potatoes were his favorite food one time while they were out. But this was a little . . .

"Tonight, I swear I'm going to barge into the kitchens and force them to cook these. It's what we deserve."

Max's laughter felt a little strained. It was the times he was the most excitable that made Iris the most worried.

As Jinn kicked the burlap sack off his feet, Iris approached Max gingerly. "Are you sure you're okay?" she asked, inspecting his expression.

Max's shoulders relaxed. He leaned down to her height, smiling devilishly, making Iris's heart jump.

"Seeing you worry about me makes me feel *more* than okay," he answered. Iris quickly inched away. "I'm okay *now*, at least," he added quietly.

Iris stared between the two of them. A young boy struggling to live after being ripped from his father's side. Another taken from his mother and his sister. And she an immortal tightrope dancer seeking the truth behind her existence—the web that weaved all of their destinies together.

"Sometimes you think too much, Iris." Max patted her on the back. "Better to let yourself *feel* in the moment and then let it all go once it's done."

Jinn scoffed. "If anything, she doesn't think *enough*. You'd be well aware of that if you'd known her for more than a few days."

That childishness was back in full force. As Iris grimaced at her partner, Max wrapped his arm around her waist, drawing a squeak from her lips.

"I don't know, mate, I think when it comes to some things, *feeling* should matter more than thinking, wouldn't you say?"

As Jinn's expression turn cold, a flustered Iris pushed Max away and stepped back from both of them. "Well, now that we're all here, I think we should go over what happened in the first round," she said. "And think about how we can make our teamwork stronger."

"How about actual teamwork?" Jinn scoffed, and Max's expression tightened.

"You sound motivated, Iris." Max folded his arms. "After everything that happened . . ." He stopped to consider his words. "This tournament is a real bother, isn't it? The reward may be high, but the price is—"

He stopped himself, turning from her slightly without saying another word.

Something *had* happened to him. But she knew he wouldn't tell her if she asked.

Iris touched the lavender bow brushing her ear as the passing wind blew her hair. "We're in it. We can't escape, not without consequences. Besides . . ." Iris looked at John Temple's book on the grass and remembered the photo she'd taken from the British Museum. "This isn't just my fight. I want to know why *we* are who we are. Is this really about evolution? The end of the world? Or something else entirely? We deserve the truth. I don't know if we'll have another opportunity to get it. I can read all the books I please. But being involved in this tournament, surrounded by others like us . . . it's given me more knowledge about myself—about *us*—than I've had in the past ten years."

Max placed his hands on his hips. "The truth wouldn't be so bad, I guess. Just have to make sure we don't die before getting it."

"Did you forget?" Iris winked. "I can't die."

"So you'll leave the rest of us to the wolves?" Max laughed. "My kind of woman."

Jinn cleared his throat rather conspicuously. "At any rate, for now let's just do as Iris says. Go over the last round, figure out what we can do better. And then . . ."

"And then." Iris looked at Max.

Then they had to survive the second round.

30

THE NEW SHOW AT WILTON'S BEGAN seven days after the first, and somehow it was even worse, with more terrible actors to recount, with ridiculous fanfare, the battles of the first round.

Two women with black makeup painted all over their faces squared off among the trees. Iris exchanged a glance with Rin, who'd taken her spot against the left wall. She knew what Rin was thinking because she was thinking it too: these actors looked positively *idiotic*. Exaggerated cartoons with terrible wigs and big red lips. And the *script*.

Actually, the script was curious. Many of the important details of their conversation had been left out—everything surrounding Iris in particular. Did Fool not hear them? Or was he instructed to leave it out? How could Fool have all these accounts in the first place?

"I think they could have chosen a better actor to play me," Max said, watching himself battle Rin's former grave-robbing teammates.

Then came a paralyzing shriek. The lights dimmed. And suddenly there was red paint on the ground and two men covered in it. The vampiric man and the priest, chanting his prayers.

"For the sake of His sorrowful passion . . ."

Iris looked at them now. Gram, the sallow-skinned man, smoking his cigarette. And Jacques sitting a few seats away, his head down as if he was sleeping, though Iris could still see the white collar around his neck. Iris had made sure to know them by name. She and Max exchanged wary glances while Jinn watched Gram, his eyes narrowed.

Apparently, this show had been playing for the past seven days, attended by members of Club Uriel. For them, it was more than just a bit of Sunday evening's entertainment. It was a vicarious experience, a chance to live the battles themselves from the comfort of a theater seat. What the bored and wealthy wouldn't do.

Jinn's soft touch grounded her back in the present. And suddenly, she remembered simpler days. Their dancing, bickering over timing and precision while Granny tried to calm them both and Egg squawked in her arms. She wondered if those days would ever come back.

The play entered its final act, performed only for them. Alice, the blond protagonist who had willingly followed Fool down the rabbit hole of mayhem, had passed the first round. Now she needed to know the details of the second.

Fool appeared from the same trapdoor, his posture bent in a gentlemanly bow. The mysterious Fanciful Freak always made her shiver.

"The second round?" He tilted his head too far to the side. "Why, Alice, the second round will be a wondrous trip around London, a true test of wit: a treasure hunt."

"A bloody treasure hunt?" said Cherice behind them.

Hawkins sighed. "You've *got* to be kidding me."

The mumblings of the other champions began to fill the hall. Elsewhere, Bately snorted, his arms folded against his chest. Max watched him out of the corner of his eye. Bately's room was on the club's fifth floor. Every so often, she or Max would cross paths with him in the halls. Bately was good at prodding Max, teasing him about the good old days, reminding him of Chadwick. One day, he mentioned Max's sister and all hell broke loose. It was all Iris could do to keep her teammate from bashing his skull. After that they exchanged no words as they passed each other in Club Uriel. Just glances. And from Bately, a wicked grin promising revenge.

Fool pulled three long cards from underneath his black jacket sleeve. Tarot cards, each with figures drawn meticulously, the surfaces painted in black, violet, and gold. Henry, who sat at the very front with his team, leaned in closely.

"Hidden somewhere in London are three cards, only three, which look just like the replicas in my hand: The Sun. Judgment. The World. Three cards. Three locations. You are to bring as many of the three as you can back to Club Uriel undamaged. Find one card. Find two. Or, if you're daring, find all three if you can. Those who bring a card will be considered a winner of this round. Remember, the *winners* of each round will receive a mysterious advantage for the finale. But surely you don't want that for your competitors, do you?" Fool laughed. "The more cards you collect, the greater chance you have at taking away that advantage from another team. Something for you to think about, no?"

He was banking on their desperation. And from the looks of the teams around the music hall, it was a safe enough bet to put money on. Only three cards in London. Not enough for all the teams here. And if a team found one card, they'd likely be attacked and challenged for it, even by another team with a card of their own.

"Oh, and please don't try to create your own cards to fool the club," Fool added, wagging his index finger. "Any attempt to turn one in will earn you a burial site. To find the real cards, listen well to our riddle. It is entitled 'Twilight of the Gods.'"

While he paused for effect, Iris could have sworn he shifted his gaze toward her. Whatever expression he wore behind that mask of his was a mystery she didn't need solved.

"Please do stay in your seats," he warned.

Fool descended through the trapdoor and the curtains closed. After a time, murmurs filled the hall—teams thinking of their strategies perhaps. That is, until a blast of white smoke drew their attention to the stage once more. The smoke covered the entire stage. Then, with a kind of elegant grace, the curtains opened again to the sound of a harp gently plucking cryptic, mystical chords.

Firelight shone from the back of the stage, now showing a picturesque valley and three tall women, actresses who hadn't yet appeared in this play, dressed in dark, shimmering drapery, their long hair covered in black veils. The first, who looked like the oldest, lay on the right under a fir tree. The second was stretched out on a rock in front of a cave. And the third, clearly the youngest of the three, sat in the center in front of the rock.

A beautiful song escaped their lips, alluring like the sirens, in a language Iris couldn't understand, but from her travels with Coolie's company, she suspected it was German. As they sang, one rope was passed between them, the thick cord the color of golden hay.

"Hold on, I've seen something like this before," Iris heard Lucille say on the other side of the room only to be shushed by Mary.

"We who see all," the women chanted in English. "Through the years we have seen them. The figures who pioneered the enlightenment of mankind and the modern age. We see their past. We see their destiny."

The oldest woman unwound part of the rope and tied one end to a branch of the tree. And then began her verses.

"In the *salle de jeu de paume,*
those men of Robespierre's Estate;
in the *salle de jeu de paume,* they made a promise.
But the upheaval they sparked was not a *parlor game.*
The ideas they formed would shape Europe for decades to come,
and lead millions to their deaths."

She threw the rope to the next woman, who wound it around the rock.

"Treaties deeply pondered
can sometimes lead to the enslavement of others.
The Earl of Shaftesbury had once believed in the divine right of kings,
and the hereditary conditions of their slaves.
But the moment he challenged the king, his fate was sealed;
his body was sealed without even a trial.
He who once supported the imprisonment of others became himself a *prisoner . . .*"

The last and youngest woman caught the rope that was passed on to her before throwing the end behind her.

"Immanuel Kant was inspired by that English man of science,
that professor whose discoveries changed the world,

and yet what a small-minded fool Kant was.

Despite his love of nature and reason,

he failed to understand the nature of humanity.

But such a man would have been welcome in that professor knight's humble *abode*,

or perhaps his academy. An institution of learning . . . an institution of misery."

The youngest threw the rope to the second. "Oh, sister, know'st thou what will befall their children?"

She nodded. "Branches of the ash tree litter the ground."

The second threw the rope to the first, who then loosened it from the tree. "Ready for the flames that will burn *all* to ashes."

The rope broke. A hush fell over the women as they took hold of the pieces.

"The die is cast," said all three in unison. "No more speaketh we. The folly of men begets folly. The cruelty of men begets cruelty. They shall hear us no more. Descend!"

In a puff of smoke red like the sunrise, the women vanished from the stage.

The hall was silent. Iris's eyebrow rose as she looked at her teammates.

"Was that it? Was that the riddle?" Cherice whispered behind her. "I can't even remember what the hell they said!"

"Quiet," said Jacob.

"The second round will officially begin tonight at midnight." Fool's voice could be heard over the hall. "You're not to touch each other until then. You'll have until midnight tomorrow to complete this round. But the round can end sooner so long as all three cards are returned to Club Uriel."

"Twenty-four hours?" Max lowered his voice, turning to Iris. "These cards are hidden throughout London. It's a big city. We're going to have to work fast to make it in time."

"This trial is not so hard if you reflect upon what was said." The gold in Fool's mask glinted. "Then, take your leave. I bid you farewell!"

The curtains closed for good. Immediately afterward, champions began filing out of the music hall, grumbling in fury. Like Cherice, Iris could barely remember the riddle. Thankfully, the little bald man at the door was giving each team a pamphlet of the play's script as they left. How nice of the Committee.

"Hey." Cherice leaned in. "We'll meet in your room in thirty," she told Iris's team very quietly before following Jacob and Hawkins out the door.

Iris looked around. Bately had already left. She'd seen him pass by with a toothpick lodged between his teeth, his eyes on Iris. Gram and Jacques were gone too. Jinn and Max got up.

"Iris?" Max said, worriedly looking down because Iris was still seated.

She felt suddenly drained. Fool's words were beginning to jumble inside her mind, which was already preoccupied with a mystery of its own.

"It's all right, I'll join you at the club. I just need some time."

"We'll wait for you outside," Jinn said in a tone that told Iris this wasn't up for discussion. Iris smiled almost in spite of herself as her two overprotective teammates hesitantly left the hall.

It was almost ten minutes that she laid back against her seat, staring up at the rafters, letting her vision double and blur before blinking her eyes clear again with a groan. Robespierre. Shaftesbury. Kant. She'd heard of some of those names, not all. Wherever in London those three cards were, their locations were related to those three men. Iris was sure of it.

Her whirring thoughts blocked everything else out. Maybe that was why she was so shocked when she turned and found—

"Fool!" Her heart jumped into her throat. He was sitting several rows behind her, staring up at the rafters along with her. "What are you doing here?"

Fool began to giggle. Loud and frenzied. His lazy slouch looked like hers just a second ago—his arms dangling behind his chair, his eyes up at the ceiling. Was he mocking her?

"Don't be scared, little rabbit. I am a fool, after all. A jester. Though one could say a fool is no fool at all." His top hat obscured the upper part of his mask without falling down entirely. He pushed it up and leaned forward. "Did you enjoy the play?" he asked with great interest. "Did you understand the riddle I wrote, 'Twilight of the Gods'? It's partially based upon that extraordinary opera by Richard Wagner. Clever, don't you think?"

"You wrote the riddle?"

"Under the supervision of the Enlightenment Committee. It wasn't too difficult. All my life I've been quite the fan of the opera, of plays and the masque. Though I must admit, when it came to 'Twilight of the Gods,' Lord Temple had quite a few ideas of his own. He's very much a fan of Wagner's work, you see."

Iris swallowed carefully as Fool tilted his head to the side as if she was supposed to get something . . . as if she was missing an important clue just by his sitting there and speaking to her.

She wasn't sure what to make of this Fool. His peculiar nature, his intense interest in her. But there was one thing about him she wanted to know, right here, right now.

Fool lay back against the bench, his face to the ceiling. This was Iris's chance.

Not too quickly, she stepped toward the mysterious man, pausing every so often to watch the rise and fall of his chest. So he *was* human, then. Not some kind of conjured golem. When she was close enough, she stretched her hand toward his face. She expected him to grab her wrist, but he didn't move, didn't even twitch. Well, that was good for Iris.

She seized his mask and pulled.

And pulled.

And again.

"It doesn't come off," Fool said, making Iris jump back. She could imagine him smiling underneath that veil of his.

"You were at the South Kensington fair ten years ago too, weren't you?"

"Why, yes. I was there to murder my doctor. Don't be surprised"—for Iris had audibly gasped—"I don't much like alienists. Lord Temple is the only one who seems to understand. We both have *terrible* fathers." He laughed.

Though this time his laugh felt a little strained. Iris didn't know what to think.

"Ah, that reminds me: he has a message for you."

Stepping back as he leaned in, Iris put a hand against her chest. "What?"

"Just that it would have done you some good if you'd taken him up on his earlier offer."

Earlier offer? Iris furrowed her brow. "You seem to talk about him a lot. Are you his personal servant or something?"

"He feels you need time for relaxation," Fool said without answering. "I agree. The truth will be learned in time. Perhaps sooner—"

He stopped, immediately placing a finger to his lips. Silence. He looked up quickly, and then: "Ah," he said finally, a little defeated, slumping back. "I guess my time is up."

Iris felt a chill and looked up at the rafters.

Fool. One. Two. Three. Three Fools. Three Fools standing upon the rafters, one crouching, one upright and pristine like an arrogant gentleman, the last fidgeting with his top hat. It was too much. Iris ran from the hall as fast as she could.

31

I SAY WE JUST CHECK EVERYWHERE." CHERICE kicked her legs as she sat on Max's bed.

Max rolled his eyes. "Oh, we'll just scour the whole city indiscriminately, will we?"

"We can throw her in the Thames and have her take a look there," said Hawkins by the door.

Cherice pouted as the two boys laughed. "You guys never take my ideas seriously."

"Because who can take *you* seriously?" Max ruffled her hair as if she were a scruffy little schoolboy. Iris could tell she hated it.

"Okay, okay." Sitting on the couch in the corner, Jacob held up a hand to stop them. At the very least, they took him seriously. "We need to think this through a *bit* more carefully."

Iris cleared her throat. "Did I happen to tell you all that there were four Fools at Wilton's?"

"Yes!" said everyone for the second time, since it was the third time Iris had brought it up.

"It explains how he's able to watch so many different teams," Jinn had said when Iris told him outside the hall.

Indeed. Perhaps Fool started out as one man and, due to the explosion at the fair, became many—or maybe he could split himself into different Fools at his leisure. Each Fool seemed to have his own way about him. His own mannerisms. His own personality. And it was very clear to her that the Fool she spoke to didn't seem all too comfortable sharing everything he wanted while the other Fools were around.

But all the champions had strange abilities, and he was a watcher, not a competitor. What they needed to do now was concentrate on the second round. The riddle.

"I read the riddle a few times." Jacob flipped through the pages of the pamphlet Wilton's doorman had given them. "There are some words here where the ink is bolder than the others."

"A clue," said Hawkins, and though Jacob stiffened a little at the sound of his voice, he nodded. Hawkins seemed to notice; though he was too proud to show it, he probably hadn't realized he was showing it nonetheless. Iris blushed slightly as she remembered shamelessly spying on them.

"There were some words that *sounded* louder than the others when they spoke," Iris offered. "What are the bolded words?"

"The first actress who spoke—the 'Norns,' they're called here—for her section the words are '*salle de jeu de paume*' and 'parlor game,'" Jacob said. "For the second Norn, the word 'prisoner' is emphasized. And in the last section: 'abode.'" He looked up, a question in his eyes. "It's a start, but . . ."

"But the key is finding out about those men mentioned in the riddle," said Iris.

"There were three, weren't there?" Max listed them off with his fingers. "Robespierre. The Earl of . . ." He scratched his head. "Stansville?"

"Shaftesbury," Iris corrected. "Immanuel Kant . . ." She thought. "And someone else. The humble 'abode' belonged to a professor knight he supposedly admired. That has to mean something."

The room fell silent as both teams thought.

"Well, Robespierre was a leader of the French Revolution," Jinn said, sitting on his bed.

"Well, we can't very well travel to France, can we?" Iris paused. "Can we?"

"I'm guessing it'd be a waste of time as the cards are supposed to be here in London," Jinn answered with a tiny teasing smile that made Iris grumpier.

"The Earl of Shaftesbury ended up a prisoner." Max grimaced. "Are these even real people? How do we know they weren't made up?"

"Robespierre was real. Why wouldn't the rest of them be?" The actresses spoke of men who drove the enlightenment of modern man. French Revolution . . . They must have been figures of history. But how were they to know the details of these men's lives? Iris crushed her pillow against her chest. "They could have given us a reference book at the very least."

Max finally threw up his hands in defeat. "Maybe this whole thing's a red herring," he said with a shrug. "I say we just check around the city."

"That's what *I* said!" Cherice growled, smacking him on the head with her fist.

But it couldn't have been a red herring. Nothing Fool said, wrote, or did seemed to be just for the sake of it. Even his message from Adam—for her to relax. What did it mean?

"The setting of the riddle was interesting. They were in front of a cave, weren't they?" said Hawkins. "Some teams might already be looking for caves in the area."

Cherice thought about it. "So should we give it a go?"

Jacob was thoughtful, quietly assessing the situation, listening for the words behind the words. Iris noticed how he considered everyone's opinions before answering carefully.

"The setting of the play could certainly be a clue as to what we're dealing with," he said. "The three 'Norns.' The rope that broke. But I think it'd be smarter to focus on the names and emphasized words in the script."

"Let's pool our knowledge," Iris said. "What do we know about each of these guys? And where can we go to learn more about them?"

"Well, there's a study on the first floor of the club. Maybe we can—"

Jacob stopped and looked toward the door. They all did—so they all saw the white note slip underneath their door.

Hawkins whipped open the door quickly and searched both ends of the hallway. They should have been the only ones on this floor. "No one's there," he said, closing it again.

"What does it say?" Max asked as he stooped to pick up the note.

"'All England Lawn Tennis Club.'" Hawkins frowned. "They can't be this obvious."

Another message from Fool? Adam? Another team looking to partner up? Cherice jumped to her feet. "All right, let's go!"

"Wait a second!" Jacob stood quickly. "We need to consider this carefully."

"I agree," said Jinn. "We don't know who the message is from, why they gave it to us, or whether the location is even real."

Jinn was right. For all they knew, it could be a trap. A team pretending to help while sending them to the wrong location. Worst case scenario: a blood-bath awaited them.

"Wait a minute." Iris thought back to Fool's words in the hall. Adam's message for her to relax. That she should have taken him up on his earlier offer. What did he offer . . . ?

"Come on, you don't think the other Patrons are cheating?" Cherice pressed, placing her hands on her hips. "All the other teams probably have the locations by now."

"The Patrons are probably watching each other," Jacob said. "I don't think they could cheat so freely. They probably have their own rules."

But sending secret messages wasn't beyond them. *What was it that Adam offered?*

The second round won't start for a while. Maybe you and I could play a round at the new Gossima parlor in town. A game of whiff-whaff should help you relax.

"Gossima!" Iris stepped off her bed. "The new parlor in town. Adam told me about it a few days ago! 'Parlor games'—that's one of the phrases, isn't it?"

Jinn turned. "Adam told you about this?" he asked slowly. "When did you talk?"

But Hawkins wasn't interested in that. "Table tennis?" He blinked. "But why—"

Iris was already putting on her shoes. "Just trust me on this."

"But—"

"*Jeu de paume*," Jinn whispered. "Game of the palm. It's an old name for tennis. I heard it from my father once when I was living in France."

"You lived in France?" Max tilted his head, grinning a little even when his amused curiosity was met with the stone wall of Jinn's silence.

"My father taught me a lot of things. Robespierre was the leader of the French Revolution," Jinn said instead, closing his eyes as if thinking back. "The Third Estate was a group that represented the people. The place where the Third Estate gathered when the nobles and clergy wouldn't allow them to assemble was an indoor tennis court."

Iris knew very little about the details of the French Revolution, but—"Gossima's kind of like tennis, isn't it?" Iris hopped about, adjusting her shoes. "Fool told me something at the hall that points to it. He said it was a message from Adam."

"Wow, he really, *really* fancies you, doesn't he?" Cherice snorted, and she leaned into Max. "Better luck next time, mate," she said in a very loud "whisper."

"I never need luck, mate," he "whispered" back, making Cherice bristle.

"Look. We can go to both locations. Split up." Iris dusted off her skirt. "But I think the tennis club is more likely to be a trap."

"We'll go," Jacob said, nodding at Hawkins. "Iris, your team will try the parlor."

Iris nodded. "The goal is for both of our teams to get—and keep—a card. Whatever advantage it'll give us in the final round, we can't let anyone else take it from us."

The room fell silent, because they all knew: the final trial would likely be the worst. And if either team was going to make it out alive, they needed that advantage—whatever it was.

Past midnight, the Gossima parlor was closed. It was a high-society game, sometimes called whiff-whaff because of the little ball they whacked with paddles across dining room tables. If the venue were open, she'd have seen people dressed in their finest to play this comically miniature form of tennis. Having nobody inside just made it easier to break in. Max did the honors behind the building, wrapping his fist in cloth and punching the window glass.

Inside, across the red carpet were rows of tables with little nets set up.

"Looks like there's two floors," Max said. Which meant two floors of tables, smoking rooms, closets. "We should split up. Scream if you find anything—or anyone."

Iris and Jinn stayed on the first floor, searching underneath every table to see if there was a card stuck in a corner or pinned to the floor by a leg.

"Tedious," she heard Jinn complain from inside one of the washrooms.

"Rather have another go in the zoo?"

"I'm looking for a tarot card inside a washstand."

"No, then." She almost giggled thinking of Jinn, with his worn-out sack carrying his bolero blades strapped to his back, checking the plumbing. Using the table for support, Iris stood from the floor when she heard Max's voice above them. "What's that?" It wasn't a scream. It didn't sound as if he was in danger. But she couldn't make out what he was saying.

"Stay here," Jinn told her, leaving the washroom and making for the wooden steps by the side of the wall. "Keep searching."

But the moment Jinn was out of sight, she saw a shadow behind the front door just before it closed. When was it ever open?

Iris investigated, running out into the street, checking each direction until the flutter of a dress caught the corner of her eye. Iris gritted her teeth. If they were enemies, it just confirmed that this was the right location. In that case, it would be better to get rid of them quickly while Jinn and Max searched. Clenching her fists, Iris slipped into the alleyway.

The two figures there were cast in shadow. It was a woman she'd never seen before that walked out of the darkness first—a handsome young woman with sun-kissed skin, short, dark brown hair curling luxuriously around her high cheekbones, eyes like coals glittering devilishly.

"Are you lost?" Iris asked her. She looked high society enough in her beautiful dress and that unopened, black-dotted parasol. Either she'd come to play a game a little too late, or—

Out of sheer instinct, Iris raised her fists, her narrowed eyes peering at the woman suspiciously. "Who are you?" she asked more forcibly, uneasy as the woman began to giggle behind her hand.

"Iris!" Suddenly a window opened from the second floor and Iris could see Max's frantic expression as he poked his head out of it. "Don't come back inside! It's rigged!"

"What—"

Quick as a flash the woman ran and smashed into Iris with her elbow, sending her flying.

"Who am I?" said the woman as Iris's body crashed onto the pavement hard. "I can be anyone I want to be."

She had an American accent, definitely from one of the Northern States. But there was something else bothering Iris as she stumbled to sit up. She'd heard that voice somewhere . . .

At the zoo. When it was trying and failing to pretend to be an old English lady. Lucille.

"What do you want?" Iris demanded, gripping her throbbing forehead where the woman's elbow had hit.

"Oh, we've got what we want," Lucille said.

Out of shadows came the second figure: a strawberry-blond girl with one long French braid tied in little blue ribbons.

"Mary. What's going on here?"

"What's going on," said Lucille, "is that you've been tricked."

32

IRIS STEPPED BACK, CAREFUL NOT TO trip over her dress. "What does my teammate mean by 'It's rigged'?" she demanded, glaring at the two of them.

"Miss Lucille," said the shy, nervous girl, her hands behind her back. "You shouldn't have gone back to peek inside."

"Oh, stop *fretting*, Mary; this is much more fun." Lucille turned to Iris. "The trap is the card, my dear—held in the hands of a tiny little Whittle's teddy bear rigged to explode at the wrong touch. Your boys try to remove it and—" Like one of the bad actors at Wilton's, Lucille made a gesture of slitting her own throat. Subtle.

In her long, tightly fitted bodice and draped bustle, all eggshell white, this Lucille, if it was even the *real* Lucille, strutted toward Iris, swinging her parasol. She walked as if she didn't have a care in the world—no, as if she owned it. As if she had such an unmeasurable kind of freedom at her fingers that, should she fail at this deadly game, she needed only to hop on a steamship and go back to the States to marry a Vanderbilt.

Iris stepped back. "Why would you destroy the card? How did you even know so quickly that it was here?" But she had a feeling she knew the answer to that last one. The Patrons. As expected, it wasn't just Adam sending hints.

"Even if you take the card, you can still have it stolen from you in the end. Might as well blow it up!" Lucille laughed. "Then nobody gets to have it."

Use the card to get rid of the competition. But didn't Fool say to bring it back undamaged? Something wasn't adding up.

"Unknit those brows, Miss Iris." Lucille pressed a violet-gloved hand against her cheek in amusement. "Such a serious girl."

"Iris!" Max called from above. "Sit tight. We're going to try to take the card!"

"No!" Iris answered quickly. "Don't bother, it's not worth it!"

Why wouldn't Lucille's team have just taken the card and run?

You shouldn't have gone back....

Iris lowered her head, grinning darkly, because once again little Mary had given something away. If not by her words, then by the way her arms trembled behind her back.

"This is a gamble for you too, though, isn't it?" said Iris as Lucille approached with her parasol. "Damaging one of the cards? You were at Wilton's; you heard the rules. Going against them? Well, who knows what kind of *agonizing* punishment awaits you back at Club Uriel?"

But it wasn't Lucille who Iris was looking at. It was Mary. The girl twitched particularly hard at "agonizing."

"Miss Lucille . . . ," Mary started.

"Quiet, sweetie," Lucille said without a hint of malice, her eyes still on Iris. "Yes, I was at Wilton's. Wasn't that play fun? Some of Wagner's *Götterdämmerung* with a little history thrown in; goodness, this whole tournament business is far more interesting than I could have ever imagined!"

She was close now, her parasol at her side, her chin raised as she sized Iris up as if examining a worthy foe. Iris had her fists ready, but the worried tears in Mary's eyes were the last bit of confidence she needed to go for the jugular.

"What's that behind your back, Mary?"

"Mary, run!" Lucille ordered just as Mary jumped and dropped the tarot card in her hands. The Sun. But before Iris could move, Lucille grabbed her wrist. Iris braced for a swing, but it wasn't a fist that met her face.

It was a deep, long kiss.

Iris was so shocked, she forgot where she was. The heat from Lucille's body made her dizzy. Lucille ravaged her lips until suddenly Iris felt Mary's dress flitting past her.

"What—" Iris blinked, still in a daze. "You . . . !"

"*You?*" Lucille repeated in a mocking tone, still holding Iris tightly by the small of her back. "Over the many years, all the women I've held in my loving embrace have had a good deal more to say than that after one of my kisses." She smirked. "There's a particularly lovelorn redhead I left in New York who'd kill to be where you are now, you know."

Mary has the card, Iris reminded herself. Lucille's kiss had indeed left her with a pleasant tingling feeling, but Iris couldn't let herself be beaten by a distraction. She clumsily turned to chase after Mary when Lucille pulled her back, readying a fist this time. With one swift movement, Iris blocked the woman's swing, causing Lucille to jump back.

"Fighting doesn't suit me, you know. All the blood and the hair everywhere." Lucille lifted her parasol, clicking a button that made the metal tip jut out, sharp and battle-ready. "Doesn't mean I won't."

"The card's a decoy!" Iris managed to yell to Max and Jinn, earning Lucille's grin as the woman charged.

"We have Henry to thank for our trinkets—including the fake card he drew just before setting out. Quite the artist. Grandpa Whittle would be so proud." She wielded her parasol like a fencer, nearly too fast for Iris to keep up.

Apparently, she *was* a fencer. "Turns out, I was taught by one of the greats in France."

And in the next second, the woman tripped slightly before regaining her footing. Apparently, not even the best fencer could overcome a bustle.

"Iris!" Jinn. "We're coming down. Don't fight her unarmed!"

Iris looked up, and a sword came flying down from the window above. One of Jinn's bolero blades. Iris caught it handily and swung it around, pointing it at Lucille.

"Did I mention I was an opera singer in Italy?" Lifting her skirt, Lucille lunged again, but this time Iris was ready. Familiar with this weapon, she battled for real as if she were on her tightrope, the steel of her blade clashing with Lucille's parasol.

"Before I did a stint as a highwayman," Lucille added, nicking Iris's neck.

"Like telling tall tales, do you?" Iris's heel caught her dress, and she stumbled back against the wall, ducking just in time for the point of Lucille's parasol to lodge in the brick.

"What I like is being able to be anything." Lucille began swinging her parasol again. "To change. To pass. It's fun. You can do anything you want. It's freedom incarnate."

"Alas, not all of us have such a privilege," Iris said, and caught the parasol with both hands, ripped it from Lucille's grip, and smashed the curved handle into the woman's forehead.

Lucille must have known her time was up. Yanking the handle back from Iris's grip and tripping Iris with a swift move, she ran toward the open street. "We must do this again! Oh—" she added, and pointed toward Iris's hair. "There's something on your bow."

A red beetle hair clip that wasn't there before. When had Lucille—?

Panic gripped Iris. She didn't have time to think. Ripping it off her bow, she threw it toward the walled end of the alleyway. It exploded the moment it hit the ground. A sizable charge, not big enough to destroy the building, but big enough to freeze Iris to the spot. A quick salute and Lucille dashed into the street, barreling through Jinn and Max just as they appeared.

Her teammates ran toward her as the smoke from the flames rose into the sky. Iris stared down at the hole in the ground that could have been her head, and by the time Iris looked up again, Lucille was gone.

"If the tennis club was a trap, then Hawkins would have gotten them out of there," Max said as they ran through the streets as fast as they could. "Back to the club. We'll regroup with them there."

But once they turned a corner into Pall Mall Street, Iris realized fast that

Lucille's team wasn't the only one that considered hunting other teams as important as hunting for cards. Iris had wondered who'd been responsible for the clue slipped underneath their door. It might have been the pompous-looking man now in the middle of the empty street in front of them, his finely combed brown hair tucked neatly underneath a gray bowler hat. One of Benini's men. So was it Kyle Leakes or Freddy Frasier? Iris had spied both in the club a couple of times, their long legs climbing the stairs completely in sync.

"Mr. Frasier and I split up," said Leakes when Iris asked, waving a gentlemanly hand and speaking as if he'd gone to finishing school. In his other hand was a gleaming cane. Iris could barely see his brown eye behind his right monocle. "He must have already done away with your friends at the tennis club by now. An alliance—how *quaint*."

And Mr. Leakes wasted no time dispersing mist from his body.

Iris, Jinn, and Max closed ranks, standing back-to-back as the mist surrounded them. Jinn and Iris readied their bolero blades and Max his fists as the mist took shape into monstrous forms. Gargoyles. How medieval.

"One doesn't need an alliance when you can create your own army," said Leakes, and his monsters immediately began attacking. Though made of smoke, their teeth and claws were somehow hard as metal. Iris and Jinn fought blade for blade. Max managed to blink behind two of the monsters. They burst into smoke the moment his hand chopped their necks, only for the smoke to gather and take shape once again.

"There's no end to them," Max said, ducking the claws of another. "Gotta get Leakes!"

"Easier said than done." Iris gritted her teeth. They were fast, overwhelming, never-ending. She didn't have time to even look for the man behind the beasts.

"Iris," Jinn called, holding out his hand and giving it a flick. With just that she knew. She ran at Jinn. She and Jinn once practiced for weeks to get that one-handed flip right. Though she was light, for that show in Birmingham, Jinn had to work on his upper-arm strength like never before. As Jinn flipped her up into the air now, Iris once again felt that peace, that calm as she became one with the sky. It also gave her the perspective she needed.

Leakes. He was apart from his army, sneaking up on Jinn like a coward.

"Jinn, behind you!"

Just as Iris threw her blade down at the gargoyle rushing to stop him, just as it dispersed into smoke, Jinn flipped back. After a full twist, his boots found Leakes's shoulders and smashed him against the pavement, knocking him out. The gargoyles disappeared.

Picking up her blade, Iris wiped the sweat off her forehead. "You probably didn't need to do a whole *back full*," she teased with a grin. "A regular jump would have sufficed."

Jinn smirked. "Quiet," he said before checking the champion's pockets. No card.

"Come on," Max said, rubbing his bruised knuckles. "I don't believe for one second the rest didn't escape. Not with what Hawkins can do. They're probably inside the club right now."

When Iris ran through the door first, she didn't expect Rin waiting for her by the front of the steps inside—without her veil, no less. "Rin?"

Jinn and Max must have reacted defensively, because Rin put her hand up in peace.

"It's okay," Iris told her teammates. "She's not here to fight." She smiled at Rin, making the girl blush. "Besides, this place is a neutral zone, isn't it?"

Now that Rin was on her own, Iris had hoped she was ready for some kind of alliance. What Rin had to tell her instead was *not* what she expected.

"You asked me to tell you if I found any information on the white crystal," she said, causing Iris to intake a sharp breath. "If you want to know the truth, today just might be your last day to do it. Give up the hunt for the cards, Isoke, before your true treasure slips away forever."

33

WHILE RIN WAS PLAYING THE PART of guard and champion, she was secretly taking advantage of Bellerose's connections. One of them had told her an interesting rumor about the West African envoys discussed in the newspapers—the ones who'd come to England to talk to the queen about their mining dispute with the National African Company, owned by the Crown. The papers had said the dispute was over the mining of *salt*. Far from it. The mineral both groups were after was an ore kept secret from the public—one that shone blinding white like a pearl.

The white crystal.

Iris and Rin spoke alone.

"Isoke, from what the legends say, you were kidnapped by the Dahomey in a village near that mining site all those years ago," Rin whispered in the lobby just beneath the stairs.

Iris rubbed her arm, deep in thought as she considered the implications. "And I had a crystal with me when I arrived in the kingdom?"

"The one now in my chest." Rin placed her hand there.

"I have to know more," said Iris quickly. "If I can just meet with the envoys—"

"They've been in England for weeks," Rin said. "They're meant to leave at sunrise."

Which meant Iris had to move quickly.

"But one cannot simply speak to those of such high political importance. I'm sure they'll be well guarded by both their own people and this country's government. You'll have to find your own method to get to them."

Her own method? "Wait!" Iris called as Rin began to walk out the door. "You mean, you're not going to help me?"

"Since one of the Patrons died, I've been ordered to work with another partner. If I don't find him at our agreed meeting place, he'll be suspicious. Not to mention, Bellerose is hosting a party at her residence tomorrow evening. She said before it starts that there's something she needs me to do no matter what."

Iris frowned. "Still doing that vile woman's bidding?"

"It was just supposed to be until I found you and returned you to the king," answered Rin. Iris gulped as Rin pushed opened the door and turned her head slightly. "But right now I *am* a little interested in the mystery of the white crystal—the stone that connects us, Isoke. I'll support your efforts, even if it's from afar. And even if it means staying in this country longer than I expected to. Besides," she added, "finding the truth is *your* mission."

"And what's yours, then?" said Iris, remembering the girl's viciousness when they first met. That deadliness was still there, but the drive . . . the drive had waned. Iris could tell. Taking her back to the Dahomey . . . Was it still her goal?

Rin fell silent, lowering her head. "I'm not so sure anymore."

She left.

Iris didn't have much time.

Max was right to believe in Team Hawkins. They were already inside Team Iris's room, waiting for them. Apparently Frasier had loose lips. Before defeating him, Team Hawkins learned that the professor knight mentioned in the riddle was Sir Isaac Newton. He was the one who'd inspired Immanuel Kant. So the card was in the abode he once lived in. None of them knew where that was.

And Iris used it to her advantage.

Iris hated herself for lying to them. But the truth was why she was in this tournament to begin with, and she just didn't have the time to explain it all or to convince them to go along with her plan. So Iris lied and told them that Rin was given a clue by Bellerose as to the location of the next card: Marlborough House, Sir Isaac Newton's "abode." They didn't have time to look through books and corroborate it.

Based on Rin's intelligence, the Oil Rivers envoys that had arrived at Plymouth one month ago had just returned to *their* residence at Marlborough House, escorted by the Colonial Office. They would have retired for the night, so they weren't coming back out. But tongues tended to loosen in private. Iris needed a way inside without being seen. She was right to ask the rest for help, telling them that the envoys were holding one of the tarot cards as part of the tournament's second round, even though she knew there was no such thing at Marlborough House. And though she hated lying to them, if she'd come clean with the truth, they might have tried to stop her from going. Pushed her to prioritize the second round while one of her important leads slipped away.

Maybe they *wouldn't* have said that. Maybe she was being too hasty in judgment, too reckless. But the thought of getting a clear hint to her past had overloaded her senses and taken precedence over everything else. Her nerves were buzzing.

She forgave herself by insisting it surely wouldn't take up too much time. She just needed to get into Marlborough House, learn what the envoys knew, and get out without being caught and arrested for breaking and entering. Max had a solution she hadn't expected.

They arrived at the house quickly. Max's birdcall was the same Cherice had used that day in the alley, an unsuspicious but loud signal that drew some attention from those still out on the street, but not enough to endanger the plan.

They'd found a couple of branches on the same tree: Max and Jinn, Iris and Jacob. Hawkins and Cherice were in the tree closest to the house. Cherice responded to Max with a second birdcall.

Marlborough House was two stories of red bricks, rusticated cornerstones, and long rectangular windows. It belonged to the Crown and their guests, which meant there were likely as many guards inside as outside. But Hawkins and Cherice weren't just checking for guards.

"That means they're coming back soon," Jacob whispered to Iris.

"You guys really have this down," Iris told him, and the gentle smile he gave her in return made her seize up in guilt.

"We've been together for so long. This is how we've survived. I came here when I was so small. I wouldn't be here today if it weren't for them—Cherice, Max, and, a-and Hawkins."

Try as he might, he couldn't hide his blush even in the darkness. She was too close to him not to see it.

"Hawkins is quite the interesting man," Iris said, and watched as Jacob nodded stiffly.

"He's impossible," Jacob suddenly said in an impatient tone.

Jacob looked like she did when insulting Jinn to Granny. The revelation made her blush along with him for more than one reason. Longtime friendships did breed closeness . . .

She shook her head. Now was not the time to think of such things.

"By the way, Iris," Jacob said, clearly wanting to move on, "I told Hawkins and Cherice this while we waited for you inside the club. But during this round, and if possible the next, we need to stay clear of Belgium's boars: Gram and Jacques."

Iris twitched at the sound of their names. "That was my plan anyway." She tried not to think about the scene they'd made in the first round. "What did you hear about them?"

"After beating Frasier at the tennis club, we took the opportunity to get some more information out of him." Jacob scratched his skin through the black hair curling around his ears. "The two men were assassins who worked for Belgium's king. I don't know what happened to Jacques to turn a priest into an assassin."

"Who knows," replied Iris, shaking her head.

"Gram is especially dangerous." His fingers dug into the bark of the trunk as they waited for Hawkins and Cherice to return. "Frasier was told the information by his Patron, who has contacts with workhouses across England. Gram grew up in one of them with five of his brothers."

"Five brothers . . ." Those workhouses had such terrible conditions that they became a central point of England's public discourse surrounding morality and the innocence of childhood. Well, there was nothing innocent about Gram now.

"They pounded horse hooves into glue. But because of famine, they had no choice but to . . ." Jacob stopped and searched for the right words. "To eat the rest of the horse's rotted flesh. Right off the bone."

Iris's stomach heaved. Her hand flew to her mouth as she remembered Gram quivering in sheer ecstasy as he bathed in blood at the zoo.

"Gram got a taste for it. After a few years, his brothers began disappearing one by one . . ."

A sense of dread swelled in Iris's chest, but she didn't have time to think about it, and Jacob clearly didn't want to continue. After a few minutes, both Cherice and Hawkins returned with their brass binoculars. They all hopped down from their branches. Max flicked his head in the opposite direction, and without a word, they strode quickly away from the area, ending up in a nearby alley. There, Cherice and Hawkins told them what they saw.

"They're on the second floor, seventh window on the northern facade," Hawkins said. "The envoys, I mean," he clarified for Iris. He crumpled the leaf he'd pulled out of his hair. "Unfortunately, they're not asleep yet. But the good news is that no other teams are in the area."

Because she'd made the whole thing up. Iris hid a wince before biting her cheek and snapping herself out of her guilt. Hers was an important mission too.

Max nodded. "Hawkins, did you get eyes on the room they were in?"

"It's a very big room, suitably fit for a royal," he confirmed. "And, I might add, there's a very luxurious bathroom inside, in which exists one of the cleanest toilets I've ever had the pleasure of setting my eyes upon. The door was open slightly."

Cherice knocked her knuckles upon his golden head. "What is it with you and toilets?"

"It's what happens when you've never had the luxury of a clean one." Hawkins flicked her on the forehead. These were people who really had grown up together. "At any rate, now that I've seen the bathroom, I can confirm it'll do just fine to hide in."

"So what now?" Jinn asked, close to Iris's side.

"We have to search the room for the card, don't we?" Hawkins said. "Preferably after they finally sleep."

Iris nodded. But she didn't want them to sleep. She wanted them to *talk*.

"How do we get inside?" Iris said.

Max patted Hawkins on the shoulder. "This guy will get you inside. From here."

"From here?" Iris gaped at the young thieves grinning mischievously at her.

"And you can take all of us?" Jinn asked.

"There's not so much space in the bathroom," answered Hawkins. "It'll fit two people at the most. I'll take Iris with me. She's the one who found out about this place. And she looks itching to go," he added, winking at her. Iris must have looked as impatient as she felt.

Jinn stepped in front of Iris as if to shield her. "I won't agree to that!"

Iris knew he meant well, but she let out a quiet, frustrated sigh nonetheless.

"Too bad. There's only room for two." Lifting his arms, Hawkins flexed his fingers.

Jacob stepped in between Hawkins and Jinn, holding his hand up to stay Jinn, who looked ready to fight him. Then Jacob turned to Hawkins and lightly laid his hand upon the other boy's cheek, thumb brushing his neck and fingers sliding across his ear, golden hairs slipping over them. Iris felt a shy flutter in her stomach from the tender scene.

"Don't aggravate things," he begged softly. Their intimacy was so quietly palpable.

Hawkins sighed, shutting his eyes but still wearing that devilish grin. "Fine, fine."

"It'll be okay, Jinn," said Max. "Hawkins is a cheeky bastard, but he's trustworthy. And Iris can handle herself, you know that."

He winked at her, which didn't go unnoticed by an annoyed Cherice.

At the end of the day, Iris appreciated both of them—the concern and the confidence. Like always. "Let's give it a go," she told Hawkins, walking up to him.

It happened too quickly for Iris to even figure out what was going on. Hawkins fell back, but not before grabbing her arm and pulling her with him. As she tumbled forward, her wide eyes managed to see a black void open up behind him, but before she had a chance to fear it swallowing her whole, she'd landed on the hard, white wooden floor of the envoys' bathroom.

"What was that?" called a deep voice coming from the other side of the door. Not in English.

"Quickly," Hawkins hissed. "Behind the curtains."

He meant the gray flower-patterned curtains covering the bathroom window, long enough to drag on the floor. It was a small space. As Hawkins grabbed her elbow and yanked her to her feet, Iris eyed the marble sink, the light fixtures hanging low from the ceiling, the ceramic tub—and yes, the beautiful, gleaming white toilet. Her head was still spinning as Hawkins pulled her behind the curtains just as the door opened.

Iris held her breath as boots clicked on the wooden floor. The swish of the bathtub curtains. A frustrated sigh.

"Segun? Is there anything there?" came another man's voice from the sitting room.

"No," said Segun, and Iris was relieved when the footsteps retreated and the door closed behind them.

As Hawkins opened the curtains, she let out the breath she was holding. "That," she started, "that was . . ." She couldn't find the words for what had just happened.

"It's called Sliding," said Hawkins quite proudly before his expression softened, his voice turning sentimental. "That's what Cherice's brother called it. Imaginative man."

"Chadwick, you mean?"

Hawkins nodded. "Creator of the Fanciful Freaks. But he was also someone who . . ." He stopped. "Who meant very much to me." He looked at Iris a little nervously, a little defiantly; a vulnerability that came from the expectation of a crude reaction. And when that reaction didn't come, he gazed out the window.

Iris wondered about Jacob but didn't dare bring up the subject. It was clearly complicated.

"Even as a child," Hawkins said, "I was always quick-witted enough to know when to run and hide. Chadwick teased me about it. These abilities of mine just ended up making it all that much easier."

"I feel dizzy." Iris's stomach gave a horrible flop. "I think I'm going to throw up."

"Be proud: you're dealing with this better than he ever did." Hawkins smirked. "Chadwick used to throw up on the spot, the poor lamb."

"And nobody saw us?" she whispered.

"In the alley? I don't think so. Not here either. And if we're to keep it that way . . ." Hawkins put his finger to his lips.

Earthen tones were splashed across the golden-brown wallpaper, giving the bathroom a rustic feel. To her right was a cabinet filled with folded towels, and to her left, a white washing pot underneath a small, square mirror fixed to the wall. Hawkins and Iris tiptoed past the sink and approached the door.

"Can you hear anything?" Hawkins whispered.

Iris laid her ear against the wood. It sounded as if they were having some kind of meeting. She could hear the clinking of cups upon plates.

"We can search for the card here in the meantime until they finally go to bed," said Hawkins, and Iris gave an awkward nod.

"Y-you go ahead and search. I'll listen for when they finally go to sleep."

Iris continued to listen as Hawkins quietly searched for a card that wasn't there. It was a good thing he couldn't understand what they were saying. She just hoped to get this over with as soon as possible.

But the conversation they were having was not one that interested her. From their discussions, they clearly weren't impressed by their stay, and why should they be? The queen hadn't budged on any of their demands.

They had done their research; their schedule mirrored that of King Cetshwayo two years before. The British were operating on protocol with no real commitment to strengthening diplomatic relations. The envoys didn't care much for the ceremonial and entirely useless tour of England's military and factory facilities, even though they were clearly meant to be. Also apparently, their translator consistently gave off a faint smell of pickles, which bothered the other envoy, named Adedayo. Perhaps he had a sensitive nose.

Iris waited patiently, listening to them drink and speak about the goings-on of their families, their homes. The local community near the mining site was split in their approval of it. For some, it gave jobs and income. But for others, rumors of *what* they were mining took precedence over economics.

Okuta funfun. The white stone. Its very existence had given some people a sense of foreboding, such that many called to leave the site and the stone untouched.

"I still cannot trust them," said Segun. "We need to find out what they're doing with our stone. It's *ours*. We should do with it as *we* wish."

Chair legs slid against a wooden floor. "The white stone has curious properties," Adedayo said. "How does such a small area in a land rich in palm oil suddenly bear a stone one has never seen before?"

"A stone that didn't exist before the Day of Darkness."

Iris sucked in a breath. Rin had mentioned it before.

"According to our spies, the Fon long noticed too. The Maasai in the east have begun to suspect. Too many strange happenings started after the eclipse almost sixty years ago. And Britain continues to take the stone for themselves to study here."

"As they take everything," said Segun.

A prolonged pause. "If they unlock its secrets, how will they use it?"

The Day of Darkness. The creation of the white stone. But what had created it? What would produce white crystal in a land rich with oil?

"Segun. After going back home, we should dispatch spies to the Crystal Palace."

"The Crystal Palace? Why?"

The Day of Darkness. Something terrible must have happened on that day.

"I have a contact at a newspaper here: the *African Times*. A young reporter from Abeokuta believes that the Crown is hiding something there. Something underground. The Colonial Office refused when I asked to put it on our schedule for this trip. It's suspicious."

It was then that Rin's voice began echoing in Iris's mind.

You were brought to the Dahomey merely weeks after the Day of Darkness...

When Iris closed her eyes and saw Anne's dead face, she wasn't able to stifle her scream. Alarmed shouts rose from the living room.

"What are doing?" Hawkins hissed, but just as he reached Iris, the door opened.

One was slight, young, and very dashing, and the other a fair amount thicker and likely older, though both had finely coiffed beards and full heads of black hair. But far from the caricatures drawn in those *Punch* magazine cartoons, these men looked handsome and princely in their blue caps and sweeping brown robes. They also looked very, very angry.

"Who are you?" the slighter one demanded. Segun, by the sound of it.

"Time to go," Hawkins whispered, and grabbed her hand once more. Segun was fast, but Hawkins was faster. Before Segun could grab him, Hawkins had successfully Slid through his black door of nothingness, bringing them back to the alleyway.

MADAME BELLEROSE STRIKES

ADAM ARRIVED AT MADAME'S RESIDENCE FOR breakfast as she'd requested the night before. Servants were hurriedly preparing for her party tonight even at this early hour. Even with the marble kitchen table filled with a sumptuous breakfast, they were already bringing in ingredients for tonight's dinner.

Pierre had taken his coat, leaving Adam in his brown vest, dark blue tie, and white dress shirt. As Madame gestured for him to sit at the opposite end of the long table, he wondered if Iris had received his message. There was an explosion at the Gossima parlor last night. He knew she couldn't die, but he hated the idea of her being harmed. The supernatural being he'd been preparing to meet again after all these years probably wouldn't have cared.

But the girl he *did* meet—Iris? No. She didn't deserve that. It was one of the reasons he still wished she could have simply stayed in his residence and regained her memories slowly, even if it took longer without the heat of battle stirring her blood, passion, and memories.

"How's your breakfast?" asked Madame Bellerose after a time, sipping her water from a white glass. "I hope it's to your liking."

"As it always is," Adam answered dispassionately, cutting into his sausages. "By the way, did you kill Cordiero yesterday?"

"That rude old man?" Madame laughed. "Whatever would have given you that idea?"

Adam swallowed his food before continuing. Eton had taught him the proper skills. "Well, he was poisoned," he said. "You've poisoned quite a bit in the past." He looked at his own food. "I wouldn't be surprised if this food were poisoned, in fact."

"My Adam, you're too pretty to kill." Madame lifted her glass as if to toast to his face.

"He also insulted you the other day."

"That he did." Madame sipped. "Men and their ways."

This tiresome banter was all a feint on his part. Adam had had Cordiero killed for his own reasons. But sometimes games like this were necessary. Bellerose didn't seem fazed by his false accusation, but sowing the seed of doubt about his own involvement made things easier for him.

"Well, we once agreed that there would be seven members of the Committee at all times. We should at least start the process of looking for a replacement among the members of the club," said Madame. "Rumors have already spread that he was a part of the Committee, and now the scramble has begun. The poor man's body isn't even cold yet." She laughed. "I was quite disappointed with the results of the first round. Two of my men killed. Dreadful! I've been trying to poach some others. For example, Van der Ven's—"

"Belgium's boars?" Adam's eyebrows raised with amusement.

"It isn't against the rules for a champion to switch teams of his or her own will, is it? At least"—Bellerose dabbed her lip with a napkin—"it wasn't a rule we made. So technically, I'm doing nothing wrong. Luckily, I've made some progress with one."

Finding loopholes was only the smart thing to do in a tournament such as this. But challenging Van der Ven took guts. The military man would not take it lying down. It was that kind of brazenness Adam actually admired in her.

"You know," she continued, "you still haven't answered my question about Belle Vue Zoo. And your involvement in the first round."

"Still on that, are you?" The orange juice was freshly squeezed. Even if it were poisoned, it would have been worth it. He *loved* orange juice. "Have you learned anything from my father's research?"

"Alas, no. But I've discovered something else that unfortunately has led me to consider all the questions I have about you a little more carefully. Pierre!"

The ghoul-like man wafted into the dining room, a dark cloud following behind him as if he were slowly dying from dysentery. "Yes, madame."

"Have you confirmed attendance for all our guests?"

"Yes, madame." Pierre nodded slowly. Everything this man did was very slow.

"And what of our special guest upstairs? He's still mending well, I hope?"

Adam carefully placed his glass back on the table. Who exactly was this special guest she kept going on about?

"He is as comfortable as he can be, madame, but he still has trouble talking."

Madame sighed. "Of course, the poor thing. That will be all." She looked at Adam. "Would you like to see him? I think he responds to company quite well."

Adam smiled cordially as he wiped his mouth with a napkin and left the table with Madame Bellerose. Just what was that witch up to? It bothered Adam to no end that he couldn't grasp the answer as he followed her up the grand staircase, even though he ran every hypothesis in his mind while responding pleasantly to her idle chatter.

"I've realized as I grow older just how important it is to keep track of your friends," she said, completely insincerely. "My friend was found floating in a river near Oxford. A nasty blow to the head. He'd been healing there in Oxford all this time, unbeknownst to anyone. But you see, I'm a very suspicious person. And so I wanted to discover for myself what happened to him."

Madame's heels were crisp upon the wooden staircase. The rhythm filled Adam with dread.

"I found him after the auction and immediately had him delivered to my house," she continued as if speaking about a package. They walked down the hallway and stopped outside a room on the second floor. "But as he stayed here, I began to wonder."

They walked inside. A group of servants and nurses was tending to an old man breathing shallowly upon a comfortable bed, the curtains and windows open. The servants bowed and curtseyed at their presence and one rushed to close the door behind them. It wasn't until Adam drew near enough to see the man's face that his blood ran cold.

"This is impossible." Adam's face paled, his lips trembling. "This can't be."

"And yet it is. Mr. Carl Anderson is indeed alive, Adam, although we sent you to kill him."

The servants and nurses were completely under Bellerose's employ. They didn't respond in any way to her words, as trained and instructed, Adam expected.

"I *did* have him killed," he said in a hushed voice, watching the sleeping man. "I was there to make sure it was done."

"But for what purpose? Or rather, for *whose* purpose." Madame Bellerose dismissed the nurses and servants, who scurried away and shut the door, leaving the three alone. "We asked you to kill John because he betrayed the Committee by taking the Moon Skeleton and hiding his research. He aimed to betray us. To find an ally who could help him escape us. But unlike you, he was never quite so good at concealing his intentions. Or maybe he just trusted the wrong man."

Neville Bradford. His father didn't know how desperate the man was to find a seat on the mysterious and powerful Committee. John had gone to both Bradford and Anderson, his friends from the old days. Anderson had agreed to help. Bradford sold them both out and then had a sudden crisis of conscience once Anderson was "dead," the idiot.

Madame stepped to the side of Mr. Anderson's bed. "He was a stupid man, your father." She scowled, looking at the barely living body as if she wanted to strangle it to death. "He really thought we in the Committee weren't worthy to guide the next stage of humanity. The audacity." She squeezed her fists so tightly that Adam could see a spot of blood developing on her white glove where her nails had been. "But the real question is, what do you believe, Adam?"

By now Adam had regained control over himself. He stayed perfectly still.

"I know we in the Committee wanted them all dead," Madame continued. "To hide our secret. To make sure that not even the Crown knows that the world is to end and how we plan to escape from the apocalypse. Only we Enlighteners deserve to have the power that knowledge brings. But what about you?" Madame cocked an eyebrow. "Why did you want them dead?"

Adam responded carefully. "For the same reason, of course."

"Really? Because I've been spending my spare time with dear Mr. Anderson, seeing if I can get him to say something intelligible. And one day, do you know what he told me?"

Adam gritted his teeth but said nothing.

"'That boy will betray you all.' That's what he said."

The room filled with silence but for the sound of Carl Anderson's labored breathing. Adam remembered that night clearly. The night he hired men to march Anderson out to the river blindfolded. Just like Bradford, Anderson had learned John Temple's dangerous secret—the one secret Adam didn't want anyone to possess. And just like Mr. Bradford, Mr. Anderson had bargained, begged for his life. But Adam wouldn't be stirred.

"Please, Adam!" Beads of sweat had dripped down Anderson's face as the hired goons readied their clubs. "The Committee is evil!"

"To hell with the Committee," Adam had told him. "I'm doing things my way."

Damn it! He should have killed the old man himself. Angrily, Adam turned around. "He doesn't know what he's talking about."

"And yet you so clearly have too many secrets," Madame Bellerose said as Adam began stalking toward the door. "I don't like men with secrets."

Adam reached for the doorknob.

"And I don't like men who lie."

Adam saw Pierre on the other side of the door before a whack on the side of the head from the man's cane knocked him out cold.

Adam woke with a gasp, stripped of his shirt and chained by the wrists to the ceiling of what could only be described as a torture chamber. All kinds of painful-looking medieval instruments hung upon the dark red clay walls. It was the bucket of chilled water Bellerose had splashed on his face that had woken him so violently. His bare chest was cold and wet, the hairs on his arms raised. He shivered.

"Oh, my dear Adam, you're awake!" Madame threw the bucket to the ground and clapped her hands together. "How do you like my basement?"

Warily, Adam glanced at the lit candles on the bloodstained table. "It's very you."

"Now, Adam, are you prepared to tell me everything you've been hiding from me?"

"I'm not hiding anything," Adam lied, earning him a slap in the face.

"What about your father's research? The secrets he kept even from the Committee. You know them, don't you?"

"Not at all."

This time a backhand. Madame Bellerose was finished playing. She took off her gloves before she gripped his chin so that he could feel her nails dig into his skin.

"What about that girl you're so fond of? What would she do if she knew you murdered your own father and at least one of his friends? Maybe I should invite her to my party and ask her. Oh, you didn't know?" Bellerose added as Adam narrowed his eyes. "This party is dedicated to Mr. Anderson—his re-debut into civilized society. Although only the Committee will be in attendance. I'm sure they'll be very interested in what he has to say."

And no doubt, if Bellerose uncovered another snake within their numbers, just like her brother, *along with* the truth of his father's research, it would earn her their respect—and fear.

"The doctor said Mr. Anderson's inability to speak is a reluctance. A psychological issue rather than simply a physical one. I wonder if he'd be in a talking mood if I sent Iris to speak with him. Of course, I'll be there too."

An ambush. Damn it! Gritting his teeth, Adam struggled against his chains.

"I love it when your mask cracks. I knew using her would be much more efficient than simply torturing what I want out of you. Do you know why, Adam?" Madame Bellerose leaned in close, tilting her head. Adam could feel her breath on his ear. "Because I think whatever little secrets you're keeping have to do with that beast you seem so inexplicably fond of."

"*We're* the beasts, Violet," he replied, rattling his chains.

But Bellerose looked content. She'd sniffed a connection. And though she didn't know what that connection was, it made her all the more dangerous.

"Guard?" Bellerose turned. "Guard? *Viens ici.*"

Through the door stepped the young champion he'd seen inside Club Uriel. The Amazon: Rin. Her face, newly unveiled, caused Bellerose to cringe and swear in French, complaining about the young woman's eye. Rin kept her face neutral, but from years of feigning compliance himself, Adam could tell she'd be happy to lop the woman's head off right where she stood.

"I'm getting ready to go out. You'll be coming with me, of course. Watch him while I'm dressing," she said in French. Rin nodded. "Adam, I've done a terrible thing." From underneath her dress she pulled the tarot card of Judgment. "It's meant to be in a grand house my father bought for me on St. Martin's Street."

"Where Newton lived more than a hundred years ago," finished Adam with a cough.

"I wonder if your champion will come if I offer her something in exchange." Bellerose seemed to relish his inability to answer. "Don't think of trying anything daring while I'm away, Adam. One of Van der Ven's men will be here shortly to watch you. Seems like I chose the right boar to bargain with."

Bellerose laughed as she left Adam alone with the girl named Rin. But Rin wasn't like the other champions or even Bellerose's servants. He'd seen her standing with Iris as Cordiero's corpse fell down the staircase. Seen her body language, her closeness to Iris. Her arm up, blocking Iris as if to shield her. That, her clear hatred for Bellerose, and her current, dispassionate expression were enough for him to make a quick deduction. Once the door closed, Adam gathered together all the Fon words he knew from his father's research, mixing them with French in hopes she'd understand.

"Iris is in danger. I need you to help me." And when Rin raised her eyebrow, he nodded. "I need you to give a message to one of Iris's teammates. Listen carefully."

34

THE DAY OF DARKNESS. THE WHITE crystal. The South Kensington explosion. The Fanciful Freaks. Iris didn't know what any of it meant. But what she did know was that she stood at the center of it all. The Crystal Palace was where she had to go next. If the British government had a stock of white crystal right here in the city, where else could she go?

She sat on her bed as Max and his friends debated their next move. Rin's information about a card being at Marlborough House was wrong somehow. She'd misunderstood Bellerose. That was what Iris had to tell them to stop them from going back to try again. Instead, as the guilt of a lie stung her, she gave them an idea: target the teams, not the locations. Henry's team had gotten a card for sure. They were the obvious choice. But where to find them? That was the debate. Some would search outside while others would stay in case they returned to the club.

Once Jinn sat down next to her, she snapped out of her daze.

"You seem distant." Jinn leaned forward, letting his elbows prop him up.

"Oh?"

"A little."

With a sigh, Iris shut her eyes. "Does it bother you?"

"Why wouldn't it?"

Iris could feel her purple ribbon tied in a great bow brushing against her ear. She hadn't taken it off since he'd given it to her.

"I understand your feelings," Jinn said softly once it was clear Iris wasn't going to answer. "Things are so different now. So wild." They both glanced over at Max and his friends, who'd all begun to bicker. Cherice was wringing Max by the neck. "In only a few days, everything has changed so drastically. Just like back then."

"Back then?"

"When my father died. Everything changed in an instant. I was on my own, alone and desperate. Eventually, I found a steady rhythm, but now things have changed again. I wonder if that means *we've* changed."

People were made up of their experiences, their memories, their understanding of themselves relative to those around them. For Iris, those three points were like parts of a wave constantly in flux, a picture changing and taking shape before her eyes. How could it not change her? But who would she be once the dust had settled? The more she learned about herself, the more complete and the more *fearful* she became. Why did she have to go through this just to know who she was? What was so special about her past that its secret had to be so safely guarded?

"There are times when I feel separated from myself," Iris confessed. "I thought participating in the tournament and discovering more about the truth would bring me together. But as this goes on, with all the information flooding in, the more everything feels out of control. There are times when it all makes sense and times when I feel . . . sectioned. Like my inside and outside aren't in harmony with each other."

"Then you need to ground yourself." Jinn placed the back of his hand on her cheek. A small touch that sent an electric shock through her chest. "Ground yourself in the familiar. In me, for example. Ground yourself in me, Iris."

As if suddenly catching himself, he withdrew his hand and stared resolutely ahead. His touch *was* familiar, as familiar as his hands gripped firmly and confidently around her waist, tossing her up into the sky. It excited her at the very same time it gave her comfort.

It was her own bubbling emotions that sent her into confusion. Because at the same time as she craved Jinn's touch, every time she heard Max laugh heartily at the other side of the room, it made her feel lighter. Like all this nonsense would sort itself out. She looked at Max now as he battled with Cherice and smiled in spite of herself. She wasn't sure if Jinn noticed. She wasn't sure if it was important even if he did. But maybe she was thinking too much. With a deep breath, she placed both her hands upon his face.

"I'll try that," she told him with a little smile.

The morning sun streamed through the window. They'd had a little sleep, but overall spent most of the night coming up with a list of places they could feasibly check before midnight tonight. Cherice overheard some club members gossiping. Apparently, many champions were checking the area. But as far as Iris knew, nobody had come to the second floor of Club Uriel with all three cards.

The game was still on.

Soon, a knock came at the door.

"Rin?" Iris looked excitedly at the girl in her long black jacket standing in the threshold of her room. "Do you . . ." She dared to think it. "Do you want to *join* us?"

To her dismay, Rin shook her head. "Come to the club room on the second floor. Someone there wants to see you."

She cast Max and Jinn a furtive glance before turning and beckoning for Iris to follow.

"Have you found a card?" Iris said. "And by the way, who's this new partner you have?"

"A card?" Rin thought as they descended the steps. "You could say that." She didn't answer the second question. Not out of malice, but something else. Next to her, Iris could see her eyes shifting nervously to the side.

Finally, they came to the second-floor club room, mysteriously empty even at this early hour but for one individual. Iris recognized her even while seeing only the back of her head.

"I'll leave you two alone," Rin said, patting Iris on the shoulder before going.

The woman's wide-brimmed pink hat had several red feathers that matched the color of her overcoat, dress, and of course, that hair, twisted expertly with little white flowers sticking out from the folds. Her white-gloved hands daintily held a steaming cup of tea and brought it to her lips. The only light in the room was through one drawn curtain over a window near the bar.

"Don't just stand there." Madame Bellerose waved to the leather seat in front of her.

Iris defiantly strode down the aisle and sat opposite the woman. She readied a slew of clever insults on her tongue, but then looked down at the table.

A tarot card. Judgment.

Iris's fingers couldn't help but twitch at the sight of it. Madame slipped it into her jacket's inside breast pocket.

"In due time," Madame said, taking another sip from her tea.

"Are you Patrons allowed to get so involved?" Iris's eyes narrowed. "Isn't this cheating?"

"We're Enlighteners. We do as we please and kill those who disapprove."

Madame Bellerose's lips stretched into a smile as she watched for Iris's reaction. Iris stayed neutral, although an image of Cordiero, gasping and bloody, rose up in her mind. Bellerose had no idea how much Iris already knew about the Enlightenment Committee—their members, for example. Iris was sure Bellerose was especially interested in how much information Adam was willing to share with Iris. And why.

With a sigh, Madame Bellerose placed her teacup on the table. "I have a proposition for you," she said, setting her elbows down, entwining her fingers, and resting her chin on them. "A trade, if you will."

"What could I possibly have that you would want?" Iris asked. "Beyond beauty, inner goodness, human decency—"

"Your time, for now," Bellerose said, her voice growing strained. "Yes, I want your time, Adam's champion. After that, I suppose we'll see what you have that would suit my interests."

Iris's body was ready to spring at the slightest surprise. "What do you mean by that?"

"I'm throwing a party tonight."

Iris rolled her eyes. "Yes, I know. Good for you," she answered flatly.

"Oh, forgive me," replied Bellerose with a dismissive wave. "I don't suppose you even have parties where you come from." Iris bristled. "But your presence is required nonetheless if you want this card."

"Let me guess." Iris folded her arms. "Your party'll be filled to the brim with champions just itching to get me out of the way."

"Such a negative little thing, aren't you?" Madame played with a strand of her hair. "Not at all. There's just someone I'd like you to meet."

Iris was just about to give her a nasty retort and make for her card.

"Adam's been keeping him from you."

Iris unfolded her arms. Once again, Madame was watching for her reaction. "So?" She scoffed. "I'm just a champion. The second I win this tournament and get my money, I'm out of London. Who cares what secrets he's keeping?" Adam's secrets had secrets. But what did Bellerose know about *her*? That was the question.

"Aren't you interested in learning?" Bellerose continued. "I am. I'm interested in finding out everything I don't know."

Iris said nothing.

"What if I were to tell you that this is a man Adam tried to murder?"

Her shoulders dropped. Iris sat a little straighter in her seat.

"That's what makes the dear boy so delectable: his skill at deception." The feathers on Bellerose's hat fluttered as she tilted her head to give Iris an arrogant look.

Bellerose touched a finger to her red lips. "It was Riccardo Benini who 'cleaned up' after him so to speak, making alibis, creating a new murder site, and bribing officials after Adam tortured Neville Bradford and shot him in the head."

The man whose picture was framed in the greenhouse? Adam had said he'd been met with an unfortunate accident, but not *this*. Iris kept her hands on her lap, trying to stay calm. She knew the sight of her distress would give Bellerose the utmost pleasure.

"Oh, you poor pet, you didn't know, did you?" she asked, amused.

"I'm no one's pet," Iris responded, hands clenched.

"Before Adam executed Mr. Bradford, there was another man whom Adam tried to kill: Carl Anderson. Do you know what the two men had in common? His father, John Temple."

It was a name that came up entirely too much. But that was the man who held in his hands the key to the truth. Did Bellerose know? Or was she only just starting to understand?

"Many of us are interested in his research these days. Why, just the other night, several men who work for Benini were found dead near Temple's burial site. Whatever were they hoping to find there? His bones, perhaps?" Bellerose laughed. "Or maybe it's just my imagination. John Temple's secrets are valuable, you see. As such, he confided in very few people. And one of them is about to have his survival revealed tonight."

"I can't imagine that would be very safe for him," Iris said flatly.

"But you don't care about that. No." Bellerose gave her a sidelong look. "You care more about what John Temple told him that was so dangerous he needed to be killed, even if Adam's attempt failed. You care about the Temple men's secrets as much as I do."

"Why don't you ask Carl yourself?"

"You think I haven't? But his tongue won't budge. I think he might respond to you, though. Since he's been saying your name."

Iris frowned. She tried to search Madame Bellerose's face, but her expression was unreadable. Her *name*? Was this woman telling the truth?

"It's all he's been able to say, I'm afraid," she insisted. "Nothing else. I'm sure you want to know why." Bellerose set down her cup. "Well, then, now that that's settled. Come."

Iris watched in disbelief as Bellerose stood, leaving her teacup steaming on the table. "*Come?* What, *now?*"

"Yes, now, or I'll rescind my offer. My servant Pierre will take us back to my residence. Come. That's all you need to do, and the card will be yours. Along with the truth."

Jinn flashed in her mind's eye. Her first instinct was to run to him, to tell him everything. To bring in Max, to devise a plan. But there was no time. This was an offer she couldn't refuse, and Bellerose knew that. Without allowing her time to think, to regroup with her team and plot, Bellerose had given her an irresistible ultimatum.

She'd go. If this was some kind of trap, she shouldn't—no, she *wouldn't* involve Jinn and Max. She'd face it the best way she could and come out on top. No matter what Bellerose had planned, Iris knew that she couldn't trust Bellerose to just *hand* her the card, not when the woman was still in the game with her own champions. Iris would have to control the situation somehow.

She was tense everywhere as she followed Bellerose out of the room. Rin trailed silently behind them down the staircase. Only when Iris spotted Bately leaning against a tree, calling crudely for his new partner, did Rin address her.

"Don't worry, Isoke," Rin whispered to Iris just as Pierre opened the door to the carriage for Bellerose. "I'm still playing my part. And as for you—" Rin kept her voice low as Bellerose entered the carriage. "Be careful. He'll be coming to help you."

"Guard!" Bellerose called her like an old farmer's maid snapping at her pen hens. It *infuriated* Iris. But Rin only smiled—a little wickedly.

"Go," she told Iris before striding toward Bately. Iris shuddered as he winked at her before she stepped into Bellerose's carriage.

The old man in Bellerose's luxurious apartment looked a stone's throw away from death. Either that, or he'd just come back from the grave. His eyes were open very slightly, and his pupils were milky and unfocused, each staring in its own direction. His mouth was parted just enough for weak breaths to come in and out of his chest.

Bellerose nodded to the only servant in the flowery, lavender room. He exited, leaving Iris alone with Bellerose and this half-dead man: Carl Anderson, bearded, long-nosed, and terribly thin as if wasting away. A former member of Parliament. A former member of Club Uriel. Now a hostage.

"Go on," Madame urged her. There was no sign of mirth in her expression. Just business, then. Fine with Iris.

Shooting Bellerose one of the worst grimaces she could muster, Iris approached Mr. Anderson with care. He looked so grizzly, so helpless. Iris felt a sympathy for him she didn't think she could have for someone debased enough to be a part of the British Crown—oh, and a death cult.

But this man had answers, answers that Adam refused to give her until *he* deemed her ready. The arrogance. Maybe *this* was the time. Time to know what John Temple knew about She Who Does Not Fall.

Still.

As Iris leaned over Mr. Anderson, she looked behind her at Bellerose, who waited impatiently in her red ensemble with her arms folded. Iris bent lower, pressing her hand against his shoulder, descending until her lips were close to the man's ear.

"I'm Iris," she whispered so that only he could hear. "The Dahomey woman John Temple was researching. The Enlightenment Committee tried to have you killed. There's a member with me right now. Tell her nothing."

"Her." His lips formed the word weakly, and yet Iris could still feel the fear in his voice, the tension in his body. "Belle . . . rose . . ."

"You really think I'll agree to you whispering things in his ear?" Bellerose began toward them.

"D-don't come near me, you ghoul!" Mr. Anderson's voice was louder now, just barely, but the terror and hatred in his cloudy eyes spoke volumes. "You ghouls, all of you! Stay away!"

"Ghouls?" Madame Bellerose looked a little annoyed. "Need I remind you, I rescued you from death. I could have let your corpse *rot*."

Mr. Anderson's voice was shallow. "And instead you brought me here and had me . . . had me tortured in your basement."

Iris glared at Bellerose, wide-eyed. But the woman only shrugged.

"And I wouldn't have had to if you'd just *told* me what John Temple—"

"N-no."

Suddenly, Iris felt his cold, clammy hand around her wrist. "If I speak, I'll speak only to this girl. You can go straight to hell with the rest of the demons in that bloodthirsty Committee."

"Well, as long as you speak." Madame Bellerose shrugged, turning around.

"I'll get the answers from her soon enough," she said, patting her inside breast pocket, where Iris knew she'd stashed the tarot card.

The tension didn't dissipate until after Madame Bellerose had shut the door behind her, but Iris was still on high alert. Carl Anderson. He looked at her as if he was gazing upon something not of this earth, just like Adam had all those years ago in South Kensington.

South Kensington . . . Iris knew she'd have to be the one to start the conversation, to thaw this man out of his sudden stupor. What better place to start?

"You mustn't tell them," Mr. Anderson whispered just as she opened her mouth. "You mustn't tell them what John told me."

"What did John tell you?" Iris knelt down next to him. "And *why* did he tell *you*?"

"We grew up together. Even in childhood, he trusted me." He didn't speak easily, but Iris was patient, waiting for him to form each syllable, to inhale and steady himself between words. "He no longer trusted the Committee. Their designs for power. The madness of the tournament. And he knew that devil child would come for him soon."

Devil child . . . Iris paused, imagining his handsome face and blue eyes. "Adam Temple?"

The name itself threw him into a fit of coughs. Iris placed a hand on his chest to calm him, fed him the glass of water next to his bed to keep him lucid. Dribbles of liquid dripped down the sides of his mouth. It wasn't until a few minutes later that he was able to speak again.

"He's not to be trusted."

Iris felt that pang again. That odd tugging sensation in the core of her being that told her Anderson was right and wrong at the very same time. When it came to Adam, she was pulled in different directions. She did not trust him, and yet she knew she could. It was a bitter sensation.

But Adam didn't have the same regard for others that he seemed to have for her. That much was clear. This old man's state was proof.

"In some ways, I understand him," said Carl, clearing his throat and sinking into his pillow. "John was a terrible father. Put his dreams, his research, and his never-ending desire to seek thrills across the world before his family.

Charlotte's brother, who stayed with him, was as puritanical as she, but a violent madman. He beat that child senseless while John was away. More so after Charlotte and the other children were gone."

Carl fell silent. Iris stared at the white sheets, torn.

"And yet that child never lost that wicked, scheming mind," Carl continued. "In fact, if anything, it only grew sharper. Once I heard that his uncle had been committed to an institution, I knew that boy had been behind it. He managed it. Somehow."

Iris remembered, a slight chill running down her back, the night Adam had casually told her about his family. She swallowed the lump in her throat.

"If John had spent more time with that boy, he would've realized what he was capable of. He would've realized *sooner* that he had learned John's secret—the truth. That *stupid* man—" Carl hacked up blood. "If he'd come to me *before* he realized his life was in danger—"

"I don't understand." Iris shook her head. "What's the secret John was hiding from—"

"The Committee," Carl finished, his eyes wide. "The Crown. The *world*. The truth is dangerous. Released into the wrong hands, it would be disastrous. Brought out into the open, it would plunge the world into blood and madness. Knowing is the ultimate power. The power to prepare for the *true* future ahead of us. The power to guide it. To save humanity . . . or to destroy it."

If Iris wasn't scared before, she was now. Deep down, she didn't want to believe Adam's nonsense about the end of the world, but this man's bulging veins screamed differently. However, the more Iris pressed with questions, the more the feeble man lost track of his thoughts. Soon, he was staring at her and just babbling, drool slipping down his chin.

"The crystal ornament in John's safe. It went dormant because of those damnable experiments." He shook his head. "It was Adam who realized it all before John did. Adam who took it and offered it up as a sacrifice. John didn't know what his son had done until it was too late. Why didn't he realize it? Why didn't he realize how much that boy hates this world?"

"Slow down," Iris hissed, gripping him tightly as if he would fly away aboard his own delusions. "Explain this to me one step at a time. Do you mean the white crystal?" When Carl gasped and went silent, she hurriedly continued. "What about the white crystal? What do you know about it? Please tell me!"

But then, silently, tears began to leak down the old man's face. Slipping down his chin one after another. He wept. For himself. For others. Iris didn't know. A light breeze from the open window brushed her back and rippled the light curtains behind her, but Iris could only watch this old man as he cried shamelessly in front of her.

"Damn that man," he said finally. "Giving them the *heart* that he broke cursed the Temple family for eternity. Damn him. Seymour . . ."

Her mind went blank. Her fingers, once gentle upon Carl's white shirt, now dug into his chest without her realizing it. Hate rose inside of her, insidiously, secretly. "Seymour," she whispered, her nails finding skin. "You mean Seymour Pratt . . ."

She didn't need to see him nod to know it was true. That the man she couldn't remember, the man she hated but didn't know why, was at the center of this mystery. She barely heard Anderson begin to shout in pain before she started barking at him.

"Tell me where he is," she said, her eyes round and menacing. "Where is he? *Where is he?*" She needed to know so she could kill him, of course. That's what she had to do without a doubt.

Carl looked upon her as if the kind girl in front of him had suddenly been taken by a demon. "Where he always is: th-the Crystal Palace," he said.

"The Crystal Palace," Iris breathed, the bulging veins in her hands beginning to soften.

The Crown is hiding something there. Something underground. That's what Rin had told her.

Carl let out a scream. Snapping out of her daze, Iris panicked, letting go of him.

"I'm sorry." She shot to her feet, horrified at the sight of his bloodied skin underneath her nails. "I'm so sorry!"

Carl wasn't looking at her but toward the window. Someone was behind her. Before she could turn, a hand held a sweet-smelling white cloth over her nose and mouth. She didn't have time to struggle before the room went dark with Carl's frightened yell.

35

IRIS AWOKE IN A COLD DUNGEON, filled almost entirely with worn
instruments of torture but for the pot of beautiful pink azaleas in the leftmost corner. Madame Bellerose's shriek was what made her snap back to
her senses, and when she barreled through the door, Iris realized she couldn't
defend herself; her wrists and ankles were tied with rope, her body crumpled
on the floor. Bellerose's sharp-heeled boot was on her chest before she could
figure out what had happened to her.

"Tell me who killed Carl Anderson," Madame Bellerose demanded, sending
a shock through Iris's system.

That frightened old man, dead? Iris's lips parted, but she couldn't make a
sound.

Bellerose stomped down hard. "Tell me!"

Iris gasped for air. "I don't know!"

"Tell me, you little beast!"

"Look at the two of us," Iris spat. "You really think *I'm* the beast in this
situation?"

Another stomp. Another.

"Madame, stop!"

Iris's breath scraped her throat as she inhaled sharply. Adam? It was Adam's
voice. Slowly, painfully, she turned her head to find Lord Temple shirtless and

beaten, tied to the ceiling by a long chain, his feet just touching the floor. Shallow cuts painted his chest red.

"You found her unconscious in his room at the same time you found the man's body," Adam said. It was astounding how he could remain calm in this situation. Then again, who could deal with an Enlightener better than another Enlightener? "I'm sure one person was responsible for both. You're smart enough to figure that out, Violet."

Madame Bellerose strode over to Adam and seized him by the chin. "Don't call me by my name, you rude little boy."

And slapped him. Adam spat out blood.

"Then again." She considered it, letting her anger calm. "Carl Anderson died before he could reveal his secrets to me. To the Committee. I'm sure you had something to do with that." Bellerose caressed the side of his cheek. "Even from in here, bound up like a little present. Just like I'm sure you had something to do with Cordiero's murder, as we both know it wasn't me."

She pushed him back violently and turned, folding her arms with childish impatience.

"Either way, the Committee will be here by eight. That old man must have told your champion *something*." Madame Bellerose slid up to Iris once again, this time pulling the tarot card out of her breast pocket. "I'm sure you'd give up that information for a reward, no?"

"Eat filth."

Iris's head nearly split apart from the kick Bellerose dealt it.

"Madame, enough," Adam yelled. *"Enough!"*

It was the first time Iris had heard him so angry. It seemed to make Bellerose delighted. The gentle knock against the door more so.

"Come," said Bellerose pleasantly.

A man with skin as dark as Iris's walked through the door, his head shaved, his robes split at the sides to reveal a pair of gray slacks, and a piece of bread in his hands. His priest collar was just the same, as were the scars all over his sharp-angled face. Jacques.

"Like I said, the Committee should be here in several hours. It's a miracle

I was able to gather them at all considering their schedules. You know that Bosch, always off selling his nightmarish weapons to the highest bidder." Madame gave Jacques a sidelong look. "This one will keep an eye on you both for now. My own champion and a spare I picked up from Cordiero's decimated team are out trying to obtain the remaining two cards as we speak."

"The terms of our agreement are the same, then?" Jacques asked.

Iris had never heard this man whisper anything more than a prayer. His voice was deep and rough, but calm and quiet like gentle waters.

"You guard them for just a few hours, and I give you a card. Very simple." Bellerose patted him on the back. "As for the other two cards, well, that will be up to you. My offer for you to join my team is still on the table. Consider this agreement a taste of our mutual alignment. Oh," she added, "and I imagine you're not the chatting type." She looked back at Adam. "Feel free to make these two sleep in whatever manner you deem fit."

Madame Bellerose left Iris and Adam alone with one of the Belgium boars.

Iris awoke *again*, throat sore, to the sound of familiar chanting.

"I offer you the body and blood, soul and divinity, of your dearly beloved Son . . ."

Jacques. He sat against the wall next to the door, Bellerose's collection of bear traps on the table to his left. With his right arm balanced on his knee, he ate a stale-looking piece of sesame bread, spitting out the seeds every so often. His gaze was pointed at the wooden floor.

Looking at him brought back flashes of memories from the first round— visions of Jacques burning incense while his partner bathed in the blood of another champion. Her body trembled. She was terrified. Still, she had to try *something*.

"Don't trust Bellerose," she pleaded with him. "She won't give you that card no matter what you do for her, I'm sure of it."

"So should I trust you?"

His words had come so quickly, it caught Iris off guard. Jacques still did not look at her.

Trust. How did she build trust? She considered it long and hard. Then she thought of Granny. Of Rin. And now this man, Jacques. It was worth a try. Yoruba was the language she was more familiar with. She tried to speak it. It was difficult, but more familiar to her than Fon with her having read *Iwe Irohin* and listened to Granny speak for years.

"You can trust me," she said, sitting up, carefully forming each syllable in the language. "You can trust me more than her, I promise. Give me a chance."

Jacques suddenly began speaking a language she'd never heard before.

"You're from the Congo," Adam said. Iris could see how worn he was.

"I speak many languages." Jacques bit into his bread, chewing carefully before spitting out another seed. He was still gazing at the floor when he spoke to Iris. "But not yours. Don't expect camaraderie from me, girl."

"Iris," Adam said, his breathing labored as he struggled to keep his head up. "Are you all right? How badly are you hurt?" And he had the audacity to sound worried for her.

"Quiet." Iris remembered the hollowness in Carl Anderson's eyes as he spoke of Adam.

"Aren't you curious why I'm here?"

"Wasn't it to kill Carl Anderson?" Iris glared at him. "Oh, wait, you tried and failed to do that already. Not with Bradford though. That was a bull's-eye."

For a time, the only sound in the room was Jacques chewing his bread.

"What did he tell you?" Adam asked.

Iris smirked. "Enough. That you're a cold-blooded murderer."

"Was Bellerose with you?"

"What?" Iris balked. "No, I was alone!"

Bafflingly, Adam seemed relieved at her answer. "Good. That's good."

"*What's* good?" Iris struggled against her ropes as she looked up at the young man swinging from the ceiling. "Did you or did you not have Carl Anderson killed? *Twice?*"

"I sent Rin a message to help you," Adam said, which didn't answer anything. "But if you're still here, something must have gone wrong." He was speaking more to himself than to anyone else, but soon his eyes were on Jacques sitting on the floor. "You didn't kill Anderson, did you, Jacques?"

"No." Jacques spit out another seed. "But I shot the one who did."

"What do you mean?" Adam demanded.

"After I arrived here, I heard an intruder sneak inside upstairs. Bellerose had asked me to guard against intruders. So I found him and shot him. He escaped quickly afterward."

"So you *know* who killed Anderson." Iris pressed him further. The way Adam's eyes slid to her did not go unnoticed. The same person who killed Carl Anderson had spared her, only knocking her out. Why? What game was Adam playing? If something had gone wrong, that meant that very same person was supposed to . . . what, *take* her?

Iris's head throbbed as she considered it. It couldn't have been Rin who'd knocked her out. She went with Bately. If she'd wanted to kill Carl Anderson, she would have accompanied them to Bellerose's home. As Bellerose's champion, she wouldn't have raised any suspicion.

"It's none of my concern," answered Jacques.

"So what *is* your concern?" Adam stilled himself, controlling his emotions likely in the midst of incredible pain. Blood dripped from his shallow wounds. "Why do you fight?"

"To feed my family." Iris was surprised Jacques would answer so simply. But perhaps it was a simple matter for him.

"Family." Adam smiled sadly to himself. "Once upon a time, family meant everything to me. And then my siblings were murdered and my mother hanged herself. I visit their grave sites every year. Place their favorite flowers by their stones. But not my father."

Iris remembered Carl Anderson's words as she listened.

"My father, who had all the resources in the world, used those resources to abandon his family and chase cheap thrills. But you, also a father, chose to engage in monstrous work all for the sake of your family." Adam smirked. "Like night and day. You couldn't be more different. I respect you."

"It would take a murderer to respect another murderer," Iris muttered.

"Is there anyone here who hasn't murdered?" Jacques asked, and Iris's shoulders stiffened when she realized she couldn't answer. She couldn't remember her old days in the Dahomey Kingdom. Maybe that was a good thing. Who knew what she'd done in the name of the king.

But Iris noticed something. It was when Jacques was defending himself that he showed more emotion—subtle, but fiery nonetheless. His family. That was what this conversation needed to center on if they were to escape. Adam must have realized it too.

"You're right," Adam said. "A man like yourself. Only someone ready to risk everything for a cause that meant everything to him would take part in a tournament such as this. You, who took up the work of an assassin to feed your children."

Jacques's hand dangled in the air with his bread. "Who told you I was an assassin?" he asked, unperturbed.

"Van der Ven likes to brag about his champions."

"Jacques," Iris interrupted, a sense of urgency gripping her as the clock ticked away. The Committee would be here soon. There was no telling what they'd do to her to get Carl's information. Or what they'd do if they knew the depth of her connection to John Temple. "You're doing all this for your family. I understand that. But there's something much greater at stake. Something that might put even them in danger!"

"The apocalypse?" Jacques answered coolly, and for the first time, he looked at her.

"Did Van der Ven tell you?" Adam asked.

"Yes. But I want proof. Proof that God means to end this world sooner than I expected."

"And I can give that to you," said Adam. "If you let the two of us go, I will. Bellerose will give you nothing, I can guarantee that."

Jacques didn't look surprised. But he considered it.

"Please," Iris pushed. "Please let me go. I have to . . ." Iris thought of Carl Anderson's dying words and shivered. "I have to get to the Crystal Palace. I have to go!"

Adam's head whipped around to look at her, but before he could speak,

Jacques stood. Iris's heart gave a jolt as he threw his piece of half-eaten bread on the hard ground.

"My mother taught me to pray," he said, rubbing his knuckles as he stepped in front of the door. "In hopes that God would have mercy on us and save us from our miseries. When she died, it was my father who taught me something different. Even enslaved, he'd been a warrior."

He approached them, his steps calm and measured. "He was forced to protect Britain's interests in the Caribbean, fighting in the early-century battles against France and in the Napoleonic Wars before settling in London. By then he was only a shell of himself, but he told me something important. Something my mother never would have approved of."

He looked between Adam and Iris. "God's mercy is only bestowed upon those he favors. And it is luck, not prayer, that determines who belongs to that coveted class."

He broke open his left index finger so that the bone of his knuckle was exposed. Iris's scream had barely escaped her throat when gunpowder sparked from his bone and a bullet pierced an instrument hanging from the wall. Iris believed it was called the "pear of anguish."

The man who'd taken Cordiero's wife hostage. The figure who'd disappeared around the corner shortly after. Iris had figured it was him based on Adam's list. This just confirmed it. But Iris was more concerned with the way Jacques pointed his hand, his *weapon*, between the two of them.

"Shall we find out which one of you is among those chosen few?"

Adam smirked, lowering his head. "A fitting power for one who specialized in targeted, long-distance sniping even before your days as a Fanciful Freak."

"I want proof that it is real," Jacques said. "The end of the world."

"And you trust me to tell you rather than your *own* Patron. Or Bellerose?"

Jacques's expression was cold, stern. "Van der Ven cares only about his own power and status. Bellerose is similarly blinded by pride. But you still have someone you care about. I can tell that about you."

"Yes, I do."

Iris clenched her jaw tight, her lips pursed as Adam's gaze slid seamlessly to her. She turned quickly. She couldn't stand to see honesty in his eyes. Not someone like him.

"And that makes you different from them?" Jacques continued. By now he was so close to Adam, he placed his fist easily underneath Adam's chin.

"I promise that when you are ready, if you set us both free, I will tell you everything you need to know about the end of the world. And if at any point you're not satisfied, or if I go against my word, you and your partner Gram can hunt me and kill me on the spot."

He was willing to go that far. For what? To protect her secret? Or was he just trying to save himself? Iris tugged against her binds as the clock ticked away. Finally, Jacques withdrew his hand.

"All I want is for my family to live," Jacques said, snapping his finger back into place. "If any harm should come to them, I will murder the Patrons myself."

Iris's heart nearly beat out of her chest as Jacques walked toward her, adrenaline coursing through her as he bent down and—

Cut her binds with the knife he had in his pants pocket.

"Go," he said. Iris didn't need telling twice. Before he could reach Adam, she was already out the door, running, running, up the stairs, through the hall, around the bend—

"Out of my way!"

Madame Bellerose barely had time to react to Iris's war cry. Iris was on her, her hands around the woman's neck. They crashed against the ground, both of them gasping in pain, but Iris was too fast. Her hand found the woman's inside pocket. The tarot card.

"I'll be taking this, you *bitch*." Then Iris knocked out the two guards standing in her way, barreled past the frightened servants Madame Bellerose had screamed for, and ran out the front door before anyone could stop her.

"I-Iris?"

Iris stopped and saw a figure limping out from around the corner of the building. His eyes widened with relief and shock at the sight of her.

"Max!" Iris ran to him. He looked as if he'd just awoken after a deep sleep.

Worn and in pain, he held his bleeding arm, grimacing. "What happened? Why are you here?"

But when she went to touch his arm, he recoiled from her. He didn't look at her. His eyes held a certain kind of misery within them that didn't feel natural at all, not for Max.

"Did something happen?" she asked, touching his face, seeing the wetness in his eyes.

The clamoring in the manor grew louder. They couldn't waste time here. Iris pulled Max out the gates by his unwounded arm, and they ran as far as they could from Bellerose's residence. Once they got to a main street, Iris pushed him inside a carriage.

"I have one of the cards," she told him, and though he narrowed his eyes with confusion, she didn't have the time to explain. She was too consumed with other thoughts to consider his strange presence here at all. "Go back to Club Uriel. Get someone to dress your wounds. And tell the others I'm all right." Her lips trembled slightly as she thought of Jinn.

"Wait!" Max said through the window as she closed the door. "What about you?"

She couldn't go back to the club, not when Carl Anderson's words repeated themselves endlessly in her thoughts. "I'm going to the Crystal Palace."

36

I *have to get my memories back.* She had to take back control. Her thoughts raced as she rode a carriage to Penge Peak, which sat next to the affluent suburb Sydenham Hill. It was nine o'clock when she arrived. The second round would be over soon. The teams must be battling each other right at that moment. She hoped Max would relay the message to Jinn, Cherice, and the others. Her team now had a card, but Team Hawkins needed their own so they could both get the advantage for the final round. They needed to decide their plan of action while she decided her own.

> *Ye gentlemen of England,*
> *That live at home at ease,*
> *Ah! Little do ye think upon*
> *The dangers of the seas!*
> *Give ear unto the mariners,*
> *And they will plainly show*
> *All the cares and the fears*
> *When the stormy winds do blow.*

Iris sighed. This cabbie, with his drooping mustache, terrible voice, and strange accent hadn't stopped singing since he picked her up near Bellerose's place. "Sir, I'm trying to think."

"Thinking! Why, life is too short for thinking, my dear! Enjoy the moment!"

With a laugh, he continued in a deep, cheerful rumble while the horses clopped along.

> *We bring home costly merchandise,*
> *And jewels of great price,*
> *To serve our English gallantry*
> *With many a rare device . . .*

Iris was happy to leave the carriage as soon as it'd stopped, though she didn't miss the troubling way the cabbie's eyes lingered on her.

With evening having already descended, a respectable crowd of people lingered on the grounds. There'd been a fireworks display earlier for some event, Iris overheard, but it was over now. Two gas lamps sparked dimly along the wide, circular red-stone pavement surrounding the fountain in the middle of the garden. There were more by the shrubs and statues and along the wide walkway leading through the garden to the palace itself. Prince Albert and Queen Victoria's Crystal Palace, to be exact: a magnificent dome of slender cast-iron rods upholding walls of clear glass. A cultural mecca that housed exhibits, concerts, and other wonders for visitors to enjoy. It was closed today, but that wouldn't stop Iris. The envoys said themselves that the Crown was up to something underground. Iris wouldn't leave until she discovered its dark secrets.

The palace may have been closed but the general gardens weren't. There were still sparse visitors here and there even this late into the evening, a few with their children. She was careful not to be seen as she made her way toward the Crystal Palace and slipped inside.

Being a dancer, Iris was able to stay light on her feet inside the empty exhibition space. No echoes. But she felt so small in this jungle of tall iron rods that, bound together in long meshwork, formed the walls and fortified the glass-plated ceiling. The inside felt unfinished. Still, moonlight streamed in from the netted glass ceiling. The beautiful evergreen trees planted along the side of the building gave off a surreal, magical effect fit for a palace.

Iris searched the area, trying to find an entryway that might take her to the Basement. After almost an hour, she heard footsteps. She stayed out of sight and followed them. Soon, another pair of boots joined the first pair, and together they led Iris through the labyrinth of iron like Ariadne's string.

When the echoes stopped, so did she, slipping behind a red curtain meant for an exhibition slot big enough to hold sculptures and paintings. Hiding within the shadows by the iron wall, Iris peeked through the curtain. Several meters away, three men in suits stood by a cluster of rods. They were too far away for her to see their faces, but their voices carried through the empty space well enough for her to listen.

"Have the envoys left?" asked one man. "The Colonial Office told me they were asking to see this place before they returned to Africa. The operation hasn't been compromised, has it?"

"Relax. The office refused their request to put the Crystal Palace on their schedule. Far as I can tell, there hasn't been any cause for concern ever since we relocated to the Basement."

Iris stepped closer to the curtains, her ear nearly touching the velvet as she listened.

"You think somebody talked? Why else would they suddenly ask about it?"

"You think one of us would tell the Crown's secrets to a nameless Negro?"

"Calm down, Mr. James. The Crown's research has been going on for twenty years. You think a few bloody Africans are going to best 'em?"

He laughed as if the very idea that the envoys could discern their secrets was so ridiculous that it was beneath consideration. Good. Their arrogance made for a strong weapon. The Crystal Palace, John Temple's research. All of it was connected to the white crystal. Experiments with the ore and an unnatural explosion had given Rin her powers in Dahomey. It could have been the same principle behind the explosion at the South Kensington fair ten years ago. Whatever the Crown was doing here, it was tied to the Fanciful Freaks.

Another set of footsteps emerged to Iris's left, and though the curtains were drawn around her, she held her breath. Slow, clinical steps passed by her, too close; his boots were right there, visible underneath the red velvet. Iris didn't dare move, even after it was clear the new figure had joined the other three.

"A wise man wrote not so long ago: 'At some future period, not very distant as measured by centuries, the civilized races of man will almost certainly exterminate and replace throughout the world the savage races.'" A voice had recited the quote from memory. A voice Iris remembered. A voice that made Iris's blood run cold.

"I agree with Darwin's conclusion," the voice continued. "The erasure of primitive societies and their replacement with more glorious civilizations is inevitable. But only a fool would let that lull them into a false sense of security."

"In other words, Doctor?"

"In other words: do not rest." Though he spoke like a teacher, a *mentor*, Doctor Seymour Pratt's voice was frigid and empty, hollowing Iris out from the inside. "And do *not* underestimate anyone," he continued. "Whoever they may be."

Hold her down, gentlemen. Do not underestimate her. This beast is dangerous.

His voice brought visions. Visions of pain and screaming. Blood and death. Hectic, chaotic memories of cold words and colder hands on her. Memories wrenching tears of wrath from her eyes . . .

Before Iris knew it, she was leaping out from behind the curtain and rushing toward the doctor in his long black jacket and black tie. His gray hair drooped down from his bald head, merging into the beard that stretched down his neck, but she struck for jugular nonetheless, screaming as she wielded her nails like a knife. One quick slash was all she needed. But she'd been too far away; they saw her coming. The other men stepped in front of the doctor, grabbing her arms and waist, struggling to hold her as she screeched for blood.

All the while, Doctor Seymour Pratt looked at her through his beady eyes. Not even a wicked grin. He simply inspected her, always *inspecting* with interest. "You see?"

"I'll kill you. I will *kill* you, Pratt!"

Iris fought against the men's grip with all her strength. One man each had an arm while another gripped her waist, three fools keeping her from the one thing she wanted to do—*needed* to do—more than anything. That emotionless old man's wrinkled face needed to be ripped off. She needed to make him suffer like he'd made *her* suffer years ago.

Yes. He'd once made her suffer. Iris may not have had the memories, but she knew it in her soul.

"It seems you remember me, Iris. Although maybe it took you some time to remember. Otherwise you would have come to kill me a long time ago. I once hypothesized that if you ever regenerated, there would be psychological consequences for you to reckon with. Fascinating."

Iris didn't hear him. A screech that didn't even sound human erupted from her throat, scratching it raw.

"She's a bloody animal!" said one of the men who held on to her even after being elbowed in the face.

"An animal? Yes. But this animal is special." Doctor Pratt rubbed his white beard, studying her with those beady black eyes. "The day of the auction, when I saw you again, I knew I'd have to bring you here eventually. Then I heard you'd escaped. Clever beast."

Her desire to kill him filled her with as much grief as it did pain. It made her knees buckle. Made her very *self* slip away.

"The five years we spent together must be engraved into your heart. That peculiar heart. Riddles we could never solve no matter what theories we hypothesized. No matter how long we worked. Now that you've been born again, I believe it's time to resume where we left off, don't you?"

Doctor Pratt turned, placing his hands behind his back with the kind of nonchalance meant to shrink Iris's being into nothingness.

"We may not have the Moon Skeleton, but her heart may serve well in its place. Take her to the Basement. With the discoveries we've made in the years since her initial capture, I daresay we'll find her body more useful this time around."

Doctor Pratt began to walk away.

"But Doctor, we can barely keep her still," said the man on her left arm through gritted teeth. "How are we supposed to take her anywhere?"

The Doctor turned his head. "Shoot her. She'll live." A simple suggestion before continuing down the hall, turning a corner, and disappearing from her sight.

"I've got a gun," said the man holding her waist. "Hold her down."

Tears continued to sting Iris's eyes as the man let her go and the remaining men gripped her arms so tightly she could feel the blood pulsating in them. They had her stretched out as if she'd been nailed to a cross built to make her suffer. And yet as they talked about going for her heart, as they joked about the man's aim, Iris realized they didn't even have enough regard for her life to make her suffer. They didn't address her. They didn't see even a sliver of her humanity as they talked among themselves. She was a beast to be put down. And that was all.

Crying, Iris shut her eyes, tears hot against her skin as the bullet pierced her breast.

And then a curious thing happened.

The metal *shattered* against her heart.

That was the last sensation she felt before dying.

She didn't know how long she was gone for. After several moments, the darkness faded. Moonlight began streaming through her closed eyelids. Shards of metal oozed out of the bullet hole. If she'd been in her right mind, she would have questioned it: What exactly was her heart made of that it could shatter a bullet?

If she had been in her right mind.

But now her mind was fury, filled with shadowy tools cutting into her flesh, magnifying glasses, rough hands inside her mouth measuring her teeth, blue and green eyes watching her.

The indignity.

As the men carried her through the Crystal Palace by her arms and legs, revenge swallowed her being. And so when she opened her eyes, before the men could notice, she slipped her right arm out of one man's grip and struck him in the ribs. Then she kicked her left foot into another's chin. She fell on her back in the midst of the confusion, but rebounded quickly, punching two of the men in the ears to knock them off balance and kicking them between their legs just to send the message home. One by one they went down, knocked out. She caught the last man before he could run away, kneed him in the stomach, and covered his mouth before he could scream for help. Spinning him around, she forced him to look at the unconscious figures of his colleagues. She relished his fear.

But as she held him in place, she could not only feel his heart pounding; she could sense something more in her blind state of blissful rage: the precious feeling of his life. His vitality. His essence. Closing her eyes, she remembered that day on the balcony with Adam when she felt life flowing through the plants and into her soul. The peaceful oneness of all things. She remembered Adam telling her to concentrate.

Breathe and let it consume you.

It was life force she sensed. The soul all living things possessed. She thought of Adam pressing her supple body against his hard chest, begging her to feel him. And she did feel him—his spirit.

His anima.

Just like she felt Granny Marlow that day she first came to Coolie's.

She felt this man too. His very source of life flowed into her.

She closed her hand tighter against his mouth, feeling his essence of life as he began screaming bloody murder.

As she set his essence of life *ablaze.*

He continued screaming, his body flushed with heat. His skin peeled off his arms. Blood trickled from his nose and mouth. She felt somehow peaceful as she burned him alive from the inside out, reducing him to ash right there in her arms.

Nothing.

Then shock.

Then confusion and horror.

The disturbing sight of a pile of ashes at her feet that was once a man.

Panic, electric and acute, pulsed through her body as she stumbled backward, unable to blink, unable to close her mouth as she took in the hellish sight of what she'd done. And then she saw not *his* ashes but the ashes of others inside Gorton Zoo decades ago.

A memory. Clear as day.

The bodies of men and women turned to dust. The sun blazing above her, the sweat dripping from her brow, mixing with splatters of blood. "Specimens of the Niger Region," her exhibit was called. And behind her, Anne Marlow lay dead from a rock to the head thrown by one of the exhibit's visitors.

Anne had died that day: the third of August, 1832. Anne Marlow, though that was never her name. Iris had never learned her true name. But she had mourned her death nonetheless. Mourned it the only way she knew how in that moment of perfect grief.

By burning everyone near her to ash.

And now Anne was here in the Crystal Palace, trying to speak to her just like at Belle Vue. She knew it wasn't Anne. Anne was gone.

No, this thing only took Anne's form. Just as she suspected during the first round. This was another being entirely reaching out to her, trying to communicate, but she didn't want to listen. She covered her ears as its voice began speaking its riddles.

Uoy Sekam Ohw I Si Ti Rof Em Morf Nrut Ton Od.

Nekawa . . .

"The Hiva . . ." Iris said it herself, but it was as if her voice was not her own, as if it had burrowed out of the ancient earth itself to find her lips.

Iris's nails dug into her scalp. "No!" she shrieked, shaking her head. "No! *Get away!*"

And then she was running, out of the palace, through the grassy field. She needed to escape.

Her heart stopped the moment her shoulder bumped into someone, fearful he'd turn to ash. Frantically, she looked for a safe route, but her eyes caught instead a tall sculpture that hadn't been there before, firm on the grass, exciting the Londoners swarming around it.

Not a sculpture—a puppet the size of a young boy of average height. Pink cheeks, pointed nose, bushy brows, pin-striped pants. It was the puppet of Punch she'd seen in Whittle's toy shop. Delighted children played by its red boots.

"Turn around, Miss Iris."

Henry Whittle. Shaking, she turned and saw him, his gray newsboy cap and his brown vest the color of his hair. But all she could think about were the ashes left inside the Crystal Palace. The memory of death and bloodshed at the Gorton Zoo.

"What is happening?" Iris wailed as she tried to shake the memory away.

"What's happening is this." Henry took his right hand out of his jacket pocket and pointed a finger up into the air. It sparked with light that vanished just as quickly as it had appeared. Then he pointed at Punch.

"The puppet I built is pretty popular, isn't it?" Henry said with the pride of a toymaker underneath his calculating tone. "We know you have a tarot card. Give it to me or I'll make this puppet explode." His finger sparked again, the beauty of its light suddenly appearing all the more menacing. "I know you just 'can't stand the thought of people dying,' right?" His voice was mocking.

Their conversation that day at Club Uriel. He remembered. And now he was using it against her.

"So?" Henry tilted his head to the side. "What shall it be, Miss Iris?"

37

THE BOLDNESS OF HIS THREAT DASHED whatever remaining memories lingered in her mind. Iris bit the corner of her bottom lip hard, drawing blood to make sure she remained in the present. Whatever had happened in the past, Henry was real. His puppet was real. His threat was real.

Calm down. Iris flexed and unflexed her hands as she watched Henry Whittle's lips curve upward. *Think this through. What's in front of you? What's really in front of you?*

"All these people." Iris flicked her head to the side. "You can't be willing to *kill* them."

Henry pompously straightened his vest. "Can't I? You've seen what I can do. I've always had a knack for building explosives just as much as toys. Now that I've *changed*, setting one off?" He smirked. "All it would take is a snap of my finger."

The moment he readied his hands, Iris stepped forward in a panic. "Wait!" she cried, her arms up as if to stay a beast. The sound of children's laughter was suddenly like wails in her mind.

Gripping her forehead, she blurted out in frustration, "I don't have a card! I *don't.*"

"Except I heard Rin tell Maximo you were heading to Bellerose's house."

Iris stepped back, dread coursing through her. "We staked out the house for hours. Then you ran out and told your teammate that you had the card. We were smart to follow you."

We? Iris scanned the field but all she could see were visitors milling about and cooing at that damn puppet. Would Henry do this? Who was she to say? The boy's grandfather was in debt. The Whittles were about to lose everything. What did she know about this boy and who or what he was willing to blow up to save his own family?

His family.

"Does your grandfather know you came all the way here to take bystanders hostage with a toy? 'Give me a bloody card or I'll blow up some kids'?"

Henry flinched but said nothing.

"You think he'd be happy to see his grandson's a murderer?"

"I'm not a murderer! Don't talk about my grandfather!" Henry flung his newsboy cap down upon the grass. He seemed to realize what he'd done because his eyes widened for just a moment. Without moving his gaze from the ground, he breathed in and out slowly.

"That old man just wants to make toys," he whispered. "But he's got no business sense. He'll make toys in the morning and cry alone at night while Mary, who has no parents of her own, brings him his meals and medicine. Soon we won't be able to afford even that."

Iris's heart clenched as she thought of Granny, who always grimaced when Iris brought her medicine but took it nonetheless.

"What would you know?" Henry glared defiantly at her, tears in his eyes. "What would *you* know about us?"

Iris pressed her hand against the dress pocket where the tarot card was. "I know what it's like to have people you'd do anything for," she said, surprising herself when another face appeared in her mind's eye beyond Granny. She saw him for just a flash in his circus attire, carrying her on his shoulders, dragging her to go practice their next routine. Back in those simpler times. "I think I know, now, or at least I hope, that you wouldn't kill those people, who aren't even involved in all this madness, just to win the tournament. I have to believe that."

She remembered him, sullen and suspicious in Whittle's. And yet everything about his demeanor changed once he was called to that friendly old man's side.

"Either you love him enough to kill for him, or you love him enough not to break his heart," Iris said, because those were the only two options she could see.

Henry tried to put up a strong front, but he was fidgeting. His unsure hands were straightening his vest and white sleeves, already perfect with no need of further fiddling. His terrorist facade was slowly starting to crack.

She remembered the way he'd smiled as his grandfather teased him that day. His eyes now weren't the eyes of a killer. They weren't like Doctor Seymour Pratt's. Thinking of *those* black beady eyes in that moment reminded her of the bitter taste of hell. Henry didn't compare.

"Can't we settle this some other way?" Iris said. "Away from the crowd?"

Was there another way? Another way for all of them struggling in this evil tournament?

Henry's frown deepened. He said nothing. The two stared at each other, waiting to see who would break first. It was Henry whose arms eventually began to tremble.

"*Heeenryyy!*" came a voice that sounded somewhere between a song and a battle cry. "My adorable boy!"

Mary? Iris was shocked to see the shy girl practically jump on Henry from behind, wrapping her arms around him. In her worn blue dress, she looked taller and bustier than before, but that was undoubtedly the pixie-like, cherubic face Iris knew, strawberry-blond braid and all.

Henry's cheeks practically burst into flames. "What. Are. You. Doing? I'm busy—"

But Henry couldn't seem to stop her from pinching his right cheek. Painfully.

"My, isn't he adorable?" Mary said as Henry winced.

Wait, that voice. Like Mary's, it was as soft as a flute's whistle, but something was off.

Henry looked as if his mother had shown up in the middle of a date. Like he wanted to crawl into a hole and disappear.

"A boy of fourteen, a genius toymaker like his grandfather, working so hard to save his family from debt. Henry, you adorable boy, I told you this wouldn't work. You're far too innocent for this kind of bluff, you sweet little boy!"

Iris's eyebrow raised. Something was *very* off. Mary let go of Henry and stepped between the two of them, taking in the sight of their enemy with a manic confidence that could never have belonged to Mary. The pieces fell into place once the blond pixie began whistling a tune—a familiar old folk song.

> *Give ear unto the mariners,*
> *And they will plainly show*
> *All the cares and the fears*
> *When the stormy winds do blow.*

The old cabbie who'd driven her here. "Mary" seemed to relish the sight of Iris's eyebrows rising, the sting of a revelation realized too late.

"Let's try this instead," she offered.

Mary grabbed Iris's forearm and fastened it against her neck.

"Help!" Mary shrieked at the top of her lungs. Iris tried to pull herself away, but Mary kept her arm pinned to her neck as if she *wanted* to break her own windpipe. "Help, police! She's attacking me! Help, I'm being attacked! Help! Police!"

Another bloodcurdling shriek, and she'd caught the attention of the policemen in the vicinity, who were now closing in on them. Iris panicked as she thought of the ashes in the Crystal Palace. What if someone had seen her go inside?

"Oh dear, help me, I'm in trouble!!" Mary cried again.

"Enough, Lucille!" Iris finally yelled, struggling to pull herself out of her grip.

Lucille grinned. "Henry, you adorable boy, will you search Iris for her tarot card before the police arrive? I'd start with her pocket. Once she's locked up, she won't be coming after us."

Iris cursed under her breath as the policemen made their way through a shocked crowd. Lucille must have known how this would look in front of the officials: Iris, a brown-skinned African, holding "hostage" a girl who looked like the poster child of cherubic innocence. It was a scheme as brilliant as it was evil.

Just then the real Mary appeared through the crowd in a frilly pink dress, two ribbons tying her strawberry-blond hair. When she saw herself in Iris's "vise grip," she looked at Henry, then at the police, and gauging the situation quickly, turned around to hide her face.

"Hello? Mr. Whittle! I know you could look at me, Mary White, your beautiful maid, all day, but you *must* set aside your secret love for me and *check our competitor for the damn card.*"

Lucille said the last part through gritted teeth because even as the police approached, Henry couldn't move. It wasn't until Lucille screamed Henry's name that he snapped out of it and pulled the tarot card out of Iris's pocket.

Playing the situation as if she'd *finally* broken free of Iris's grasp, Lucille barreled toward Henry. "Oh, Mr. Whittle, let us escape from here! Take me away, you handsome boy, you!"

"*Don't* overdo it," Henry whispered with a scowl as the real Mary ran toward them. He grabbed her by the hand, and the three fled the scene just as the police closed in.

"Put your hands up, you brute!" one policeman cried, wielding his black club menacingly. A cluster of them with clubs and guns stood before her as onlookers kept their distance, ravenously eating up the scene. Six. Seven. Iris put up her fists, ready to fight them all.

Then she blinked.

And suddenly Max was there with her, right in the center of the group, his back to hers.

"Ma—" She stared, but before she could finish her sentence, two of the policemen were already on the ground, their clubs tossed to the side. "Max, when did—"

Two more down, one choking on a blow to his neck that came too quick for Iris to see.

Iris closed her eyes and blurted it out. "When did you get here?"

By the time she was done with her sentence, each policeman was on the ground, defeated, their clubs scattered on the grass next to their dismantled guns. Sweat dripped off Max's brow as he breathed deeply and greeted Iris with a smile.

"What was that?" He wiped his forehead and leaned over. "Didn't catch what you said."

He didn't look as pale as he had in front of Bellerose's home, but there was still a pinch of sadness behind his cheeky grin that she couldn't ignore.

"Did you bloody see what I just saw?" said one onlooker.

"He just . . . so quickly . . ."

But the visitors didn't have time to gossip. Just then a stream of fire shot over their heads in a perfect arc. Screams erupted from the crowds as they gaped at the flames.

Iris turned back to see Jinn emerging from behind a cluster of visitors with slow, deliberate steps, wiping his mouth. With a deathly serious look, he said, very simply: "Fire."

"Fire!" another visitor screamed. *"Fire!"*

Everyone began running in every direction as Jinn reached Max and Iris. Iris grabbed both of them by the wrists, relieved and overwhelmed to see the two of them.

"Are you all right?" Jinn said, immediately checking for wounds.

"I didn't need you to come save me," she said defiantly, though she couldn't help but relish the feel of their skin in her hands.

Jinn rolled his eyes. "Right."

She expected Max might join in, but his eyes were unfocused, staring at the grass. His bleeding arm was bandaged. In her frazzled state of mind, she could think of nothing else but relief that he'd gone back to Club Uriel and gotten it dressed.

"Max," she said, touching his other arm, giving him a jolt of energy. "Are you okay?"

Max only stared at her.

"We can talk later." Jinn grabbed her hand. "It's bedlam here."

"Yes, because of you!" Iris reminded him, almost giddy from the blood rushing either to or from her head; she couldn't even tell anymore. Her body felt worn, her shattered mind held together through sheer force of will. She didn't want either of them to let go of her.

"Come on," Max said finally, grabbing her other hand.

"Wait! Look!" Iris pointed toward the Crystal Palace. Mary, Lucille, and Henry were standing a few meters away, their backs to her. "They're still here. We could get the card back!"

And what: Win the second round? The tournament? Did it even matter anymore? Something dark inside of her needled her, reminding her of the ashes of a man she'd just murdered. Incinerated from the inside out.

Win the tournament. Win the tournament . . . and then what? Iris couldn't recall.

"We should try . . ." She swallowed, suddenly feeling dizzy as she remembered the heat from the man's body as he burned at her touch. "We should at least—"

"Damn," Max breathed. "Damn!" He jumped to his feet, pulling Iris up with him. "We have to go. Now!"

Because Mary, Lucille, and Henry were looking up at two men who towered over them. And Iris recognized them both.

Belgium's boars.

Jacques had taken one of the axes she'd seen in Bellerose's dungeon. And then there was Gram. His nearly jaundiced pallor. His stringy gray hair just clinging to his scalp and brushing his shoulders. His large, bloodshot eyes and black lips. His buttoned-up dark gray jacket. But something was different. There were cuts on his face: two long gashes on each cheek.

"Jacques," Gram said in a deep, hollow voice that sounded as if he hadn't spoken in a hundred years. "Jacques . . ."

"That voice," Jinn whispered next to her, his fingers twitching.

Mary, Lucille, and Henry were quaking in fear. Jacques . . . Why appear here? Why now? He'd wanted to know the truth, and yet he was still playing the game. Like she was.

In one hand, Gram held his cigarette. In the other, his top hat, which he placed on his head before saying to his partner: "Jacques."

"Yes, I know. They managed to injure you earlier, didn't they?"

Lucille's team?

"I need to heal. I need to feed . . ."

"We do what we must," said Jacques, lowering his head. Just like Henry. Just like Iris and so many of the other champions. Whether for money, family, truth, or freedom, they were all doing what they felt they had to for the carrot the Committee dangled over their heads.

Except Gram. Iris had an inkling that Gram just liked to kill.

It was then that Jacques shook his head and turned his gaze elsewhere, anywhere other than the three frozen in fear in front of him. "I am truly sorry," he said. "But I can't stop it."

He sounded sincere.

And then Gram's hand was on Henry's vest. With his pale fingers curling into the fabric, he lifted the boy up with one arm and, with the force of a demon, slammed Henry back onto his knee.

The ugly, loud crack was so horrific, it stole the air from Iris's throat. Mary was screaming enough for the both of them, but Lucille hadn't the chance. As Henry's motionless body dropped to the ground, Gram's quick hand reached for Lucille's fake face and *tore it off*. Iris stared in utter horror as blood slopped from Lucille's head, from Gram's hand, and from the fresh flesh dangling in his dirtied fingers. Soon, Lucille's body was on the grass at his feet.

Iris finally began screaming when she saw Gram put the soggy flesh into his mouth.

38

GRAM'S BODY ARCHED BACK AT THE taste of Lucille's flesh. Jacques didn't touch him. He took the Judgment card Henry had been holding instead, then searched the boy's pockets until he found the Sun card his team had taken from the parlor. But when Jacques found Iris standing there in tears, he motioned with a flick of his head for her to run. She couldn't. She couldn't tear herself from the sight of Gram slurping and crunching. As if he'd lost himself in the taste, he stumbled back, writhing, holding his hands to his mouth greedily while the wounds on his face closed without a scar. His power . . .

"We have to go," repeated Max, tugging Iris's arm. "We have to go *now*."

But she just couldn't move. Neither could Jinn. Next to her, his brow furrowed, his lips parted, and his feeble voice was just loud enough for her to hear the words "No, it's not him . . . is it?"

If Gram had ever been at Club Uriel, he'd never shown himself. Iris wasn't even sure which floor he was on. Jinn had only ever seen him at Wilton's. But each time they crossed paths, Jinn's suspicious eyes followed the man, trying to place him. It was as if Gram were a monster he'd seen in a penny blood he'd read long ago.

While Gram was distracted, a terrified Mary fell to her knees and turned Lucille onto her back, grabbing onto her faceless head. Iris stood transfixed as the same bright light she'd seen during the first round danced from her fingers. When she lifted her hands again, Lucille's true face must have returned, because Mary blocked it from view and whispered to her. Lucille turned around quickly as Mary moved on to Henry, but by then Gram was ready for more.

"We have to go!" Gripping Iris's shoulders, Max began to pull her away.

"No!" Not while Mary was still desperately trying to heal Henry's broken back. "He'll kill them!"

Gram reached for Mary's head just as a stream of fire erupted from Jinn's mouth, missing the three on the ground, aimed squarely for Belgium's boars. The two jumped out of the way, but Jinn's fire chased them, forcing them to split up. It wasn't Jacques who Jinn was after. That was clear. He spat out his flames like a dragon until Gram had disappeared behind a statue.

"Jinn, what are you doing?" Iris linked both her arms around Jinn's bicep, but he shrugged her off frantically.

"That man . . ." Jinn could barely breathe, his mouth still smoking. "That man! I . . . I think I know him!"

"Of course, he's one of the champions!"

"No!" He shook his head. His hollowed-out expression as he stared at his trembling hands sent a shiver down her spine. "I *know* him." And suddenly, his head was in his hands. "No." He shook his head again. "Was it him? No, I don't know . . ."

Iris had never seen Jinn so frenzied. The cool veneer he kept around him at all times had shattered in an instant upon seeing that horrific ghoul of a man. Patches of fire spread throughout the grounds. It would attract the authorities soon, but how long until they arrived? How long did Iris have to spirit Henry, Lucille, and Mary away from these beasts?

Through a patch of fire, using his black cloak to shield his face, Gram charged at Jinn, so fast it was like he was gliding across the grass. Jinn froze, his mouth gaping.

"Is it you?" Iris heard him whisper.

A long sword launched at Gram's head. A blade of pure white. Jacques was too quick, maneuvering himself forward and throwing his ax to knock the blade off its trajectory. Both weapons clattered to the ground, the sword shattering into white smoke.

"I'm sorry. I have to win the tournament. And so I can't let you kill this man," Jacques said to the girl who'd emerged from behind the Punch puppet.

Rin. She weaved around patches of fire, her long braids fluttering behind her.

And on the other side of the puppet:

"Bately." Max's fists were ready.

The usually cocky Bately was a shadow of his former self. He looked both traumatized and feral, intent upon revenge. He held his gun in his left hand now because his right was missing three fingers. Iris could tell by the way it was bandaged. Bately glared wildly at Gram.

"I've got you now, you sick bastard," Bately said. "Now that I tailed you here, I'm going to end your miserable life myself for what you did to me!"

Just what the hell happened after Iris left for Bellerose's house?

Rin tried to summon her sword again, but Jacques reached his ax first. Iris ran toward him, and as he brought his weapon down upon Rin's head, Iris blocked his blow with her hands on his wrist. Her knees buckled underneath his strength, but it gave Rin the time she needed to grip the hilt of her sword and lunge for him. Jacques flipped back until he stood on the fountain ridge.

"Why are you here?" Iris asked in her best Fon.

Rin understood. "We met Gram on the great bridge and fought. He ate the mercenary's fingers." Bately. Her expression darkened as she lowered her head, the dark purple of her scarred eye facing her enemy. "Isoke. That white man needs to die. This tournament and its prizes mean nothing to him. I can see it in his eyes. He lives to feed." Rin scrunched her face in disgust.

Like the horses' rotted flesh he ate as a child to survive, according to Jacob. And like . . .

Iris almost threw up. Meanwhile, Jacques stood silently on the ridge of the fountain beneath the moon, his ax in hand. Waiting.

Another stream of fire. The way Jinn was going, all of Penge Peak would be engulfed in flames soon. Gram dodged his flames, his strides long, his expression dark like the devil.

Amid it all, atop the Crystal Palace, stood Fool—or at least *one* of him—his black cape fluttering, his face covered with his harlequin mask. The watcher of their misery, documenting their bloody battles, soaking in the mayhem.

There were only monsters here.

Bately fired at Jacques, but his left hand was clearly not his dominant. One bullet would have torn through Rin if Max hadn't appeared behind the two girls just in time, pulling them to the ground.

"You see this fool I've been saddled with," Rin muttered as she sprang to her knees, keeping her head down as Bately kept firing.

"Bately!" Max screamed, jumping up. "You bloody bastard, watch your damn aim!"

Bately had no qualms about aiming his gun right at Max. Max dodged each bullet using his ability, but Bately had known he would. So he let him come, let Max's anger drive him forward.

"Max!" Iris struggled to her feet, fearing the worst. "Don't get close! Cover your ears!"

But the moment Max was near enough to grab him, Bately whispered something Iris couldn't hear. Max's hand froze on the barrel of his gun.

"Oh no." Iris squeezed her fists. What had Bately whispered with his charmed tongue?

The gun was aimed at Max's chest. She thought Bately would shoot him point-blank, but instead, Bately let go of the handle, giving the gun to Max, who took it obediently.

"Max?" Iris said again as Max pointed the gun at Jacques and fired while Bately laughed.

Jacques returned fire, breaking his index finger and shooting out of the bone. The projectile traveled too fast for Iris to see. It pierced through Max's wrist, causing him to cry out in pain and drop Bately's gun.

Just like Adam said in Bellerose's dungeon, Jacques had the deadly eyes of a sniper. This was business to him. But Jacques didn't kill him. Max held his wrist, moaning in pain.

"Kill him, Maxey!" Bately sounded a lot more confident now that he had someone to do his dirty work for him. "*Kill* him!"

"No, stop! It's too dangerous!" Iris screamed, but Max was already running for the fountain, fists at the ready.

Iris pumped her legs as hard as she could and tackled him to the ground just as Jacques jumped and brought his ax down upon them. Iris had no choice but to block it with her waist as she moved to cover Max, gasping as the blade pierced almost to the bone.

The sound of her pain snapped Max out of his stupor. Bewildered and horrified, he scooped up Iris and carried her out of harm's way while Rin leaped into action, dueling with Jacques.

"Iris!" Max sank to the ground, watching the blood pouring from her wound. "Iris! Look at me! Come on, look at me! Oh God, why did you . . . ?" Breathing heavily, he attempted to keep her head from flopping about. "Look right at me, all right? *All right?*"

She could barely open her eyes. "It hurts," she whimpered. "It hurts . . ."

"It's all right, she can't die, she can't die," Max whispered to himself as if the mantra would keep him sane as he held her.

But he knew as well as she did; she could still feel pain. She could still quiver from the putrid horror of it.

"Jinn!" he cried out. "What the hell are you doing? Iris is hurt!"

Iris's head flopped to the side helplessly as she watched Jinn swallow his fire immediately and look toward them. In another second, after spraying fire to keep Gram from following, he was running to her.

Iris's consciousness flitted between two worlds. Was she on the grass bleeding in Max's arms? Or was she in a dimly lit room bleeding from a wound of another kind? The sharp pain in her waist. Monsters above her speaking among themselves, making their calculations. Terms she couldn't understand. Numbers and measurements.

"Pratt . . . ," she whispered, her eyes growing wide as she saw the man hovering above her.

"Iris!" But why did that awful man have Jinn's concerned voice? "Iris, look at me!"

She felt a new set of hands on her as the other applied pressure to her wound. Then her head was on someone's shoulder. With each touch, she grew colder.

"Max, do you have something to stop the bleeding?" Jinn.

"No. No, I—" Max sounded beside himself. "I'm sorry. This is my fault. I've done so much wrong. Iris, it was *me*. I was the one who—"

"Concentrate!"

"Even if she dies, she won't stay dead." Max nodded again and again, reassuring himself, sometimes speaking English, sometimes slipping into Spanish. "She'll come back. She'll come back to us, won't she?"

Do whatever you wish to her. She can't die, did you forget? A terrible voice mocked Iris from within her memories. Like soggy hands rising from a black swamp, it grabbed her and pulled her deeper into the darkness.

"But I don't want to die," she said weakly. "I never wanted to die. Not even once."

"Iris . . . *Iris!*"

She heard Jinn. Heard Max too, but she couldn't see him. She could see Anne instead, trying to speak to her. She was hallucinating. She needed to break out of it, return to herself, but Anne's whisper was so loud in her ears:

Nekawa.

"Stop it. Please! Stop! I can't understand you! Leave me alone!" she cried, trying to writhe away from her. "The Hiva. The Hiva! The Hiva begins anew!"

"Iris?" Max asked, frightened.

"Get away from me!" Iris shut her eyes. "I'm sorry, I can't understand you. I'm sorry. I'm not who you think I am! I'm sorry! I'm sorry!"

"Iris, listen to me. Listen to my voice." Jinn. He sounded desperate. That desperation carved out the contours of his graceful face from within the darkness. His high cheekbones. That sharp nose. Those cat eyes. Those lips that always grinned a little after he nitpicked her mistakes. "Listen to me," he said again. "Wherever you are right now is not where you need to be."

"I killed him," Iris cried as the pain in her side reminded her of the ashes in the Crystal Palace. "I killed a man. I did, didn't I?"

As Jinn and Max struggled to respond, Rin grunted in battle from a distance, steel clashing against steel, but it sounded miles away.

"Gram and Jacques are still . . . Damn it!" Max swore. "Jinn—"

"That girl, Rin. She'll handle them," Jinn hissed as Iris gasped for breath.

"She can't take them both on for long!"

"Then *you* help her!"

"But Iris—!"

"Max," Iris said, her eyes fluttering open. "Jinn. What am I? What am I? What—"

"Iris, listen to me." Jinn hugged her. "When I throw you up in the air, you always close your eyes. I know. I've seen it. Do you know why that is?"

She felt his rough hand brushing the sweat dripping from her forehead as she trembled.

"It's because you know that no matter how long you stay suspended in that boundless space, my hands will find you again. Right now, just like that, come back. Come back to these hands. Come back to this moment. Here with me. Ground yourself in me, Iris. Ground yourself in me and *survive* it."

This time. This place. This *her*. She was more than just shattered memories. More than parts and pain. Jinn's voice stretched forward, offering her a lifeline. She took it. She embraced the pain that would not kill her but caused her entire body to quake.

Looking up at Jinn and Max, she tried to smile. But then Henry's panic and fury rang out from the din of battle.

"If you two demons don't leave, I'll blow you all to hell! Even if it means taking everyone with me! I don't care anymore! *I don't care!*"

Iris was in too much pain to respond, but she could hear the quiver in his voice. He meant it. He would do it just to be rid of them.

"Gram. Enough." Next to Gram, Jacques jumped back from Rin, lifting his hand up in surrender. Sweat dripped down the girl's forehead. She was a soldier, but the stress of having to fight both boars was clear. "We have the cards," he said. "I won't fight just to satiate your grim appetite."

But Gram wasn't finished. From the corner of her eye, Iris could see

Gram approaching, causing a panting Rin to back off immediately. Shouts of approaching officers could be heard.

"Not enough," said Gram, and in a flash, he took Jacques's ax.

It flew.

And then Bately was screaming.

Iris lifted her head in time to see Bately's right arm drop to the ground.

"Good God . . . ," Max whispered as Iris shut her eyes. Bately's shrieks pierced the air.

When she looked again, Gram was skulking off behind a patch of flames, letting Bately's arm dangle in his grip. Jacques escaped in another direction. Rin tossed Iris an apologetic look before tending to Bately so he wouldn't bleed to death. As for Iris, she was already being scooped up, lifted into Jinn's arms.

"Damn it." Henry fell to his knees. "Damn it all to hell." His voice cracked as he wept.

39

TWO DAYS AT CLUB URIEL. IRIS stayed in bed. Jinn and Max left their room only when they needed to. As Mr. Mortius delivered their meals to them, that wasn't often. Iris held on to the pocket watch Max had stolen for her. Its song comforted her.

Every so often, Cherice would come in to cheer her up and gossip.

Ah, so the final card was at the Tower of London. That was where the Earl of Shaftesbury had been imprisoned after turning against King Charles II. Iris couldn't care less. After taking all three cards, Gram and Jacques had been the only ones to pass the second round. It didn't matter.

Everything was jumbled in her head. Carl Anderson's words, his death. The dungeon. Pratt and the man she'd reduced to ash. Gram and Jacques. Everything weighed her down to the point where Jinn had to lift her up and force her to eat two nights in a row. One night, when Max was asleep, he simply held her as she wept in his arms, crying for Granny.

This was a mistake. This was all a mistake. The only time she voiced this out loud, Jinn was on the first floor getting more of Club Uriel's medical supplies. It was Max who'd told her gently not to give up. But even as he insisted, he had very little of his usual charm. It was like he couldn't look her in the eye.

Every day she woke up knowing that the members of Club Uriel were likely gossiping about their battles based on Fool's reports and Wilton's new show. She hated them all.

Then on the third day, Mortius appeared at the door. "Miss Iris, Lord Temple would like to see you at the terrace on the second floor."

Oh yes. Adam. After promising the Enlightenment Committee the moon, Bellerose had been left with a dead Carl Anderson, a tortured Adam, and no new information gleaned from the little champion she let get away. According to Adam, there was no information to give. Just Madame's sick desperation. She couldn't stand up to the Temple name.

Max dropped the newspaper he was reading on the table. "He can eat shit," he barked with the kind of fury that startled Mortius—startled even *Iris*. Jinn was on his feet.

"It's all right," Iris told the boys. She felt strong enough. "This won't take long."

At least she hoped it wouldn't. At some point, Max and Jinn must have made a pact to try to keep her mind off things, for they took turns trying to make her laugh, bickering with each other so obviously for show. It'd helped, somewhat. But now that she was walking back into the room of beautiful green flora, anxiety filled her once more.

Adam stood on the terrace waiting for her in a brown jacket and vest. If he had any lingering trauma from his time in Bellerose's dungeon, she couldn't see it.

She hated this feeling. She hated being on the terrace despite the much-needed air. She tightened her hold on the white shawl Granny had made her. Where to start.

Ashes in the Crystal Palace. Secrets in the dark.

Adam held out his coin. "Try to set aside everything that's happened," he said.

Iris was too tired to even be baffled at what he was suggesting. Had Carl Anderson's corpse been buried yet? But there it was, that honesty again. The silent plea for her to believe him just this one more time.

"No matter what you might think of me, I *am* on your side," he insisted. "We need to practice so you can find my father."

Find his father. For what again? For the truth? As she looked into Adam's eyes, Anne's voice called out to her. The word escaped from her lips before her mind could catch up:

"The Hiva."

Adam gave no reaction. His expression remained still.

"Hiva," she said again. "The Hiva."

He leaned back against the balcony rails. "What do you know of it?"

"You know what it is, don't you? The Hiva? And . . ." She searched her memories. The outline of Doctor Seymour Pratt emerged from the darkness, causing a violent shudder. "The white crystal. And the Crystal Palace. My heart." She remembered the bullet shattering against it. "My bones. And . . . and—"

It was all jumbling together.

"What do you know of these things?"

"And *you*." She didn't dare step any closer, though his gaze seemed to beckon for it. "You, as a child, looking up at me that day at the South Kensington fair with a white dress in your hands." Her hand began to tremble against her chest. "The explosion. And we Fanciful Freaks."

"No, Iris. You're not like them."

A heavy silenced passed between them as they studied each other underneath the cloudy sky, the sounds of carts, wheels, and trotting horses filling the empty space.

"Tell me everything," Iris whispered.

"If I did, would you be able to handle it? Are you handling it now?"

"Tell me!" She pounded the balcony railing, letting part of her shawl slide down her body. "Is my life a game to you?"

"No, Iris. *No*." With two strides he closed the gap between them. "The truth isn't something that should just be told to you. You have to discover it yourself. To feel it in your bones. Lay the pieces one at a time in a way that'll help you understand. What has rushing gotten you? Jumping in headlong has only hurt you."

Iris scoffed. "And you care so much about my well-being."

"I do, Iris." His fingers lingered near her but dared not touch. "I think I really do."

Iris stepped back, leaving his fingers to grasp the breath left in her wake. "I can't tell if there's anything about you that's real."

Adam turned his head slightly but couldn't seem to meet her eyes. "I didn't kill my father. But Neville Bradford did die at my hands. Before that, I also tried to kill Carl Anderson."

Iris backed farther away from him. "Why?"

"It was my father's fault." Adam's expression turned vicious as he thought of the man. "By telling them his secrets, he sealed their fate. Those are dangerous secrets, Iris. If either the Committee or the Crown ever got ahold of them, they could be used as a weapon."

"Against who?"

"Against *you*." Adam swiveled around, his face reddening just enough to show his frustration. "Your true identity. That's what my father was researching. That's why he left my family and traveled around Africa looking for clues. He still has those secrets in his journal. Even though he was an Enlightener, he couldn't agree with the Committee's tournament, their plans for the world."

"Plans . . ."

Adam's hands tightened around the railing. "The Committee wants to leave this world to die. They believe they have a way out—to another world."

Iris was so numb at this point, she simply let the information wash over her. Another world. Maybe that was where she'd come from. Maybe that was what had made the Fanciful Freaks. At this point, whether he was telling the truth or not, anything was possible.

"I told you that the Committee believes *they* should be the ones to guide humanity's transition," Adam reminded her. "My father disagrees, and without his research, his secrets, the Committee won't be able to follow through with their plans. Right now he's hiding from their spies. But I'm sure he's searching for someone worthy to give those secrets to. Someone worthier than the Committee. Worthier than the Crown. And whichever rival finds out the secret, it'll be *you* in danger. That's why I lied and told the Committee I killed my father. That's why you have to find him first before they realize he's alive."

Iris fell forward, letting her forearms hold herself up on the railing. He was right. Being told all these things made her head ache. Her breathing quickened as she watched the street below without seeing the pedestrians, the carriages, the newsboys selling their wares. A pinch in her chest and ribs caused her to shut her eyes and breathe in deeply as she let her mind catch up to the information flooding her.

Adam finally cupped her face with his hands. "When I first talked to you at the amphitheater, I was shocked. I didn't expect to see so much good in your eyes. So much innocence and life. And now . . ." He trailed off, looking deeply into them. "Now I know that the moment you learn the truth, *that* will be the moment your misery will truly begin. But I—"

He stopped, fighting with himself. Iris's lips curled inward as fear gripped her. Just what kind of hell was waiting for her on the other side of the truth?

"But you still need to know," Adam said resolutely as if to convince himself. "I had Cordiero killed because he threatened to come too close to your secret. I would do the same to the other members of the Committee. Make no mistake."

Iris couldn't move, couldn't even speak as he stared at her with the intensity and honesty of a beautiful monster.

"I am a murderer and a deceiver," he said. "I know that. But I still wish you'd believe me. Let everything be done at the right time, in the right order, under the right circumstances. Continue with the tournament. Let the heat of battle dislodge those sleeping memories. Find my father. During the final round, I'm sure you'll remember. Once you find my father, I promise, everything will fall into place."

"The tournament . . ." Iris thought of Gram and shuddered. "If you care so much about me, then why ask me to participate in such a horrible game?"

"Because it's *through* that game, *through* the horror and violence, that your true self will awaken."

My true self . . . Iris gripped the peach-colored lace around her neck as she thought of the ashes littering the floor of the Crystal Palace.

"Trust me," Adam pleaded, and gave her the coin. "Everything at the right time."

———— • ————

Trust him. But how could she? Trust a monster? Trust a devil? A demon? Though his pleas pulled her in, deep down she knew this man was leading her into hell, even though his desire to protect her was also his truth.

Truth.

An unknowable, unavoidable conclusion awaited her. Something so terrible that Adam wouldn't dare utter it except at the right moment.

Despite her fear, she lay underneath her bedcovers, night after night, holding Adam's coin, attempting to feel his father's essence of life.

That unstoppable drive to know. Her insatiable need for *self* even if it drove her so far into the dark that she ended up losing the parts of her that she most cared about. John Temple had gone to the Dahomey in search of She Who Does Not Fall. If his son would not tell her, then she would make John do it.

Club Uriel announced that the final round would take place at the end of the week. For the next two nights, Iris practiced. She practiced feeling the life forces of those around her, Jinn and Max in particular as they slept in their beds, never letting herself go too far for fear of what she might do to them. She controlled her breathing, closed her eyes with the back of her head on her pillow, felt the fluttering of her eyelashes and the weight of her eyelids, and imagined their essences entering into her, warming her skin until her entire body pushed them out again with a shiver.

Max and Jinn tasted different: one sweet like grapes, the other savory bread. It was silly to imagine it like that, but the differences helped her discern between their essences.

No, their anima, she thought. She somehow knew that was the right term.

And so one night, she poured all her energy into the Temple coin. Psychometry, Jacob had told her a few days ago when she asked whether or not it was really possible. A scientific theory that one could pierce through pasts and presents, lives and afterlives by sensing the flow of life through an object. A coin, for example. Or a man's body. Even the air. The flow of life was everywhere. She just needed to pluck the right string.

Finally, she did. John Temple. This string that she felt pulled her from the inside. While Max and Jinn slept on, she physically followed the string out of her bed, out of Club Uriel, out into the cold, dark night. It was leading her to someone living and breathing—and in London.

She navigated the dark streets of the city until she came to the steps of a train station. She looked up at the large, bright clock on the white brick building. It was nearly three in the morning. That would explain the lack of people, but as she descended deeper into the station, passing the wooden signs directing passengers to their platforms, she quickly realized that the station was quite suspiciously empty.

Iris tied her shawl around her head like a bonnet and, inspired by Rin, used the white fabric to cover her face, keeping her head down as she descended another flight of steps.

Then she heard voices.

"... your entourage ..."

"Mr. Bosch told us he'd be sending his head man ..."

Bosch of the Guns and Ammunitions Company? An *Enlightener*. Her heart sped up along with her steps. As she approached the underground platform, the voices grew louder.

"Ridiculous! Do you expect us to believe *this* is the head of Bosch's development team?"

Iris hid behind a wall of white-and-dark-green brick. Then, sucking in a breath, she peeked around the corner.

The platform was a cold gray strip stretching into a dark domed tunnel. A train had already disappeared into it in a whirl of steam whistles. On the gray strip, two groups stood close to a wooden bench not far from Iris. On one side: three men in brown bowler hats and jackets. And with their back to the train tracks, another group of men flanked a beautiful brown woman.

The woman had light brown skin with long black hair flowing loose down to her waist. Her navy-blue sari hugged her body tightly, sucked in at the waist by a black skeleton-like corset worn on the outside. Upon her head dangled bronze and silver headpieces, shaped like little suns chained together around her small skull. The silver nose ring piercing her right nostril looked like a cluster of gears to match those dangling from her ears. She returned the upset stares of the men in front of her with a confident puff of smoke from her long golden pipe, her heavy-lidded eyes watching them like a mocking cat.

"Uma Malakar," she introduced herself. "Head of Bosch Guns and Ammunitions' Weapons Development Team. Pleased to make your acquaintance, gentlemen."

"This is absurd!" One man swiped away the smoke she'd breathed into his face. "Bosch's man is supposed to be . . . a *man*. A genius weapons maker. An inventor. And you're telling me *this*—" He could barely finish his words.

"Watch what you say," cried one of the men behind Uma. The rest of her followers nodded fervently until they stopped on the cue that was Uma's black-gloved hand in the air.

"Mr. Brightly, was it?" The woman had an English accent as proper as theirs, but hers was a barrel more confident. "You shouldn't be so hostile, Mr. Brightly. We've come to share our research on an agreement Mr. Bosch made with *your* team. If you're unhappy with what you see"—she motioned down her own body—"then you're certainly free to explain to the Crown why the weapons we've been developing on their behalf will soon go to another willing customer. And trust me, there are always willing customers."

Bosch was making weapons for the Crown? Did the Committee know? Mr. Brightly's chestnut mustache quivered from an angry exhale through his nose.

"You've received the *wares* we sent seven days ago, I'm assuming?" Uma continued.

"Yes," Brightly answered stiffly.

"And I'm also assuming that although your people have been studying it meticulously, you still have *no idea* how the weapon works." She smoked her pipe.

Mr. Brightly looked offended by the mere fact that a woman, especially one with her skin color, dared to speak down to him. But he couldn't refute her. Brightly's eyes lowered to the brown pouch strapped to her side. "John Temple's research—his journal. You have it with you . . ."

John Temple's journal? How did she manage to get ahold of it?

But the moment he reached for it, guns were in the air. Uma hadn't moved,

THE BONES OF RUIN

of course. Her men acted fast, ready to kill on her word as if they'd been baptized as her willing disciples.

"It's not polite to touch a woman's body without permission." The look in Uma's eyes made it clear she knew as well as he did that she could order his death with a word, and he would be gone in the blink of an eye. As Brightly withdrew his hand, Uma's men withdrew their guns.

John Temple's journal. Iris pressed her back against the wall. Was that what she had been sensing rather than the man himself? Adam thought it was in his father's possession. The Committee ordered the man's *assassination* because they feared he'd eventually give it to one of their enemies. Apparently those fears weren't so unfounded. Unless . . . Did Temple really give away such a precious possession or was it *taken* from him?

"Temple's work still needs to be fully decoded," Uma said. "But what I've discovered so far will help us learn more about the properties of the white crystal—and how to manipulate it."

The white crystal. Iris covered her mouth with her hands. John Temple's secrets.

"Either way, I'd like you to take me to your base of research and show me the progress you've made. I'm intrigued to see what you've done after *decades* of research."

"We haven't found the Moon Skeleton yet," said Brightly.

"Not surprised." Uma smirked as Iris frantically tried to commit their words to memory. "According to Bosch, John Temple had it when he *supposedly* died."

"Supposedly?"

The conversation abruptly ended. A hush fell over the group. Iris narrowed her eyes, confused, wondering what happened, until she realized she could hear a wheezing sound coming from her open lips—her own breathing.

"My," said Uma. "I do think we're being spied on."

Panic began to set in and Iris clumsily moved her feet toward the staircase, only to trip ungracefully and crash to the brick floor. But this was okay. This could still work. As the frenzied footsteps approached her, Iris quickly lowered the shawl over her face.

"Please," Iris said once the men were upon her, surrounding her at the foot of the staircase. "I . . . I b-beggar." She spoke in broken English, hoping they'd believe she couldn't quite understand them. She held out her cupped hands, bending over in supplication. "Spare please."

When she looked up, she saw Uma looming above her through her white shawl. Perhaps it was an odd turn of fate, but the woman's deep brown eyes softened at the sight of her. Gone was the mischievous grin, replaced now by an inscrutable expression.

"How much do you think she heard?" asked one of Uma's men.

"Miss Malakar, shall we get rid of her? She's only a beggar. Doesn't look like she even knows English. Still, it is better to be safe than sorry, isn't it?"

Uma hesitated.

"What's wrong, Malakar?" Brightly laughed. "She's just a colored girl squatting in a dirty corner of the train station. Or are you unwilling to kill someone like yourself?"

At that, Uma's shoulders relaxed and lowered, her chin rising in defiance. "There is no one like me, Mr. Brightly," she said coldly, and raised her hand.

On cue, one of Uma's disciples aimed his gun at her.

"Wait."

Iris was prepared for a bullet in the head. Then she'd escape once they were gone. That was her plan. What she received instead was Uma's mercy.

"This girl is just a beggar," Uma said. "Leave her be."

Brightly smirked. "You truly are soft toward *your kind*, aren't you—?"

A gunshot rang, loud and violent, shaking Iris's eardrums. This time it was from the pistol Uma had taken from inside her sari. Brightly's hat clattered to the ground with a brand-new hole smoking through the brim.

"I'm an impatient woman, Mr. Brightly," said Uma, handing the gun off to one of her men before taking another puff from her pipe. "You'd do well to keep your mouth shut from this point forward. Come."

Uma spared Iris one last piteous glance before she flicked her head. Her disciples followed her dutifully out of the train station. A lucky break, maybe.

But if Uma was an employee of an Enlightener, Iris would have to tread more carefully from now on.

She waited a few more moments before escaping the empty train station.

The white crystal, initially discovered in the mining site in the Oil Rivers Protectorate. Stolen by the Dahomey and taken over by the Crown, each for their own experiments.

The Crystal Palace: the Crown's research base.

The Moon Skeleton: out there somewhere in John Temple's possession.

And Iris. The Fanciful Freaks. Iris thought of them battling in this tournament, none of them knowing exactly where they'd come from or why they existed. It felt like everyone else had more information than they did about their own selves.

After what felt like hours of walking and thinking, she found herself at Wilton's Music Hall. The Fanciful Freaks of London. Their lives turned into a show. Their misery entertainment for others. She stared at the poster for some time before entering. She found Fool once again sitting in the back row, his head against his seat. Resting.

Iris scoffed. "For all the work you do for them, they don't let you sleep at the club?"

"The theater has always been a comfort to me, dear Iris."

Fool turned his head to the side, and the sight of his harlequin mask suddenly sparked a sense of panic. She looked up to the rafters. Empty. There was only one Fool here today.

"Tell me." She hovered above him, body still cold from her time outside. "What do you get out of this tournament? Do you like being the Committee's dog? Adam's little messenger?"

"Lord Temple understands me," said Fool, tilting his head too far for a normal man. "And the Committee feeds me." At this he giggled.

"They feed you?" Iris cocked her head to the side. "Feed you what?"

She couldn't tell whether Fool was staring at her or not, not with that blasted mask covering his face. He was an enigma she wanted nothing to do with.

"Do you know what the final round will be, my rabbit? Why you were given two rounds preceding it?" he asked, and when she couldn't answer, he laughed. "One final contest between the remaining teams. A fight to the death."

Iris gaped at him in horror.

"In front of the good gentlemen of Club Uriel. This battle will take place on the lowest floor of the building: a secret basement your Patrons have taken to calling Cerberus."

Iris flinched at the name. Cerberus: Uriel's underworld.

"Those who won the first round by receiving two pairs of keys and those who won the second round by receiving at least one card—*they* will be the ones to fight each other. The opening act of the show will be the slaughter of those remaining who did not win either round."

Names and faces flashed through Iris's mind in a frenzy as she thought of who was doomed to die before the third round even began.

Rin. Iris's whole body seized. She didn't get a card in the second round. Iris was the one who'd taken her key in the first round. She grasped her blouse over her heart, stumbling back. What kind of nonsense was this? What kind of . . .

"From this point forward, only one team of Fanciful Freaks will survive. The team that does will win the tournament. And so you see, Iris? I am well fed." Fool turned his head sharply to the other side. "With merriment!"

Iris had had enough. She'd had enough of the Committee and their secrets. She'd had enough of Club Uriel watching their pain. She'd had enough of killing and death. She grabbed Fool by his white collar, dragged him out of his seat, and tackled him to the ground.

Fool's top hat fell from his head, revealing a small patch of brown hair clinging to his scalp. She glared at his false face.

"There won't be a fight to the death," Iris hissed, pinning his arms to the ground. "Not if I can help it." She could feel his blood pumping fast in his veins. "You can let your masters know if you want; it doesn't matter to me."

"Once you agreed to enter this tournament, you entered a pact of sorts," said Fool. "Those who try to escape the final round will meet with certain death."

He flicked his sleeve. Out came one of the tarot cards.

"Judgment," whispered Fool as Iris stared at its surface: the naked men, women, and children reaching out in desperation from their graves toward an archangel whose apocalyptic trumpet blew nonetheless. "The sound that blows in the final days. How very suitable."

Iris wouldn't let it come to that. She swore upon her immortal bones.

Enough was enough.

PART THREE
Enlightenment

The forces which are working out the great scheme of perfect happiness, taking no account of incidental suffering, exterminate such sections of mankind as stand in their way, with the same sternness that they exterminate beasts of prey and herds of useless ruminants.

—HERBERT SPENCER, *Social Statics*

She had been disassembled into her relevant parts. She was "fetishized"—turned into an object. This substitution of a part for the whole, of a thing—an object, an organ, a portion of the body—for a subject . . .

—STUART HALL, *Representation*

40

S HE SPREAD THE WORD SECRETLY WITHIN the walls of Club Uriel: "Meet me at Wilton's. Midnight. Champions only. This is a truce. I have what this tournament can't give you." To stop the madness of the Tournament of Freaks before they all ended up dead. That was her goal.

Everyone had agreed to participate in the tournament knowing that their lives would be on the line. Everyone wanted their winnings. In that case, Iris would have to offer them something she hoped would be far more tantalizing: the truth.

It was a gamble she prayed would pay off.

When it came to a truce, not everyone was interested. Rin strode through the doors of Wilton's in her beaded blouse and sunlit skirt, her sword in her hands. Iris bit her lip, relieved to see her. This affected the young warrior too, after all. But Bately didn't follow. Max, who sat on the arm of a chair, didn't look relieved or disappointed.

Hawkins's team came several minutes later. After what she'd seen and heard in the train station last night, Iris would need to know everything they did about their Patron, Bosch.

Finally, in walked Henry, Mary, and a woman she assumed was Lucille. She had on the unremarkable face of a middle-aged woman you could find anywhere on the streets of London, her black hair parted down the middle and tied to the bottom of her neck in a bun. That frumpy black dress and white apron were definitely not Lucille's style. Then again, even Rin had her sword. Even during this parley, everyone was on guard.

In the middle of the theater, everyone found a place to sit or stand. The tension between them was palpable, but it was Henry's team that was largely on the outs. They stayed closer to the stage while Rin had her back to the exit. Ten past midnight.

"Belgium's boars are a no-show, then," said Max from his chair. "Right. So we can cross cannibalism off tonight's event."

His confirmation gave everyone permission to relax. One by one, they began speaking.

Hawkins hung his head in relief, releasing an audible sigh. "Good to know."

"You've faced them before?" Though Henry's arms were crossed confidently over his chest, the trauma of their last battle was clearly etched in his sallow face.

Jacob sat on the arm of a chair next to Hawkins, who'd chosen to stand. The two glanced at each other. "We've been lucky enough to escape every time we ran into them."

"But we heard about all that nasty business a few nights ago," added Cherice, her pumpkin hair brighter under the music hall lights. "Sorry 'bout your back, mate."

Henry straightened it uncomfortably, as if making sure it still worked. It did, thanks to Mary, who stood next him, wringing her hands shyly.

"Just what in the hell are those monsters anyway?" Lucille may have been wearing another face, but her real, haughty voice was as strong as ever. "I'm still having nightmares."

"You sure you wanna know?" Cherice swung her legs from the arm of the chair she was sitting on. "Gram's story's pretty damn grisly."

"Gram? That's the one who *ate my face*, right?" Lucille scoffed. "Yeah, I think I have the *right* to know."

The tip of Rin's sword scraped the wooden floor. "One must always know their enemy."

That was probably the only reason she agreed to come. But only Iris understood her.

"What'd she say?" Cherice's legs froze in the air. "She making fun of us? Hey!" She leaned over. "Plotting something, girly?"

"Cherice, calm down," Jacob scolded, but she only pouted like a child in response.

"Y-yes. I agree." Mary clung to Lucille's arm. "We mustn't fight among ourselves. This is a neutral zone, after all."

"If it's so neutral," said Henry, "then why's that girl carrying her sword in plain sight?"

"Perhaps for the same reason you've got a few marbles hidden in the back pocket of your jacket." Max pointed at him, causing Henry to stiffen. Iris hadn't even seen. "Planning to set them off if things get rough?"

"Always ready." Hawkins laughed. "I like this brat."

Cherice slapped him in the back of his golden head. "Like what? Getting a limb blown off? Not me. Iris, you should have left those punks out of this. How're you gonna trust someone who doesn't even show their real face?"

Lucille sighed rather theatrically. "I don't like rude little girls. I dealt with far too many of them during my vaudeville days, though I suspect that was largely due to jealousy."

"It's okay," chimed Hawkins without bothering to look at her. "You're probably secretly ugly anyway. I get it."

"*Excuse* me—"

"Everyone, please!" Iris cried over the arguing that suddenly erupted. Beside her, Jinn lowered his forehead into his palm. "Everyone!" She looked to Max, who shrugged. "*Quiet!*"

Her voice echoed in the rafters. Silence. Iris began rubbing her temples.

Rin considered her with interest. "Why did you call us here, Isoke?"

The Fon that only Iris could understand reminded her of something Max had brought up minutes before the meeting. How did they know that Fool wasn't also present, somewhere behind the curtains, perhaps, listening and waiting to tell Club Uriel of their discussions? She, Max, and Jinn had checked backstage before everyone had arrived, but it still didn't give her confidence. However, Max had come up with a plan—a plan that required everyone's cooperation.

"I called you here because the third round is about to begin, and despite the money the Committee has promised, I doubt any of you are really eager to fight to the death for it."

Restless legs, fidgeting hands.

"Has that been confirmed?" asked Henry.

Iris nodded. "Fool told me himself last night. Round three is a fight to the death. And whoever hasn't passed a round by now will be killed outright the second we all step onstage."

Anxious glances. Mary almost began to cry as Henry and Lucille comforted her. Their team hadn't managed to pass either round despite their efforts. She tried her best to repeat it in Fon so that Rin could understand. Rin, ever the warrior, didn't seem moved at all. Well, Rin was confident enough in her skills. Maybe she thought she could fight back. But there was no telling what kind of death the Committee had planned for the losers of the tournament. Iris cared enough for the both of them. For all of them.

"Fool has no reason to lie," Iris told them. "He wants the mayhem. You got a taste of mayhem a few nights ago, Henry. How did it feel?" She looked around the hall. "How do you all feel about being slaughtered for Club Uriel's enjoyment?"

The champions glanced at each other, none daring to speak.

"I have something I'd like to discuss with you," Iris continued. "But before we do, I want to make sure our conversation remains private." She turned to Max, who gestured toward Jacob.

"What do you say, Jacob? Just like when we were kids?" Max's expression brightened a little with nostalgia.

Jacob tucked his black hair behind his ear. The two shared a connection, Max told her; they were both scouted and brought to Europe by the same headhunter: the Norwegian Johan Adrian Jacobsen. They came at different times and at different ages. They lived in different zoos before escaping to the London streets. But their common history had built a close connection.

Jacob brushed, first, Cherice's throat with the back of his hand. With Hawkins, his touch was a little more tender. Their eyes connected softly for just a moment. Once he was done, Hawkins gave him a little wink before Jacob moved on to Henry, blushing. Lucille. Then Mary. No one fought him. It was clear that gentle Jacob was hardly a threat.

"Jacob here has a special gift," explained Max. "The gift of language. He can make people understand and speak different tongues. Or forget how to. He even made up his own. Cool, right?" Max laughed, wistfully remembering simpler times. "When we were kids, we needed a way to communicate among ourselves. The effect only lasts a little while, but it should be long enough, wouldn't you say, Jacob?"

"That depends on what Iris needs to tell us," Jacob answered, moving to Rin.

Once Jacob had finished, they were all speaking a language Iris had never heard before. A language that existed only in Jacob's imagination.

"When I first came here as a child," Jacob said, returning to his spot next to Hawkins. "I was so overwhelmed by the language. The loudness of the streets. The faces. But nothing was more terrifying than the language. That feeling of listlessness, of loss. It's never left me."

Hawkins took Jacob by the wrist. "You don't need to explain yourself, Jake," he said, but Jacob shook his head.

"I want to. I think we should all try to know each other a little more. To understand why we're each in this tournament. Being able to communicate with others is so important for too many reasons."

"Jacob and I made a pact when we were children," said Max in the newly acquired language Jacob had given them. "That we would find Jacobsen. If we can just find him, he could lead me to my sister. And Jacob may have a way to go back to Labrador."

Cherice jumped off her chair. "What? You're not still thinking of going, are you?"

Jacob's nervous look toward Hawkins was met with a noncommittal shrug. "At the very least, I'd like to visit. See my people again. But finding Max's sister takes precedence."

Max stared at his hands as if he saw something fresh and warm upon his palms. "The night we were separated, that moment I saw the carriage ride away with my sister inside, it felt like a lifetime. And I . . ." He paused. "I told myself I'd do anything to get her back."

Max's gaze slid toward Iris, but she was too busy thinking to pay attention. Communication. A moment lasting a lifetime. A strange thought came to mind.

"Hawkins," Iris said. "You once told me that you were always good at hiding."

"Still am." Hawkins slyly brushed his hair out of his face. "As you've seen yourself."

"Cherice's gambling scams," Iris whispered, absently tracing a line on her lip with a nail.

"Oi, they're not *scams!*" Cherice insisted, bristling when the others rolled their eyes. "Okay, they're scams, but so what? Look, I've always been good with cards, right?" Some slipped out from underneath her white sleeve and floated in the air above her. "My big brother taught me. And we weren't doing anything wrong anyway, you know; everyone needs a bloody retirement fund. And besides—"

As Cherice babbled on, Jinn nudged Iris in the ribs. "What are you thinking?"

"What I'm thinking is," Iris said loud enough to stop Cherice in the middle of her tirade, "these aspects of yourself. You'd consider them important parts of you, wouldn't you? Important characteristics. Moments. Each defining you. What if that has something to do with the *nature* of the abilities you got after the explosion that day at the South Kensington fair? I'm sure you've thought about it by now."

Everyone exchanged looks. They probably had.

"Something that defines you," Iris continued. "If you all think deeply about your abilities, I'm sure you'd find a connection."

She glanced up at Jinn, who seemed lost in his thoughts. Perhaps of his father at the fair. He'd told her himself that he remembered the flames burning the ground so strongly. An image that stuck in his mind for all these years. An image that became a secret power he despised. Iris slid her hand into his so that he wouldn't float too far into his memories.

"Even if what you're saying is true, why are we discussing this?" Henry demanded.

"Because I'm sure our Patrons are aware of this." Iris gripped Jinn's hand even tighter as she thought of it. "I'm sure they're aware of much more. They hold all the cards. They're battling among themselves. Do you really think it's just for a bit of macabre entertainment?"

Iris told them what Adam had said. The Committee's belief that the world was ending and only one among them had the right to choose the next steps of mankind. But when Iris prodded the others for information, she received baffled looks.

"And you believed him? My, you are a gullible young woman, aren't you?" Though Lucille looked like a drab fisherman's wife, she gestured like an extravagant opera singer in the middle of an act. "We've received no such information from our Patron—in fact, I'd say your Patron has a bit of a loose tongue. Maybe he likes you."

She winked, making Jinn glare daggers at her.

"It sounds like a crock," Lucille added flatly.

"Because he's always on business, we've only been in contact with Bosch through a surrogate," Jacob said. "But England's rife with spiritualists and cults. The end of the world is a bit hard to believe."

"Some say the same about us Fanciful Freaks." Iris wouldn't back down. "Don't any of you want to know why we are *what* we are? What the bigger picture is that our Patrons are keeping to themselves? Or are you happy to play the puppet and slaughter each other for their sport?" She stepped down the aisle, making sure all eyes were on her. "How do we even know if the final round will be the end of it? The Patrons can do whatever they want; Fool said so himself. It's already a fight to the death, with only one team surviving. Maybe after they declare the victor, they'll kill even the winning team to keep their secrets secret."

Iris had thought about it over the past few days. By the way the champions squirmed and fiddled with their clothes, it was clear they were considering it too.

"I want to know what they know." Iris jumped onto the stage and sat on the edge. "Truth is power. And with the truth, we may have the leverage we need over the Patrons to stop any further bloodshed."

"You mean blackmail?" Jinn folded his arms.

"Once we have their secrets, we can use it against them. And for that, I'll need your help."

But unlike Adam, the other Committee members hadn't told their champions of their true motives. Why would they? Adam had a special connection with Iris . . . a special affection, though she hated to admit it. For the other Patrons, their champions were just a means to an end. Frustrated, she spoke terms and phrases, hoping they'd recognize them. Until—

"The Moon Skeleton."

Rin.

"Madame Bellerose often speaks less carefully around me because she thinks I'm not as fluent in her language as I really am. That phrase . . . She's uttered it more than once."

"We've let these bastards play around with us for far too long," Max said. He hopped onto the floor. "The only way to get the upper hand is the hard way."

A little smile played on Jacob's lips. "This isn't heading anywhere good, I'm sure of it."

Max flexed his arm. "We find a Patron and make him talk. Beat him senseless if we have to." And he added darkly, "I say we go after Adam. It's finally time for him to get his due."

"I second that," Jinn said a little too quickly.

Iris waved her hands. "Wait a moment."

"Why?" Jinn pushed back. Iris didn't like the look Jinn was giving her. "He isn't someone we should be trying to protect."

"I'm *not* trying to protect him," Iris insisted in a huff. "I just know he's not gonna give up his secrets that easily."

"Because of all the time you've been spending together," Jinn mumbled.

"What?" A flurry of heat swelled in her cheeks. "You are such a *child*," she blurted out.

"Excuse me?"

"Can you get over yourself and concentrate for a *second*?"

"Oh my, lover's quarrel." Hawkins laughed as Jacob covered his smile with his hand.

Now it was Max's turn to flare red. "*Lovers?* What? Hardly!"

"Why, are you jealous, Max?" Jacob teased.

"Jealous? Of *them*? You two, I *swear*—" Cherice punched Hawkins hard in the arm and went in to strike Jacob, only for Hawkins to catch her wrist before the hit could land.

"Oh, it's some kind of love polygon? This is so much fun!" Lucille clapped her hands in delight as the room continued to descend into chaos.

"Enough, enough, *enough!*" Iris let out a growl that silenced the room. "There's someone else on the Committee that will be much easier to trap and question. *Ease of operation* is what I'm aiming for," she added, shooting daggers at Jinn, who scoffed and turned away. "Italy."

Everyone understood. Riccardo Benini. He was clearly the blabbermouth of the group, and judging from what Bellerose had told her at Club Uriel the other day, he'd been investigating John Temple as well. It would be much easier getting him to talk than Adam.

"But h-how do we trap him?" Mary squeaked, stepping out from behind her teammates.

At this, Hawkins stroked his chin mischievously. "Benini, you say. Well, if it's him, I might have a way. Though it won't be for the faint of heart."

"Are you acquainted with him?" Iris asked, sitting up straight.

Hawkins shrugged. "You could say that. Though not directly."

Barely able to contain her excitement, Iris jumped down from the stage. "All right. This is good. This is great! So? How do we find him?"

"Before I tell you my idea, I need to know this one very important piece of information." Hawkins looked her dead in the eyes before his lips slid into a smile. "How comfortable are you in a brothel?"

41

THE GROUP PROMISED TO MEET AGAIN tomorrow, Friday, at midnight to discuss their next move. According to the information Cherice gained from spying on some club members gossiping about the tournament, Saturday night would be the show at Wilton's and then, promptly after, the third trial would begin. According to Hawkins, only a handful of participants were needed for this operation—whatever that operation was.

Team Hawkins and Team Iris were on his side, he reasoned, so they would be the ones involved. Rin was skeptical but agreed. Henry was the only one who pushed back, wanting to know the full details of his scheme. Though Mary looked unsure, Lucille seemed somewhat annoyed she couldn't come along.

"Best to keep the mystery," Hawkins had told them while he made his "arrangements."

The next afternoon, he took Iris, Jinn, and Max to the Granby apartment of a gorgeous woman who looked only a few years older. Her hair, a curly reddish brown, was tied up messily upon her head. She'd buttoned only the top two rows of her long, dark blue jacket to show the gold-and-blue floral-patterned dress she wore underneath, her black gloves the same color as the lace choker around her neck. And she wasn't alone. Other well-dressed girls were sitting on couches with handfuls of dresses.

"Lily Giralt." Hawkins's prim friend offered her hand to Iris without looking at her; she was already directing the women to clear the teacups off the kitchen table to make room for the dresses—very large, fancy, *uncomfortable*-looking dresses.

"Excuse me, Miss Giralt?" Iris said timidly, and when she finally did catch Lily's eye, the woman stared at Iris, amazed as if she were a wonder.

"Why, Lawrence, you didn't tell me you had such a pretty friend." Lily walked over to Hawkins, who sat next to Max on the couch as Jinn watched, leaning against the wall. "You seem to collect them so easily."

"As evidenced." Max gestured down his own body, making her laugh. "Hello, Lily."

"Maximo." Lily placed a dainty hand below her chin. "It should be a sin to remain so eternally handsome. But no matter how many times I compliment you, you never visit me."

Hawkins laughed. "If he were to visit you alone and Cherice were to find out, she'd kill you both in your sleep."

"Yeah, I like my head where it is," mumbled Max, shuddering at the thought.

Lily brushed the hair from Hawkins's cheek affectionately like a mother. "How old is that girl now, sixteen? She should be more mature by now. I'm sure the little thing's still running about behaving like an unruly schoolboy. And Jacob?"

Hawkins nodded with a soft smile. "He's well."

"And you're keeping him well, I presume?" Lily tilted her head with a mischievous smile as Hawkins let out an exasperated sigh, barely audible.

"Lily—"

"Yes, yes, I know. I haven't forgotten Mr. Winterbottom, and clearly neither have you." Before Hawkins could respond, she tapped Hawkins underneath the chin.

"I take it you all know each other?" asked Iris, listening to them with interest.

"Since childhood. We share a certain taste of the extra-legal." Lily winked and turned to Jinn, who watched them all with a stony expression. "Goodness, handsome men abound. Though this one looks a little dangerous. The quiet ones always are."

Jinn narrowed his eyes and said nothing.

"They'll both do, won't they?" Hawkins said, looking between Iris's two teammates.

"Wait." Max watched the women arrange the dresses and their accessories carefully on the table. "We'll do for what?"

Lily swiveled on the heels of her long black boots. "You'll be going to Chelsea this evening. When Hawkins described your mark to me, I thought this would be the perfect trap. I don't work there myself, but I have friends in the establishment that'll help us set things up quite nicely. Apparently, Benini can be quite the annoyance—and late in his payments." She faced Iris and shrugged. "And who wants a customer like that?"

Hawkins thumbed through the dresses on the table. "With all the investigations going on in the city, I'm surprised your friends would agree to do this. They could end up in jail."

"They won't." Lily chuckled. "Since most of the men investigating them are also frequent visitors themselves. There's nothing to worry about."

All Iris cared about were the words "Benini" and "trap." "What are you planning?"

Lily looked her up and down with interest. "Beautiful, to be sure. You'd fit in as one of their Tuesday Girls if you wanted to work for them."

"Tuesday Girls?" Iris wasn't sure if she should ask, but Lily offered up an explanation nonetheless.

"Riccardo Benini, you see. He frequents quite a few high-class establishments around London, but he comes to the Chelsea place particularly because they're aware of his . . . specific tastes. He's a scatterbrained man, but when it comes to his desires, he's quite meticulous."

One of the girls behind her scoffed but otherwise kept her thoughts to herself.

"Tuesdays he delights in the *exotic*," Lily said, wriggling her fingers. "Those from around the world who would keep his company. You're an exquisite vision, Miss Iris; I'm sure he wouldn't mind—"

"And?" Iris said a little too loudly, because the thought of keeping Benini's company made her shudder, not to mention that the term "exotic" irked her to no end. "You're saying he has a specific fetish for every day?"

Lily shifted uncomfortably. "You didn't have to say it so *brazenly*. But yes. Wednesday is Ancient Rome Day, togas and all."

"Friend of mine told me he asked her to call him *Caesar*," said one of the girls, and the others cringed. So did Lily.

"Right." Max shook his head. "I think I've heard enough."

Jinn boosted off the wall. "So what do we have to do with this?"

Lily folded her arms with a cheeky smile. "Today is Friday. Friday is very . . ." She paused. "Let's say late-eighteenth-century France. It's very Marie Antoinette."

"Maximo," called Hawkins from the kitchen table as he held up a red dress. "I think this one matches your eyes, don't you?"

The room fell silent but for the giggles of Lily's female friends, who'd finished arranging the items painstakingly across the kitchen table. It took several moments for both Jinn and Max to realize the plan at the same time: the trap they were to set, and who would play the starring roles. Iris burst out laughing at the same time Jinn began stammering, his body flush with embarrassment. Max, on the other hand—

"Bloody amazing!" He practically skipped over to Hawkins and began staring across the table. "You mean I get to wear some of this?"

Lily shook her head in amusement. "I should have known. Yes, dear, you get to choose any dress you like. But since you're to seduce Benini, and I'm an expert in such seduction, I'll be the one to make the final decision as to what you'll be wearing this evening." She turned to Jinn, frozen by the wall. "You too, my dear. You'll make a lovely working girl."

It was the kind of hilarity Iris needed in the midst of so much misery and confusion. But not everyone shared her sense of amusement.

"I refuse!" Jinn managed to spit out. "I utterly, utterly refuse! And you! Stop laughing!"

His eyes kept darting to Iris, collapsed onto a chair, clutching her sides as if they'd burst.

"Don't be closed-minded." Max picked up a gold-colored broach. "I've always wondered what you ladies have to go through, all those layers of clothes you wear. Iris's worn the same thing for days now."

Iris stopped laughing and sat up. "Excuse me for not having a closet full of ball gowns."

"I see this as a learning experience." Max tried the broach on.

"You're just completely mental, aren't you?" Jinn looked at him as if he wasn't sure if he should be impressed or baffled.

Argument filled the room until Lily stomped her boot on the floor. "Pardon me," she said, and the room fell to a hush. "I seem to remember Lawrence telling me that you three are the ones who want to interrogate Benini."

"Yes," Iris said, her laughter gone as she remembered the purpose of their mission.

Jinn lowered his head. "But doing something like this—"

Lily shot him the stern look of an older sister, one Max and Hawkins seemed all too familiar with as they didn't dare challenge her. "Something like this is a job many before you have taken up and many after you will continue once your mission is done." Lily folded her arms. "In order for me to arrange this with the establishment in Chelsea, they had to temporarily relieve the Friday Girls Benini usually sees. Which means that for the sake of your mission, those girls will go out of work for a day. That's money out of their hands. Money many of them need."

Lily straightened out the lace gloves of one of the dresses on the table with her fingers. "You may look down on this, but for us, this is our livelihood. And I'm not ashamed of what I do." She glared at Jinn. "Be a bit grateful for this opportunity you've been given."

"All right, all right," said Hawkins. "I think they're ready to try a few of these on. Right?"

Iris jumped to her feet, suddenly feeling rather embarrassed herself. "This seems a little intrusive. Should I stay in the room, or should I leave? Or should I turn around?"

Max and Jinn exchanged sheepish glances.

———•———

On a cool Friday evening, four royal beauties ascended the white stone steps of an extravagant home in Chelsea. Past the dark columns, the mahogany door opened before they even reached it. A white-bearded man in a black jacket straightened his top hat as he passed them, though not before giving them an appreciative glance. As his carriage rolled down the street behind them, the beautifully dressed old woman standing at the threshold of the front door welcomed them inside with a gracious bow. She and Lily exchanged proper greetings.

"Is Benini here yet?" asked Lily as she walked through the door.

"He's due to come at eight on the dot," said the woman. So they had half an hour to wait. The woman peered over Lily's shoulders. "And are these—"

"Why, yes!" Lily looked upon her work with utmost pride. And she had every right to; it took two painful hours and four sets of hands to complete. "May I introduce you to Miss Iris, the most beautiful among them." She placed her hand on Iris's shoulders. "And the two cowering behind her are Miss Jill and Miss Maxine. Do be kind—they're new. Girls?"

The three curtseyed as they'd been taught to.

Max and Jinn were a vision. Jinn looked particularly dashing in his embroidered velvet gown, a lovely midnight blue, lace and beads around the bodice with a dark peach undergarment. His sleeves ended with a frill of silk revealing the white of his gloves reaching up his elbows.

But Max would not be outdone in his layered dress, an eggshell white with red flowers, the skirt fanning about him like a blossom. The sleeve of his jacket of the same color exploded with fabric that dragged across his dress when he lifted his arm to adjust his silver belt. He *insisted* on the sun hat. It was Iris who suggested their dresses, and Lily who ultimately gave the seal of approval.

Iris wondered which of them was the most uncomfortable. Iris's dark-violet silk day dress was cinched in at the waist with a black belt while her puffed sleeves were dreadfully tight. Her layers had layers. Marie Antoinette indeed.

The powdered white wigs they wore, along with their carefully drawn makeup, made them unrecognizable. Still, would Benini really not know that his three new Friday Girls were champions?

"Don't worry about all that," Lily said when Iris asked. "If the plot goes accordingly, he'll be subdued before he has a chance to make the connection."

They walked into the crowded establishment. Red velvet curtains covered gentlemen of wealth as they drank from their wineglasses, laughing with beautiful women in white dresses.

The plan was a simple one: Iris would hide in a room awaiting Benini with one of the other Friday Girls. Once he appeared, so too would the other girl and, with the door shut behind them, the interrogation would begin. If anything, their attire helped them to maneuver through the establishment without attracting many stares from the regulars, who expected a taste of imperial France on Fridays. Besides, even if Benini recognized them, based on what Iris knew about the man, he'd probably be flattered to know Adam's champions were willing to spend quality time with him before the tournament's final round.

"Now remember." Lily faced them. "Benini always visits the rooms in a counterclockwise direction."

"You've got to be kidding me." Jinn pressed his hand against his forehead as Max fiddled awkwardly with his corset.

Lily took Max's hand and gestured toward the room in front of him. Iris could see the wooden doors through the red curtains. "Max, that's your room at eleven o'clock."

Max nodded. They all knew Lily'd meant the direction, not the time.

"Iris, you'll go with him. And Jinn, the ten o'clock room has been left empty for you. We'll make sure the man's plied with enough alcohol that his tongue's looser than his belt."

"I have to warn you," said Iris, "I'm not sure what'll happen in that room. It's an interrogation, after all. Things might get a little . . ." Iris cleared her throat. "Violent. For him, of course."

"The rougher, the better!" Lily dismissed her concerns with a wave. "This establishment is used to Benini's eccentricities, so if he lets out a yell or two, I don't think anyone would be curious in the least."

Business as usual, then.

"Listen for my knock," Lily told Max and Iris. "That's the signal he's about to arrive."

"That's that." Max grabbed her hand. "Come on, then, Marie *Antoine-Iris.*" He pulled her to their eleven o'clock room, and Iris could have sworn she saw him toss a rather childish look toward the brooding Jinn behind them.

Iris noticed the oak night table ahead of her first as they crossed through the double wooden doors. Two lit candlesticks flickered near the vanity mirror. Iris and Max stepped onto the brown, orange, and violet Persian rug on the floor.

"Okay?" Max asked, because Iris was blushing.

"Y-yes!" she stuttered, accidentally hitting her powdered wig as she saluted him. "Nothing to worry about here!"

Erotic oil paintings. To her left behind the red curtains hung quite a few of them. Max seemed to like them. And to her right, a red canopy the same color as the covers draped the cast-iron bed. Fluffy golden pillows trimmed with lace, the red lamps affixed to the walls, the crystal chandelier hanging from the low ceiling. No expense was spared.

Max closed the door behind them and sat on the bed. "And now we wait."

Iris giggled as he adjusted his skirt. "Awful, isn't it?"

"You women are heroes for bearing this crap." He smoothed out his skirt. "Still." He lay on the bed, plunking his foot down and holding his head up with a hand. "At least this gives us a little quality time together."

Iris chuckled in disbelief, sitting in front of the vanity mirror. "Maximo. You can't be serious."

She waited for his silly retort, but it never came. Through the mirror, she could see Max sitting upright, leaning over his legs, intertwining his fingers.

"What's wrong?" She cocked her head to the side. But Max didn't answer. Her back straightened. "Max?"

"I think Berta would have enjoyed things like this," Max said quietly. At the sound of his sister's name, Iris placed her hands on her lap, gazing at him with concern. It wasn't like him to talk about her. "She was sillier than I was when we were young. I wonder if she's still like that?"

Right. It was hard to forget sometimes that she wasn't the only one suffering. No matter what was happening to her, there were times when Iris had to be a champion for someone else when they needed it. And so she smiled, hating herself when she realized that was all she could do for him.

"You'll find her again, you know that. I'll help. You know that too." And when Max looked at her, her smile grew even sweeter. "I mean that. You can't get rid of me that easily. And then we can see together how silly she is. If she's anything like her big brother—" She whistled.

But what she said only made his expression more solemn. What was going on?

"We're teammates. You've said that to me before." Max scratched behind his ear, shutting his eyes as if all he wanted to concentrate on was the feel of his nails against his skin. "No matter what's happened. We're a team." Like he was trying to convince himself.

Suddenly he let out a sigh and fell back onto the bed. His hat tumbled onto the covers. "Just let it go, Maximo." His arms spread out across the covers. "Throw it away. And forget it."

"Throw what away?"

"All this nonsense worrying. Thinking round in circles. It's been my flaw since I was a child. It's why I went along with that damn headhunter. I thought, if I could just get some good work like he promised—" He stopped himself, shaking his head. "No, Maximo. Just throw it away. Worrying never leads anywhere good. When you worry, you make desperate, stupid decisions. You get yourself in bed with the wrong people. You believe their promises . . ."

You believe their promises . . . Iris checked her makeup courtesy of Lily's girls. But when she looked into the mirror, she saw Adam instead. "I'm not so good at throwing my thoughts away," she confessed. "I'm always worrying. You're right, it leads nowhere good."

Iris lowered her head, looking at the sleek varnish on the night table. Deep within her thoughts she heard Adam whispering his warnings. Just how far was she willing to go for a truth she may not be prepared for?

Looking at herself like this reminded her of those moments before a show. Her heart would be beating in excitement for the rising of the curtains. Well, this was a performance too, of sorts. She had to do now what she always did then. Quiet her heart. Listen to her own breathing.

"Iris, do you take me seriously?"

Seeing Max through the mirror, she couldn't help herself. She burst out laughing, into her hand, of course, so as not to make too much noise.

"Thanks," Max said sarcastically.

"Don't look like that," said Iris, giving him a wide, sidelong smile. "You're far too beautiful to wear such a heavy expression! I won't allow it any longer. It's almost sinful."

She waved him over. He came dutifully, bending down to her level so they could look at each other, powdered wigs and all, in the mirror. With a hand, she cupped his chin and grinned.

"Look at the two of us! Aren't we pretty?" Iris winked.

Max was silent for a long time. "You're beautiful, Iris," he whispered.

His voice was soft as silk. Iris's heart jumped a little, but she covered her nervousness with a little laugh. "You too, Miss Maxine." She swallowed after her voice cracked.

"I've thought so since the moment I saw you," Max confessed. "But it was all fun and games then. Business and promises." Iris wasn't sure what he meant, but he didn't seem to notice her puzzled expression. He was looking at himself. The secrets in his eyes. The hint of shame.

"But then I came to know you. Your charm. Your struggles. Your sadness. Your strength. And I didn't want to . . ." He bit his lip and straightened up. "I didn't want to leave you."

Iris's body stiffened. She should be hiding behind the red curtains, waiting for Benini to come, but she couldn't move from her chair. She stared at the ribbon in her hair through the vanity instead. Lily had suggested replacing her ribbon with a black one to contrast the color of her dress, but she couldn't bear it.

This was the ribbon Jinn had given her, after all. This was *their* ribbon.

She shivered as she felt the back of Max's hand brush her neck. "Only you can think of something like that in a situation like this."

"I agree. Maybe it's the ambience?" He looked around at the red-lit room, the candles, and the ready bed. "But truthfully, I've been waiting to spend time alone with you."

Iris pulled her tight sleeves. "We're attempting to ambush and interrogate a member of the Enlightenment Committee in a brothel on the eve of a battle to the death," she reminded him.

"You're right." And then she felt his strong arms around her neck, soft but secure. "But I've never met anyone like you. Mysterious. Dangerous. Proud. Daring."

He was far more open than Jinn. But at the thought of Jinn, Iris's heart beat that much faster, guilt prickling her warm body. Iris gripped Max's arm. "Not now."

"If not now, then when?" Max lifted her up and, taking her by the shoulders, pulled her close, looking deeply into her eyes. "Tell me. What do you think of me, Iris?"

This was ridiculous—the dresses, the frills, the lace, the bed, the scheme— and yet her breath hitched nonetheless as she felt his hard chest heaving.

"Don't," she whispered, but she didn't move. Instead she remembered the night Jinn had asked her the same question. Then too, Iris had no answer. Why couldn't she answer?

"You're too bold," she scolded Max. "And sh-shameless."

"Shameless. I agree. After everything I've done, I agree." Max's grin was a little sad.

Everything he's done? Like what? Iris furrowed her brow, but then he brushed a finger down her cheek. Her body flushed. Her mind went blank.

"But sometimes you have to be bold. I told you before: I'm not a fool but a trickster. I do as I please. Maybe I should just admit that. Maybe I should relish it. And forget everything else."

"A trickster never takes anything seriously." Iris looked away to hide her flushed expression. "Including feelings."

For a moment, she wondered if she'd finally struck a nerve. But Max only gazed down at her with a challenging expression, his grip around her shoulders loosening. "Right. Well then, let's just test that theory, shall we?"

Iris almost let out a yelp as Max swept her off her feet and carried her to the bed.

She couldn't believe this. They had to wait for Lily's signal. Maybe they'd already missed it. Benini could be here any moment. So many protests whirled in her mind while her lips stayed parted in a silent gasp.

No protest mattered more to her than the reminder that Jinn was in the other room, waiting for the mission to begin, but once Max had placed her gently on the bed, once her back felt the silk sheets and the weight of Max's body was on top of her, the protests silenced one by one.

Max's lips were upon hers before she could catch her breath. Deep, long, meaningful kisses that disarmed her just enough that she couldn't shield herself from the feeling of his warm fingers sliding up her leg, pulling her dress up with it.

She wasn't an expert in passion. Years of having no memories had made her mind rather one-track. Ever since she fell from that tightrope by the bakery and broke her neck, her mind had felt under attack. Every new development left her floundering in painful mysteries. At night, when she closed her eyes, she saw Anne trying to speak to her. And in the morning, as the first rays of sun peeked through the window, she mistook her heavy eyelashes for falling ash.

So in that moment, as she placed a hand upon Max's neck, she wondered if maybe "throwing it all away" would soothe her. Forget about it all. Maximo Morales, that handsome, charismatic rogue who never stopped making her smile from the very depths of her being . . .

It *did* soothe her. Once she let herself go, her whole body arched toward him as he deepened his kiss. Her body tingled with pleasure, with warmth, with passion that made her feel alive as Max clumsily slid off her jacket. At this rate, both their makeup would be ruined.

No, stop worrying. Stop caring. Iris's other hand somehow found his back, but then quickly flopped at her side. It wasn't that she didn't know where to put it; she was unwilling to put it there. Because if she did, it would sink even lower. It would grab his flesh and pull him closer. Too close. Too close . . .

Her hand flopped about until it caught the handle of the chestnut drawer beside the bed and pulled it open. Max peeled himself away from her to peer inside.

"Ropes . . ." Iris blinked as Max reached inside and pulled a long cord from the drawer. Then he gazed back at her, a wild look in his eyes. Iris's heart lodged in her throat. "Don't you even *think* about it!"

They must have missed Lily's knock, because in walked Benini at that very moment in a purple sleeping robe, shorts, and not much else. He stepped enthusiastically inside, too excited by the sight of the two with a rope between them to close the door.

"I see the evening's already started without me." He rubbed his hands together, drinking in the sight of them. Then, stepping toward the bed, he squinted for a better look. "Wait a moment. Aren't you—?"

"We are." Jinn. He was the one to close the door behind him. "And we have a few questions—"

Jinn stopped, his arms dropping to his sides as he stared at Iris and Max on the bed, the two frozen as if they'd been petrified. By now Jinn must have known that distinct feeling intimately, for he stood rooted to the spot.

"Wait, what's the meaning of this?" Suddenly, Benini grinned, pointing at the three of them. "I see. Letting off a little steam before the final round, then?" Benini laughed. "Well, I can understand your wild appetites, but I wonder if Lord Temple knows about—"

Jinn's hand flew to Benini's throat. Gripping it tightly enough that the Patron could barely squeak, he shoved Benini onto the bed, forcing Iris and Max to roll off the other side.

"Like I said, we have a few questions for you," Jinn repeated darkly.

"What! What is the meaning of this—"

Jinn pulled off his left glove and shoved it rather roughly in Benini's mouth. For a second, Iris thought he'd choke and die before they even had a chance to ask anything.

"You." Jinn's narrow eyes slid toward Max, who peeked out from behind the bedspread. Picking up the rope left on the bed, he threw it at him. "Help me tie him to the bedpost. *Now.*"

Max wiped the makeup from his face, a mixture of both his and Iris's, and did as he was told without a word. Jinn was wild with anger. His body tight, he threw off his wig and wiped the lipstick from his mouth with a dark expression that told her he was aching to maim something.

Panicking, Iris jumped to her feet, wringing her hands together. "Jinn, this wasn't—"

"And you." His venom was not directed toward her. Completely unrestrained now, Jinn pushed the sock down hard in Benini's mouth, shoving his head into the bed. "It would be in your best interest to answer my questions quickly and honestly. I am *not* in a good mood."

42

BENINI'S ROBES WERE SPREAD OUT UNDER him across the bed, revealing his white underwear, his ankles and wrists tied to the wooden bedposts. With Jinn's glove inside his mouth, his screams were muffled. Jinn watched him struggle for a moment. Max scratched his head with a sigh. Even with Benini helpless before them, neither seemed willing to do or say anything. Jinn wasn't even looking at the Enlightener at all. The emptiness in his faraway gaze enveloped the whole room.

I can sort this all out later. I will sort this all out later. With a quiet but determined sigh, Iris brushed passed Jinn and removed the sock from Benini's mouth.

"Help!" he screamed predictably. "Help! Somebody!"

Behind the door came Lily's light laughter. "Oh, that's just one of our customers, Benini. Most of you frequent customers should know his tastes already. Do ignore him and carry on."

"Hear that, Mr. Benini?" Iris let a little of her real frustration show in her menacing tone. "No one's coming for you."

"What is this? These ropes!" He tugged his arms again to no avail. "I demand to know why I'm being bound and gagged in this establishment when it isn't yet Saturday!"

Iris blinked and, shaking her head, shoved away the nasty images that had begun running rampant through her mind. "I'm asking the questions here, and you'd better listen to me."

"You really should," said Jinn quietly. "As she's the type to break you into pieces when you least expect it."

Iris looked at him for a moment, taken aback, but quickly refocused on Benini. "I know you're a member of the Enlightenment Committee."

Benini gasped loudly.

"Oh, *please*," Iris snapped. "You told me the first time we met in the Pit."

Benini let out a weak laugh. "Oh, did I? That certainly sounds like me."

"I also know you've been looking into John Temple. I want to know why. Is it to do with the white crystal? Or the secrets underneath the Crystal Palace?"

Before coming here, Iris had calmly practiced the questions she'd ask. But now that she had Benini tied down, the questions flew out of her rebelliously and sloppily. Nonetheless, Benini expectedly gaped at her, shocked.

"Did Adam tell you?" After cursing, he bit his lip. "That boy is *far* too fond of you."

"Certainly isn't the only one," Jinn mumbled, and as Max gulped, Iris shot him a dirty look. Jinn looked unapologetic, continuing as if he'd said nothing at all. "What do you know?"

Benini's was the laughter of a soon-to-be dead man: high-pitched and terrified. "I might as well sign my obituary if I tell you everything here."

"But if you don't tell me, you'll die by my hand." Iris tried to make it sound believable. Judging by the whimper he let out as she wrapped her hand around his throat, it was working.

Jinn smirked. "I suppose killing comes easiest to a woman who can't die."

Iris released Benini's neck. "And what is *that* supposed to mean?"

"This is an interrogation," said Jinn, finally meeting her eyes with a glare. "Or are you finding it difficult to concentrate?"

"I cannot believe you right now!"

Max waved a hand. "Well—"

"Quiet!" they both yelled at the same time before he could get a word out.

Iris boiled inside, her hand nearly shaking. "Are you really so fragile that you can't get ahold of your feelings even in *this* situation?"

"And what exactly am I supposed to be feeling in this situation?" Jinn gestured toward Max. "Seeing the two of you—"

"This isn't about any of us!"

"Well, it kind of is," said Max.

"I said, 'quiet,'" spat Iris through gritted teeth. One more word from either of them and she might burn everyone alive.

"No, I *won't* be quiet." Max straightened out his dress rather dramatically and folded his arms. "This wouldn't be such a mess if you could just sort out your own feelings."

Iris let out an incredulous laugh. "Excuse me?"

"It's quite clear how the two of us feel."

This time, Jinn looked her dead in the eyes, his body quivering just slightly. But slightly was enough. Iris pressed her lips together, overwhelmed as the walls closed in.

"But I don't know . . ." She stopped and swallowed a whimper. "This is so unfair."

And through it all, Benini found it within himself to giggle, actually *giggle.*

"Well, this is a right mess, isn't it?" he said.

He shouldn't have. Soon Iris's boot was in between his legs, ready to crush. "Tell me everything you know, *now*! Or the rest of your Fridays will pass by rather uneventfully."

She began to press down as sweat beaded Benini's forehead.

"Okay, okay!" Tears leaked from Benini's eyes. "Oh, you horrid cow. You awful witch!"

"Why did you order your men to dig around John Temple's grave?" Iris pressed down harder, causing Benini to sing like a canary.

"Because he has research on the white crystal that not even the Committee knows!"

Iris released some pressure off him, just enough to let him take in a shallow breath and keeping talking. "What is the white crystal?"

"We still don't know." Benini blinked tears from his eyes. "From our research, it appeared on the twentieth of September, fifty-six years ago. The day of the global twenty-four-hour eclipse. It didn't exist before then."

The Day of Darkness. Iris shivered but kept her foot firmly where it was. Out of the corner of her eye, she could see Max and Jinn exchange glances.

"And then again a small piece of it was discovered in 1863. The Muvian Expedition funded by the Crown."

"Muvian Expedition?" Jinn whispered.

"Within Lake Victoria, they found more white crystal—and parts of a machine."

Wait. Iris remembered John Temple's book. The Crown's expedition that cared more about the treasures inside Lake Victoria . . .

"The Crown is researching it right now, aren't they?" asked Iris.

Benini managed to smirk. "Underneath the Crystal Palace. But after decades, those idiots have no idea what they have in their hands."

"And what machine is that, then?" Max leaned over the man.

At this, Benini's grin deepened. "That which will define the fates of all mankind. The Helios."

The term echoed deep within her as if she knew it intimately. As if she remembered it. . . .

"The Moon Skeleton is the key that can be used to operate the Helios. Adam's dear father had it once upon a time. The Helios, on the other hand, is the device that will open the door."

"The door to what?" Jinn gripped the bedpost that Benini's left leg was tied to.

"Other dimensions."

Silence. None of them knew what to make of it. Only Benini seemed amused.

"Why do you think us Enlighteners decided on this tournament?"

Iris gripped her sleeve. "Adam told me. It was because you madmen believe the end of the world is coming. And you seek to guide humanity or some such foolishness."

"It's not foolishness, my dear." Benini's eyes glinted savagely. For the first time since meeting him, Iris was afraid. "The Hiva."

Iris's blood ran cold.

"What in the bloody hell is that?" demanded Max.

"An event. The cataclysm destined to befall earth and destroy all of mankind. It's called the Hiva. And the Hiva's arrival has been foretold."

Jinn squeezed his hands into fists. "By who?"

Benini rested his head against the pillow. "Now, if I were to tell you that, I'd *really* die."

Upon his right palm, Iris could see the mark of the Oath Maker. That's what Adam had called the pink scar of a skull with a sword through it.

"The global eclipse lasting a day," said Benini. "The first appearance of the white crystal. Those were signs." Benini chuckled. "Like with Noah's flood, soon this earth will become uninhabitable. The Helios will be the key to man's revival. The Crown believes they've found new material they can use as weaponry to wage war upon other nations and strengthen their empire. But we of the Enlightenment Committee have a deeper understanding of things. And we're already looking ahead to the *new* empire to come. An empire that will be of *our* making after the end."

"Perhaps he's really gone mad," Max whispered. "It could be trauma."

It *did* sound mad. It *was* mad. As Jinn had once said, the Enlightenment Committee was nothing but a doomsday cult filled with the bored, supernatural-obsessed elite. And yet why did Iris's heart quiver? Why did her stomach lurch from both fear and need? Taking her foot off Benini, she stumbled back. Jinn watched her, reaching for her hand with a worried look before refocusing his attention on their captive.

"What did John Temple know that no one else did?" he asked.

"*I don't know*, you slow beast of burden."

In two steps, Jinn was hovering over him, his hand gripping the collar around his neck.

"B-but!" Benini stammered. "We believe it's all in his research—especially in his journal."

The journal now in Uma Malakar's possession.

"We haven't been able to find it, as much as we've looked. I really don't know exactly what he discovered," Benini continued. Did he really not know that Uma had it? "But I *do* know that he had a deeper understanding of the cataclysm to come. It's why he betrayed us. I suppose the more he learned about it, the more feasible it became that he could one day stop it."

"You don't want to stop it?" Iris whispered.

"You can't stop what's foretold," Benini said, too peacefully. "But imagine becoming the king of a new era. What untold wonders await us after the apocalypse? What kind of society can we create with those fortunate enough to survive the cataclysm and become our future subjects?"

But this man already had everything. Enough money and leisure to frequent brothels in between watching the poor and desperate murder each other for promised winnings.

Iris felt sick. She couldn't be in the room with this man another second. But there were two more questions she needed to ask. One was simple but led to a dead end.

"The South Kensington explosion. How did it create us Fanciful Freaks? What exactly happened that day of the fair?" she asked.

"That, I don't know." Benini nearly screeched when Iris came at him. "I'm telling the truth! I swear! Please! Oh, won't someone *restrain* her?"

The last question she was too afraid to ask.

Where do I fit into all this?

No, she couldn't dare speak it. But there was a way to find out.

It was clear as day that finding John Temple was crucial, just like Adam had said. But since she couldn't yet sense the man himself, stealing his journal would be the next best option.

Iris looked at the clock hanging on the wall beside the bed. Half past nine in the evening. As she thought of their meeting with the other teams at midnight, a plan began to hatch.

"I need to know everything you do about the experiments happening in the Crystal Palace." Iris refused to give Benini the pleasure of seeing her fear. Instead, she made him quiver underneath the red canopy. "And you *will* tell me how to get inside the Basement there."

Benini swallowed. "Will you kill me, you cruel thing? You should. For with the information I'll tell you, you're as good as dead too, even if you manage to win the tournament. Once I tell the Committee what happened, they'll hunt you down."

"Not before they kill you," Jinn reminded him.

Benini squirmed in dismay.

"So I guess this'll just be our little secret, then?" Max winked and patted him on the leg.

"Even so," Benini continued, "the journey you're embarking on is a dangerous one. You're all in over your head. Isn't it better to remain blissfully unaware while you fight for your winnings? Imagine what you can do with all that money."

Iris glanced at Jinn and Max, who, with stoic expressions, waited on her word. "I think from now on, *I'll* decide what I do," she answered him. "Now talk."

43

"JAMES! YOU'VE COME BACK, OLD CHAP! Where've you been?"

The man Iris had burned to ashes dragged a weak Iris, back in her regular clothes, through the empty Crystal Palace. Her leaden feet could barely keep up with the rough tugs of the double-knotted cord holding her captive. Behind her, a solemn Jinn and Max followed, their heads bowed, their hands tied.

Three men in vests and brown corduroy jackets ran up to them underneath the cast-iron domed ceiling, their expressions changing from hostile to bewildered once they saw their colleague, who'd mysteriously disappeared the night a strange wildfire had almost set Penge Peak ablaze. Jinn's fire had likely been a convenient excuse to keep visitors away while the Crown continued their experiments underneath the Crystal Palace—including those on the Fanciful Freaks not participating in the tournament, if she remembered Adam correctly.

To save themselves from the final fight to the death, experimentation was precisely what Jinn and Max chose. Turning their partner in was a sign of good will.

After Jinn had confessed, the men nodded. "Good, good. We can always use more experiments. The ones we have aren't faring too well." One of the men rolled up his sleeves and inspected Iris. "This is the female specimen that disappeared that night, right?" said one of the men. "The one Doctor Pratt's been asking for?"

Iris reminded herself to keep her head low and her expression despondent. She was a defeated "specimen," after all.

James nodded. Iris had told him not to speak. Every time he was about to form a syllable, for show of course, he ended up hacking and coughing, causing his colleagues to believe that he'd been sick. It was the only way they could think of to keep up the ruse.

"All right, then. Come on, bring these freaks to the Basement."

After the men had turned their backs, Iris, Max, and Jinn exchanged glances before following them down the empty halls of the Crystal Palace.

It had been only a few hours since their midnight meeting at Wilton's. It'd taken that long for Lucille to mold her face into a close approximation of James according to Iris's detailed descriptions. She could never forget the face of the man she'd killed.

"The interrogation went well, but there are still details I need to confirm," Iris had told the group after she, Max, and Jinn had changed back into their normal attire. "About us and our gifts. About the Committee's plans. Give me time. I swear I'll get to the bottom of it all by daybreak. But I'll still need your help."

Jacob's secret language. Hawkins's Sliding. Lucille's shape-shifting and exuberant willingness to wear men's clothes. Everything had worked to bring them to this exact place and moment. One of the men they followed now took them around the corner. Then, after more winding hallways, he threw open the curtains hiding a small space near the rightmost wall that normally would have been used for an exhibition. Gripping a metal handle in the floor, he opened a hatch. And down the stairs the captives descended.

"The end of the world," Cherice had whispered nervously. "Sounds mad as hell, but if it's really why they want us all to kill each other . . . I mean, it is, right?"

"Whether it is or isn't, we'll know soon enough." Jinn's hands were clenching and unclenching, something he did before particularly difficult performances.

"Remember: to get out of the Crystal Palace, you need to get back up to the area Hawkins Slid you to," Jacob reminded them before their mission had begun. "It's the only area of the Crystal Palace he's ever been to, though it was years ago."

"That was a fun day of looting, wasn't it?" Hawkins had said with a whimsical sigh of nostalgia. He looked to Max, but the expression of his friend was uncharacteristically grave. He knew as well as Iris did how dangerous this infiltration scheme would be. According to Benini's loose tongue, the Crown's aim was not only to research but to *weaponize* the supernatural.

There was no telling what they'd find there. Iris wouldn't let herself forget it as they walked down the wooden steps deeper and deeper beneath the Crystal Palace.

Behind her she could feel the heat from Jinn on her right side, and Max to her left. The two shouldn't have come. She hadn't planned on them coming, but they'd insisted. The gas lamps affixed to the brick walls flickered with light. So much had happened between them. But she was grateful, at the very least. Grateful that they insisted.

"Thank you," she said in the temporary language Jacob had given them. It would last only a few more hours at the most. "Thank you for being here with me." She didn't want to admit the fear rising within her, but she was sure it was obvious.

"I'd never let you do this alone," answered Jinn. Max looked at the two of them but said nothing. Out of the corner of her eye, Iris could see Lucille's lips curve into a sly smile. She must have thought the three of them were positively adorable.

"Oi, shut it!" said one of the men a few steps below them, turning and sneering at them.

Soon, they came to a set of iron doors. The sneering man opened it with a key, bringing them inside a dark cavern of corpses.

The dirty clay walls, dimly lit with lamps, did not provide quite enough light for the men with rolled-up white sleeves, brown vests, and scalpels to work. The candles on the desks next to them helped them cut into their dead subjects lying on the wooden tables set up in two rows at each end of the room. A sudden pressure inside Iris's skull tightened as the putrid smell of death slipped into her. The naked corpses were clean, but not the earthen floor beneath them or the buckets of organs carried to and fro. Adam was right. The Crown was far crueler than she could have ever imagined.

The sight of one man, his body cut deep down the center, caused her to convulse into awful memories. Memories of knives . . .

"Iris!" Jinn gripped her arm.

"This's the one Doctor Pratt's been interested in, eh?" said a thick man with a brown mustache as he measured the skull of one corpse. "He went out but should be back soon. Why don't you take these three to the Testing Chamber with all the other live ones?"

The man who'd led them down to the Basement turned to Lucille. "There should be an empty preparation room you can store 'em in. I've got business. You can handle this on your own, right, James?"

Lucille, whose false face had grown rather pale, coughed in the deepest voice she could muster and nodded resolutely, giving him a pat on the back.

From the intelligence they'd gathered from Benini, they knew that the Basement was shaped almost like a giant keyhole, inside of which were four main chambers. They'd just visited the first: the Resurrection Chamber, affectionately called the Graveyard among the surgeons who made extra money by forming part of the Crown's secret team of researchers. The next would be the Testing Chamber, where all manner of experiments were conducted upon living subjects. Farther back, the Research Chamber, colloquially referred to as the Factory. This was where the scientists would have taken the white crystal to study and tinker with. As for the last:

"You'll find the greatest secrets there," Benini had told them. "The proof you want will be in the Grand Chamber—appropriately named, for it is the largest among them."

Underneath the high, flat ceiling of the Testing Chamber, dozens of rooms lined each side of the hallway. Benini had warned her that the Basement was labyrinthine—as expected for an underground hangar spanning the vast Crystal Palace. Aboveground, visitors could enjoy the spectacles of discovery and spoils of imperialism.

But below:

"Dear Lord," mumbled Lucille.

Wails. Iris heard wails coming from some of the closed wooden doors. For those doors left slightly open, she was able to peer through the gap. In one, a man lay on a metal table, his head hooked up to wires attached to a metal contraption hanging from the ceiling. The electrical current made him convulse down to his feet. Iris looked away the moment his mouth began frothing. In another, she saw two girls in a tank with shallow water brushing their heels as scientists surrounded them, measuring the temperature, watching their heavy eyelids flutter. A feeling of dread washed over Iris as she recognized their long locks of black hair.

"The Sparrow twins," Iris whispered. The doll-like girls who'd attacked them outside the British Museum. Even in this state, the two were holding hands. Squeezing.

As researchers streamed in and out of rooms with bloody instruments and clipboards holding papers filled with numbers and scientific jargon, Jinn gripped her wrist.

"Don't make any hasty moves," he said. She hadn't realized she'd begun moving toward the twins. "We have to stay focused. We can't afford to be trapped in a place like this."

Iris had known infiltrating the Basement would be dangerous even before Benini told them the details. But she wasn't prepared for *this*—for this suffering and death.

But she wasn't alone. It comforted her while also fortifying her resolve. They came here with her. She had a responsibility to keep them safe and deliver what she'd promised: the truth.

No matter how terrible it was.

One of the researchers directed "James" to an empty room where the three captives were to wait before being transferred. It looked like a torture chamber from the Dark Ages. Bellerose would have been delighted. The iron candelabra. Walls made of clay and dark, misshapen bricks. Buckets of water upon a cushion of hay in the corners and small wooden tables filled with instruments. Very medieval.

A researcher came in to tell James someone would relocate the specimens shortly.

"And Miss . . . Uma Malakar?" Lucille said, coughing into her hand.

"That odd woman's still holed up in the Factory. I don't like her attitude, but the wonders she's brought us?" His blue eyes flashed with an eerie, macabre kind of excitement. "I've never seen anything like it. Bosch and his group will truly revolutionize the British Empire. At any rate, wait here a moment. Someone will be with you in ten minutes."

As soon as the door closed, Lucille's smile collapsed. She let out a groan. "I'm not sure how long I can do this," she said as she unfastened their ropes. "My faces don't last very long."

Iris walked over to the central table and grasped the long white sheet crumpled on top. "Benini said there were double agents working in the Basement to spy on the Crown's research developments on behalf of the Committee. John Temple did too once upon a time. There are at least a few in each chamber, some working as researchers, some as security patrollers. We're champions. We need to find the Committee's men and convince them we're here on behalf of our Patron."

"I don't need to tell you your plan is bafflingly dangerous." Jinn crouched down by a water bucket in the corner, running his hand through his dark hair. "And Benini's suggestion on how to get through this place seems so risky it borders on ludicrous."

"But you came with me anyway." Iris shyly shifted on her feet as she added, "Crank."

Jinn bit his lip, taken aback, as the two looked at each other without saying a word.

"Sounds like an adventure to me." Max smirked, breaking the silence.

Jinn cleared his throat. "Not to be rude, but hearing that from someone incapable of grasping the gravity of situations isn't exactly comforting."

He clearly meant to be rude. Iris's cheeks burned as she thought of what happened inside the brothel. And yet, even after everything, before they'd left Wilton's Hall, Jinn had whispered this into her ear:

"No matter what happened before or what happens next, I won't let this go wrong. I'll do everything you need me to. And I won't let anything happen to you."

He'd said it with an almost noncommittal air, and yet the gentleness with which he squeezed her hand spoke volumes—volumes of a language she had yet to fully understand.

"Hey, I'm serious. We can do this, no matter how big the risk." Max looked around at the others for affirmation. "Right, Lucy?"

Lucille gaped. "Don't dare lump me in with you. I'm *terrified*." She was picking at James's hair. "Ugh, it's starting to itch. Oh, to be done with this ordeal so I can return to my former beauty."

Her exaggerated gestures while wearing a man's face almost made Iris smile before she remembered it was the face of a man she'd burned alive.

She gripped her own wrist, clamping down on its steadily rising pulse. All she wanted was resolution. Peace. For that they needed to find Malakar.

After a deep sigh, she spotted a fire poker in the corner of the room. She didn't want to imagine what "scientific purpose" it served in a place filled with human experimentation. But maybe it was better to picture the kind of horrors that could be awaiting her. She had to be prepared for anything.

Their ten minutes were almost up. Lucille retied their hands, this time looser as Iris instructed. Soon a researcher opened the door and beckoned them forward.

"Rooms 3A2 and 3B3 are prepared. We'll be taking the two male specimens there. As for the female, a special room has been prepared for her." The man gave an almost wicked grin. "We've sent word to Doctor Pratt. He'll be quite happy to see her."

Iris flinched, but she kept herself composed. Gritting her teeth, she stared the man deep in the eyes and said: "The Enlightened."

"What?" The man tilted his head. "This one speaks English? But does she know what she's saying?"

Their first failure. No matter. Iris had anticipated this.

The researcher walked with "James" down the halls, and whenever she spotted someone rushing by, either she, Max, or Jinn would say it: "The Enlightened."

But all she received were odd stares.

"James, can't we shut them up?" said the researcher, annoyed when all James did was cough and shrug.

Around several corners and halls, they continued to speak those two words. At one point, Iris heard the researcher sigh and mumble, "Well, they'll be shut up soon enough, won't they?" With his slight figure, he didn't seem the fighting type. *Whining* was his way of dealing with their constant eruptions. Lucky for them. It wasn't time for them to raise a fuss—not yet.

Eventually they reached the third section of the Testing Chamber.

Damn Benini, thought Iris, the rope hot against her wrists. He'd made it seem like there were double agents littering the halls. If they didn't find someone soon, they'd be separated.

This hallway was more crowded than most. They were approaching Jinn's room. This was her last chance.

"The Enlightened!" she cried, her voice echoing down the halls, making everyone stop and stare at her. Researchers even poked their heads out through the doors of their rooms.

It worked.

As things started to settle and researchers returned to their work, one very short brown-haired man with chubby cheeks and a pair of burgundy suspenders slyly switched his trajectory, heading for them. He seemed interested in his notes as he approached and soon was walking with them. The moment he whispered to Iris, "Shall never die," she knew she'd crossed the first hurdle.

The Enlightened shall never die. The code phrase to identify the spies of the Committee.

Together they walked into 3A2. This man, Mr. Jonas, dismissed the men inside, citing some excuse. He almost shoved James out the door, but Iris stopped him. "He's one of us."

"Mr. James?" Mr. Jonas peered at him. "I had no idea."

When Lucille nodded, Mr. Jonas gave him a suspicious look but didn't press.

Iris lowered her voice. "We're here on behalf of Lord Temple. We're his champions. He's sent us to find out the progress of Uma Malakar's work."

The Committee knew Bosch cared only for his own business. But they let him do as he pleased. This way, they could steal Malakar's work for the Crown when it was ready.

"A progress report is due to the Committee in just under a month," said the man.

"He needs it now. We don't know why," Jinn insisted. "We work for him just as you work for the Committee. Otherwise, how could we be here?"

From Mr. Jonas's perspective it made sense. There was no way anyone was supposed to know about this place, least of all the Committee's personal entertainers.

Mr. Jonas nodded. "She's in the Factory. I'll lead you four to her."

Around another few corners and finally through a set of iron double doors, Mr. Jonas led them into a spacious room that looked like an actual factory. There were so many wires hanging down from ceiling rods, attached to rows of wheels. But what they were spinning wasn't gold.

The white crystal . . . Iris felt a shiver deep in her flesh. Crystal shards rolled over the wheels like sheets of chain mail. How they'd even managed to break it down and re-shape the ore was beyond her. There were boxes of gears and nails by the far-left wall in front of a row of strange metal tubes. Iris was surprised by how many plain-dressed women were inside, working the wheels, and men sweeping the floors of white dust round the long clay columns. Mr. Jonas took them to the front of the room, where there was no machinery but sacks filled with unknown substances piled next to a wooden door on the left. He knocked politely and walked inside.

"Miss Malakar. The servants of one of Bosch's colleagues are here to see you."

"Well, I wouldn't say servants—" Max started, only to be nudged in the ribs by Lucille.

"Bosch's colleague, you say."

A few men Iris had seen accompany Uma at the train station stood quietly at the end of the room. The woman set down her magnifying glass on a table filled with shattered rocks of white crystal and, sweeping her blue sari to the side, turned to them. Mr. Jonas left them alone, shutting the door behind him just as Uma's brown eyes locked onto Iris.

"You." She picked up her monocle from the table, cleared off a bit of white dust, and peered through it at Iris. "Aren't you that beggar I spared?"

"That was a misunderstanding," Iris said, gulping nervously. She looked behind her to make sure Jonas was really gone. "We didn't tell Mr. Jonas, but we're actually Mr. Bosch's champions," she lied.

"Oh, that silly tournament." Uma raised a pierced eyebrow. "Are you now?"

"He doesn't want anyone to know we're here on his orders," Iris elaborated. Approaching Malakar as Bosch's agents, pretending to be on his side. Iris hoped to the heavens it would work. "I've been sent to fetch the journal that belonged to Lord Temple's father. Mr. Bosch needs it."

Uma slanted her neck. "Does he now?"

The woman barely ever blinked. Her gaze was uncompromising. It didn't seem like Benini or even Adam knew that Uma had the journal. How in the world did Bosch retrieve it without any of them knowing? The members of the Enlightenment Committee were playing a dangerous game among themselves. Iris couldn't afford to make the wrong move.

But what if Uma already knew the identity of Bosch's real champions? Iris's pulse raced at the sudden thought. She stayed calm, readying another excuse before Uma shrugged, pulled out the black leather-bound journal from her brown pouch, and held it out. Everyone stared, bewildered.

"Take it," she said with another shrug.

Iris hesitated. Was it a trap? She couldn't be sure. But she couldn't pass this up. As her hands were still tied, she beckoned for Lucille to go ahead. Tiptoeing closer, Lucille snatched the journal as if from the jaws of a lion. But when she opened the book . . .

"What are these?" Iris leaned over, baffled, as Lucille flipped through quickly.

Symbols. Shapes. Letters and numbers out of sync and order.

"It's a code, of course. You really think Temple would leave his research unguarded?" Uma gave her a mocking, piteous look.

There was, at least, one symbol Iris recognized as Lucille flipped through the journal. A picture, rather. A picture of a key she recognized.

It was small. Two rings overlapping. A crown upon its head. A sun and its shadow.

Jinn, Max, and Lucille knew it too as they peered at the page together. It was the same shape as the skeleton keys from the first round.

"The Moon Skeleton," Uma told them, brushing a loose strand of black hair from her face as she approached them. "An ancient artifact excavated from Lake Victoria decades ago. It's lost to us now. And what a shame, because there's one thing John Temple's work makes clear: without the Moon Skeleton, we can't operate the Helios. Finding his journal was hard enough. But wherever Temple is now, I imagine he's not giving up that Skeleton so easily."

Wherever Temple is now? Did she . . . did she and Bosch know that Adam's father was alive? Iris searched the woman's unknowable eyes.

Uma stopped in front of her. "But now that you're here, Iris, perhaps we can rectify that."

Iris's muscles seized as Uma snatched back John Temple's journal and flipped through the pages. "Miss Iris. Doctor Pratt said you'd be coming," Uma said casually. "That it was only a matter of time. But to think it was the beggar girl all along." She laughed at the happenstance of it all, shaking her head. "John's work details the experiments conducted on you in grim detail, at least from what I've decoded so far. I'm actually quite sorry you had to go through that," Uma added, her voice softening a little, and in that moment, even in Iris's stunned state, that softness felt genuine. "Such a pretty girl. The description of you fits perfectly."

Experiments. Iris closed her eyes and could feel the knives cutting into her.

"Gorton Zoo."

Uma's words stopped Iris cold. The woman flipped the book shut, tapping the black cover. "On that horrible day, after your rampage, you were subdued and taken to Cambridge University. Pratt was a budding scientist then, but given the description of what he did to you, he was as ruthless then as he is now." She narrowed her eyes. "I hate men like him. Unfortunately, I have to work with filth every so often. My job is what it is. And to be honest, I'd be lying if I said I wasn't curious." Her eyes widened, glinting sharply like glass. "Curious about you . . . about the truth of your monstrosity . . ."

"Shut your mouth!" This time it was Jinn, gripping Iris by the arms from behind as she swayed unsteadily on her feet.

"Yes," Iris whispered darkly, her head dangling forward as she attempted to steady herself. "I didn't come here to chat." Clenching her fist, she nodded to Jinn and Max. "Do it."

The ropes came off. Jinn reached inside his vest and pulled out two of the blades he'd been hiding and tossed one to Max. As Jinn pointed his at Uma's jugular, Lucille, clearly excited, let herself fall whimsically into Max's arms as his hostage. After all, if they had an in with James at the Crystal Palace, they couldn't let themselves waste it.

"Give me John Temple's journal now, and we'll be on our way," Iris demanded as Max and Jinn held their blades close to their hostages' throats.

The men behind her raised their guns, but Uma only looked impatient at most as she raised her hand to calm them. "Come now, there's no need for all that. I have what you want just as much as you have what I want."

"And what's that?" Iris asked.

"The truth of who you really are."

Iris's lips quivered for just a second.

"Outside this room and behind the iron doors is the Grand Chamber. There lies the Helios—or at least, the version of it we've constructed through the pieces found in Lake Victoria." Even with Jinn's blade to her throat, Uma waved Temple's journal. "And if I've decoded these words correctly, then we might not even need the Moon Skeleton, because you, Miss Iris, may be the key to waking up that sleeping machine. Well, part of you, anyway."

Iris didn't like the alarming glee in her eyes—the look of a mad scientist. "Which part?" Iris asked, and immediately wished she hadn't.

Uma smiled. "Why, your crystal heart, of course."

THE QUICKENING

WHAT?" ADAM'S TEACUP FELL FROM HIS hands and shattered on the ground.

One of the Committee's spies bowed their heads as they confronted him in his living room. "Your champions, my lord. They've infiltrated the Basement. We didn't realize it until we saw her there shouting the secret code words."

The Enlightened shall never die. But how did Iris know? Someone on the Committee must have talked. And there was only one person with a loose enough tongue.

The other spy seemed reluctant to add his next detail. "I'm not quite sure what their objective is, but they're pretending to have donated themselves to the Crown's experiments—"

"What?"

The men cowered as Adam glared at them, though he didn't even see them at all. He saw Iris locked up in that dreadful hellhole surrounded by cadavers and the stench of sorrow.

"Ready the carriage," he told them as he strode out of the room and started up the steps.

They knew he didn't like asking twice. Or once. "Yes, Lord Temple!"

Adam was already on the second floor of his home by the time he heard the front door close.

It was hard lifting his arms with the bandages he'd wrapped around his chest. Madame Bellerose's torture still smarted. Regardless, he slipped on his gray vest and black jacket, tightening the tie around his neck. His hair was still a mess. He could see it mocking him in the mirror. His own sapphire eyes mocked louder. Eyes of worry. Fear. Fear for a being more powerful than what the human mind should have been able to imagine.

Death? The stench of sorrow? But isn't the real Iris used to such a thing?

It was true. From the first time he'd learned about her from the research that the Temple household kept under lock and key, he knew to expect nothing but power from Iris. The research had prepared him. The Bible had prepared him. That divine being did not need him to run to her rescue. But meeting her at the amphitheater that fateful day had flipped everything upside down. Seeing her worry, her pain. Seeing her fear and determination grow as she continued her journey toward discovering her holy purpose. He wasn't running to save his father's Iris.

He was running to save *his* Iris.

Yes, she was his, and no one else's. Given to him by God as solace for the deranged life he'd lived. His purpose for living. And soon, she would be his purpose for dying.

If Iris was in the Basement at this time, she'd undoubtedly run into Malakar. That woman wouldn't be able to resist. She'd force Iris to remember. She'd find a way. And when she did, what would become of Iris? Would she be ready for those horrific memories to return?

But it was always going to come to this sooner or later. He straightened his jacket. She was always going to learn. It was a matter of time. Perhaps the time was now.

He simply had to make sure he was there to guide her when she did. To shield her identity from prying eyes. To give her protection and shelter once she awakened.

And to make sure she didn't end the night killing everyone in the vicinity.

"It's not time to make enemies yet, Iris," Adam said as he left his room and descended the staircase. His one solace was that she wasn't alone. She had her circus partner. And Maximo. Yes, that boy was by her side, exactly where Adam had positioned him. As long as Adam had his sister as a card to play, Maximo would still do as he wished. As always.

Adam climbed into the carriage. "Quickly!" he commanded. "There's no time to lose!"

The horses' hooves dashed against the pavement as the carriage took off into the night.

44

CRYSTAL, MISS IRIS. WHITE CRYSTAL. ACCORDING to this journal, your heart is made of it."

In Iris's mind, Uma's words repeated in a vicious cycle as she, Max, and Jinn followed her to the cast-iron gates that separated the Factory from the Grand Chamber. Lucille had been held back by one of the factory workers. Apparently, James had worked in the Research Chamber, and it was now up to Lucille to fumble her way through whatever tasks they needed "James" to work on while Uma slid open the gates.

With Max and Jinn close beside her, Iris entered the chamber as if in a dream. Round and vast, bigger than all the other chambers. Iris felt like a fly lost in the heavens. Grand. The peak of a keyhole just as Benini had described. Marble floors. Windowless walls. A high ceiling suspended on cast-iron rods, domed like the Roman Pantheon.

Lining the walls were machines of different sizes, some up to Iris's knee, others larger than an average-sized human. They were covered in burlap sheets. Cases like treasure chests were arranged in rows. Weapons, perhaps. But no greater treasure existed than the one inside Iris's own chest.

It felt like flesh and blood, *beat* like flesh and blood. But Iris remembered the night she was shot in the chest in the Crystal Palace. The bullet had shattered against her heart.

"The white crystal . . ." Iris found her voice as Max and Jinn watched over her, concerned. "Is it the source of our powers? Us Fanciful Freaks."

Uma's laughter echoed in the rafters. "Is that what you're calling yourselves? Well, I suppose you have to call yourselves *something*." Uma had taken her pipe with her before leaving the room and now sucked in a hearty inhale, exhaling it steadily through her nose. "What do you know about the South Kensington explosion?"

"Investigations ruled the official cause to be some kind of gas leak," Jinn answered for her. "But we know that was clearly a lie."

Uma tapped her brass pipe with a finger. "The Moon Skeleton," she said. "It's partly made of white crystal. It's exactly as it sounds—a skeleton key. But it's not *pure* white crystal. It's been heated, cooled, and processed with other strange materials through an elaborate refining system I've never seen before. The kind of engineering John Temple describes in his journal . . ." Uma shook her head. "Those are specific scientific techniques that are simply not of any current civilization on earth."

Max's chuckle was as fearful as it was incredulous. "What are you saying? That this key was made by bloody Lilliputians or something?" When Jinn looked at him, he added, "What? I'm an avid reader, I'll have you know."

"At this point that guess is as good as any," said Uma. "But one thing is for sure. It was created by a civilization that existed long ago. Long before *us*."

Another iron gate lay several feet into the chamber. Uma stood in front of it, considering the brass design: sun and moons, connected by a never-ending vine. A string of fate, perhaps.

"On that day of the fair, the previous heads of the Basement were ready to showcase the machine they'd pulled out of Lake Victoria in order to signal to the world that the British Empire had made advanced strides in technology never before seen in mankind. Progress!" Uma yelled suddenly, and whipped around with her arms outstretched, her sari fluttering about her. "Progress," she repeated, quieter. "Well, if it's in the name of progress, all is fair, right?" She took another puff of her pipe. "Of course, if I'd been there, I would have told them not to rush to show off a technological advancement when you're not even sure what it does. They thought it was just an energy source. As it was,

I was *not* there. And when they tried to activate the Helios without using the Moon Skeleton, which was still in Temple's possession at the time, a rather . . . *unexpected* reaction occurred."

"Unexpected reaction . . . ," Iris whispered. "The explosion."

"Well, the Crown aren't quitters. The explosion wasn't an 'explosion' in the traditional sense. More vaguely, it was a large emission of energy that left the Helios intact. So the Crown continued their experiments. They still think it's an energy source. Well, it is. But more than that, it's a door. A door to other worlds." Uma's eyes sparkled as she said it. "Another frontier for mankind to explore—and conquer."

Uma slid open the gate.

"I present to you, the Helios," said Uma with a bow.

That a steel cage was still separating them from such a small machine made Iris wonder just how dangerous it really was. It reminded Iris of a snow globe but stretched up to her knees. Blue glass framed by bronze and iron outer frames. And at the top of its dome, a keyhole.

The Moon Skeleton is the key used to operate the Helios. The Helios is the device that will open the door.

Max ran a hand through his curly hair. "Looks made in a craft shop."

A door to other worlds . . .

"Unbelievers." Uma narrowed her eyes. "The Moon Skeleton, according to Temple's research, moderates and controls solar energy within what is called the Solar Furnace, a chamber within the Helios made partially of processed white crystal. We're not sure how, but its presence allows the Helios to channel untold amounts of energy to carry out its operation. That day at the fair, without the Moon Skeleton as a stabilizer, operating the machine caused a terrible reaction; the Solar Furnace released a wave of energy the likes of which we've never before seen. Thus far we haven't come up with a suitable name—"

"Anima," Iris whispered, approaching the machine in a dreamlike trance. "It is called anima." As if she'd heard these terms in another life.

Uma watched her thoughtfully. "Anima, you say. Hmm . . ." She smoked her pipe. "Ani-matter, perhaps? Well, who cares about the name just yet? As for why it transformed some and not others . . ." She shook her head. "Well, that's why we continue our research, isn't it? After the incident in South Kensington, the Crown continued its studies here. But what do *you* think, Miss Iris? You seem rather taken with the machine."

"Iris!" Jinn ran up to her, but when he gripped her arm, she shrugged him off, almost violently. No more waiting.

"We've been testing other pieces of white crystal to stabilize the machine— carefully, of course, to avoid another explosion. But nothing ever worked. Not powerful enough. The mysterious civilization that made this machine must have known too, which is why they always refined the crystal with other metals and materials, some of which *we* have not yet invented. But I wonder . . . The crystal allegedly inside *your* body." Uma's smoke seeped into Iris's nostrils. "How powerful is it?"

Feeling John Temple through Adam's coin. What did Jacob call it? Psychometry. Sensing the flow of life. Piercing pasts and presents. Her ability . . .

Iris already knew what she had to do.

Iris turned to Uma, the rise and fall of her chest quickening with each breath.

"Don't be afraid, Iris," Uma said. "Embrace where the Helios takes you."

"Iris," Jinn whispered. "Don't." He was afraid. Her partner. Her Jinn. She touched his face gently. She gazed at Max too and nodded. Both of them were scared for her, but she had to do this. She was tired of wondering. She'd spent ten years doing it. Ten years of fearing an uncertain future borne from an unknowable past. Enough was enough.

"I'm sorry, but there's no going back," she told them, and touched the machine with both hands. The Helios lit up with white light.

"Iris!" Max and Jinn called at the same time, for the moment she'd grabbed it, her body froze. The heat of the white light enveloped her, seeping out of her open mouth, her blank eyes.

Max's and Jinn's desperate cries were so far away. She could feel them attempting to pull her away from it. The strong arms around her waist were Jinn's. She knew the size of his hands, the texture of his palms.

The Helios shook and sparkled with white lights that burst across the room like shooting stars.

And then the scene changed.

There was no dome. No machine. No Jinn and Max. Only a society crumbling. Towers as high as the sun collapsing. Flying ships bursting into flames. Men and women in white robes running for their lives, burning to ashes. Burning. Burning from the cataclysm that had struck them, wiping them away like Noah's flood. This was dozens of millions of years ago. Iris remembered the cries of terror and woe as she stood in the center of Wotan's garden, a beautiful flowery oasis, the last in all the earth after its people had destroyed the rest with their industry. Nothing was left behind, but it was of no consequence. All would be reborn that should be reborn.

The scene changed to a mechanical paradise. The Zabachian Empire. Several million years ago. A place of soot and ash that blocked the skies, a world where no life was allowed to live but inside black fortresses littering each continent. Only those of wealth wore gas masks and were able to breathe the air. Flowers the size of elephants whimpered out poisonous gas. Mutated monstrosities from experiments gone wrong. Once again, humans had made a mess of the world, and once again, it had to be destroyed.

Then there was the Naacal. They'd worshipped the sun. The signs of the sun and its shadow were drawn all over their religious texts and ancient tablets. In their arrogance, they had used technology smaller than the eye to allow a chosen, privileged few to grow wings. Classes within classes. Blood, pain, and slavery of the weak. It was the kind of hubris that needed to be stopped. Their wings burned to ashes on judgment day in a rain of blood and terror.

Iris felt disembodied. The woman she was staring at in her memories looked like her, but it wasn't her. It couldn't be—not those cold eyes. She trembled terribly as another apocalyptic scene bled into darkness. And then she saw herself, inside a crater within the fertile ground, naked and fully grown. She was created inside the earth. To announce her arrival, the ground had quaked and split apart, caving in around her. She climbed out of the cavern using roots and bits of rock, finally finding her footing in the middle of a forest. The white dust she'd left in her wake sparkled slightly in the ground, barely noticeable to the eye. But when she opened her palm, there was a chunk of white rock in her hand. And soon, the sun faded to dark.

Yes, Iris remembered. This was her latest rebirth. This was why the sun had died.

The Day of Darkness, a voice inside her whispered.

She had been called again. But first, as always, she was to observe humanity without judgement to understand why they needed to die.

A Dahomey raid near a Yoruba village. The time she'd spent with the locals had come to a violent close. She was now a captive of King Ghezo. His warrior. And under his reign she was to fight intruders and rivals and kidnap others into service for the king. Iris saw herself in a sleeveless, plain blue-striped dress with a black belt and shorts down to her knees. Inside her red clay household, underneath the pointed thatched roof, she finally finished attaching the string she'd weaved to the white crystal and placed it around her neck. A trinket to remind her of her purpose lest she become too involved with mankind, too lost in their politics and day-to-day curiosities.

Isoke: She Who Does Not Fall.

The scene shifted, stars shooting in her eyes. She saw herself bloodied and enraged in Gorton Zoo. Thanks to the cruelty of an English schoolboy, Anne lay dead on the ground, but Iris had made sure she would not go alone. She now knew. She now felt it: the reason why she'd been called to serve judgment. And she would fulfill her purpose.

Ashes. Dead bodies. And her own bloodied hands. Iris remembered Agnus Marlow crying next to her in the human exhibit turned graveyard. And then she remembered looking right into the eyes—black beady eyes—of a young man with the tamed blond hair of a gentleman. With his family reduced to ashes at his feet, he pointed at Iris as policemen shot at her.

Too many memories were flooding into her at once. Cambridge University. The experiments that lasted five years. Five years of barbiturates and other drugs they used to keep her mind dulled and confused. Five years of torture once they realized the creature before them couldn't die. And through it all was the blond man with beady black eyes, young and brilliant, taking the lead in the Crown's research. The man she hated most in this world.

Doctor Pratt . . .

By then he knew as well as the other scientists did that as long as her crystal heart stayed intact, her body would always regenerate. She would never die, no matter what they did to her. No matter what wrath and suffering they brought upon her in the name of discovery. Finally, her heart *refused.* It went dark and would regenerate no more. Once it was clear that his experiments with it would take him no further, Pratt gave her heart to the Temples as a gift. And there it sat, no more than a chunk of white stone, for years, until . . .

Iris's body began to convulse as the Helios held her, not letting her go.

This next scene was one she'd seen many times.

Muscle latching onto bone. Flesh layering over muscle. Nerves humming. The agony of a body forming once again, growing around a heart of white crystal. Her crystal heart that had laid dormant for many years to stop the experiments had been taken to the South Kensington Exhibition and sensed the Helios somewhere nearby. Her heart felt the Helios's energy—energy that also lay deep inside the heart itself—and knew it was away from danger. Knew it was safe. And so she regenerated—regenerated at the same time the Helios turned on.

Waves of energy interacting, *communicating.* The reaction was explosive.

After she'd awakened inside a room filled with Egyptian artifacts, she looked into the eyes of a young Adam Temple. He gazed up at her in fear, in awe. And he asked her a simple question: *Madame, tell me . . . are you . . . a goddess?*

But to protect this new woman, newly regenerated, her heart chose not to regenerate the memories of the pain that had come before. So this woman knew not who she was. She knew not of the horrors she'd wrought upon civilizations. The cataclysms borne from her hands in her other lives.

She did not know that she had been reborn to begin her work anew.

As the cataclysm known as Hiva.

45

HER HEART KNEW THE HELIOS. NOW, as she came in direct contact with it, her heart released the memories it had been holding inside. Jinn and Max tugged with all their might as the energy of life and memory gushed into her—through her. Iris felt her hands peeling from the machine, painfully as if her skin was ripping. Soon she lay flat upon the floor. Her mind emptied of thought, her body of feeling.

It wasn't until she heard heavy breathing that she drew herself up and looked behind her to see Jinn and Max frozen to the spot, their eyes wide. She did not need to ask. She already knew from their expressions.

Just by touching her, they'd seen everything. The life and memory that had gushed into her and through her had flowed out of her and into them.

The cataclysm known as Hiva. The planetary *cataclysma*.

Hiva.

The end of the world.

It was *her*.

Iris lifted her shaking hands and grasped her head. Through the vast emptiness within her, a howl escaped from her lips, so empty and frightening it made the two jump. A sharp pain rocketed through her skull as she slammed her forehead against the floor again and again.

"Iris!" Jinn yelled, running to her. "Iris!" He lifted her up and squeezed her against his chest, enveloping her totally. "Iris. Forget what you saw," he pleaded. "Forget it all. None of it was true. Do you hear me? You're *Iris*. You're *still* Iris. You will *always* be Iris. *My* Iris!"

She couldn't stop. Her cries, the memories of pain and death. The terrible truth of her purpose. The cataclysm. The end of the world. The worlds she had ended before.

Max. Max didn't move, didn't even look at her as Jinn lifted her to her feet and dragged her toward the iron gates.

But Uma would not let her leave.

The massive machine that blocked the iron gates had been crafted into the shape of a monster. Made of metal, brass, and iron, its bulky frame looked like nine different mythological beasts sewn together by a madman. Iris could distinctly see a large, snapping beak, a dragon-like head, and two bent metal legs reminding her of a stork on water. Spinning gears moved the two long gun barrels that could have been mistaken for arms. Uma mounted the giant beast like a horse, using two levers to maneuver its clunky frame.

"This is one of my recent prototypes," said Uma, and Iris could see a burlap sheet discarded by the walls. "I call her *Nava*. A technological creation owing to the white crystal's energy source, though I don't think the Crown was too happy with my design when I showed them. I, however, find it suits my tastes perfectly."

Indeed, inside the belly of the beast was a chunk of white stone spinning by some kind of force field inside the steel cage. The stone gave off a dull, white light as it whirled.

"I don't have anything against you, Iris." Not in the least comforting coming from a woman aiming the barrels of guns at her from atop a mechanical monster. "In fact, I admire your boldness. Tricking me when we first met, risking your life to find out this hellish place's secrets. You remind me of myself." She trailed off thoughtfully. "Unfortunately, for me, my research takes precedence over everything. And though regrettably I don't know what the Helios showed you, it's clear as day that to complete my research, I need you. So. No. *Leaving.*"

Iris thought of Doctor Pratt's black eyes and burned to her core. "Everyone wants a piece of me, don't they?" But then her lips curved into a lopsided smile. "Shame I can't die."

Uma raised the machine's guns. An empty threat.

"Go ahead." And within her, nightmares of pain became dreams of vengeance. "Let's see if you can make me fall."

The guns fired, round after round, Gatling-style. Iris saw the sparks as she ran toward the great beast, her fists ready. In a flash of anger, Iris dug deep inside her, summoning that monstrous power she'd used on James in the Crystal Palace, on so many others in the past. She could feel the power there waiting for her to burn her enemy to ashes.

But she couldn't do it. Just as she managed to touch the power, a wave of pure panic struck her, freezing her to the spot. Uma aimed.

And then Iris blinked.

Soon she was tumbling off to the side, out of the line of bullets, in Max's arms.

"Let me go!" she screamed, beating his chest, and to her surprise he did. He looked at her like he never had before.

With fear. Not for her, but *of* her.

A stream of fire burst from Jinn's mouth, causing Uma to nearly slip from the mechanical monster in her attempt to dodge. It would have been a nasty fall to the floor, but she hung on by a hand to the brass rung of a ladder.

"That's quite enough."

Iris's blood ran cold as the iron gates slid open. In walked Doctor Pratt with a fleet of researchers behind him.

"When I saw James's remains, I knew I'd be seeing you again, Iris," he said. "I hoped." When he lifted his hand to rub his white beard, her fury erupted. The cuff links of white stone on his sleeve. She remembered now. They were hers. Maybe not her heart. But it was because of her that the white crystal existed. They belonged to *her*.

"Iris!" she heard Jinn yell, but it was buried by her own screaming. She ran toward him, ready now, truly ready to kill him, to make him pay for everything he'd done to her. Her blood pounded in her ears, the tears flying from her eyes.

But when Adam stepped through the group of researchers, his gun pressed against the side of Pratt's head, she stopped, utterly confused.

"Alas, it seems there's been a mistake," said Doctor Pratt, unperturbed. "I didn't know you were under Lord Temple's wardenship."

"Indeed, she *is* a ward of the Temple family." With his free hand, Adam straightened his black tie underneath a pristine white shirt and gray vest. "And as a ward of the Temple family, she can't be held in this place against my will."

His will. *His* will . . .

Doctor Pratt's beady gaze slithered toward him. "Ah. Is that so, Lord Temple?"

Adam grinned amicably. "It is indeed, Doctor Pratt."

A silent but deadly battle of wills bristled beneath the friendly banter. But in the end, Doctor Pratt lowered his head.

"It would turn into somewhat of a mess if we went against the esteemed Temple family's wishes." Doctor Pratt cleared his throat. "Then, I suppose it's decided. We will release the subject according to your wishes."

For now. Iris could almost hear the words upon his lips.

"What about the other two volunteers?" one researcher from within the group asked.

Adam smirked and lowered his gun. "Oh, you can do what you want with them."

"No!" Iris screamed, rushing to him and grasping his black jacket. "You can't! You can't take them from me!" Her knees buckled, but she kept herself upright, her head pressed against Adam's chest. "I won't let you people take any more from me!"

"It was a joke," Adam said. Very simply.

"A *joke* . . ." Slowly, as if in a trance, Iris raised her head. She gazed at him. At the boy whose family had once owned her crystal heart. The crystal ornament Carl Anderson had mentioned. "You disgust me," she whispered.

"I told you to wait," he whispered back into her ear. His hot breath made her shiver. "That no good would come from you rushing into the truth. Everything in its own time."

"Everything in its own time," Iris repeated with a half-crazed grin, swaying on her feet. "Like the end of the world." Her laughter sounded too polite to her own ears. Almost as if she were humming on her way to the apothecary to buy Granny's medicine. She laughed until she finally collapsed into Adam's arms.

46

THE NIGHTMARES SANG TO HER. LIKE children, they jumped on her chest. She whimpered and fidgeted underneath the bedcovers, wishing them away, as if those cruel things would soften at the sight of her tears.

"Iris," came a soft voice somewhere just beyond the darkness. "Iris . . ."

She pried her eyelids open and found herself resting in a soft bed underneath extravagant mauve-colored bedcovers made of silk. Next to her, in front of a chestnut night table, sat Adam in an oak chair.

"You're finally awake," he said softly.

Iris understood. This was his residence at 19 Melbury Road. The same room she'd been in after she escaped from Coolie. Her body was cushioned on the grand bed by many pillows, ribbons, and flounces, but it didn't make her feel any more comfortable. Marble-topped cabinets to her left lined the corner of the wall, tucked in behind the dark gold curtains blocking the evening light and the sounds of the horse hooves and carriage wheels on the streets below. Strange to hear them again after she felt as if she'd been trapped in another world.

Iris tried leaving her bed, only for her feet to feel weightless upon the soft-loomed rug. She collapsed back onto the bed.

"How long have I been asleep?" she asked Adam without looking at him.

"All day. It's half past nine. The final round of the tournament will start soon."

She must have missed the official Wilton's show, but she already knew what the instructions were: a fight to the death. It would begin at midnight inside Cerberus. She fell back, her body leaden, her eyes only half-open from drowsiness.

"Max and Jinn?" She pushed the half question out of her throat.

"Max has been roaming London since last night. Jinn, on the other hand . . ." Adam stood up from his chair and leaned against the door. "He hasn't left the front steps of my home since we brought you here. He didn't even struggle when they wouldn't let him inside. He must still be out there now. Waiting for you."

Max . . . Jinn . . . The horrors they had witnessed inside the Basement. What were they thinking now? What did they think of her? She couldn't stop the worry squeezing her chest.

"Adam." Iris chose her words carefully. "Did you know that I could kill like that?"

"Iris . . ."

She couldn't stand it—that expression of concern, of empathy. He had no right. "When I feel people's life force—their anima—if I concentrate hard enough, I can use it to burn them alive." Except the last time she tried to use her powers, that flash of extreme panic had stopped her. She wondered if it was a blessing in disguise. "Is that what you were training me to become?" She squeezed a pillow to her chest, her nails digging into the fabric.

"Iris, I—"

"Sensing the life in others." The rims of her eyes stung. "And using that ability to destroy them!" She tried to step off the bed but collapsed to the ground.

"Just like you've done to many civilizations before ours, as my father hypothesized."

Adam walked over to her and, gathering her up in his arms, placed her back on the bed. "I wanted to keep you right here," he said. "Right here away from that violent tournament so you could slowly learn . . . slowly awaken those gifts. *Slowly.*"

"Everything in its own time." Iris felt as if she'd been given an anesthetic. "Slowly awakening me to become a beast."

"Not a beast," Adam corrected, and he grabbed her hands softly. "You're not a beast, Iris. You are the cure for this world. You are our salvation. Divine."

"A goddess?" Iris repeated the same words he once spoke to her as a child. "A god of death, maybe." Her voice choked up with emotion as she considered it fully, and a sense of dread slipped into her, carried by the air from the cold window draft. "A monster."

"Never a monster." The back of Adam's fingers were soft, warm. "You're our light, Iris."

"I'm the cataclysm!" Iris stared at the silk sheets without seeing them at all. "The cataclysm to bring an end to the world."

The words sounded mad as they sprang from her lips. And yet she knew it to be true from deep within her crystal heart. The visions she'd seen . . .

Adam wiped the sweat from her forehead. "And as such, *you* are the way for all mankind. Not the Crown. Not the Committee. *You*."

She looked up at him, terrified to see his beautiful face so serene. "That's the secret you wanted to keep from both the Committee and the Crown at all cost," she whispered. "The secret you murdered over. The reason you want to find your father before anyone else does. Not that the end of the world is coming. The Committee already knows that." She remembered the maniacal glint in Benini's eyes. "But only your father knew what form the cataclysm would take. That's why he went to the Dahomey village. His research. He realized I was the Hiva."

"Yes."

"You killed Neville Bradford. You had Carl Anderson killed even while we were inside Bellerose's home."

"Yes. To protect you."

A moment of silence passed. Adam was too close. She could feel his back against her arm, but she couldn't move. Her stomach churned as she tried to calm her breathing.

If the secret of her identity was indeed in John Temple's journal, then Bosch would find out just as soon as Uma finished decoding it. And she already seemed well on her way to the truth. It was only a matter of time before Iris had a target on her back.

"When I awoke again in South Kensington ten years ago, you were waiting for me," Iris said.

"I brought your heart to your bones," Adam said. "I read my father's research. I thought I could awaken you that way. Bring you to life."

A schoolboy with unruly black hair, sapphire eyes, and a suit far too adult for him. A little baron in training. A boy just starting his adolescence gazing up at a wondrous creature: a goddess of death reborn.

"After your heart went dormant, Doctor Pratt gave it to my grandfather, an old friend, once he thought there was nothing further he could learn from it. A Cambridge souvenir. He had no idea. But I knew. After I read my father's research, I knew. Or at least, I thought I did."

Iris gripped her chest, feeling her crystal heart pumping inside her.

"Without your heart, Cambridge University donated your bones to Paris's Museum of Man for one of their exhibits. And the museum lent them for viewing at the 1874 South Kensington International Exhibition. That was where I tested my theory. I thought I could rejoin your heart to your bones and bring you to life once more. But that's not what happened. You didn't need your bones. Just your heart alone—and the Helios. Indeed, right before my eyes, you exploded into life once more."

Her revival along with the Helios's operation. One crystal's energy speaking to another. The resultant explosion had created the Fanciful Freaks.

Jinn. Max. Cherice. All those whose lives had changed forever. Because of her . . .

Iris grasped at her chest once more. She couldn't breathe. An electrical pulse shivered painfully through her body. It wouldn't stop.

"It's okay," Adam said quickly, his hand on the small of her back. "Breathe. It'll pass."

His words, his touch were comforting and yet terrifying all the same. She wanted to push him away, cry in his arms. Her mind was a mess of contradictions. But there was one thing she knew for certain: "You. Pratt. The Crown. The Committee. You're the savages," she whispered. "You're wicked. So, so wicked."

"The whole world is wicked," Adam said. "That's why you exist." Adam grabbed her shoulders and forced her around. "This world is evil. I've known it since the moment my family was murdered so pointlessly. You are needed, Iris. We need you."

Iris's lips parted; her eyes budded with tears. "To end it?"

"The global eclipse was a sign that the end was near. It signaled your rebirth. The Committee wants to escape into another world, but for that they need the Moon Skeleton to open the gate. My father has it with him. That's why I need you to find my father, Iris. You need to find my father, find the key, and destroy it." He squeezed her hand tight. "Then there'll be no escaping your judgment. And the wicked men and women of this world will fall."

Was this the truth she'd been searching for? Iris pulled her hand from his grasp and stared back at the young baron in terror. "You're mad, aren't you?"

"Not mad. Just ready." Adam lowered his head. "'Let your loins be girded about, and your lights burning,'" he said. "'And ye yourselves like unto men that wait for their lord, when he will return from the wedding; that when he cometh and knocketh, they may open unto him immediately. Blessed are those servants, whom the lord when he cometh shall find watching: Verily I say unto you, that he shall gird himself, and make them to sit down to meat, and will come forth and serve them. And if he shall come in the second watch, or come in the third watch, and find them so, blessed are those servants.'" He paused as she stared at him in confusion. "Luke."

Iris trembled. "The Bible?"

"My mother made me memorize it the moment I could read. She said I should be prepared. And I am." He slid his hands away from her. "Iris, like me, you've seen cruelty. You've suffered at its hands. You've *seen* how evil the people of this world can be. So what do *you* think humanity's fate should be?"

Iris pounced on him, pinning his arms to the bed as she let her anger explode. "And if I say destruction, what about you? Are you willing to die?"

"Yes," he said with a voice and expression so calm, so at peace, it shook her heart. "I've been ready for a long time, Iris."

Iris's shaking hands found his neck. This boy raised by a doomsday cult and a puritanical mother. This boy destroyed by his trauma and cursed by his own intelligence. She squeezed so hard she could feel her nails digging into his skin.

And yet Adam only looked at her with affection.

In a moment of insanity, she pressed herself against him and kissed him deeply and desperately, letting the wetness of his lips slide across her mouth. Surely this was all he wanted. He'd be satisfied with this. But when she looked at him again, his eyes, now half open, hadn't changed. He was resolute. The slight hint of lust in his expression did nothing to change that.

The clock struck ten with a deep, low knell. The sound reverberated through her flesh. Through her . . .

Through her bones.

"This is too much." She slid away from him and jumped to her feet, pulse quickening as she scurried to the desk. "This is just too much. I don't know what to do."

"Then I'll give you time," said Adam as he rose and headed for the door. "Ten o'clock. The final round will begin soon. You and your team should still fight." He opened the door. "It'll be good practice for you as you prepare for the end."

47

Dear Agnus,
I have a confession to make.

Iris sat at the desk, writing with a quill she'd taken out of its inkwell.

You were right. I was once a military woman of the Dahomey.
Decades ago, I tried to kidnap you and your sister, Anne, in the
middle of a raid. It's what we did. I would have brought you
back to King Ghezo as slaves, or perhaps you would have joined
the ahosi *like I did. But as fate would have it, the three of us had*
another foe. And after an unsuspecting attack, we all ended up be-
ing taken to England as Marlows. As entertainment for Europeans.

But there was nothing at all entertaining about the life we lived.

With a frustrated sigh, Iris crumpled the paper and threw it onto the floor along with the rest. Then she lowered her head into her hands. She just wanted to see Granny again. To hold Egg in her arms. To go back to knowing nothing. She felt as if she'd flown too close to the sun. Where she was now . . . where she was going. She didn't know. She just didn't know.

It was almost eleven o'clock. The final round would begin at midnight. Soon, the people she'd come to know would be battling to the death for the entertainment of evil men.

No. She wouldn't let it happen. No matter who she was, she couldn't let that happen.

And so she prepared herself. The moment Adam walked through the door again, she punched him hard in the face and shut the door behind him. Then, after he'd collapsed to the floor, she gripped his neck.

"Uma has your father's journal, by the way," she said, relishing the sight of Adam's eyes narrowing in confusion as he struggled to breathe. Finally, something she knew that he didn't.

"My body is my own," she hissed. "My heart is my own. My fate is my own."

"If it . . ." He coughed, his windpipe crushed beneath the strength of her hands. "If it be your will, Iris. But our story . . . isn't yet over . . ."

Her breath hitched. She released his neck and took in the sight of him, utterly distressed. No, she wouldn't kill. Never again. Instead, she knocked him out with another punch.

She would disappear. Yes, that was what she needed to do. After she did, Adam would be too busy dealing with Bosch and Uma to look for her. Hopefully, she'd never see him again.

Her will was her own. She wouldn't devolve into a killer no matter which cruel god had created her to be one. That was why she needed to end this tournament. No more killing. No more pain. No more loss. No more death.

Hiding Adam's body on the other side of the bed, Iris ran out of the room, down the stairs, and through the door only to find Jinn still waiting for her on the steps of 19 Melbury Road. The moment he stood up and turned to her, she fell right into his arms.

"It's okay." Jinn squeezed her so tightly it almost hurt as she cried. "Remember what I told you."

Forget everything. But she couldn't forget. She couldn't avoid it.

"Jinn," she said, quickly wiping her face. "The final round of the tournament will start soon. I have to stop it."

She half expected Jinn to stop *her*. Instead, he gave her a solemn nod. "Then we need to hurry," he said.

It would've been an hour on foot, but Iris had taken some loose coins she'd found in Adam's room and used them to pay for a carriage. "Please, as fast as you can!" she told the driver.

"What's the plan?" asked Jinn as the horses whinnied.

"I originally promised them the truth," Iris answered, staring out the window, her heart thumping in her chest. "Adam told me once that the Committee wants a monopoly on the secrets of the world because with knowledge comes power. I can blackmail them: stop the tournament or I'll share those carefully hidden secrets in front of all of Club Uriel. Let them all fight over what to do with them. It'll become a catastrophe worse than their Spring Massacre."

"I suppose that's the only card we have to play."

There was too much traffic on the road, more than Iris had expected—carriage joyrides, barrels of produce, carts of hay, and pedestrians crossing without a care in the world. Iris checked the pocket watch Max had given her. At the thought of him, the pit in her stomach only grew larger. "Have you seen him? Max, I mean?"

Jinn shook his head. But they'd see him soon. She was sure of it. Max was their teammate. He would support them in the end.

It was eerily silent when she stepped through the entrance of Club Uriel on Pall Mall Street, probably emptied out by the Patrons for tonight's event. No Max. Deserted lobby. Not a sound, not one person inside the gentleman's club—

"Iris." Jinn grabbed her hand and pulled her behind him because he'd seen it too. They both saw it at the same time.

The trail of blood leading up the staircase.

Splatters. All the way up to the second floor.

Iris's steps sounded louder than they should have for how lightly and carefully she placed each foot. Like the clang of a blacksmith's hammer against an anvil, ricocheting through her very bones. The moment she stepped onto the second floor, the sound of boots on wood captured her attention. Hurried footsteps—Max's. He rushed out of the gentlemen's room with a sickly pallor, covering his mouth with his hands as if he'd seen hell.

"Max!" Iris ran toward him.

The moment they locked eyes, he stumbled forward and gripped the railing with a hand. She held him up, both hands on his waist, trying to look up into his face, but his gaze stayed on the blood on the staircase below.

"Max, what's happened here?"

"Iris . . ." His chest trembled against her hands. He could barely speak.

"Max," she started, but then stopped. It was past midnight. Had the fighting already begun? Was she too late? But all the mayhem was going to take place in Cerberus, the underground arena. That was the plan, wasn't it?

Jinn went ahead to the gentlemen's room while Iris stayed with Max, trying to calm him down. She bit her lip, trying to think of what to say. Finally, she placed a hand on his cheek. "I know everything is upside down right now," she said. "I don't know what you must think of me. But just know that I'm still me. I'm still Iris. Please don't be afraid of me. I . . . I do not want you to be afraid of me."

"I killed Carl Anderson," Max whispered. "I poisoned Cordiero."

Silence. Iris pulled back, staring up at him as if he'd gone mad. "What?" she breathed.

"Adam asked me to be part of his team from the beginning. Before you came to the Pit. He told me about you. Asked me to help push you into joining the tournament. If I did, he would give me a lead on the headhunter who took my sister." He shook his head. "I had to do it. I had to. I couldn't afford not to. But that wasn't enough for him. He had me do other things . . ."

No. It couldn't be. Max wasn't a murderer. Jacques had shot the man who'd killed Carl Anderson. And Max—

And she found Max inexplicably outside Bellerose's residence. Wounded. So much had happened since then that she hadn't even had the chance to think on that.

"That man shot me after I did it. I had no choice but to escape out the window."

He was the one. The hand she felt covering her mouth with a cloth, putting her to sleep before Carl Anderson could say too much too soon. All under Adam's orders.

An unexpected tear rolled down her cheek as Max finally turned back to her, his face already wet. He shook his head. "I'm sorry," he whispered, his hands gripping the railing so tightly his veins protruded from his skin. "And Iris . . . I've done another terrible thing."

It was then that she finally heard a weak sound coming from inside the gentlemen's room. She hadn't realized Jinn had been standing in the doorway this entire time, shocked into silence. And when Iris ran to join him, she could see why he'd stumbled back.

The floors, the red leather seats, the bar table and stools—all were littered with the corpses of Club Uriel's esteemed members.

At the back, in the leftmost corner of the room, cowered Cortez and Madame Bellerose, stunned as they stared at the two men, the only ones living, at the front of the room. Jacques's bloodied ax rested against the wall on its own as he bowed his head. His right fist, which he held close to his lips, was clutching a rosary, the crucifix dangling in the air. And next to him—

Iris's stomach heaved. Gram, his stringy gray hair, wide face, and pale white skin. He sat upon a desk that once held wineglasses and platters of hors d'oeuvres: the particular tastes of the wealthy who'd thought they could control those beneath them with simple promises of riches and rewards. Now, as Gram's long black jacket draped to the floor, the flesh of the rich satiated *his* particular tastes.

"You—" Jinn whispered, his hands suddenly shaking against his legs.

After Iris's scream cut him off, it was Jacques who addressed her. "It was all a lie," he said. "This tournament is meaningless. The world *will* end. Nobody's family is safe." He looked up at her. "Are you the one, girl? The one who'll bring calamity upon us all?"

Iris's mouth parted and closed again. The smell of death seeped through every pore, leeching all feeling from her skin, making her numb.

"How did you . . . ," she finally whispered, stepping back and bumping clumsily into a figure behind her.

It was not Max.

She turned her head. Behind her, Hawkins gripped her wrist, his expression grim. And beside him, Max shook his head again, his plump lips stained with his own tears.

"I told you," Max said. "I've done a terrible thing."

A black hole opened up behind Hawkins, and he took Iris with him into the dark.

48

CERBERUS WAS INDEED A MIGHTY ARENA, perhaps not as big as those during the times of the Colosseum, but one fit for the upper echelons of a gluttonous society nonetheless. Except they were all dead and gone now. Only the gladiators were left inside this dark space illuminated by gas lamps hanging from the flat ceiling.

Max and Jinn had followed Hawkins through his dimensional rift. It made no difference to him. Hawkins went to join his teammates at the opposite end of the ring as Jinn ran to her side.

Hawkins, Cherice, and Jacob.

Lucille, Henry, and Mary.

Rin and Bately, still missing the arm Gram had taken from him.

They stood and faced Iris inside the arena, a fair distance away, though the tension among them was no less palpable.

It was Jacob who spoke first. "Is it true?" he asked, and though Iris found sympathy in his voice, his expression was stern and ready. "Are you going to kill us all one day?"

To her right, Jinn stepped in front of her. "How could you possibly know? Who—"

"Max . . . ," Iris whispered, and glanced back at him.

Her teammate, who remained a ways behind her, couldn't look her in the eye.

"S-so? You have a problem with it?" Cherice piped up, folding her arms. "He was spooked to hell yesterday and needed someone to talk to. Of course he told us everything. I can't believe you lied to us! You've been fooling us all this time, haven't you? *Haven't* you?"

The look in her eyes. This was the girl who'd brought her food when she was upset, who stayed up with her and gossiped. A friendship that shattered right before her eyes.

Max crouched down, sliding his fingers in his thick, curly hair.

"You gave her up?" hissed Jinn.

"No." It sounded as if it had taken every ounce of strength he had left just to speak. "Cherice . . . I didn't want this."

"This isn't about what you want, Morales." Henry rolled his colorful glass marbles in his right hand ominously. "This is about survival."

From the other side of the ring, Iris caught Rin staring at her intensely, mouthing something in Fon that Iris couldn't understand.

"Is that why you had Gram and Jacques butcher Club Uriel?" Jinn asked darkly.

"They did that themselves," Hawkins replied, and couldn't suppress a shiver at the thought of them. "Not what we intended. But they also had a right to know. You offered us the truth, Iris. This is the truth we've been told." He pointed at her. "That you were born a demon meant to destroy us. That you *created* us Fanciful Freaks. That you exist to end the world. Do you deny it?"

"W-was that your goal all along?" Iris was surprised the timid Mary would speak, but she did, her strawberry-blond braid bobbing against her back as she shook next to Lucille.

Iris couldn't believe what she'd just heard. "My . . . my *goal*? No. No!"

"Did you know the whole time?" Henry pushed.

"*No!*" Iris cried. "I didn't know! I didn't know any of this!"

Bately smirked. "So you don't deny it."

To see Bately, Hawkins, and the rest of Max's friends standing together despite their history. To see them advancing on her. Only one common goal could bring them in lockstep with each other: survival. Iris drew in a shaky breath and kept silent as she thought of what to say next. She looked back at Max, but his head was on his knees. She looked up at Jinn, but he was struggling as hard as she was to find an argument to make in this arena that had somehow become the setting of an impromptu trial.

"Wait a second, now, wait a second!" Jacob stretched out his hands to stay the mob. "Iris is our friend. Let's not jump to conclusions. We need to hear her out. She deserves that."

Everyone stopped where they were. Hawkins lowered his head while Cherice sniffed back tears. Despite their harsh words, Iris could see the toll this was taking on them. The slight quiver of Hawkins's fists. The trembling of Cherice's little body. This wasn't fair. This wasn't *fair*.

"Iris." Lucille. She was wearing a new face now, grim like a schoolmaster's. "What happened to the man you had me impersonate to infiltrate the Basement?"

Iris's body seized up. She clenched her teeth.

"You said he was a member of the Crown's research team who disappeared. Everyone we met in the Basement seemed to think he'd disappeared too. So where did he disappear to? And how could you know his face in such detail? A random man you saw for just one second inside the dark Crystal Palace?"

Iris lowered her head.

"None of that matters," Jinn said, waving her off. "Stop trying to trap her. Iris isn't your enemy. She's only—"

"I killed him."

The words flew out from her lips before she could stop them. Team Hawkins stared, mouths open, aghast, heartbroken, unable to say a word. As Jinn looked back at her, as Max lifted his head, as Rin's eyes narrowed, as the Fanciful Freaks glared at her, Iris stood her ground. She no longer wanted to lie. She was tired of it. Tired of secrets. Tired of hiding what she was. So she told them.

She told them what she saw in the Helios.

Told them what she'd done to Mr. James with only a touch.

Told them about her visions. The massacres she'd committed. And how her regeneration in South Kensington changed the course of their lives forever.

As she spoke, a burden lifted off her. She felt lighter than ever before. The truth. The treasure she'd sought for so long, had fought so hard for. And yet, ironically, it was the truth that dug the pit beneath her that much deeper.

"Those envoys mentioned the white crystal and the eclipse at Marlborough House," said Hawkins, stunning Iris. "Everything they said seems to correlate with what you've just told us. But sadly, that only corroborates how dangerous you are, Iris."

But the envoys had spoken in *Yoruba*, a language Hawkins shouldn't have known.

"How did you understand them if you—" she started, and then she remembered that day, the strange brush of Jacob's thumb against Hawkins's throat before he Slid her into the bathroom. That's right. Jacob could make people understand *any* language. Which meant they had planned to eavesdrop all along . . . all without telling her.

"Please believe me, none of this matters," Iris said, pushing past Jinn, pleading her case. "I'm *me*! My mind, my body, my soul, my will. It's mine. Please believe me! I don't want to kill anyone!"

"But . . . but you already have," Jacob reminded her quietly. He sounded hollow. Lost.

"Tell me it isn't true, Iris!" Cherice said, her hands clasped together as if in prayer. She stepped forward, but Hawkins pulled her back protectively. He was protecting Cherice from *her*. "Come on, just . . . This is all a joke, right? Right?"

Iris's lips snapped shut. She looked to Rin, but the girl said nothing. In any case, the sight of her only reminded Iris that she'd been a murderer long before the Crystal Palace.

But five years of experiments and decades of dormancy had taken her memories from her. She wasn't the same person. She was Iris. She was who she was. Wasn't that enough?

But then, who was to say she wouldn't turn and begin her massacres anew? Who was to say she wouldn't find a reason, like that day Anne died at Gorton Zoo?

None of them were safe. They knew it too. Whatever denial existed between them had evaporated, leaving nothing but the cold hard truth. Those among the Fanciful Freaks who once looked at her with smiles and laughter now saw her as the enemy. Iris knew right then and there.

The final round would still be a fight to the death.

And since she couldn't die . . .

"Look, none of our hands are exactly clean," Bately said as he waved the one he still had. "There are a few murderers among our lot, I presume. But as for me, my personal philosophy's rather clear: survive by any means necessary. Ask them." He flicked his head toward Hawkins, who sent him a withering look, but said nothing. "They're well aware of how far I'll go to keep living. So, uh, do me a favor, won't you?" He pulled a gun out from the back of his britches. "Walk a bit forward, will you, love? It'll make it a lot easier to shoot you."

His voice echoed throughout her body. Her mind felt blown with a sudden case of vertigo, but it passed quickly, and soon her lips stretched into a wide, willing grin.

"But of course, Mr. Bately," she said, and walked forward as he'd commanded.

"Bately!" Jacob cried.

"You bloody bastard, wait!" Cherice growled.

A bang. The first bullet pierced her left thigh. She cried out in pain, and yet somehow she had to keep going. She knew it was Bately's silver tongue compelling her. She tried to shake off his influence, but she happily limped along, waiting for another bullet to burst through her flesh.

It was Rin who saved her from further pain, taking her sword of white crystal out from her chest. Flipping it around with expert grace, she stabbed Bately through his rib cage. Blood gushed from his open mouth as he gaped in shock. There was no pity from the other contestants. But Iris could see the same determination to live in their eyes. Whether they believed in her words or not, there was only one way to ensure their own safety.

"Damn it." Cherice wiped away her tears. "Damn it all to bloody hell! I don't want to do this, Iris, but I also don't want to *die!*" Her cards flew toward Iris, sharp as knives, and Henry dashed forward, rolling two of his marbles on the ground. Iris dove to the ground to avoid Cherice's attack, sliding back when she noticed Henry's marbles sparking like firecrackers. By the time they finally exploded, Iris had jumped out of the way, but the force propelled her forward. She landed hard on the ground with a shuddering gasp.

Fire burst from Jinn's mouth as Hawkins dashed out through the smoke from Henry's blast, coming straight for her.

"Sorry, Iris. This isn't personal," said Hawkins as he ran.

And yet it felt so very personal. She remembered the way they'd laughed together as they dressed Jinn and Max for their infiltration mission.

Just as she blinked away the tears threatening her focus, he stopped in front of her. "After Chadwick died, I made a promise that I would always protect those I love, no matter the cost." He grabbed her. "And no matter the foe."

Iris was frozen, looking at the apology written across his delicate, rosy face.

"Iris!" Jinn cried, noticing too late what Hawkins was doing. As Jinn began dashing toward her, as Hawkins's black hole opened behind her, Iris sucked in a breath.

And blinked.

"Max!" she cried, having been pushed to the side by the teammate who'd just appeared in front of her. *"Max!"* she cried again, louder, when she saw him.

Because when Hawkins had moved to shove Iris into the black hole, he'd shoved Max in her place. Hawkins grabbed at Max to try to stop him from falling, but he lost his balance and tumbled toward that hole with him. To where, Iris couldn't fathom. But Hawkins had planned to get rid of her forever. That much was clear.

"Iris." As Max fell, he gave her one last smile. "You'll forgive me, won't you?"

And they disappeared into the black void.

"Max!" Iris screeched, only for Jacob's and Cherice's screams to join hers.

"Hawkins!" Jacob was beside himself. "Max!" He dropped to his knees, holding his hair. "Oh God, oh God, what have we done?"

Cherice was still wailing, and soon the little thief's cards were targeting Iris again. Jinn's fire burned some to a crisp, and Rin's sword cut down the rest that Iris couldn't dodge. Iris hadn't even seen the girl running forward.

"Give him back!" Cherice shrieked, her eyes wide with horror. "Give Max back!"

"Isoke!" Rin cried. "Come!"

"Why?" Iris rasped as her body went nearly limp. "What does it matter anymore?"

Without warning, Rin slapped her out of her stupor. "It matters," she said. "To me."

Rin took her wrist as Jinn sprayed the room with more fire, blocking the others from following as the three escaped Cerberus. Up a long, winding stretch of wooden stairs to the lobby, then out of the club, where they found themselves in the courtyard. She remembered once upon a time when she'd had her first real conversation with Rin here, the hardened warrior letting down her defenses to show the kind girl underneath. Iris silently thanked her. But their battle was not over. An ax flew at Iris's head and was blocked by Rin's sword.

Jacques. "Are you the coming devil meant to end all mankind?" The rosary dangled in his left hand, the crucifix bobbing up and down with each heavy step he took toward her, Gram slithering behind him.

"If there's any devil on this earth, it's *you*." Jinn stepped toward them, his chest heaving as he stared at the ghoulish Gram, blood dripping from the man's mouth. "I *do* recognize you. From the fair. I thought I was going mad, but . . ." Jinn's voice broke. He shook his head, his whole body lurching. "You were the one I saw as a child. It was you standing over my father's body that day next to the fires. You who dragged him away as he screamed for me!"

Jinn's horrible revelation hit Iris so hard she clutched at her chest, feeling her crystal heart beating through her blouse. It couldn't be. But Jinn had never looked so desperate, so terrified, so filled with rage and despair as he did now, staring at the vampire before them.

"Why? You two are assassins, aren't you? Why did you target my father?"

"I know not of this," confessed Jacques. But Gram said nothing.

"I'm talking to *you*!" He pointed at Gram. "You're the one I remember there.

What . . . ," Jinn tried again. "What did you do to him?" His voice broke.

Jacques shut his eyes and turned his face away in penance. But Gram still didn't answer.

"Refik Ibrahim!" Jinn burst, unable to control his rage. The name of his father. The name of the man whose disappearance had cast him into a world of strife and loneliness. "What did you do with him?"

It was then that Gram opened his bloody mouth. "I never remember the names of my meals."

Jinn's arms dangled at his sides, his breaths growing progressively faster. And then, suddenly, Iris's partner was howling and charging for Gram, spraying fire everywhere.

"Jinn!" Iris tried to run for him, but Rin's rough hand gripped her wrist to hold her back. "What are you doing?" Iris's frenzied mind was blank of everything but the fact that Jinn would face off against these monsters alone. That he couldn't possibly survive. That she needed to save him. "Rin, let me go!"

"Isoke, it's your life they're after. We have to leave."

Rin attempted to drag her off, but Iris fought back, tugging wildly.

"Let me go! Let me go!" Iris's screech tore at her throat as Jinn's fire burned everywhere, everything. In that moment, she remembered the days they'd laughed together. The days they'd practiced their routines, both dripping sweat. Those precious moments when he'd tossed her up in the air from their tightrope. Jinn had been wrong. Iris didn't always have her eyes closed while she was up in the sky. Sometimes she gazed at him from up in the air . . . watching him smile.

"This place is dangerous."

"Are you still taking me to the king, then?"

Rin hesitated, shifting on her feet, staring unfocused at the sword in her hands.

"Well, are you?" Iris barked.

"I . . ." Rin stopped. "It's already been arranged." But she didn't sound like her confident self. She sounded apologetic. Unsure. "I'm sure your Jinn would have wanted this too."

"How could *you* know what Jinn wants?" Iris bellowed, and with a giant burst of energy, she pushed Rin aside and tackled Jinn to the ground, knocking him out. Iris hadn't the time to wipe the tears from his face.

"We're leaving," she said, her Fon suddenly perfect. "Jinn and me. And we're not going to your king. You have two choices, Olarinde: come with us, or get out of our way. If you try to stop us, *I'll burn you alive.*"

Jinn's thick barricade of fire wouldn't keep Gram and Jacques back forever. But it didn't take Rin long to see what she'd been yearning to see since she'd arrived in Europe. Isoke. The one called Child of the Moon Goddess.

She Who Does Not Fall.

Rin's eyes brimmed with the utmost awe and respect. She bowed her head. "We go tonight."

Lifting Jinn's body over her shoulder, Rin motioned for Iris to follow her.

Iris turned around one last time to look at Club Uriel, collapsing under the ravages of burning flames, and taking her once friends still in Cerberus with it.

Everyone . . . I'm sorry . . .

Iris held back her tears as the three of them escaped into the night.

A Young Man
Thinking II

APACK OF ICE IN ONE HAND. A queen in the other. Adam Temple held the former against his forehead but considered the latter with interest.

The letter he'd just been sent by Cortez, delivered by one of his servants, lay unopened on the living room table next to his chessboard. In front of the window, Fool watched him carefully through his harlequin mask.

"You won't open it, Lord Temple?"

"There's no need," Adam responded, setting the sack of ice back down on the table. "I already know what it says."

Club Uriel was no more. It had burned down just a few hours ago, everyone inside murdered. They were still looking for survivors. The Committee was to call an emergency meeting to address what had happened. But Adam already had some idea.

"Iris," he whispered, the name sweet and terrible on his tongue.

"Let me look for her, Lord Temple," Fool offered dutifully. "If I move quickly enough, I'm confident I can find her by sunrise."

But Adam shook his head. Night still ruled the sky. Somewhere underneath the stars, she was running. Running from herself. From her destiny. From her duty. From his deepest wish.

"She's been through enough. Leave her be for now. I'll let you know when it's time to start tracking her. Just make sure you keep this a secret from the other Fools. They're not loyal to me like you are. And I don't want the Committee to chase down Iris." Adam considered the black chess piece in his hand. "I'll be the one to do that."

But not before finding a way to deal with Bosch. The bastard had found his father's journal somehow. That meant there was a high possibility he knew John Temple was still alive. Why Bosch was moving on his own and how much he knew about Iris, Adam didn't know. But Bosch's treachery was exceeded only by his own greed. He wouldn't so easily share the most valuable information in the journal with the other Enlighteners.

Well, Adam couldn't be sure of that. The one thing he *did* know, however, was that he'd have to deal with this mess sooner rather than later. What would each member of the Committee do if they knew Iris *was* the coming apocalypse? Kill her? Or use her as a weapon to help them conquer the New World and whoever—or whatever—may be there awaiting them? There were too many possibilities. Dealing with Bosch and Uma would be the first step in keeping the Committee away from Iris, and it would keep Adam quite occupied.

Which was most likely why Iris had told him in the first place. Clever girl.

Fool swept off his top hat and bowed deeply. In the next moment, he was gone, the window curtains billowing in the wind.

Iris was quite right. Adam was a beast. He was well aware of that. But this was a world that created beasts. It was only fitting that a beast would help to end it.

Poverty and lies. Empire and hatred. Sickness and greed. The grief of the weak conquered and enslaved by the "enlightened." Injustice. Torture. Pain.

One day, she would realize it. With destruction came creation. From death came birth. The world that he believed in was the world that she would create. And whether she accepted him or not, he would help her create it. There was no doubt in his mind that he was brought into this wicked world and made to suffer for that reason—and that reason alone.

Now that Iris knew who she was, the true game would soon begin.

"You'll embrace me soon enough, Iris," he said. "On the day that you reach your limit, once you too become sick of this world, then you'll know. Then *you'll* come to *me*."

Adam placed the queen back into her coveted spot and smiled.

THE NEXT STAGE

November 15, 1884

On the other side of the world...

FABLES WAS NOT HIS LAST NAME. And when people asked for his first, he told them "Tom." It was a good enough lie. And Fables had been lying since the day he was born.

His birth was a lie. His father was not his father, and his mother was not who his father thought she was. Her light brown skin helped her pass in Kansas. He'd fallen in love with her at first sight. He didn't know that Fables's mother had fled Missouri to Kansas seeking freedom. It shouldn't have mattered. But to that green-eyed son of a mayor, it was a blight when he found out. Worse still was when he realized his wife had had their first son by another man. His mother mysteriously disappeared after that.

Or maybe that was a lie too. Fables spent his childhood concocting story after story as to why his father hated him until stories couldn't sustain him anymore. Soon, he fled too. Maybe fleeing was in his blood. He liked to imagine it was. He liked to imagine many things as he wandered the dusty cities begging for food and a place to rest his head.

A tall, skinny boy of eighteen. Lanky limbs. Slightly crooked teeth. Curly brown hair and brown eyes like his mother. Square jaw like his father. And quite handsome, he liked to think. If it weren't for his looks and the lonely men and women he kept company on occasion, he would have starved to death by now. Though he had other skills. Beyond his gift of storytelling, his mother had given him one more thing.

"Play another song!"

"Yeah, go on, boy. Play. Play!"

"What do you wanna hear?" Fables called out into the rowdy saloon, though he doubted they heard him. Drunken cowboys and seedy gamblers grabbed women by their chests and swung them around onto bar stools—or was it seedy cowboys and drunken gamblers? A fight had broken out behind him. People were yelling. Someone threw a man across the bar, causing the bartender to swear and jump back as he crashed into murky glasses, booze bottles, and plates of food. Just the usual day.

Sighing, Fables turned back toward his piano, stroking his prickly chin. He should play a song. Any song. As long as he was entertaining someone, he was making money. As long as he was making money, he could do the one thing that would make his father furious: survive another day.

"What do you wanna hear?" He tried again. An older woman wrapped her arm around his neck, bent down low, and whispered into his ear. "Ah, okay."

He played "Turkey in the Straw." The light tune seemed to enliven the saloon. People were stomping their feet, hooting, dancing, singing along. He played again and again until abruptly, his fingers came to a full stop against the piano keys.

"Hey, why'd you stop?" said a grizzly, black-bearded man at the table nearest him.

But Fables didn't hear him. He'd played the song so many times, the notes had started to blend together until it became meaningless background noise. Just like the people here. Just like what his life had become. A mayor's grandson, scraping for food, getting by. Surviving another day. He'd traded fine clothes for the torn pants and dilapidated shirt he wore now. A far cry from the manor he'd once lived in just miles from here.

"How did I get here?" Fables ran his fingers into his curly hair.

"Hey!" Black Beard slammed his chips on the table. "I said, why'd you stop playing?"

"Because I felt like it, you ugly bastard."

Fables never could keep his tongue in check.

The table toppled over as the bearded gambler jumped to his feet. Fables didn't know what was happening until the bottle of beer had collided with the back of his head with a smash. The sound of laughter harmonized with the searing pain as he felt himself being picked up by many hands and thrown out the front door onto the dusty ground.

He lay there in the hot sun, crying. Nobody helped him. He didn't expect them to. It was fine. He wanted to die. Might as well get it over with.

He slept.

The sounds of shrieking brought him back to consciousness. Gripping the back of his bloody head, Fables winced and looked through the wooden swinging doors.

The saloon was eerily quiet.

Dragging himself up into a sitting position, he looked around. The streets were empty too. Some food stands knocked over. Shoes left behind. Almost as if people had fled something in a hurry. Fleeing was his specialty, so he could tell. Soon, he'd likely have to move on too.

But first he wanted to know what had happened to the rowdy bar.

Still cringing in pain, he dragged himself back into the saloon. The bartender, the prostitutes, the businessmen. The cowboys and the gamblers. All gone. Their chips and beer were still fresh on the table.

Only one figure was inside. A man he'd never seen before. A man he couldn't make up even in his wildest of dreams.

Fables held his breath. The man's back was to him, so Fables couldn't see his face. The man was . . . He was naked. But his long, brown hair covered most of his body, curling almost down to the floor. Weeds and flowers twisted out of his locks as if they'd been planted there.

And his skin—his skin was gold or bronze like one of those ancient statues. He had the body of one too, perfectly sculpted like a Roman gladiator. His blue veins were visible through his skin, and Fables could see them bulging, pulsating as if slurping down blood.

The saloon was dustier than usual. Without taking his eyes off the man, Fables inched over to the piano by the wall. The ivory keys were covered in dust.

And where were all the people?

It was then that the man turned. Fables, eyes wide, was stunned to the point where he couldn't feel his pain anymore. The man was beautiful. Perfect.

Fables began trembling, his arms limp at his sides. This man was unlike anything he'd ever seen before. Unlike anything that had ever existed. Better than a fairy tale. Sweeter than a song.

The man's golden eyes had no pupils and needed no whites to peer into Fables's soul. Upon his forehead was a band of sharp emerald laurels, like a wreath—and a shining white jewel glittering in the center. A white stone. A white crystal . . .

His power was so palpable, Fables dropped to his knees and cried. He'd always thought his father was the most powerful man he'd ever met. How wrong he was. How *wrong* he was.

Fables looked up at the creature with awe. He couldn't stop the words from escaping his lips even if he wanted to. "Sir, tell me . . . are you . . . a god?"

The man answered, "Yes."

Fables nodded quickly, clasping his hands together. Of course he was a god. What else could this wondrous creature be? "Where have all the people here gone?"

At this, the man smiled a little. Just that *little* was intoxicating. "Dead." He gestured around him, and Fables finally realized that the bar was covered in *ash*, not dust.

Fables's heart was racing. He scrambled to his feet. He'd never been this close to divinity before. This close to power. Power—the one thing he'd always wanted but never had, not since the day he was born in a lie.

"Where did you come from?" Fables continued, because he couldn't ask enough questions. "Heaven? Why are you here?"

The man was staring off into the distance. It was only after Fables had asked the last question that he turned and looked at him once more. "I'm here to punish the wicked."

Fables backed up against the piano bench. "Who's the wicked?"

"Humanity."

If Fables was honest with himself, it was what he'd always wanted.

Someone who punished those who deserved it. This world was awful. Wicked. And the more he stared at this wild, golden man who appeared before him like a Greek god, the more the deep-seated desires he never dared to speak before bubbled to the surface. A desire for revenge. For blood.

This was a wicked world. The people in it were better off dead.

And like a dream, the man stretched out his hand. Fables stared at it in awe. "I would like to learn more about this world. Will you follow me?" the man asked.

Fables didn't need to think. "Yes. Yes, I will! I'll teach you everything I know!" He was elated. All those lonely, hateful nights. Someone had finally answered his prayers. Though, this probably wasn't the good Lord above—or maybe it was. It didn't matter. He would take it. He would take it.

"But," Fables continued, "what do I call you? What's your name?"

The man looked around him. At the ashes of the people he'd burned alive. The alcohol spilling down the bar. The overturned tables and leftover cards and chips.

"Hiva," the man finally said, his gold eyes bright like fire. "My name is Hiva."

ACKNOWLEDGMENTS

There was a time I would freeze on the spot worrying about how I was going to write this book. It came together because of the help of some amazing people. Thanks to my brother, David, who was the first person to hear the kernel of this idea and was actually excited to see more. Thanks to my agent, Natalie Lakosil, who enthusiastically sold it. Thanks to Simon & Schuster's team, especially my editor, Sarah McCabe, who encouraged me throughout this journey. Thank you to the authors of every resource I found and read through in order to bring this setting of apocalyptic Victorian London to life. Thank you to God and my family, who never fail me.

And thank *you*, Auntie. You were there when I did my first reading in a little local bar. You were there when I held my first ever book launch. I remember when I was ten years old and you visited my house. It was the first time I properly met you. I was sitting on the ground, watching TV, and you were sitting on the couch behind me. I turned around and asked you, "Are you my *real* auntie?" Because Black girls have lots of aunties, you see—blood-related and friends of the family and the like—and I didn't know exactly what *kind* of auntie you were.

Thank you for being my real auntie.